GHOST HUNTER: THE HOLLOW MEN

Peter J. White

CONTENTS

Title Page	
Foreword	
Chapter One	3
Chapter Two	7
Chapter Three	10
Chapter Four	15
Chapter Five	20
Chapter Six	23
Chapter Seven	30
Chapter Eight	33
Chapter Nine	37
Chapter Ten	45
Chapter Eleven	53
Chapter Twelve	56
Chapter Thirteen	59
Chapter Fourteen	64
Chapter Fifteen	71
Chapter Sixteen	77
Chapter Seventeen	81
Chapter Eighteen	87
Chapter Nineteen	90

Chapter Twenty	94
Chapter Twenty One	96
Chapter Twenty Two	98
Chapter Twenty Three	100
Chapter Twenty Four:	107
Chapter Twenty Five	111
Chapter Twenty Six	114
Chapter Twenty Seven	117
Chapter Twenty Eight	121
Chapter Twenty Nine	130
Chapter Thirty	140
Chapter Thirty One	149
Chapter Thirty Two	154
Chapter Thirty Three	158
Chapter Thirty Four	171
Chapter Thirty Five	175
Chapter Thirty Six	184
Chapter Thirty Seven	187
Chapter Thirty Eight	195
Chapter Thirty Nine	209
Chapter Forty	213
Chapter Forty One	227
Chapter Forty Two	236
Chapter Forty Three	246
Chapter Forty Four	257
Chapter Forty Five	266
Chapter Forty Six	276
Chapter Forty Seven	285

Chapter Forty Eight	295
Chapter Forty Nine	306
Chapter Fifty	312
Chapter Fifty One	322
Chapter Fifty Two	330
Chapter Fifty Three	340
Chapter Fifty Four	349
Chapter Fifty Five	359
Chapter Fifty Six	377
Chapter Fifty Seven	383
Chapter Fifty Eight	405
Chapter Fifty Nine	416
Chapter Sixty	422
Chapter Sixty One	429
Chapter Sixty Two	435
Chapter Sixty Three	441
Chapter Sixty Four	454
Chapter Sixty Five	471
About the Author	475
Afterword	476
Read on for more Ghost Hunter:	478

FOREWORD

Foreword

I hope you like this book. A combination of real-life events inspired the story and the character. Visit PeterJWhite.weebly.com/the-hollow-men.html to read about them.

If you liked the book, please leave a review on Amazon. We indies rely on people like you to get the word out. Thank you!

Sign up for the Ghost Hunter Newsletter at PeterWhite.Weebley.com/news to get the second book in the Ghost Hunter series: *Slouching Towards Tenancingo* for **FREE.** (And to be apprised of approaching publication dates, character info, interesting links and stories related to the series as well as free short stories and other bonuses. It's a win-win situation here. And how often do those come along? Go for it!)

To learn more about the five books in the Ghost Hunter series (number six is in progress) and other titles by the author, go to PeterJWhite.weebly.com

Ghost Hunter: The Hollow Men

Ghost Hunter: Slouching Toward Tenancingo

Ghost Hunter: Bangkok Redemption

Ghost Hunter: The Bad Beginning (prequel)

Ghost Hunter: What Lies Beneath

Ghosts of a Coven Past: A Tale of Witchcraft, Spirits, Satanism, and Possession

Between the essence
And the descent
Falls the Shadow
"The Hollow Men"
T.S. Eliot

CHAPTER ONE

Max killed the big Kawasaki Ninja.

A hot wind whistled, blowing sand and dust cross-wise. A tumbleweed the size of a large dog scratched its way across the road and into the desert.

He stepped up onto the old fashioned boardwalk, his boots clomping on the weathered wood, and made his way into Riker's Bar.

Inside, the room was dim and smoky, despite laws to the contrary.

A few scattered cowpoke-looking men sat at tables with varying amounts of empty beer bottles in front of them, three men at the bar.

No one looked.

Max strode to the bar and threw a leg over a stool.

"Bushmill's. Beer back," he said.

The bartender gave him a long look, nodded, and turned to serve up the drinks.

Max put his elbows on the bar and used the mirror to scope out the room.

Just as he thought.

He'd counted eight men at the assorted tables on his way in.

Now there were nine. And a woman in a red dress.

"A goddamn red dress," Max said. "Shit."

What the hell is it with dead women and red? Do women attracted to danger and bad men like red? Did their men dress them before they killed them?

"Excuse me?" said the bartender.

Max looked away from the mirror.

"Nothing," he said. "Thinking out loud."

The bartender gave him another look.

"I seen you before?" he asked.

"Doubt it," Max said. "Never been here."

"Huh," said the bartender, "I would've sworn...."

"I get that a lot," Max said. "Common type: Bald guy, goatee."

"Huh," said the bartender again.

Max looked around the bar: booths against the wall, tables scattered at the periphery of a dance floor, some pool tables and actual pinball machines in the back. Standard. He didn't imagine there was much need for anything to draw in customers: those who drank would come.

"Bar's been here a while?" Max said.

The bartender leaned back and crossed his arms.

"Yup. Big times here in the old days."

"It goes back that far? Oil boom days?"

"Yup. Black Callahan's place, originally."

Max frowned.

"Black Callahan. He the one that got himself hanged?"

Max scrutinized the man next to the woman in the red dress in the mirror.

Big fellow. Old-fashioned fancy, shirt with a string tie, black leather vest, cowboy hat. Jet black hair, beady eyes, five o-clock shadow like sandpaper on his face.

The man's gaze stayed fixed, riveted. Unnatural. He didn't move. Didn't blink.

Neither did the woman beside him.

She was a beauty. The red dress complimented her red hair. Fair skin, with a dusting of freckles. Bright eyes that never moved or blinked.

The couple looked as if they'd been captured in amber, a static holographic image.

The bartender stepped forward.

"You know the history?"

Max nodded.

"Heard of it."

The men in the room worked their drinks, their talk low.

The couple at the table shifted.

The big man's face colored and contorted, a mixture of rage and pain rippling across his features, bending them into the mask of a devil.

The woman's bright eyes bulged, and the top of her head dented in, blood and brain matter running down her pretty face.

"Killed her right here in this bar," the bartender said.

"Figured," said Max.

"Bashed her head in, that table over there." The bartender gestured at an empty table in the back. "With a hammer."

"Hmm," said Max. "Looks more like the butt of a pistol, to me."

"What?" said the bartender.

Max shook his head, looked away.

"Heard different. That's all."

Max picked up the shot of Bushmill's.

"Bottoms up."

He threw the shot back in a fluid motion, grimaced, picked up the short glass of beer and tossed that down on top of the whisky.

"Better," he said, wiping his lips with the back of his hand.

"You sure I ain't see ya before?" the bartender asked.

Max shook his head.

"I told you. I'm a common type, that's all."

The bartender's eyes didn't waver, "Nope. Something tells me there ain't nothing common about you at all. Not a thing."

Max's smile never touched his eyes.

"So I've been told," he said. "What do I owe you?"

He reached back to pull the wallet from his pocket, and the bartender jumped a little.

"Easy," said Max. "Just getting my wallet."

"Sorry," the bartender said. "Just feeling a little spooked, I guess. Been feeling that way since you come in."

Max met the bartender's gaze until the bartender turned to polish the glass in his hand.

"Yup," Max said. "Get that a lot."

He slipped a ten dollar bill out of his wallet and laid it on the bar.

"Keep the change," he said.

The bartender offered him a nervous smile in return. "Thanks," he said.

Max nodded, took a last look at the tableau in the mirror—the demonically twisted face on the big guy, the bulged eyes and brain matter on the face of the redhead—then turned to go.

Just eight men in the room.

"Right," Max said.

He eased the door closed behind him on the way out, pulled it shut.

Boots on the boardwalk and back to his motorcycle.

"Shit," he said. "Cannot get a break."

He threw a leg over the bike, kicked it off its stand and started it up.

"Seriously."

The bartender picked up Max's shot and beer glasses, carried them to the sink as the rumble of Max's motorcycle faded.

He spun quickly, shot a look at the room, relaxed a little, and turned back to the sink.

CHAPTER TWO

Max read the sign as he flashed by.

Aston: Food. Gas. Rest.

Looked to be a town of a couple of hundred at best. Just another farm town slowly dying in the 21st century.

The sun was low against the rolling green hills, and Max figured this was his best bet for the night. He kicked the bike down into fifth, the 998cc engine howling, slowing the bike, fourth, third, then eased the bike off the main road into the town.

Simple but surprisingly wide Main Street for such a small town.

One with an active city council: lots of potted plants and floral arrangements hanging from hooks with well-kept wooden signs welcoming one to town.

In the dusk, the flowers looked black, the words on the sign a ghostly white glow.

Just off Main Street, a motel. Classic sixties model: two story, doors painted different colors, white with blue trim.

Max wheeled his bike into the spot in front of the office, dismounted, stuck his helmet on the mirror and clomped in.

An old farmer type was sitting in a chair behind the desk watching some reality show, hands clasped on his big belly. He raised an eyebrow at Max.

"Room?" said Max.

The old guy laughed.

"You got your pick," he said. "Got a trucker in 207, back corner there. That's it."

Max nodded.

"How about the other top corner, then?"

"That'd put you right on Main Street," the old guy said.

Max looked out the window at the empty street.

"Wouldn't say traffic was a problem," Max said.

The old guy laughed again.

"Well, I suppose you got that right," he said. "Name's Slim."

Max's lips turned up a bit.

The old guy laughed.

"One of those opposite things. Never was. Slim, that is."

"How much for the room?"

"Thirty bucks a night'll do."

Max took another look around.

"You have a busy season around here?"

"No, not hardly," said Slim. "Got the Onion Fest in April. Fourth of July. Labor Day. Occasionally a group of farm workers come into town for a big night. Like that."

Max pulled out $30 in cash and laid it on the counter.

The old guy groaned and hoisted himself out of his chair to shuffle down the counter and grab a form.

"Fill this out," he said.

"That room got any history?"

"History?"

"History. As in suicide, murder, any kind of unpleasant death. Like that."

Slim gave Max a long look.

"No, I don't believe it does. That matter to you?"

Max nodded.

"It does. I'm…sensitive that way."

Slim's face lit up.

"You like, one of them whatchamacall'ems? Mediums?"

Max did not smile.

"Just sensitive. Key?"

Slim sighed and reached under the counter and came up with a key with a room tag labeled 201.

"Not much of a talker, are ya?" Slim asked.

Max shook his head.

"Don't generally have a lot to say. Thanks for the room."

Max palmed the key and slid out of the office.

Slim watched Max fire up his motorcycle and move it to the space under his room. He was a little pissed the guy didn't want to talk. A medium, or whatever. That was interesting. Come morning, he'd bet the traveler would have something to say.

Max climbed the stairs, stuck his key in the door, and disappeared inside.

CHAPTER THREE

The room smelled like mold. Musty, unused. Queen-sized bed, little TV mounted in the corner across from the bed. Tiny bathroom.

A sense of the surreal settled on Max, the objects and walls of the room taking on a dull shine. His olfactory sense clicked up a few notches, something ephemeral and unreal awakening atavistic survival mechanisms.

Max sniffed.

Dirt. Freshly turned earth. The smell blossomed and turned putrid. Like a rendering truck passing by on a broiling summer day.

Ah, God, Max thought. *I asked him, too.*

Max looked in the mirror over the bureau and sure enough —there she was in the bed. Wasn't a lot to look at in life, Max figured, and death hadn't improved anything.

Bruises discolored her cheek bones. She had one split eyebrow, a broken nose, a fat lip, and her jaw hung loose. And that was what Max could see without trying.

Her neck was canted at an unnatural angle. *Cause of death,* Max decided.

"God damn it."

Back in the office, Slim protested.

"I"m telling ya, mister. Never heard of anything like that."

There was a glint of malice and delight in his eye that Max didn't like at all.

"Give me a ground floor room. Right in the middle." Max surveyed the motel, opening himself a tiny bit.

He regretted it instantly. Misery echoed through the

courtyard, reached all the way into the office. A lot of unpleasantness had gone down in this motel.

Max considered getting his money back and heading up the road a piece, but figured it'd take him a couple more hours to come to a place with a decent motel, and he didn't want to sleep out in the open. He wanted a bed. Untroubled sleep.

That seemed out of the question here, though. He might get some sleep, but it was certain to be troubled.

"Ah, the hell with it," Max said. "That one."

The room with the purple door, dead center on the ground floor, felt the least troubled.

Slim reached back under the counter, came up with a key.

The setting sun glinted off the key, and just for a flash—reflected red in Slim's pupils.

Room 113 had a similar musty smell to 207. Max braced himself and waited, but nothing else came...just a musty room. With mold.

Max stood with his back to the door and took in the room in the reddening light of sunset. Same as 207. Through the darkening gloam, Max checked the mirror. It reflected the same view his eyes saw.

"OK, then," Max said.

He stepped away from the door, turned and closed the curtains, then turned on the overhead light.

So far, so good.

Bathroom. A surprising number of deaths occur in the bathroom.

The bathroom was pleasantly clean. A touch of mildew spoke through the smell of bleach, but nothing else. The mirror reflected the whole room, and both were empty of visions, ghosts, or views into the world of the dead.

Max reached over and slid the shower curtain back. Sparkling clean tub and fixtures. Looked over his shoulder at the mirror. All sparkle and clean.

"Thank God," Max sighed.

He went back to the bedroom, and started unpacking his saddlebags.

Lying in bed, fingers interlaced behind his head, Max stared at the ceiling.

Thailand, he thought. That's what kicked it all off. Fresh off the teams, there to train Muay Thai. The place was steeped in spirit lore, animism, dark practices, open debauchery, institutional corruption—absolutely chock a block with dark and dangerous entities.

And yet...there was a sweetness and docility to the people, a nobility and a grace that counter-balanced all the negative.

The Muay Thai camp he'd gone there for was superlative. Run by an old Thai boxer, Ong, who'd been a legend—one of the first to open his camp to foreigners—it taught the discipline with no frills, just a strict adherence to time-honored methods that produced some of the best fighters in the world.

It'd started so well...

Max shook his head at himself.

Nostalgia. Bullshit.

Yeah, the first year was solid, and the second started well. By then he was taking on fights against real Thai fighters and holding his own. Even had a girlfriend—a spectacular beauty with a mean left hook.

Max fingered the ropy scar tissue bristling through his eyebrows.

He'd been cut by elbows, pounded by kicks, dropped by flying knees, but he'd stood his ground and earned respect.

The gym owner, Ong, had taken him on. For real. Old school stuff—as serious about the spiritual aspect as the physical. Meditation and morning prayers at the temple.

And then....

The dark side had opened up.

Hookers a dime a dozen.

And...the night that cracked it all wide open.

Max blinked, remembering.

A door had opened in his head. A door there was no shutting, or at least, no shutting all the way.

Since then, Max was constantly leaning against that door, leaning hard, but it always stayed a crack open. He could step back and let it swing wide at any time, but that was never good.

Too much misery behind that door. Too much death.

The bed was surprisingly comfortable, and Max's eyes grew heavy. He let sleep take him.

The slap of flesh on flesh startled Max awake.

The hell?

He sat upright, his whole body tense, listening with his nerve endings and his ears.

Slap. A thump of something hitting the wall.

The room next door.

Max got up and padded to the window, cracked open the curtains, and peeked out into the parking lot.

Empty. Just the trucker's rig off to the side, his motorcycle in front of his room and a lot of empty space.

The light in the manager's office was on, but no one occupied the chair behind the desk.

Moaning. A scream cut off...

Max opened himself a tiny, tiny bit...

Red blossomed inside his head: blood on walls, blood on the bed, blood on the mirror, blood on the floor. Blood. The room next door drowning in it.

What the hell is this place?

Max slid to the door, opened it carefully, slipped through and over to the window of the room next door.

The curtains were open, the same bloody tableau he'd had splashed inside his head on view.

Max backed away from the window and let the door in his head open a notch—that shimmery sense of the unreal silvering his view.

He spun a quiet 360, arms out.

Waves of misery and pain radiated from every room of the hotel.

Women had died here. Lots of them. All of them nasty, brutal deaths. Images of brutish sex flooded Max's mind. Men using their fists and their sex as weapons. An ugly, savage current of emotion swept through him, almost carried him away.

Max leaned back against the door in his head and held it as shut as he could.

CHAPTER FOUR

Max came awake with a jolt.

The rest of the night had passed without incident, but some sense of purpose had settled into the depths of his soul and was pushing at him.

He pushed it away.

Slim was back on duty, watching Max load up his saddlebags from behind the counter in the manager's office.

Max tightened the straps, gave the bags a couple of sharp tugs to make sure they were set, then strode over to the office to drop off the key.

"Sleep well?" Slim asked.

"Tolerable," Max said.

"See anything..." Slim let the question hang in the air.

Their eyes met and locked. Max saw the same glint of malicious humor in Slim's red eyes he'd seen the night before.

Son of a bitch, Max thought. *This amuses him.*

"Had a lot of good times here, have you?" Max asked.

Slim raised his eyebrows, "Depends on what you call good times," he said.

"I'll bet," Max replied. "You grow up here?"

"Born and bred," Slim answered.

"Bet not much happens in these parts that slips by anyone's attention," Max said.

"Ever live in a small town?" Slim asked.

"Mostly passing through, but...yeah," Max replied.

"Then you know how it is," Slim said. "Gossip and drinking..."

Max nodded.

"When was this hotel built?" he asked.

"Around '62, I think," Slim said.

"Reasonably well maintained," Max said.

"Owners like it that way," Slim said.

"And who would they be?" Max asked.

"Bannisters. They're a big deal in these parts, heard of 'em?"

Max shook his head. He narrowed his eyes, considering Slim. The old guy had an edge, a soul-deep meanness, but could he have been one of the...*things*...that created the misery pouring out of this hotel? Max figured he didn't have the balls. More of a behind-the-scenes type, a voyeur, someone who gets a kick out of shit like that. Someone who wouldn't mind stirring the pot.

"So, Bannisters," Max said.

He leaned on the counter, brought his face eye-level to Slim's.

"What kind of people are these Bannisters?"

Slim's face closed.

"They the mansion-on-the-hill types? The Lords of the wheat, some shit like that?"

"Fact is, they do have a mansion on the hill, the one just out of town. You'll see it on your way out, if you head out the direction you were going."

"I plan to," Max said.

"They were one of the founding families of the town," Slim said. "Them and the Ingersolls."

"Ingersolls still a big deal around here?" Max asked.

"Nope. Big fire took down the whole family, turn of the century," Slim said.

"This century?" Max asked.

Slim laughed.

"Nope, not hardly. 1900."

"Huh," said Max. "Well, thanks for the hospitality."

He turned for the door.

"Y'all come back now. Anytime," Slim said.

Max let the door shut behind him.

A mile down the road, he pulled his bike to the shoulder.

Just like Slim said, a mansion capped the largest hill on the outside of town. Big white stucco walls surrounded the place, Southwestern style. Probably had ground glass embedded on the top, Max figured.

A picture window on the house behind peeked out over the big walls.

Max caught the glint of light off a lens in the window.

"Yup," Max said. "Figured ol' Slim would've been on the phone to you..."

He considered, then raised his hand in a salute/wave to the house.

"Time to go," he said.

The nearest town was about fifty miles away. A near replica of Aston, only smaller--Main Street not as wide, the motel off main not quite as large, signs put up by the city council fewer, but just as well kept: "Welcome to Ramsey."

A low, uneasy feeling swept through Max, something stirring behind the door in his head.

What the hell? Max thought. *What is it with this part of the country?*

The whole plan had been to get hell out of Thailand, back to a place with less history, fewer ghosts, less misery soaked into the land. Thailand had millennia of history; the U.S. was a relative newborn.

The thing was, Max was discovering, there are no places without death, without misery. Some have less, but death has touched every inch of the globe, and miserable, unhappy death has cast its pall over the world entire.

The plan had been to escape. To leave the door in his head behind in Thailand.

Max remembered the feeling he had as the nose of the plane lifted off the runway in Bangkok: *freedom*. Like a great shackle had been loosened and dropped to the ground, setting him free.

And then...there was the dead guy in the stall in the airport in Seattle. Needle still in his arm. Only—the dead guy wasn't there.

And that was when Max knew: there would be no out. No freedom.

And so the plan had shifted: get out into the lonely spaces, places with less death.

But no. Every rest stop, hotel, motel, apartment house, pull-over, even sign post had death on it. Car crashes, murders, suicides, accidents: horrible deaths all over the place. It seemed to Max that more death was more often miserable and unresolved than peaceful and right—but his gut told him that was not the case. Plenty of souls passed on without a ripple—that was the norm. It took a great deal of misery and denial for the dead to linger. Only the worst cases stayed behind, and not by choice. They were stuck, caught in a specific place and time like fossils in stone.

Most were just that: fossilized views of their last moments. Unmoving, quiet, macabre monuments to an unhappy death.

The worst ones retained a life of sorts: a moving tableau of their last moments, their misery echoing through eternity. Deaths played out over and over and over, sending ripples through the fabric of space and time that played like songs etched into the vinyl of an old LP.

You just had to have the proper equipment to view them.

Max hadn't asked for it, hadn't wanted it, and didn't want it, but there it was: his "gift." A legacy of the ring maybe. Of a certain genetic makeup, perhaps. Of opening doors through the spiritual practices Ong had set for him.

Dammit. There had to be a reason for this. Had to be.

Maybe...maybe if he used his "gift," put it to work, did something with it. Maybe then....

He needed to think. Somewhere quiet, free of the restless dead.

He spotted a sign, “Scenic Outlook,” and followed the road behind it up a hill.

CHAPTER FIVE

Max aimed his motorcycle at the shade of a big Mountain Hemlock on the top of the hill outside Ramsey, thumbed off the engine, and let the big bike coast to rest at the base of the tree. The ground was hard and dry, and had no trouble supporting the kick stand.

Max leaned back and took in the view.

Other than the big tree at the top of the hill, all was alternating green wheat fields with furrowed ground. A big man-made-looking lake sparkled in the June sunshine. Off in the distance, tented orchards of some kind. Vineyards, maybe.

A body swayed in the tree above and behind him.

No escaping the dead.

He heard the creak of the branch the rope was tied to, smelled death, but refused to turn and acknowledge the suicide.

Your choice, motherfucker.

Max cupped his palms behind his head and stretched, bringing the upside-down-looking corpse into view.

A young-looking Hispanic girl. Pregnant, by the looks of it.

Ah, hell.

Part of the problem with the spirit world, Max reflected, is there's no cutting them down. Nothing physical to take down, bury, and give the soul peace. Nothing to do but to let them swing.

Max returned his gaze to the hills and lake below.

Would've thought there'd be some peace here.

The branch creaked.

Max took in a deep breath, blew it out.

Why do I keep seeing these things? Am I cursed? Blessed? What is the point?

He'd wanted to doubt his sanity, take refuge in the idea of madness, maybe find a way to blot out the visions with the right cocktail of chemicals, but the details were always right.

Always.

All the way back to Bangkok, the first one...the ghost in Nit's room.

Ghosts.

Max closed his eyes, could still see the little girl standing there, frozen in time, a look of horror on her face. She had to have been somewhere between five and seven. Not more than three and a half feet tall. If that. A red and white checkered dress that fell to mid-thigh and washed so many times it was becoming transparent, the little girl's skin showing through.

And the...head, next to her. White guy. Long hair, looked a little like Reverend Jim from the old TV show, *Taxi*—same guy played Doc in all those *Back to the Future* gigs.

The head had looked torn. Like some gigantic force had reached down and pulled it from the man's body, the skin ripping and shredding jaggedly, a look of eternal surprise frozen on the man's face.

The first vision.

He never nailed down the backstory on that one. When he asked around, the Thais gave him startled looks, mumbled things about ghosts and monsters, forces...enough for him to understand something very, very bad had happened in that room.

The main thing that surprised them, he got the sense, was that he could see it. A white guy. White guys, foreigners, weren't supposed to see shit like that. White guys were supposed to be, well, white. Foreign. Un-clued in. Literal. Guys with money, there for the pussy, etc. etc.

The next one he saw in a barbershop.

That one was a murder. Crazy jealous girlfriend came in and stabbed her boyfriend to death in the chair. Everyone knew about that one.

And now, here he was. Stateside. Running.

He'd been so damn sure that leaving Thailand would do it. Certain that whatever door he'd opened belonged in Thailand, would stay in Thailand. He remembered the glorious feeling of freedom as the big jet's nose lifted and the wheels rose into the belly of the plane and clunked home as the Boeing Dreamliner ascended and arced its way back towards the US of A.

The sun cast long shadows across the hills and Max watched the farm workers in the orchard head for their cars, all parked in a line along one edge of the orchard.

The branch creaked overhead.

Max sighed and leaned forward, got his feet on the ground, kicked the kickstand up, fired up the big bike and rolled down the hill toward town, the sun at his back.

Time to get something to eat.

CHAPTER SIX

Back in Ramsey, Max nosed the bike into a slot in front of a bar. The powerful smell of a working grill wafted over him.

Hamburgers.

His stomach rumbled, reminding him he hadn't eaten that day.

He stepped off the bike and up to the door, pushed it open, then paused and surveyed the place.

No mirror over the bar.

That was good.

More times than not, mirrors revealed things that weren't right there on the surface.

They didn't always give it up right away, though. Sometimes, he'd be sitting in a place like this, happy, doing OK, and then a strange haziness would appear somewhere in the mirror. He'd glance over his shoulder, casual like, at the spot reflected in the mirror, and see the apparition taking form.

He remembered a vision from the early days, in Pattaya City, not far from his training camp. He'd been sitting at a Go-Go bar, his back to the dancers, minding his own business when that hazy thing happened: A blur, like a smear in the mirror, but moving, kind of like a heat mirage. It sat on the top of a table in an unoccupied booth in the back.

Max had snuck a look over his shoulder, nothing. Just a table.

Back to the mirror: the haze growing, solidifying.

Over his shoulder: the haze was visible on the table.

The mirror: taking shape. Human.

Table: solidifying.

Mirror: a girl in a bikini, the standard Go-Go outfit. Blood everywhere. All over the table.

Table: taking shape.

Back and forth, back and forth until the full apparition was solid and 3-D. Not quite solid enough to touch, but like a hologram, enough to walk around and view.

Max shook his head to clear the memory, then walked in and seated himself at the bar.

The bartender moseyed over, raised his eyebrows at Max.

"Bushmills. Beer back," Max said.

The bartender nodded, turned, found the bottle, poured Max a shot, grabbed a glass, filled it with beer, set them both in front of Max.

"$3.75," the bartender said.

"You kidding me?" Max asked.

The bartender raised his eyebrows at Max again.

"Cheap. That'd be ten bucks back on the coast."

The bartender nodded, "We ain't on the coast."

Max nodded in return, raised the shot glass to the bartender in salute and downed the Bushmills.

It went down and exploded in his empty stomach like a Molotov cocktail.

Max turned his head and grimaced then set the shot glass down and grabbed the beer, sipped it.

The alcohol went to his head almost immediately.

It felt terrific.

Max started to raise his finger at the bartender, order another, then fought off the urge.

Alcohol and the sight were not good companions. Too much alcohol and Max wouldn't be able to hold the door in his head shut at all, and the spirits would come pouring in—every god damned wretched death from the beginning of time raising up to bear mute witness to its misery.

When that happened, Max could feel the edges of his mind beginning to crack, the dead too much for his head to hold, and yet they kept coming, relentless, pouring in, displaying their gruesome wounds, their impossibly bent anatomy, their blood, the smell of them overpowering and noxious.

Nope. No more getting drunk. Once was enough. Forever.

He'd been getting his party on in Pattaya after a successful fight, slamming shots with the boys, buying drinks for the girls, when all the dead in the room popped into view. Not just the ones from recent history, but *all* the dead. All the way back.

The depth of it had taken his breath away.

The last thing he remembered was ordering a Tequila shot with a couple of his fighter pals, and the shot had pushed him across some kind of liminal boundary and the dead rushed in, clamoring for the door in his head, swarming like a pack of sharks in a feeding frenzy.

Too much.

He had flashes of the taxi ride to the hospital, the dead lining the streets, pushing their way in, and then he was in a place dominated by bright white lights and probing hands, a sharp pain in his shoulder as the doctor on call drove a needle in, sedating him, and then...blackness.

He'd awakened the next day in a hospital room, fighter buddies and girlfriend there looking on anxiously, with a universe full of spirits hovering just at the edges of his vision, a sense of impending doom waiting to claim him.

That was when he knew he had to get out.

Or die.

Max turned his attention back to the bartender, caught his eye.

"'Nother round?" the bartender asked.

"No," Max said. He studied the menu posted over the bar, one of those lighted board types, with little black plastic letters stuck into grooves that marched in horizontal lines down the length of the board.

"Bacon cheeseburger," Max said.

"You got it," the bartender replied. He walked down to the

refrigerator by the grill at the end of the bar, pulled out a Tupperware container of prepared hamburger patties, another of bacon slices, a third of sliced cheese, and walked down to the grill, started everything.

Max grabbed what was left of his beer and turned his back to the bar and studied the room.

A series of battered wooden tables scattered about the room, pool tables in the back, a juke box machine. About thirty patrons. Some eating, a pitcher of beer on nearly every occupied table.

Not a ghost in the place.

Max opened the door in his head a sliver and looked again, hard.

Not a one.

"Huh," Max said.

"What's that?" the bartender asked.

Max turned around to find the bartender there.

"Nothin'," Max said. "Just getting the feeling this bar isn't as old as it looks."

The bartender laughed.

"I suppose not," he said. "Building went up about five years ago, owner bought all the furniture and shit from another bar down in Pecorino went out of business."

Max nodded. "I figured something like that. How about you? You been here long?" The bartender considered him.

"Born and bred," he said.

"Never felt the urge to get out?" Max asked.

"No, not really," the bartender said. "Did the travel bit in my 20s. Joined the Navy, saw the world, that kind of thing. Traveled around the states a piece after my bit. Never found anyplace I fit better, so I came back. It just feels right here."

"That must be nice," Max said. "Name's Max."

The bartender reached a meaty hand over and shook.

"Raymond. Passing through?"

"Yep. Planning on heading out tomorrow. Hey, you know a good place to stay? Quiet? Last hotel I was at was a lot less than restful."

"I'd stay at the Old Shady, if I was to need a hotel in town."

"Quiet?"

Raymond nodded.

"Discrete?"

Another nod.

"How old is the place? Name like The Old Shady makes me think it's been around a while. I'm partial to newer construction."

Raymond studied Max.

"Huh. Would've picked you for the rustic type, into atmosphere, like that."

Max shook his head, "Nope. Newer the better."

Raymond cocked his head, studied Max a minute, pursued his lips to say something, thought better of it, then replied, "The Old Shady's just up the street a piece. You can see the sign from the door. It was built about the same time as the bar."

Max raised his eyebrows.

"Lot of new construction about then?"

Raymond nodded again.

"Yup. Big fire. Took out pretty much this side of the street."

"Huh. That's the second big fire I've heard about in as many days."

"Yeah?"

"Yeah. Other one I heard about was back in Aston. Considerably longer ago, though."

"Ah. You heard about the fire of the century."

Max gave Raymond a long look, sizing him up.

"Got to tell you, I got a real hinky feeling about Aston."

"Yeah?"

"Yeah. Dark."

Raymond looked around the bar.

"Get you another shot and a beer?"

Max checked his watch. He'd been there for half an hour. Another shot and a beer would give him a buzz, probably put him a notch over the .08 law here. He'd have to stay another hour to let it burn off. Small town like this, cops might have an eye on the bar traffic, be all the quicker to pull over a stranger, enhance the local coffers a little bit...

"Just the beer this time, thanks," Max said.

Raymond snagged a glass off the shelf, flipped it up into the air and over, caught it one-handed, right side up, and pulled the beer with the other.

"There you go. $1.75."

"Damn. Things are cheap over here."

"Some things," Raymond said.

Max raised his glass to Raymond again.

"Cheers," he said.

Raymond nodded and watched Max take a drink.

"Where you coming from?" Raymond asked.

Max rolled his head, thought about it. He eyeballed Raymond, let the door open a bit, closed his eyes briefly.

Nothing evil rolling off of this man. No sense of darkness.

"Well, depends on how far back you want to go. Pretty much all over is the short answer."

"And the long?"

"Well...that takes a little time. Nutshell version is I'm on a cross-country ride. So kinda all over. Started in Seattle. Now I'm here."

"Huh. Haven't gotten too far yet, have you? How far you going?"

Max yawned and rubbed his face eyes and face with one hand.

"I don't know."

"So you got nowhere to be? Nobody to see?"

Max shook his head.

"Nope. Haven't had anybody in so long it's kind of hard to remember what that's like."

Raymond looked at Max, shook his head.

"That must suck," he said.

Max shrugged.

"I don't know. Never really known much else. Been on my

own since I was a kid, and never really got the hang of people. Been in places, done things, got involved with people, even got pretty tight with some of 'em, but now..." Max raised his glass, "I drink alone."

Raymond smiled, "Like the old George Thorogood song."

Max smiled back, "Yeah, like that."

Raymond glanced down the length of the bar toward the grill.

"Burger's about ready, let me grab that for you."

Max watched Raymond walk down and start putting together his bacon cheeseburger.

CHAPTER SEVEN

The Old Shady was neither old nor Shady.

Max rolled the big bike into the slot marked "Office," dismounted, and strolled in.

The kid behind the desk had on a red T-shirt with the emblem of the university a couple hundred miles away emblazoned on it. Blue jeans. Crisp hair, cut short and standing tall like the wheat outside.

"What can I do for you?" the kid asked.

"Room for the night," Max said.

"$30," the kid said.

Max pulled out his wallet and peeled out a twenty and two fives, handed them over.

The kid raised his eyebrows, "Cash?"

"That a problem?" Max asked.

"No, not at all," the kid said. "It's just...guys who pay cash..." He let the sentence trail out.

Ah, Max thought. He let the silence sit.

The kid looked away from Max, pulled out a form.

"Here you go, mister. Fill 'er out and we'll get you set up."

Max grabbed the form, filled it out, flipped it back toward the kid.

The kid was still looking at him funny.

"Something else?" Max asked.

"No. Not really, sorry. I was just wondering...maybe you were looking for some company?"

Max brushed away a flush of irritation. Kept his face calm.

"I'm flattered, but I don't swing that way," he said.

The kid's eyes rounded, then he let loose with a guffaw.

"Good one," he said. "You got me."

He grinned at Max as if they'd established some sort of connection.

"I'm talking about pussy. A little party action."

"Hookers? I wouldn't have thought there'd be a lot of that out here in the sticks," Max said.

The kid shrugged, "What else is there to do out here? Drink, fight, and fuck, that's what."

Max closed his eyes, let the door in his head slide open the tiniest bit.

The wave coming off the kid blasted Max. Lust and greed poured out of him. Nothing flat-out evil, but the kid was on his way. A sleazy little shit with no moral compass, and nothing to rein in his impulses.

"How long you been working here?" Max asked.

"Summer job," the kid said. "This is my second summer here. Why?"

"No reason," Max said. "Just making conversation. Been on the road a while. How 'bout getting me a room now?"

"Oh, yeah. Of course. Got a preference? We're pretty wide open here."

Max looked out the window at the motel. Another rectangular two-story box.

"Give me something over the street on the second floor," he said.

"You got it," the kid replied. He reached under the counter, pulled out a key and handed it to Max.

"26B. Top corner over the street. Right there," the kid gestured.

"Thanks," Max replied.

Max turned to go.

"Let me know if you need...anything. Anything at all," the kid said.

Max didn't break stride. Just waved a hand over his shoulder at the kid, dismissing him.

The room was on the newer side. Clean as a whistle and not

even a whiff of death.

But the kid bothered him. This was the second town Max'd been in in as many days where he'd gotten a strong sense of prostitution. Whatever was going on here wasn't near as nasty as back in Aston, but something was not right.

What the fuck is it with this place?

Despite his unease, for the first time in recent memory, Max's sleep was undisturbed. Vague dreams of blood and pain stuck with him like cobwebs on arising, but if that was as bad as it got, he was pleased.

The sun was just cresting the hills of the wheat fields as Max rolled the big hog onto the road and pointed it out of town.

Whatever the hell was going on, he wanted no part of it.

He was back on his original mission: find a place where he could live undisturbed by the dead. No more visions. No more gut-churning stench. No more blood, no more rotting flesh, no more ghastly sights that curdled his soul. Just normal life. Normal death. The way things were supposed to be.

CHAPTER EIGHT

He'd put nearly 150 miles between himself and Aston when his stomach started to growl and had him scanning the road ahead for signage indicating a place to eat. In another thirty minutes and as many miles, he saw it: "Good Eats: The Spotted Owl, Dusty."

He kicked the beast down a gear, blasted into town and pulled to a stop outside The Spotted Owl.

Roadhouse. Dusty parking lot with cigarette butts ground into the dirt, big one-story building with rusty trim and faded barn-red paint. Black tinted windows.

Real shit-kicker, Max thought. He scanned the parking lot for the kind of dark spots that spoke of serious ass kickings. Wouldn't have surprised him to find a tooth.

It didn't seem a likely place to find breakfast, but the neon "Open" was lit, and smoke was coming out of the fan over the grill. Smelled like the deep fryer was already cranking out fries.

Max's boots scrunched through the dirt and gravel toward the door.

Just as his hand reached for the door, it slammed open and would've caught him in the face if he hadn't slipped to the right. A big man in black jeans, square-toed, steel-tipped cowboy boots, plaid cowboy shirt tucked in behind a big-ass rodeo-looking buckle and a white cowboy hat barreled out, paying no attention to Max, practically shoving him out of the way.

A flash of anger rushed through Max. The visions over the last few days, the darkness of the area, had gotten to him, and he let his control lapse.

"Hey! Watch where the fuck you're going," he said.

Square Toes spun around and faced Max.

"Maybe you ought to shut your fucking mouth," he said.

Max let his helmet drop to the ground.

"Fuck you, cowboy," he said.

Square Toes rushed him.

He was quick, probably pretty damn good in a bar fight, especially once he'd gotten a sucker punch in, but he was an amateur. High-school wrestling, maybe, but no real training.

Max slipped to the left, dodging him easily, and helped him along with a shove to the back of his head.

Square Toes smashed into the wall of the building and roared. "I'm going to kill you for that!" he said.

"Bring it, cowboy," Max said.

Square toes rushed him again.

Classic, Max thought. His rage drained away as he entered the zone: a state of calm calculation where time slowed and he became a fighting machine.

He slipped Square Toes' rush and this time slammed in a leg kick to the back of his thigh that dropped him onto his back.

The door opened and three men slid into the parking lot.

"What the fuck, Mack?" said one of the men, this one in a black cowboy hat.

Max circled to keep all four men in his line of sight.

The three men looked down at Square Toes confusedly.

"Get that motherfucker!" Square Toes screamed.

"Knew you were a bitch first time I laid eyes on you," Max said.

Square Toes lumbered to his feet.

"God damn it! I said get him!"

Square Toes advanced towards Max.

The other three hesitated as Square Toes set himself and kicked as hard as he could.

Max stepped to the side, lifted Square Toes' boot as it whistled by, then stepped in with a straight right to the jaw.

Lights out.

Square Toes crumpled into a heap as if he'd been shot.

The three men looked at one another uneasily.

"Next?" Max said.

The one in the black hat raised his hands.

"Hold on, mister," he said. "Let's slow things down."

"Then tell that motherfucker to stop right there," Max said, nodding at one of the men who was attempting to flank him.

Black hat laughed.

"Hold on, Dennis," he said.

Dennis ignored Black Hat and stepped in with a big, looping overhand right.

Max closed the distance, pulled on Dennis' arm, adding to his momentum, then reared back and brought the crown of his head flush with Dennis' nose, stopping him in his tracks. The combined momentum of the two men caved in Dennis' nose, and Max felt both of his orbital bones go as well.

Dennis moaned and brought up both hands, as if trying to catch his face, then fell to his knees and then collapsed forward.

Max danced back, his hands up, ready.

"Now hold on, God damn it," Black Hat said. "I told him to stop."

"All I wanted was some breakfast," Max said.

Black Hat shook his head.

"Best keep movin', mister, you ask me," he said.

Max met Black Hat's gaze, glanced to his left to make sure the other man wasn't pulling anything, then returned his eyes to Black Hat.

"'Spose you're right about that, dammit," Max said.

Black Hat turned to the man next to him.

"Help me get them back inside. We'll clean them up in there," he said.

Black Hat didn't take his eyes off Max as he and the other man leaned down, got a grip under Square Toes' arms, and hauled him to his feet.

Square Toes' head rolled and he snorted as he begin to return to consciousness.

"You best hit the road and hit it hard, mister," Black Hat said.

Max nodded.

"You just took out Mack Bannister. Bannisters don't fuck around. They'll kill you, so you'd best keep going."

"What I thought," Max said.

Max stood there as the two men disappeared inside with Square Toes, leaving him with the man moaning in the dirt.

Max reached down and picked up his helmet. "Nice little town you got here."

CHAPTER NINE

By noon, Max was fed, watered, and draped over the Ninja, feet on the rear pegs, whizzing down the back roads at a steady 80 mph.

Bannister, Max thought. *Gotta be the same Bannisters ol' Slim was telling me about back in Aston.*

Max let the vibration of the beast comfort him, the road whipping by lull his angsty mind, and the sway and weave of the ride soothe him.

It was beautiful country, if you liked that sort of thing: wheat fields and orchards, rolling hills of green and yellow and brown, a car here and there, a tractor arcing over a hill, the smell of dirt and fresh fields on the warm wind.

Max eased the Kawi up a long hill. As he crested the hill, the whole area was laid out below him.

Wheat fields gave way to an enormous apple orchard.

A line of shacks edged the vineyard: worker's quarters, third-world stuff. The shacks were about the sizes of motel rooms, slapdash constructions of dilapidated, untreated wood.

A plume of dust marked a van making its way down an access road, headed for what looked like some kind of equipment shed.

The van sucked Max in. There was a dark energy there that made him sick to his stomach.

God damn it.

He tried kicking the door in his head shut, but it blasted open instead, sucking him down into a dark hole. His stomach plummeted, waves of vertigo spun the world around him, and he felt himself spiraling down into a dark tunnel that swirled into an inky-black abyss.

He barely got the bike to the shoulder and the kickstand down before waves of imagery and emotion tore through him, overwhelming his sense of the physical world around him.

The imagery brutalized his soul.

Nasty, evil shit: *girls on their backs on dirt floors, skirts up, shirts up around their necks; men lined up....* In the dark spiral of the vision, some of the men were focused flares of rage and sadism, throttling the girls, beating them.... Bones were breaking, women gasping in pain and for breath...and in this dusty misery, one evil fuck watching the whole thing, the slave master....

Max snapped to.

He was still seated on his bike, view of the orchard and shed below.

The van had pulled to a stop by the shed.

Now what?

He'd never experienced anything like this, not even in Thailand where there'd been some crazy evil shit going on. Never had he gotten an image of anything...not dead. This was more than a peek into the world of the dead; this was....

The men in the orchard were coming.

A tall man with a white cowboy hat got out of the van, strolled around to the far side of the van from Max, slid open the door.

He yelled something, and then women began filing out of the van and heading into the shed.

Max counted six women.

They all looked to be Hispanic.

There was a uniform posture to the girls...heads down, shoulders rounded, a defeated shuffle.

One of the girls didn't move quickly enough for Cowboy Hat, and he kicked her in the ass hard enough that she lost her balance and went sprawling in the dirt.

She never looked back. Just picked herself up, and disappeared into the shed.

The men arrived at the van.

Cowboy Hat had them line up, started taking money from them.

Max felt bile rise in his throat.

The men filed into the shed and disappeared.

Cowboy Hat took a look around, counted his money, stuck it in his front pocket, then strolled to the door of the shed, and poked his head in.

Satisfied, he pulled out a cigarette, lit it, leaned back against the door post and gazed out over the vineyard.

Get the fuck out of here as fast as you possibly can, Max thought. *Put a thousand miles between this shit hole and you. Find an open, empty plain where there is no death, no nastiness, just open spaces. Cows maybe. Buffalo, yeah. Buffalo'd be good.*

Max shook his head, put up the kickstand, let the bike roll down the hill, toed it into second gear and jump-started it.

The bike rumbled to life, low, throaty, powerful.

Cowboy Hat glanced up towards Max, blew smoke, looked away.

Keep going.

As the road leveled out, Max lost sight of the shed and Cowboy Hat.

Better.

As he pulled abreast of the line of sheds, the vision hit him again, more powerfully than before.

Men lined up, women on their backs in the dirt, brutal, animalistic sex. One of the men appeared to be trying to kill the woman under him and fuck her at the same time. He thrust his hips, punched the woman square in the face, flipped her over, twisted her arm up...

Max found himself beside the road, inches from rolling off into the ditch, his bike dead.

The woman was...

Her arm broke with a meaty snap. Excited, the man thrusted more enthusiastically as she bucked in agony. He reached both hands around her neck....

Max felt his own vision restricting, reddening, flashes at the periphery, pressure in his head...a pop.

He fucking killed her. Fucking son of a bitch. Shit.

Max got off the bike.

Tears blurred his vision as he staggered into the vineyard, legs unsteady. A growing sense of rage strengthened him with each stride. Soon he was jogging, his feet quiet on the rich earth of the vineyard.

The smell of the sun baking the earth, of the vines, of water —the beauty of it startled Max. He could see the fringe of every leaf, every clipped edge where the vines had been pruned. He could feel his heart pumping strongly, his lungs working, the blood rushing through his body—a sense of lightness and strength such as he had never experienced.

The edge of the vineyard appeared as a brightening of the light ahead.

He slowed, approached the open area warily.

Cowboy Hat was nowhere to be seen.

Workers slid out of the shed, eyes on the ground. They glanced over their shoulders nervously, headed for a series of tables where lunch boxes and thermoses were set.

Someone was yelling in the shed.

"That's my fucking property!"

Cowboy Hat.

The workers had their backs to the shed, and to Max.

Max eased over.

"I said, that was my fucking property, boy! You gonna pay me for this? She was worth more fucking money than you make a year, you fucking lowlife wetback!"

An angry retort in Mexican Spanish.

The workers studiously ignoring it all.

Max stepped into the shed.

Five women huddled in a corner, quivering with fear.

Cowboy Hat was faced off against a stocky Mexican.

The woman...right cheek ground into the dirt, arm twisted behind her back at an impossible angle, bare ass in the air, blank eyes staring at nothing.

The Mexican looked like he was thinking about taking on Cowboy Hat.

Both men swiveled to look at Max as he stepped closer.

Everything slowed.

Cowboy Hat's mouth opened slowly, teeth glistening with saliva, the crease forming in his jeans as he lifted a foot to meet Max.

The Mexican's eyes rounded and bulged, began to fill with rage.

And Max was into them.

A surreal, dreamlike sense settled upon him, his own movements graceful and lucid, the two men's slowed and exaggerated. Max stepped to an angle and brought his shin to the chin of Cowboy Hat, putting every ounce of strength and technique he could into the blow.

Cowboy Hat's head snapped back, his eyes rolled back in his head, his hat flew off and he fell stiff as a board.

The Mexican barely had time to turn his eyes toward Max before Max had him in a full Thai clinch and was kneeing him in the face. Over and over and over. The man went limp, but Max held him by the hair with both hands and continued kneeing him in the face, feeling it crumble inward, watching the Mexican's teeth drop to the dirt, like bloody pearls.

A whimper.

Max looked up.

The women were staring at him, mouths open.

Max let the Mexican slump to the dirt.

Cowboy Hat was flat and motionless.

The Mexican was a bloody mess.

Both alive, Max figured.

Too fucking bad.

He pictured stomping them both to death. Thought better of it.

He walked over to the dead woman and gently eased her down, covered her ass with her skirt, rolled her onto her back, brushed the dirt from her cheeks, delicately arranged her arms so that her hands were folded over her chest, then took a knee beside her.

"I'm sorry this happened," Max whispered.

He reached out and closed her eyes.

"May you rest in peace," he whispered, desperately willing this prayer of sorts to be a delivery, to spare the woman an eternity of anguished endurance, condemned to haunt this patch of ground.

Max looked up.

The women were still staring at him.

Max stood, raised his hands.

"It's OK," he said. "I'm not here to hurt you."

"What you do?" one of the women asked.

Max shrugged.

Cowboy Hat snorted, started to sit up.

Max skipped over and kicked him in the head, hard.

Cowboy Hat rolled over and didn't move.

Max leaned down and went through Cowboy Hat's jeans, pulled out his wallet, keys, and a thick wad of money.

He pointed at the women.

"You. Come with me." he said.

Max walked out of the door of the shed straight for the van.

The workers had vanished.

"Looks like we got the place to ourselves," Max said.

The women stayed in a knot, close to one another, giving Max wide berth.

Max walked up to them.

They cringed away.

Max raised his hands again.

"Look, I'm not going to hurt you, I promise," he said.

Four of the women kept their eyes on the dirt, but the one who had spoken met his gaze.

"What now?" she asked.

She was older than the others, but still couldn't have been much more than about 21. She had the thick look of a country girl, stocky.

"Can you drive?" Max asked.

She looked at him.

Max pantomimed driving with his hands holding a steering wheel.

"Oh!" she said. "Yes, I..." She stopped, unable to find the word.

Max nodded.

He turned to the van and opened the driver's door.

"Get in," he said, motioning to her.

None of the women moved.

Max stepped closer to the leader.

"Here," he said, putting the keys in her hand.

She stared at him.

"You go," Max said, glancing at the shed. No telling how long Cowboy Hat and the Mexican were going to stay down. "You go now!"

He pulled on the woman and got her into the driver's seat.

He had to herd the other women, but they were conditioned to it, and fell to following his directions.

Once he had them in the van, he slid the door shut, walked to the driver and faced her.

"Here," he said, handing her the thick stack of money he'd taken from Cowboy Hat. He dug though Cowboy Hat's wallet, pulled out another stack of money, this all hundreds, and handed that over as well.

He gestured to the women in the back, pantomimed dealing the money out like cards.

"You all split that, get it?"

The women nodded.

Max glanced back at the shed, worried now.

"You go now," he said.

The driver met his eye and something flared deep down in her eyes—something like...hope.

"*Gracias*," she whispered.

"*Vayos con dios*," Max said.

The driver started the van, turned it around, and aimed it down the access road to the road that lay beyond.

Max watched it until it disappeared from sight, gave the shack another glance, then turned and slipped back into the vineyard.

CHAPTER TEN

Max stepped quickly through the field, his boots sinking deep into the fertile dirt. He was anxious to get on his bike and be gone. Flipping through Cowboy Hat's wallet as he walked, Max dug out the man's driver's license and stopped cold: Roger Bannister.

Bannister.

Slim: "Bannisters...big deal in these parts...."

The mansion on the hill with its white stucco walls, the glint of a lens pointed at him.

Black Hat: "You just took out Mack Bannister...Bannisters will kill you."

Roger Bannister's angry face stared out at him from his license photo, Cowboy Hat in place.

"Shit, you really stepped in it this time, Maxxy, old boy," Max muttered.

He tapped the license against his knuckles as he stared into the green of the field surrounding him.

He wanted to get clear of it all: the ghosts, the visions, the Bannisters, the violence—the evil that haunted the world, coloring every place man had set foot.

Never asked for this, Max thought. *Never had any interest in ghosts, none of that shit. All I ever wanted was to fight. Didn't want shit to do with life in the US of A. Didn't want shit to do with women. Didn't want shit to do with politics. With religion, with anything.*

Max slipped the license into his shirt pocket, balled his fists, and looked up into the burning blue sky above.

He stood there a long moment: rage, frustration, despair, and pain rocking through him.

The whole god damn world is evil, Max thought. *I want no part of it.*

He had zero interest in killing himself, especially with what he'd seen: from the woman swinging in the tree the other day to a dozen other messy suicides he'd seen since the door in his head opened...no: suicide was off the table.

Just keep going. There's got to be a place somewhere where evil hasn't completely taken over. There has to be a patch of sacred ground somewhere.

Sacred ground.

That was it.

He moved through the field of vines toward the light ahead, the world bright and green, eager to get on the bike and hit the road.

Three hours and two hundred miles later, Max was even further into the farmland. Long, two-lane roads that curved through the back country and the occasional little hamlet of a couple of hundred, fewer and fewer people around.

Darkness hung at the edge of his vision as he rode: he could feel the pull of tragedy and evil out here, little knots of misery that he flashed past at 70 - 80 miles per hour.

He had in mind a place he'd read about: some New Age shit about a confluence of "energy," "where four dimensions met" or some such shit.

Before this had happened to him, Max had never really given a thought to anything spiritual or religious. It'd all struck him as a load of crap people used to make themselves happy. Like the old Simon and Garfunkel song; "All lies and jest, and a man hears what he wants to hear and disregards the rest..." Bullshit. Escapist claptrap that people used to try to control others.

Things had changed.

He still figured most of it was bullshit, but he now had solid evidence that there was something beyond this world, some other plane of existence.

He needed some answers.

So. Four Corners. The "confluence of energy."

What the hell.

Another hour's ride brought him within sight of the hill that marked Four Corners.

The road carried him alongside a coulee about a mile wide, the plains below littered with glacial boulders, then peeled off and led up the steep walls of the canyon formed by the massive glacier that'd passed through millennia ago, up past layers of orange and red, up to the green hills above.

Towering above all the others, Four Corners was the commanding peak of the area. The natives had held off the U. S. Calvary there once, and the bones of all the dead Calvary men and Indians called out to Max as he sped through the green fields toward the peak.

Despite its reputation and allure, the roads were nearly empty.

Max climbed the peak on the Kawi, winding around, back and forth, dizzyingly, to the top.

Asphalt parking lot, chemical outhouses, a chain keeping motorized traffic off the final path to the top.

The river at the center of the coulee was a line of blue water cutting through orange rock which described a line through green fields. Not a building in sight, other than the outhouses by the parking lot.

Max dug into his saddlebags and pulled out a daypack, loaded it with his camping gear, shouldered it, and stepped over the chain onto the trail.

The graveled trail soon gave way to dirt, then narrowed further. A wind cooled the sweat on his brow, and Max gave himself over to the climb, feeling the pull and stretch of his muscles, his heart beating in his chest, breath steady and deep, his boots' purchase on the sloping trail.

Reaching the top, Max looked around: a flat niche in the

rock, bushes off to one side, emptiness on the other. While it was possible to scale the remaining fifty feet of rock to the pointy peak above, it'd take some scrambling, and Max figured this was good enough. He moved over towards the bushes, and found a trail there. Curious, he followed it further back into the foliage, surprised at its depth. Fifty feet in, the trail opened up into a picturesque clearing: mountain flowers dotted the twenty-foot space, stunted trees lined the edges, and the view was breath taking.

This'll do.

He found a flat spot in front of one of the stunted trees, slipped off the day pack, and sat down, the tree forming a perfectly comfortable back rest.

Suppose I should cross my legs and mumble 'Ommm,' or some such shit, Max thought.

Ah, lighten up, shithead, he told himself. *Just enjoy the view.*

As he sat there, the clearing slowly buzzed to life. Little birds twittered in the trees, butterflies and bees moved from flower to flower, the gentle wind background music.

Just...be, Max thought. *Relax.*

A warm glow started in his belly and grew.

Just the sun on my belly.

The warmth spread through him, filled his spine, his legs, his arms, his hands, and his feet. His head filled with light. Max closed his eyes and let the warmth surge through him. His heart relaxed and all tension dropped from him.

Something to this "confluence of energy" after all.

He let himself float in comfort.

And then, at the edges of the red warmth behind his closed eyes, sparkling flashes of golden light. Popping. Darkness encroached. Light and dark. Pop, pop, pop: golden stars exploding behind his eyelids, replaced by darkness.

Good and evil.

The whole fucking world is a stage for the battle of good and evil, of light and dark, he thought.

A stage.

Lines from a play he was forced to read in high school rose in his head: "*All the world's a stage; And all the men and women merely players; They have their exits and their entrances, And one man in his time plays many parts....*"

As the light show carried him away, Max remembered his purpose for coming here: some kind of answer. Some kind of purpose. His part in the play.

"*... life exists, and identity; that the powerful play goes on and you may contribute a verse.*"

"Why me?" Max whispered. "What do you want with me?" surprising himself.

Who was he talking to? God? The spirits?

A black door appeared in the red field of his vision, its golden knob glistening in the light.

The door.

Anxiety kicked Max in the gut, accelerating his heart rate. His eyelids fluttered, his arms raised, and he found himself in full fight-or-flight mode.

No.

No running. This is what I'm here for.

Calming his heart, Max willed himself back into relaxation.

In his mind's eye, he moved toward the door.

The door grew as he approached it. His hand reached out and grasped the knob, turning it...

Skeletal fingers scrabbled out of the gap, grasping the door jamb like a hundred spiders. A force pushed the door from the other side, and with a flash of panic, Max turned a shoulder into the door and pushed.

The door closed, chopping off a clattering pile of bony fingers that scrabbled like crab legs around his feet.

Max took a deep breath.

It's OK, he told himself.

I can do this.

He tensed his gut, set himself, and reached for the door again.

A black wind howled through the gap.

Max stepped back and let the wind blast the door all the way open.

An icy cold, inky black presence overtook the vision.

Pure malevolence and hatred.

Max's head swam, the world tilted and spun.

He felt himself being sucked down into a black hole of the soul.

As he spiraled down into the blackness, he flew past visions of unspeakable cruelty and savagery: *Men cutting open the chests of spread-eagled victims, ripping out their beating hearts as the victims screamed in agony, holding the hearts up to shower blood down upon themselves.* Every form of torture and rape and sadism he'd ever heard of presented itself, and many, many more. *The open eyes of the dead girl on the dirt floor back in the shed at the orchard. The blood-splattered walls of the hotel room in Aston.*

The images magnified, splintered, grew into others, each more horrible than the last.

Bad as the images were, it was the dark malevolence that most rocked him. This was a living, sentient force of pure hatred, pure evil: it hungered for pain and agony. It grew more powerful and hungry with each scream, each death rattle, each spurt of blood and semen.

Max could feel the force reaching its icy fingers for him, scrabbling at his heart, squeezing it.

Panic flared and he fought to calm himself, but the force was too strong and he felt himself slipping away into the black iciness of the pit, the world narrowing down to a black hole that sucked him in, the darkness spreading and consuming more and more light in the vision, red warmth pushed to the periphery.

The force pried at his heart with icy fingers that scratched and scrabbled and tore.

Just let go, Max thought. *Let it take you. So easy—and it'll all be over…*

It was a brutal attempt at dominance coupled with the

seductive siren call of suicide. With a start, Max realized what the force was after: his very essence. *His soul.*

This was no three-round bout, loser helped from the ring and off to train and return.

This was for keeps.

Max pushed back.

The force responded in kind, and Max felt an icy blade penetrate to the center of his being.

Everything was wild and chaotic and filled with pain. Darkness spread until it met what remained of the golden warmth of the vision that had led him to the door.

Relief spread through Max: *the answer.*

As his panic diminished, Max felt the golden force swell and grow, pushing back at the consuming blackness.

The golden force was the opposite of the consuming malevolence. Where the darkness was icy cold, the golden force was warmth.

Max let the warmth overtake him.

His racing heart slowed, his shallow breaths deepened, light returned to the vision.

This is the battle, Max thought. *This is good vs. evil.*

The answer is really as simple as that.

There is no why, there just is.

The Bannisters had allowed the dark force to consume them. Where there should be warmth and communion, good will and the building of bonds and relationships, there was cold malevolence, the desire to dominate, destroy and devour.

The house on the hill, a black radiance oozing from it to spread across the land, its tentacles reaching out of sight, forming nodules of misery here and there: the hotel in Aston, the dirt shack at the orchard: hundreds of others stretching to the horizon of his vision and beyond.

My God, Max thought. *It's like the dark beating heart of a huge monster.*

Max's eyes snapped open and he found himself in the clearing: butterflies danced from flower to flower. He followed a particularly large Monarch-looking thing with his gaze and was startled to find he was not alone.

A beautiful blond woman sat across from him, her legs folded into some kind of yoga position, her arms resting loosely on her knees, palms up to the sun.

She blinked and a radiant light shone from her startlingly blue eyes.

Her smile revealed perfect ivory teeth.

"Hello, Max," she said.

CHAPTER ELEVEN

Max rose to his feet, startled.

"Do I know you?" he asked.

The woman's teeth shone in the sunshine.

"You were looking for me," she said. "Just now."

Max crossed the clearing and stood before her.

"You're going to have to explain that," he said.

The woman nodded her head at his feet.

"Sit, and we'll talk," she said.

Max sat.

"The path you are on is your own, and each step you take is a choice," she said. "You may turn back at any time. Press forward, flee, embrace, try to drown your gift—you are a free being, Max."

Max's head swam again, the past imposing itself on the present: all those early mornings in the *Viharn* with Phra Saksith, the spiritual guide Ong had chosen for him, the old monk's words echoes of the woman's.

"'Gift?' 'Free?' How do you figure that?" Max asked. "I didn't ask for any of this."

The woman smiled.

"You have penetrated the veil, and glimpsed the ground of all being. That is a gift, no matter how you feel about it."

"Don't want it. Take it back."

The woman smiled.

"You have seen, Max. There is no taking that back. What you do with what you have seen is your choice."

Phra Saksith: "one cannot unsee, Max..."

Max closed his eyes in frustration.

"Be blessed, Max," the woman said.

"I didn't ask for this, damn it!" Max said.

He opened his eyes, and the woman was gone.

Max leapt to his feet.

"Wait!" he called. "We're not done here!"

Only butterflies, bees, the quiet breeze.

"Damn it!" Max said.

His frustration peaked, and he felt like kicking the shit of someone, or something, and then he felt a pop in his chest, and a newfound calm in his heart. A centeredness, a solidity that had been lacking.

I'm a free man, Max thought. *I have a choice.*

Max walked to the edge of the clearing where a cliff dropped a couple hundred sheer feet before angling out and meeting the plateau below.

The breeze dried the sweat on his brow and chest, cooling him, calming him further.

What to do.

The vision of the house on the hill returned—those long, black tentacles reaching out across the country.

Max shook his head.

Nonsense, he thought. *Evil empire? What kind of shit is that? Go find your place in the sun, son. Get back on that big bike of yours and ride into the sunset, and keep riding until you find a place where the dead don't haunt you, where death is what it is supposed to be. No agony, no evil, no wrongness.*

The setting sun made the green fields below glow, brought out the orange of the rock lining the river, the blue of the water, the yellow and purple and red and white and black of the mountain flowers in the clearing. Butterflies little miraculous bursts of bouncing color.

Max shouldered his day pack, surveyed the clearing.

Worse places to set up for the night.

He sat in front of his tent cross-legged, watching the water come to a boil in the pot on the camp stove, steam rising into the reddening glow of the clearing, the burning gas from his camp stove hissing. A few birds tweeted, but the butterflies and bees were gone.

As the water came to a boil, Max opened a pouch of freeze-dried food: Noodles and Chicken.

Max poured boiling water into the pouch, stirred it thoroughly and carefully, experience having taught him to make sure no clumps of freeze-dried food remained unsaturated.

Staring into the pouch, Max thought again of the woman.

That good and evil existed was something Max had never questioned, but now he saw life itself as the battle of good vs. evil. The battle raged everywhere man set foot. That was what separated man from beast: the ability to choose and nurture evil. Or good. Free will.

Max opened the pouch and stirred it some more, walked to the edge of the clearing and watched as the red faded from the sky and the stars came out.

The brilliance of the stars startled him. Even though he'd been in the countryside for a while, ambient glow of cities not a concern, the stars here seemed especially bright.

Max sat and ate, the stars dancing in his pupils.

CHAPTER TWELVE

Max rolled the big bike to the crossroad at the foot of Four Corners.

Left led to Aston, right to parts as yet unknown.

Not my problem.

He aimed the bike to the right.

More farmland. Still in wheat country, but heading east, bound to hit the heartland sooner rather than later. Corn.

The country roads suited Max just fine. Winding, two-laned, less trafficked, slowed by the occasional tractor, but overall less populated, less death, less shit to deal with.

The blond woman's image burned brightly in his mind. Max turned it over, inspected it, replayed the conversation, tried to make sense of it.

She hadn't felt like a ghost. The peace that radiated from her had touched Max in a supernatural way, left him calmer, more centered, less angry. She was like a female version of Phra Saksith, and the thought gave Max pause: Had the old monk passed on, taken on a new form?

Her presence had pulled him from the inky abyss that had sucked him down into that Other—the black evil, the living malevolence that lurked at the edges of all creation.

A war on between good and evil. Max thought. *No surprise there.*

What was a surprise was the extent of it: the magnitude. A war waged everywhere man existed.

With a start, Max realized that even his thought process was part of it: his decision to turn right at the road and to seek escape, respite from the visions of the agony and death and ugliness was capitulation—surrender. To evil. How did that line go? *The only thing necessary for the perpetuation of evil is for good people to stand by and do nothing.* Something like that.

Max geared down and pulled over.

Wheat fields checkered green and brown in various stages of development: replanting, recovery, harvest.

The fields could be taken metaphorically: growth and harvest, culling, and replanting, the battle against insects and other foragers—even wheat fields could be read like the I-Ching, or a fairy tale, or the Zodiac, or some such.

There is no escape. To keep going is to surrender. Once you've seen...you either have to do something to help, or you are part of the problem.

Max paced back and forth alongside the road.

Most likely, I'll get myself killed. How on earth will that help?

Max climbed back on to the big bike and thumbed it to life.

Sitting there, revving the engine, he wanted to keep going: head straight out, put his back to the problem and find some peace.

But deep down he knew he'd find no peace that way.

The hell with it.

He throttled up and spun the big bike in a 180, rubber screeching as he cranked the beast up to 80mph and flew down the road back in the direction he'd come.

He pushed the bike hard, carving lines through corners at 80 and 90mph, hitting 120 on straight stretches.

An element of potential suicide mixed with the adrenal thrill of speed, and he embraced it.

If it's meant to be, it's meant to be, he thought. *If God, or Buddha, or whatever or whoever wants me to be a part of the "solution" or some such, he'll keep me from splattering myself off the side of a big ol' truck, or post, or whatever....*

At the speeds he was riding, there wasn't much room for reflection; it was all reaction and the physical response of leaning, taking the centripetal force of the curves, blasting into the straight stretches, eyes far ahead, watching for road detritus, cars, gravel, gophers: anything that could take him out.

As Max gave himself over to the ride, images popped up in his head: *the blond woman and her smile mixing with Phra Saksith's serene face, the consuming peace which filled each of them*, and then...*the bartender in that second town he'd hit*--the one outside of Aston. As Max's mind touched on him, the blond woman smiled.

Not sure if any of this made sense, Max pushed the bike and himself harder, riding it like Thor on a thunderbolt.

He had a destination now.

CHAPTER THIRTEEN

Max killed the bike and let it drift to the shoulder, just short of the "Welcome to Ramsey. Pop 1280." sign. White type on green background, with little curlicues of wheat at the borders.

He closed his eyes and tried to shut down his racing mind. Fight or flight was running the mental show, but that decision had been made hundreds of miles ago, and he was not turning back.

His gut told him to find the bartender,

Ralph? R-something. Raymond.

He had a strong sense the Blond Woman wanted him to connect with Raymond.

He opened his eyes. Picturesque farm houses surrounded by acreage. A nice wide Main Street up ahead, old-style facades fronting freshly painted businesses, shiny and new looking. Which figured, seeing how as Raymond had told him half the town had burned down five years ago.

A jacked-up pick up raced by, death metal booming out through a sound system that had the panels in the big truck vibrating in a way that rattled Max's guts. A wave of blurry imagery washed over him with the blast of air carried by the passing truck. Fists smashing into flesh, blood running, bones breaking—and through it all—above, below, in the middle, tasting every drop of blood, relishing every scream and groan, feeling the resonance of each meaty snap of bone breaking —the presence: Red and black as hell. Ice cold and demonic. Salivating, laughing, sucking in the agony and torture—growing more powerful with each act.

"The blood-dimmed tide is loosed, and everywhere; The ceremony of innocence is drowned..."

Shit.

The blond woman came to mind again, and Max realized that although the imagery had shaken him, the new-found solidity of peace and calm held. There was a foundation of peace at his core now, a calm sense of purpose in the face of evil.

Would it hold?

Nothing for it but to bite down on the mouthpiece and step forward.

Thumbing the beast back to life, Max throttled up and aimed the bike at the bar in town.

The kid wasn't behind the counter of The Old Shady. *Probably out somewhere dumping a roofie in his date's drink,* Max figured.

The ol' geezer working the counter hardly gave Max a look, just slid the key over for 26B for $30 cash without taking his eyes from the television on the wall.

Back in the room, Max opened himself a little: nothing. The place was as clean as before: no untimely death, no souls lingering between the two worlds, stuck and unhappy. Whoever had passed over here, if anyone had, had passed well.

He walked to the window and gazed out.

A few pickup trucks dawdling down Main, a couple of people on the sidewalk, nothing unusual.

Max closed his eyes and let the door in his head open some more.

He could feel the inky red presence hovering, prowling, looking for someone to feed it. The ol' geezer behind the desk downstairs was a little knot of blackness, but it was a misery mostly pulled in on itself, a self-consuming bitterness.

Off to the edge of town, a dark ruffling movement of the presence. Evil prowled the borderlands of this town, getting thicker the further down the road toward Aston.

Safe enough here, for now.

He stood at the window long enough for the sky to redden

and darken. Street lights blinked on, and neon signs in the bar/restaurant down the street spread their glow of primary colors onto the sidewalk.

His stomach rumbled, and Max decided it was time to move.

Raymond was manning the bar as Max strolled in, his boots loud on the wood floor.

Max threw a leg over a stool at the bar and sat.

"Back so soon?" Raymond asked.

"Just couldn't stay away," Max said.

"What can I do you for?"

"Bushmills, beer back."

"You got it."

Raymond poured the drinks and set them in front of Max.

"Still $3.75?"

"Yep. Good memory."

"It's Raymond, right?"

"Yep. And you're Max."

"Your memory's not so bad either."

"Mandatory for a good bartender. Not like we get a lot of strangers in here, though. So what brings you back this way?"

Max looked Raymond in the eyes, picked up the shot glass, toasted him, and tossed it back.

"Kind of hard to explain. Historical interest, mixed with some personal business, I guess you could say."

Raymond's eyebrows rose.

"How's that?"

Max closed his eyes and let the door open a sliver.

A flutter of darkness far off to the periphery.

Light poured out of Raymond. An image of the blond woman flashed into Max's mind—smiling at him. The light from Raymond reached into Max's heart, connected with the inner foundation of new-found serenity.

Max'd never sensed anything like it.

Could the blond woman have opened another door for him? This one showing the flip side of the presence?

"Fair dinkum," Max muttered.

"Huh?"

Max took a look around the bar. Same crowd from the last time he was here, he figured. Regulars. None of them gave off an overwhelming sense of darkness or light—just a toned-down mix of the two. Civilians. Regular, ordinary folks.

What did that make Raymond?

Max studied him carefully.

"You're different from most folks, aren't you?"

A glint of humor alit in the depths of Raymond's eyes.

"People keep telling me so. I suspect people tell you the same thing."

Max nodded, "Can't say anyone's ever said it in a very friendly way, other than you."

"I get a sense of that. I also get a strong sense of purpose coming off of you. So, I'll ask you again: What brings you back? What's this mix of 'historical and personal interest'?"

Max took a deep breath and let it out.

"Let's just say I keep running into Bannisters, and I do mean running into 'em."

Raymond's face clouded.

"Bannisters are not good folks."

"That's putting it mildly," Max said.

"Where'd you run into them?"

"A couple of places. Vineyard a ways down the road. Road-stop diner a bit before that."

Raymond's eyes rounded.

"Holy shit. That was you?"

"What do you mean, 'that was you?' You say that like it's something you know about."

"Me and just about everyone else. Nothing like that has happened to the Bannisters in over a hundred years."

"Turn of the century fire?"

Raymond nodded. "When they burned everyone out. Everyone."

"What do you know about that?"

"Plenty. My full name is Raymond Delbert Ingersoll."

"Ingersoll. That's the family that got burned out."

"Almost. Still a few of us in these parts."

"We've got to talk."

Raymond looked around the bar.

"Let's put that off for a bit. I'm not too worried about the boys in here, but I'd rather talk to you up at my place."

Raymond pulled a pen out and scribbled a map on a cocktail napkin.

"Tell you what. You come by and visit me after I close up. We'll talk then. I can give you some of the historical interest you're after and you can tell me about the personal business end of things."

"Deal."

"Another shot and a beer while you're waiting?"

"That sounds just fine."

"Let me rustle that up for you."

Max watched Raymond turn and go to work, a faint glow of light surrounding him, like an aura.

CHAPTER FOURTEEN

Max and Raymond sat at the kitchen table, a bottle of Bushmills between them.

"So you just started seeing the dead, then?" Raymond asked.

"That's about the size of it," Max answered. "Started one night in a condo off Jom Tien beach in Thailand. Ghost of a little Thai girl and an older, white guy."

"And you went up to Four Corners and had yourself a vision of a blond angel and now you can see a glow off some people."

"Just one, so far. You."

"Huh. I don't see things, exactly, but I have a surefire sense of good and evil. Light and Dark. Most people are a bit of a mix, and neither the good nor the bad weighs very much. With you...I don't know. You're the first man I seen with real power...and it's a mix. When I seen you before, you were real hard to read. Lots of darkness hovering around you, but somehow not *in* you, if you catch my drift. And the light is stronger."

"Before, I was running."

"And now?"

"I still want it to stop. But I figure I was given this 'gift' for a reason, and I've got to do whatever it is I'm supposed to do before it'll leave me in peace."

"And you figure whatever it is you're supposed to do has to do with the Bannisters?"

"Why else do I keep running into 'em? Into the evil they're spreading?"

"Could be because they're everywhere around these parts, and they're into everything. Can't spit around here without hitting one of 'em."

"And nobody does anything?"

"Ain't anyone around strong enough to take 'em on. Anyone gets in their way gets squashed real quick."

"That what happened with your family? Fire of the century?"

Raymond grabbed the bottle and poured himself a shot.

"Sort of. You could say the Ingersolls got in the way. You could say they had something the Bannisters wanted. You could say a lot of things, and people do. Bottom line is the Bannisters burned us out. The way they did us sent a strong message. Anyone didn't like their ways up and left. They've been running things since. Got Bannisters in local government, police, real estate, farming—any position of power or money, and they're in it."

Raymond threw the Bushmills down his throat, grimaced, and slammed the shot glass down on the table.

"You intend to take on the Bannisters, you best know what you're getting into."

"I know they are evil. I can feel it. I can see it. And I've seen what they're up to. They're all over the prostitution around here, but it's more than that. It's worse than slavery. They have no problem killing these girls, or letting people kill them. They *feed* off of that shit."

Raymond ran a hand over his head, then reached for the bottle again and poured another shot. He pulled the shot glass in front of him and cradled it in both hands, gazed into the amber liquid, swirled it and watched it spin.

"Fire of the century. Five generations ago. Was my great-great granddaddy, Rick Ingersoll who first settled these parts. He was a farmer. Grew wheat. Generous spread. Had livestock and horses and whatnot, a garden, you know. Those days, people had to be self-sufficient. Great-Great Grandaddy was a peaceful man, but strong. Took no shit from anyone.

"Bannisters came around about then, cattle people. Ranchers. Old Man Bannister, Mack, was a mean son of a bitch. Kind of man that'd get drunk, sucker punch someone, then beat them halfway to death. For fun. Only man ever to hand him his own ass was my Great-Great Grandaddy. Way my family tells it, Old Man Bannister was kicking some poor SOB about to death, and my Great-Great Grandaddy stepped in to pull him off, and caught a punch to the face for his trouble. Great-Great Grandaddy tried to back off the fight, but Old Man Bannister kept coming at him, so Great-Great Grandaddy put him down. He'd been a boxer in his youth, and Old Man Bannister was just a mean ol' son of a bitch of a bar fighter.

"Well, that was it. Old Man Bannister decided the Ingersolls had to go. There was some back and forth, and Old Man Bannister started the harassment, let his cattle into my Great-Great Grandaddy's land to trample up the crops, like that. At first, Great-Great Grandaddy just run the cattle out, but when Old Man Bannister kept it up, Great-Great Grandaddy started shooting them. Then one of Great-Great Grandaddy's workers got shot, an "accident," and that was when Great-Great Grandaddy had enough.

"In those days, men could settle these kinds of things between themselves. Great-Great Grandaddy called Old Man Bannister out...like in the Old West, you know? Well. Old Man Bannister wasn't the kind of man to fight fair, so he set up a man in a barn just off of Main Street, and when the two of 'em met on Main Street, that man in the barn shot my Great-Great Grandaddy in the back."

Raymond gave the whiskey in the shot glass another swirl, then drank it.

"Well, that wasn't good enough for Old Man Bannister. He sent men out to the farm. They killed everyone and torched the whole place: farm house, barn, silos, crops, all of it. Fire was so big it spread to town and took most of the town down.

"People were upset, of course, but after people who stood up to say something started disappearing, most of the good folks just pulled up and left."

"Some of your people must have stayed," Max said. "You're here, after all."

"My Great Grandaddy. He was just a boy of ten when the Bannisters burned it all down. Sole survivor. Local family, the Burns, took him in, raised him up."

"He never went after the Bannisters? And the Bannisters left him alone?"

"Wasn't his nature. Quiet boy. These days, we'd call it PTSD and send him into counseling, get him medicated to the gills and whatnot. In those days, people just shut it out of their mind, didn't think about it. I think Old Man Bannister tested him a time or two, satisfied himself there weren't nothing to worry about there, then left him alone. Been an Ingersoll in town ever since. Most of us take off and leave when we get to an age, but there's always one who stays put. This generation, that's me."

"How many Bannisters are there?"

"Right now? There's the Old Man, Karl, and the three boys. You met two of 'em, Mack and Roger. You ain't met Bill yet. He's the worst one."

The dead woman on the dirt floor, arm twisted up behind her, bare ass up in the air, cheek on the dirt, eyes wide open staring into nothing.

"Worse than Roger?"

"Worse. What exactly went down with Roger, anyway? Word is he came back to the house all busted up. Some stranger blindsided him, street fight or some such."

Max told him about the vision that had almost run him off the road. About the dark sense of evil. How the other workers looked away. About the dead girl—and the palpable sense of evil hovering over it all, feeding off of the pain and misery. About putting Roger Bannister down. The other girls. The discovery of Roger Bannister's identity.

"And that's how I ended up back here. Mix of personal business and history. I figure the only way to get shut of these visions is to do something with them. Balance things out. Maybe once I've done whatever it is I'm supposed to do, all this shit will leave me in peace."

Max pulled the bottle of Bushmills to his side of the table and poured a shot.

"Now you're telling me Bill Bannister is worse than Roger? Worse than Mack?"

"Mack is a bully. Plain and simple. Mean, stupid, ready to kick the shit out of anyone at any time, but aside from that kind of thing, he's not overly cruel—just a mean stupid redneck. Roger's more of an operational guy. Runs things. He's pure business. Don't get me wrong. Mean as a snake, just as dangerous...but not quite as...active, I guess you could say. Bill, he's another kettle of fish entirely. He's like Mack and Roger and Old Man Bannister squared. He's smart. He's the one that's being groomed to take over for Karl. Karl's getting on now, but nothing gets past him. Bill is his second in command, makes sure whatever it is Karl wants done gets done. Roger is boots on the ground. They've got Mack doing the go-fer shit. Collecting. Enforcing, like that. But Bill...

Raymond's eyes lost focus as he peered into the past.

"There was a time, back when I was in high school. Bill's about the same age as me—a couple of years older. He'd taken a shine to a girl, Mary Jane. Mary Jane was something. Most beautiful girl in these parts. Well, Mary Jane didn't reciprocate, you catch my drift."

Raymond's hand drifted absently toward the bottle, pulled it closer to him.

"Well, one day Mary Jane just...disappeared. Nobody saw anything, nobody heard anything; she was just gone. Never a hide nor hair of her turned up."

"Nothing? No rumors?"

Raymond snorted.

"Rumors galore, and all of 'em had Bill Bannister at the center. Rape scenarios. Torture. Kidnapping. Some people felt he was keeping her locked up somewhere. Bottom line? Nothing."

"Huh. How long ago was this?"

"Well, I'm 38, this all went down when I was a junior in high school...say 20 years or so."

"What do you think happened?"

"I think bad ol' Bill Bannister grabbed up Mary Jane, played with her for a while, beat on her, raped her, then burned her and scattered her bones out in the fields."

Max looked at Raymond. The aura around him still glowed faintly, but red spikes radiated outward.

"Why didn't anyone do anything?"

Raymond spread his hands.

"Who? Do what, exactly? No evidence. Cops are all tied to the Bannisters, anyways. Nothing to do."

"You telling me her family just sat quiet and docile? Just said, 'Oh well'?"

Raymond shook his head.

"Far from it. Mary Jane's father went up to the Bannisters to ask. Got the shit kicked out of him for his trouble. Two weeks later, his wife found him hanged from a tree in their back yard. Cops said suicide. Most of us figure otherwise. Mary Jane's ma just crumpled up and sunk into herself after that. Never really left the house. Neighbor found her dead about three years later. Hadn't seen her around, finally went over to check. Dead in a rocker in the living room. Medical Examiner said natural causes. Most of us figure otherwise about that, too."

Max let the silence hang in the air for a few minutes, stared at his hands while Raymond swirled whiskey in his shot glass and watched it sparkle.

Max closed his eyes and a man's face appeared in his mind's eye: a hard man, face lined and weathered, angry crow's feet, sloped brow, heavy five o'clock shadow. The man was completely consumed by a roiling darkness Max could see in the man's pupils. A sticky, red black aura radiated from him, a level of evil that took Max's breath away. A man totally given over to evil, who reveled in it. The kind of man who would flay someone alive and record it to use as a soundtrack to his life.

Bill Bannister.

Max stood up.

Raymond looked up at him.

"Well, guess I know where to start. Where does this Bill Bannister live?"

CHAPTER FIFTEEN

Max let the big bike roll to the shoulder and come to a stop.

Bill Bannister's spread was just outside of town, down the hill from the Old Man's.

A full moon lit the big complex: a sprawling ranch-style home that looked to go 3000 square feet, a barn, a couple of work sheds and other buildings laid out over several acres, fields stretching off to the horizon on two sides, Karl Bannister's considerable complex on the hilltop above abutting the third, a half-mile driveway leading up to a circle drive in front. An electrified steel fence surrounded the complex, gates set into each of the four walls like an old fortified town.

A light burned on the front porch. Motion-sensor floodlights flanked each of the four gates, and close inspection revealed several poles set into the ground with more motion-sensor lights mounted on them.

A fortress.

Max wondered whether all the security was keeping the world out or something in.

Nothing is impregnable.

He looked some more, and then the corners of his mouth turned up in a grim smile.

Bingo.

His eyes traced the exposed power lines running into the compound off poles set along the road.

Max thumbed the big Kawi back to life, and quietly throttled it up and around, headed back to the hotel.

Twenty-four hours later, Max rolled his bike off the shoulder and into a clump of bushes. He pulled out the night-vision binoculars he'd scored from Raymond.

Just what Raymond was doing with night-vision binoculars was not clear to Max—there was more to the man than met the eye. In addition to the binoculars, Raymond had the kind of weapons room that wouldn't be totally out of place in a SEAL bunker. In fact, the memorabilia that festooned the walls of the weapons room lent credence to the idea that Raymond had served as a SEAL—or something very like it.

The big complex was silent and dark other than the front-porch light.

The night-vision binoculars lent a greenish cast to the view.

The house looked quiet. The sheds and barn silent hulks on the plain.

Max lowered the binoculars and took a deep breath. He looked up at the sky, the waning moon, nearly full, the stars. An image of the blond woman rose in his mind. Whoever/whatever she was, she had started him on this path.

He still wasn't clear why he was skulking around the borders of Bill Banister's complex, but an inner compulsion he couldn't resist pushed him forward. His encounter with the blond woman had shifted something central in him, given him a new purpose and drive—and a new foundation of calm strength.

Let's do this.

He moved back to the bike and pulled out two helium balloons—the metallic kind that stayed inflated forever.

"Thank you, 'Breaking Bad,' if this actually works," Max whispered.

Max made sure the wire holding the balloons together was secure, then walked to a spot he'd chosen under the power lines leading into Bannister's complex.

He licked a finger and held it up to test the wind.

None.

He released the balloons and craned his neck to watch their ascent.

Just as he'd hoped, the balloons rose straight and true

straight to the power lines. Trapped by the power lines the balloons bobbled.

Nothing.

Damn it. Serves you right, believing in TV bullshit.

The balloons bobbled some more, then each made contact with separate lines, bobbled again and bumped up against one another. Sparks flew, an electric crackle and snap! and the light on the front porch of the Bannister home winked out.

Moving back to his original position, Max raised the binoculars and scanned the complex.

All was as before. If Bill Bannister had an alarm, as Max was sure he did, there didn't appear to be any back-up power for it.

Max had hoped that was the case, but wasn't counting on it: what kind of farm house didn't have a generator?

Fifteen minutes of continued silence and lack of motion satisfied him.

This is as good as it's going to get.

Max stayed low and worked his way to the fence.

Pulling a strand of wire from his pocket, Max tossed it to the fence, making sure it hit two of the wires to complete a circuit.

Nothing.

I'll be.

Big Bad Bill Bannister had no back up power—to the fence, at least.

Max threw his backpack over and quickly scrambled after it, then lay in the dust.

Nothing moved.

Fair dinkum.

The approach to the house was completely open.

Max shouldered the backpack, and keeping low, padded to the side of the ranch house as silently as he could.

None of the motion-sensor lights lit.

Max closed his eyes and listened.

Nothing.

Though he wanted into the ranch house, wanted to see what Big Bill might have in there, Max knew he had zero chance of turning over the house without being caught. And he sure as hell didn't want to be caught by Bill Bannister.

The gut feeling that had compelled him to come this far was pushing at Max to explore the outer buildings. Max's heart bumped as he scanned them. A wave of palpable evil rolled off of the buildings—a physical presence that turned his stomach.

Max moved quickly to the building closest to the house.

A workshed about 20' X 20'.

Max put his hand on the latch and tried the door.

It opened.

Huh.

He slipped quickly into the building and shut the door behind him and leaned against it.

Nothing moved.

The sense of evil rolled over him again, and Max fought against the vertigo it induced in him.

An earthy, coppery smell in the air he recognized as dried blood.

He pulled the flashlight off the loop of his pants and shone it around the room.

The room was like a museum of BDSM. Whips, chains, manacles, leather gear, ball gags, and gigantic dildos. Medieval-looking instruments of torture filled racks and hung off pegboards on the wall. Several of the tools showed the tell-tale flaky stains of dried blood.

"Sweet baby Jesus help me," Max muttered.

A wave of imagery swam over Max and dropped him to his knees.

It was everything he'd seen since he'd been cursed with the "gift," and then some.

Max leaned over until his forehead rested on the dirt floor by his knees, fighting against the urge to either puke or flee.

Dozens of women had been tortured to death on these grounds. Dozens.

A kaleidoscopic vision of torture flashed through Max's head: *Women bound and burned, dangled from the ceiling and* *whipped, tased, lit up with cattle prods, arms and legs broken over big wheels...*the imagery coming faster and faster, more and more brutal, filling his head with things he had never imagined in his worst nightmares.

And over it all, Big Bill Bannister leering, sweating, naked and rampant, exulting in his power and the women's sufferings.

Bill Bannister must die. No one could be allowed to live who had done these things. The man was a demon. Pure evil.

Max focused on the calm at the center of his soul.

A woman lying on a cot. Forty-something, beautiful. A heaviness lay on her, a hopelessness like none he had ever imagined.

Max bolted to his feet.

Mary Jane.

Somewhere on this complex. After all these years.

Max clicked off the flashlight and exited the shed.

A stairwell to the right of the shed led underground.

Max looked back toward the ranch house.

He could feel Bill Bannister's presence now: powerful, almost unstoppable, a force of evil, a chink in the universe letting in a supernatural amount of power; evil capable of swallowing souls whole.

Nothing moved in the stillness of the night. Not even a breeze.

Max padded down the stairs to come to a metal door set in concrete. The door was double-barred and secured with two heavy padlocks.

Shit.

He tugged on the padlocks and froze: the woman in there, Mary Jane, had jolted awake at the sound and Max could feel her racing heart.

He slipped up the stairs and back into the shed. Flicking on his flashlight, Max scanned the walls for a suitable tool.

A heavy steel rod, sharpened at one end like the edge of a chisel, hung on two hooks.

Max lifted the rod off the hooks.

An image of the rod, its end glowing red, wavering in the dark as it was held in front of a cowering, terrified, broken, bleeding woman stopped Max's breath and he bobbled the bar, nearly dropping it.

Flakes of charcoaled flesh floated down from the tip.

Max gagged.

Bill Bannister must die.

Trying not to shudder, Max moved quickly back to the double-barred door and stuck the chiseled end of the steel rod into the loop of the first padlock and leaned hard into it.

The six-foot length of steel afforded some serious leverage, but it took all of Max's strength to snap the lock.

Max repeated the process with the other lock.

He could feel the woman's panic and bewilderment.

"It's OK," he whispered. "Max is here to set you free."

He laid the rod carefully on the stairs, not wanting to make more noise than necessary, then removed the locks from the bars, slid the bolts back, and pulled open the door.

CHAPTER SIXTEEN

The open door revealed a narrow bunker, outfitted like something out of a 50s bomb shelter: twin bed mattress on a metal cot, metal toilet with a sink inset, a shelf of books.

The room smelled of sweat and despair.

A woman sat upright on the cot, eyes wide.

Her mouth moved. "Wh-wh-who are you?" she asked.

Max held up his hands, raised a finger to his lips.

"Name's Max. I'm here to get you out."

The woman blinked, uncomprehending.

"Mary Jane?"

The woman blinked again, confused.

Max felt something like thunder roll across the psychic landscape. The coming evil was so large, so powerful, it felt like a tropical storm rolling in.

Bill Bannister was awake.

"Quickly," Max said, "We've got to move. Come on."

He reached a hand out.

Mary Jane cowered away from him, curling her arms up defensively.

"It's OK," Max crooned. "I'm here to help."

Mary Jane began trembling with terror.

Max's words echoed inside his head, and a vision opened up of another man, crooning and cooing the same way to Mary Jane, comforting her, then leading her up to the shed above and delighting in her terrified discovery of what actually awaited her.

She'd heard this before, a thousand games had been played on her. She was incapable of trusting or believing in anything good. Perhaps ever.

Evil rumbled like thunder in his head. Bill Bannister was getting ready to move. The time was now.

"Mary Jane. Mary Jane, listen to me," Max said. "I know you've been lied to and hurt. Badly. But you must believe me. I am here to get you out of here. And we have to move now."

"No...." Mary Jane folded into a fetal ball.

Max reached down and picked up Mary Jane as gently as he could. She was trembling violently.

He figured she weighed about 120, not too heavy, but nothing he was going to go running across the complex with in his arms.

And time was tight. Bill Bannister's presence was so palpable, so evil, that Max was fighting off terror himself.

With a quick move, Max threw Mary Jane over his shoulder in a fireman's carry and climbed the stairs.

"Clay!" a man shouted from inside the house.

Mary Jane bucked violently and trembled. The man's voice dripped with command. With cruelty. Evil.

"Boss?" another answered.

"What the fuck is with the power? Why aren't you doing something? Get your lazy ass out and see what's what."

Max set Mary Jane down carefully against the side of the house.

"Stay here. Don't move."

Mary Jane whimpered.

Max laid a finger across his lips.

"Shh. I know you don't believe me, Mary Jane, but I am truly here to get you out. Please be quiet. I'll be back as soon as I can."

Max slid around the corner of the house just as Clay flew out the front door and onto the porch.

Heavy boots clomped across the porch and stopped at the top of the steps.

Max crouched in the lee of the house and watched as Clay scanned the complex from the top of the stairs, surveyed the power lines, stilled as he noticed the balloons still stuck under the power lines.

"What the hell?" Clay muttered.

Clay climbed down the steps, something dangling from his right hand.

A gun with a long banana clip.

Max closed the distance.

Clay sensed the movement behind him and spun.

Max stepped at an angle to his left and leaned as he brought up his right leg in a kick that used all his momentum and every ounce of power he could muster.

His shin landed perfectly in the cleft of Clay's neck, and Clay dropped like a sack of bricks.

Max reached down and relieved Clay of his gun.

The touch of gun metal on his hand sparked a flash of imagery: *Clay laughing as a naked woman ran across the field, aiming for her limbs, methodically shooting her up bit by bit, slowing her down by sending a bullet into a shoulder. Then an arm. Then a leg.*

Laughing, roaring with pleasure.

The woman down, groveling, pleading, whimpering in pain.

Laughing.

Max's vision cleared and he found himself looking down at the prone figure of Clay.

Rage overwhelmed him.

"Fuck you, Clay. Bad day for you," Max said.

He raised his foot and dropped his boot on Clay's temple.

The rage in his head sparked and flared—an evil joy blossoming.

Max stomped again. And again. He felt the skull crack. He stomped some more. Stomped until Clay's head was a jellied mess, brain and blood splattered over the ground.

The sound of the front door opening behind him snapped Max back to reality.

The rage snapped off as quickly as it'd come, leaving Max nauseated in its wake.

A crackling in his head, and suddenly his awareness floated out of himself and rose above to show him the whole scene.

He could see Bannister standing behind him, Mary Jane curled in a fetal ball against the side of the house, a man passed out in a bed in a room of the house, himself crouched over the still bleeding body of Clay.

He watched as Bannister's arm came up in slow motion, a gun in his hand.

Max stepped to the left, spun, zig-zagged, and was on Bannister before he had time to draw a bead on him.

Max chopped the gun out of Bannister's hand and brought his elbow back in a vicious backswing that clipped Bannister perfectly on the chin, dropping him to his knees.

Max leaned into a rear side kick and smashed Bannister's nose, driving him back into the house.

He grabbed Bannister by the hair and dragged him away from the open door.

When he got him through the foyer into the living room, Max dropped a couple of hard blows to Bannister's face until he felt him sag.

Max felt the man passed out in the room down the hall flicker into a confused consciousness.

He quickly padded down to the man's room and with a few well-placed blows sent him back into unconsciousness.

The room faded.

The man at work in the shed, pulling at a rope to raise a woman off her feet by the wrists, her hands bound behind her. Felt the man's sexual glee at the woman's agony.

Max landed a few more blows, felt the fragile occipital bones fracture and shatter.

Bill Bannister stirred behind him.

Max stepped out of the room and into the living room.

CHAPTER SEVENTEEN

Bill Bannister sat on the floor of his living room, wiped blood from his shattered nose.

"You're going to die, boy," Bill said.

Max laughed.

"You laugh?" Bill roared. He attempted to climb to his feet.

Max slapped him down with an open hand.

"I am going to die; you've got that right," Max said. "But you aren't going to have anything to do with it. Today is your day, my friend."

As Bannister struggled back to a sitting position, Max pulled up a wheel kick from the floor and sent him back into unconsciousness.

He slipped quickly out the front door, moved to Mary Jane where she lay huddled in the dirt by the side of the house.

"Mary Jane," Max said.

Her eyes squeezed more tightly shut.

"I'm back. And I swear to you, I'm getting you out of here, but I have something to take care of real quick. Hold on. Fifteen minutes, I swear."

Max reached out to comfort Mary Jane, then withdrew his hand.

The woman hadn't had a kind hand touch her in two decades. His touch might send her into a screaming panic.

Max moved into the shed, carefully selected a few items, then returned to the living room where Bill Bannister was coming around again.

"Why, hello there, Bill," Max said.

Bill's eyes swam into focus.

"Fuck you, dead man," Bill said.

Evil power rolled off the man, and Max hesitated for a second, struck by a wave of violent imagery so strong it physically moved him back a step. Above and through the imagery hovered the red black presence: ancient, implacable, gibbering, seductive, evil.

Max could feel the presence feeding off of his rage. It swelled and crooned in pulse to the beat of it. A back and forth between him and the thing commenced as the presence attempted to work its way into Max's heart.

Max approached Bannister and readied the items he'd brought back from the shed.

Bannister laughed.

His laughter enflamed the roiling emotions inside Max, and Max seized Bannister by the hair, raising him to his knees, then drove a perfectly placed knee into Bannister's liver, dropping him again.

He dragged Bannister over to a sturdy kitchen chair and manacled him to it.

Bannister retched and a stream of puke ran down his chest and into his lap.

"We're going to have some fun, you and me," Max said. "Your kind of fun, Bill. Something to even out the forty years of miserable shit you've doled out. It's going to take some time, but I promise you, it'll be fun."

As Max's hand closed over the steel pincers he'd carried in, a wave of imagery rolled over him—screaming, pleading women, Bannister and his buddies gibbering with evil glee.

And then Max saw the blond woman glowing in the clearing he'd found her at Four Corners.

He dropped the pincers.

The evil presence scrabbled for purchase in his heart, a physical sensation, tiny metal claws tearing at him, and Max raised a hand to his chest and focused on the image of the blond woman.

The scrabbling slowed, became fainter, then stopped.

Max felt the presence withdraw.

Bill Bannister looked at Max with rounded eyes.

"You're a crazy motherfucker," Bannister said. "And still dead."

Max sensed the presence in the room, hovering, but for the first time, he also sensed confusion. Fear. Vulnerability.

Max stared at Bannister.

A powerful man, heavily muscled. Puke stuck to chest and belly hairs, and pooled in his lap, staining through his pajama bottoms.

Bannister was a hollow man.

Evil completely filled him. Max could get no sense of humanity; it was as if Bannister had given over his entire being—body and soul—to the presence. Welcomed it in so completely that it had taken over.

The presence felt less threatening. The evil might threaten, gibber, and make noise, but it had no power over him.

"So. Tell me, Bill. How many evil pies you got your fingers in? Huh?"

Bannister spit blood at Max.

"That's about what I thought," Max said.

Max began moving about the house, opening drawers, pawing through bookshelves. The same gut-level compulsion from earlier drove him down the hallway into a room next to the unconscious man.

A study. Dark wood paneling, heavy wood desk, nice teak bookcase. A room of surprisingly good taste.

Neatly labeled three-ring binders lined the top two shelves of the bookcase, each binder labeled by fiscal year.

Max pulled the two most current years down, scanned them quickly.

Most of it was a foreign language to him, but he scooped up the binders and carried them back into the living room.

Bannister watched him approach. His posture and gaze made Max think of an inbred rabid dog. Something about the near-crossing of his eyes, the heavy brow, the curl of the lip.

"Afraid I'm going to have to put you down, Bill. You've been a bad boy. And there's just no way I can allow you to live."

"Fuck you!" Bannister roared.

A rabid, inbred dog growling.

Max set the binders down, then slipped out of the house.

Mary Jane was sitting where he'd left her. Quiet. Her eyes watched Max approach. She was a long way from trust or anything like it, but seemed to have settled into belief that nothing horrible was imminent.

"Just a few more things and we're out of here, Mary Jane."

In the shed, Max found the cans of gasoline where he'd spotted them.

He grabbed a five-gallon jug in each hand and carried them back to the house.

Bannister had managed to turn the chair over and break one of the legs, freeing one of his ankles.

"Well, look at you!" Max said.

Max set the jugs down and walked over to Bannister and squatted down.

"Here's the deal, Bill," Max said. "You've had a long run, but I'm shutting you down. You and your kin are an abomination. Something not meant to be free in this world. And so...I'm going to send you all back to hell. Plain and simple."

Bannister bucked and writhed.

"You are dead!" he roared. "When Pop gets a hold of you, you're going to wish you'd never been born!"

"Pop? You mean Karl? Don't you worry, son. I've got plans for Pops. And Mack. And Roger. Your whole damn clan, I kid you not."

Max reached out and brushed Bannister's hair out of his eyes.

"You're a dead man!" Bannister roared.

"And you're a broken record," Max said. "Remember how to fix that?"

He leaned back and punched Bannister squarely between the eyes. Bannister's eyes rolled up in his head, and the skin between them split, blood oozing up to drip across his forehead.

Max stepped back and watched Bannister slowly come back into himself.

When Bannister's eyes swam back into inbred focus, Max squatted down and aligned himself with Bannister's gaze.

"Here's the deal, Bill. You're going to die today. In about five minutes, I'd say. If there's anything left of your soul, anything at all, you'd best make peace with God, 'cause you're about to meet him."

Bannister took a deep breath and spit at Max again.

"OK. 'From the depths of hell, I spit at thee,' and all that. I get it," Max said.

He sighed, brushed hair away from Bannister's face once more. Bannister twisted his head violently and tried to bite him.

"OK," Max said again. "We'll do this your way, then."

Max straightened up and went into the kitchen. A box of wooden matches sat on the table. Max pulled one out, stuck the wood end in his mouth, then walked back to the living room and carried the two binders out of the house.

Reentering the house, Max headed straight for the jugs of gasoline.

He started in the back hall by the unconscious man's room, dousing down the hallway and walls. He moved quickly down to the living room, emptying the jug in a circle around Bannister.

Max picked up the other jug, stepped out onto the porch and doused the front of the house.

Then he stepped back into the foyer and watched Bannister writhing and bucking, trying to break free of the sturdy wooden chair.

"Damn fine chair you've got there, Bill," Max said.

He gazed at Bannister and felt pity, but not enough to dissuade him from setting the place ablaze.

He moved to the outside of the circle of gasoline, the fumes in the air making his eyes water.

"Damn shame, Bill. You've lived a fucked-up life...'meaningless as rats' feet on broken glass...'"

Max turned his back on Bannister and strode from the room.

"Dead man!" Bannister screamed.

Max stepped down onto the path, grabbed Clay's body with its mashed-in head by the shirt, and dragged him up the stairs onto the porch.

Max stepped back down the stairs, glanced up into the night sky.

The moon had set, and the sky was in its first stages of lightening as dawn approached.

"Good-bye, Bill," Max said. "'This is the way the world ends....'"

He pulled the match out of his mouth and used a thumbnail to strike it into flame.

Max let the match burn halfway down, then tossed it onto the porch and stepped back ten paces as the porch went up with a whoosh! and the flames snaked into the house.

Max stepped around to the side of the house. The front of the house blew open as the fumes and gasoline inside ignited.

Bannister was screaming and raging and Max had an image of him in flames, his eyes and mouth pits of fire—a demon screaming in hell.

Max had the two binders under one arm, and with his other he gently helped Mary Jane to her feet.

Her eyes were wide and apprehensive, but something like hope glinted out of the deep pools of fear.

"Time to go, Mary Jane. Let's get you home."

CHAPTER EIGHTEEN

Dawn lightened the sky as Max leaned into the curves leading up the hill to Raymond's cabin.

Mary Jane held on to him with a languid grip, docile and compliant, allowing the force of the curves to direct her leaning, a perfect passenger.

Max wondered what was going on in her mind—how long it'd been since she'd seen the sun.

He shook his head.

God, if you're there, he thought, *I've got someone who could use some help. More than I can provide.*

Raymond had told him the local police were more or less controlled by the Bannisters, so it didn't seem wise to take her to them. There were no federal offices within five hundred miles—a long way to run with a posse of Bannisters hunting him.

Max didn't expect he'd burned down Bill Bannister with impunity. He expected consequences and conflict.

Which was fine. For the first time since his "gift" had manifested, he felt something like real peace. Which was odd: he'd just stomped one man to death, beaten another into a coma, and burned yet another fully awake and aware individual to death.

And yet, he felt like whistling.

No ghosts, visions, or dominating sense of pounding evil.

Evil haunted the shadows of Aston, and he could feel its roiling pulse over the hills—it had lived here for so long it had become part of the countryside itself—but Max's newfound peace was its opposite.

More than that: this peace had the power to obliterate the

evil as easily as a flashlight defeats darkness.

Max thought about Bill Bannister as he neared the top of the hill, Raymond's cabin a few turns in the road away.

He grimaced. Hopefully, in those last moments, Bannister had received a measure of justice. The fire had killed him too quickly to balance a lifetime of sadism and murder, but Max had a sense that the flames and humiliation had hurt him badly enough to at least give him a taste of what all those women had felt.

And if there was a hell, Bannister was twisting in its flames. Now and forevermore.

Raymond's cabin rose in his headlight, and Max rolled to a stop in front of it, next to Raymond's truck. He cut the engine and carefully pulled Mary Jane's hands from his waist and slid off the bike.

He was helping her from the bike as the cabin door opened and Raymond exited, rubbing sleep from his eyes.

"Max," Raymond said. "What are...?"

Raymond's mouth opened and closed as he sought words.

He took another step forward, eyes wide.

"Mary Jane? Is that...you?" he asked.

Max turned to look at Mary Jane.

She had been standing compliantly by the motorcycle, apparently ready for whatever Max had in mind, but with the sight of Raymond, her spine had straightened and her whole body had started to tremble.

The trembling grew more and more violent; her hands came shakily up to her cheeks.

Raymond stepped forward, arms out, and Mary Jane fell into him, sobs wracking her.

Raymond gave Max a look of disbelief and wonder, then picked Mary Jane up as carefully as he might a wounded child, and turned and carried her into the cabin.

Mary Jane screeched and flailed in momentary panic as the door shut behind them, but allowed herself to be calmed as Raymond crooned to her and set her carefully down on the couch, stroking her hair and speaking softly to her.

"It's OK, Mary Jane." Raymond said. "We've got you now. You're safe."

Max stood for a moment. Watched as Raymond's touch and words soothed the frightened woman.

CHAPTER NINETEEN

Mary Jane slept peacefully on the couch, feet curled under her butt, hands under her chin. Raymond gently tucked a comforter around her and stood back.

"Un-fucking-believable," Raymond said. "She was on Bill Bannister's complex this whole time?"

"That's my guess," Max said. "He had a little bunker slash prison dug down beside one of his work sheds."

"Bill didn't build that complex until he'd been out of school for five years. Mary Jane disappeared his senior year of high school. That's six years..."

"The Old Man. He knew about it," Max said.

"Nothing gets by Karl Bannister," Raymond agreed.

"Well, I suppose he's next," Max said.

Raymond looked at Max incredulously.

"Are you actively looking to die?" he asked.

"Not really, but there are things I have to do," Max said.

"Max. The Bannisters are going to be on red-fuckin' alert. They're going to be going batshit. People are going to get hurt as they start tearing shit up trying to find out who did this to Bill. Not to mention what you did to Mack and Roger. They are going to go to fuckin' war, man."

"Bring it," Max said.

Raymond stared.

"You are either fucking stupid, or flat-out crazy."

Max shook his head.

"Nope. I just know what I have to do, is all."

"Max. It's suicide to go up to Old Man Bannister's. He'll pull Roger and Mack up there. He'll have men patrolling. He'll crank up security so high a mosquito won't be able to sneak in."

"That's why I'm not going in," Max said.

Raymond's shoulders sagged in relief.

"Ah. Good. The man can see reason," he said.

"I'm going to get them to come after me," Max said.

"Ah, shit. So much for sanity."

Max gestured at the two ring binders that lay on the table.

"Come here a minute, sit down," he said.

Max sat and opened the first book, started leafing through it.

"Look here," Max said. "Accounts. This details every penny the Bannisters bring in. If I can start interfering with that, I can get their attention. They'll come to me."

"You've already got their fuckin' attention, Max. That's not the problem. The problem is staying alive."

Max closed his eyes, thought of the blond woman. Felt the profound sense of peace she'd left at his center. He opened the door in his head a little more and let his mind drift. Imagery of women on their backs on dirt floors. Women used, abused, tortured, and killed. Women hanging from chains. Whips, red-hot pokers, pliers, cattle prods, a thousand instruments of torture. Hot blood splashing the walls and faces and torsos and bodies of the women and the naked, laughing and hooting men who reveled in their pain, their agony, their bewildered lostness, their hopelessness.

And over it all that evil presence.

Max opened his eyes.

"I've got a mission, Raymond. Simple as that. I've been given this 'gift' for a reason. He tapped the binders with his finger. And I'm not getting rid of it until I've accomplished the mission. Right now, that means ridding the world of anything Bannister. I'm going to burn them to the ground. Make the 'fire of the century' look like a birthday cake candle. I'm going to root out every lousy whore house, torture center, prison they have. I'm going to free every woman they've got. I'm going to put an end to this."

"You're crazy, Max."

"Maybe."

Max poked a finger at various headings in the three-ring binder.

"Look. These are labeled by town. The Bannisters have shit going in every county east of the river. I'm going to start with the closest, work my way out. Leave a trail of fire that Old Man Bannister won't be able to miss."

"Max. Please. You're talking some seriously crazy shit. Let's go to the Feds. You can't take this on alone."

"Well...that's part of the plan, sort of," Max said.

Raymond breathed out a sigh of relief.

"Finally, the man has an ounce of sense."

"You're going to bring the Feds in."

"What? Me?"

"You."

Max gestured at Mary Jane.

"She remembers you. You're a calming influence on her. And she's not safe here. Like you said, Bannisters are going to be going apeshit trying to find me, and her. If they're as infiltrated into the police as you think, they might start pulling random traffic stops trying to find us. And there's no way I'm getting her out of here on my motorcycle. You're going to have to get her out. Far out. As in West Coast. Seattle. Aim at the federal offices there. Get her to Seattle and into Fed custody. Kidnapping and false imprisonment ought to get the Feds out here. That will make a difference."

"Take my truck and do it yourself, Max. You'll have a better chance."

Max shook his head.

"No. That's not my role in this. I'm going after the women."

"The women?"

"Raymond. Mary Jane is just one. The Bannisters have hundreds of women. All over the county and further. Look at this."

Max tapped a finger on the pages of the three-ring binder.

"They've developed an empire of torture. They're supplying women to every evil pussball in this state. Whole counties are infected with the Bannister virus."

"And you, one-man army, are going to stop this?"

Max grinned.

"I'm going to give it my best shot. I can do things no government agency can. I can burn these people to the ground. And I aim to."

Raymond shook his head.

"Still seems like suicide to me, Max."

Max shrugged and stood.

"Time to move, Raymond. Like you say, Bannisters will be going apeshit. Best to get moving before they get organized."

CHAPTER TWENTY

Karl Bannister balled his fist and thumped it down on the solid teak dining table.

"What the fuck do you mean, 'gone?'"

Mack looked down at his boots.

"The whole place's burned out, Pops. Farmhouse is smoldering ashes. Shed is halfway down—got a lot of exposed shit in there we can't let anyone see."

Old Man Bannister jumped to his feet, the force of it scooting his chair back until it slammed into the wall behind him.

Shoulders and guts tensed across the room as Bannister's men prepared themselves for his wrath.

"Check to see if the security camera is intact. Pull the film. How many play toys did Bill have on the compound?"

"Just the one he always has. We shipped the others out last week."

"Thank Christ for that. Where have you got her?"

Mack gulped and looked down at his boots again.

"Uh. That's part of the problem, Pops. She's gone."

Old Man Bannister's face swelled and the veins in his neck popped into sharp relief.

"What?" he roared.

"Gone, Pops. Bars pried off the door, bunker empty, no sign of 'er."

Old Man Bannister picked up his mug of coffee and hurled it at the wall where it shattered, splattering hot coffee in a starburst pattern.

Every man in the room had his eyes on his boots, and moved swiftly out of the way as Karl paced and raged.

"So what are you doing about this?" Old Man Bannister

asked. “Who’s on the roads? Who’s got patrol duty this week?”

“Bill had Curry and them on the road this week. Danny and his boys are running some play toys over to West Coleman this week. Billy and his group went south to take in a new shipment at the border,” Max said.

Old Man Bannister gave a quick nod.

“Get that security film quick as you can. I want Curry and his group to know what to look for. In the meantime, have ‘em stop anything and anyone who looks in any way unusual. We can’t have Bill’s fuck toy out there loose. That could cause some complications.”

Mack nodded and gestured at a bearded giant of a man.

“Sherman. You take a few of your boys and start combing the ruins for that security camera and footage.”

Sherman nodded, “I’ll radio Curry from my truck,” Sherman said. “I’ll have him set up with binoculars and watch the roads.”

Sherman strode from the room, two of his men on his heels.

Old Man Bannister nodded.

“Everyone get his shit done and let’s find the motherfuckers did this. I want them hanging in my playroom by noon.”

The room cleared, leaving Old Man Bannister alone.

He glanced around the room, spotted the coffee splatter and mug shards.

“Clara!” he bellowed. “Get the fuck in here.”

Clara appeared at his elbow.

Dressed in a French Maid’s outfit, she was a cross between a Playboy centerfold and something out of a Dungeon Master’s wet dream.

Old Man Bannister reached out a casual hand and pinched one of her exposed nipples, hard.

Clara gasped in pain.

“Clean that mess the fuck up,” Old Man Bannister ordered.

CHAPTER TWENTY ONE

Max watched as Raymond fired up the truck.

Mary Jane was curled up against the passenger-side door with a fuzzy blanket wrapped around her.

Raymond leaned out the window.

"OK. I'm heading out of town on the main road. You sure you're clear on the back roads?"

Max nodded.

"Not too much to it. Take the first dirt road on the right, just before the Post Office. Follow the barbwire fence until I get to a flock of sheep. Take the first left after that. Go to the red barn, second right after that will lead me back to the interstate and I'm on my way."

"Good. You be careful, Max. Bannisters are likely already looking for a guy on a motorcycle after what you did to Mack. And by now, they may also have figured out it was you that did Roger as well. And if one and one make two, then three ain't so far behind, if you catch my drift."

"I do," Max said.

Max and Raymond looked at each other for a beat.

Raymond reached out a fist and he and Max fist bumped.

"Good luck, Max."

"And to you, Raymond. Be seeing you."

"I sure hope so," Raymond said.

Raymond put a hand on the gearshift and slid the truck into first gear.

Max watched the truck head down the long driveway and

disappear around a curve in the road.

"Well, here goes nothing," Max said.

The big Kawi roared into life, and Max followed Raymond down the hill, heading east.

CHAPTER TWENTY TWO

Mack sat in his truck just outside Old Man Bannister's compound.

The town lay below, roads leading in and out like a spider web across the fields.

A finger of dust rose on the road that ran outside the Smith's wheat fields, pointing east.

A steady trickle of cars on the main road.

Through traffic, mostly. Not much leaving town.

Mack recognized Raymond Ingersoll's truck as it rounded the last curve out of town, headed west.

He picked up the mic of his radio and keyed it:

"Curry? You boys got eyes on Ingersoll?"

The radio crackled.

"Yep. He's up early."

"Send someone after him. See where he's headed."

"Gotcha, Mack. You want me to pull him over?"

"No. Just follow him and see if he's heading over to Paluma for supplies or what."

"Mack? You spot that motorcycle out by Smith's?"

"Motorcycle? Huh. Nope. Just seen the dust. Got anyone on the back roads out that way?"

"Nope. Could send a team down the Interstate a bit, see if that bike pops out there. Got one posted real close to where the road comes out there."

"Do it. Until we figure out who did this, we're tracking everybody. Got it? And Ingersoll is high on my list."

"10-4, Mack. Don't you worry. We're on it."

Mack drummed his fingers on the steering wheel. Thinking.

He switched frequencies and keyed the mic again.

"Sherman? Report."

"We're cleaning up. Got the shed cleaned out, nothing for anyone to see."

"What about that security cam?"

"Camera's a melted piece of shit. We're combing through the ash looking for the box that holds the disk drive. That should be fireproof."

"Let me know the instant you got that, understand?"

"You know it, Mack."

"Good."

Mack leaned back and shaded his eyes against the morning sun, watched the plume of dust outside the Smith's place settle back to the earth.

CHAPTER TWENTY THREE

"Shit," Raymond said.

High up on the hill, sun glinted off the windshield of a truck parked just outside Old Man Bannister's place.

"They're already organized," Raymond said.

He turned and put a gentle hand on Mary Jane's shoulder.

"Mary Jane. You're going to have to keep your head below the window, got me?"

Mary Jane's eyes widened and she started trembling.

"Shh. It's going to be OK, Mary Jane. I've got you. But we've got to be careful here. Looks like the Bannisters are already watching the road. They see just me, they'll figure I'm heading over to Paluma for supplies. They see me and you, they're going to wonder who I'm with. Just a precaution, understand?"

Mary Jane slid low in the seat.

"That's a girl. We got this, Mary Jane."

Raymond shaded his eyes.

In the speed trap just outside of town, he spotted the wheels of Curry's police cruiser behind the Welcome to Ramsey sign. Raymond slid a hand along the back of the bench seat of the pick up to rest on Mary Jane's shoulder.

"Easy, Mary Jane. Be still for a piece, you hear?"

He could feel Mary Jane trembling under his hand.

It pissed him off. As the truck drew even with the sign, Raymond lifted a middle finger casually, waved it at the police cruiser.

"Fuck you, you piece of shit," he muttered.

Felt Curry's eyes on him as he moved past.

Glancing in the rear view mirror, Raymond caught the glint of the sun off binoculars.

"Damn. They are serious. Scoping cars as they leave."

He patted Mary Jane, calming her.

"Just stay still, Mary Jane. We're easing our way out of town here. I don't expect any trouble once we're on our way."

Currry watched Ingersoll's truck recede in the distance.

Motherfucker had flipped him off.

That would not do.

Curry clicked a dial on the radio to change frequencies, then picked up the mic and keyed it.

"Monte. That piece of shit Ingersoll just drove by me. You up at the fork?"

The radio squelched, and Monte's voice came through.

"Yep. Like you told me to. Nobody come this way. Everyone sticking to the main road."

"OK. When Ingersoll passes you, fall in behind and see where he goes. Then you let me know, got it?"

"I'm on it, boss."

"You'd better be, damn it."

Curry's eyes narrowed as Ingersoll's truck dropped behind a hill and disappeared.

"Motherfucker," he said. "I'll get you one of these days."

Max was almost to the highway when a sense of the presence washed over him. He geared the big bike down, let it roll to a stop, then thumbed the kill switch.

Silence. A breeze through the fields. The gentle swish of cars on the highway a half a mile distant.

And yet.... The presence was so strong that it blurred his vision. The fields felt tainted. The peaceful, pastoral scene threatened by a dark underbelly—a hungry predator looking for prey.

Max closed his eyes and inched the door in his head open.

Two sets of eyes. Two minds and souls given over to the evil presence.

Each man nurtured his own fantasy, yet they were facets of the same diseased set of desires: both men hungered for victims. Each lusted for blood and violence, lived for the meaty snap of bones breaking, screams of agony, orgasm timed to the shuddering death of tortured victims.

A truck hidden in a copse of trees just short of the highway. Dusty blue Ford F-150 on jacked up wheels. Death metal on the stereo, heads bobbing to the beat, hearts pulsing to the twisted fantasies playing in their heads.

The men were looking for him, though they didn't know it.

Which was OK with Max.

He opened his eyes and scanned the road behind and ahead.

Nothing. Not a car, not a wisp of dust on the breeze.

Ahead was a large oak tree.

Max fired up his bike and wheeled it behind the tree and parked.

He could feel the men in the truck just over the hill.

Max worked his way up the hill, following an animal trail in the grass. As he neared the crest he lowered himself to his belly and inched up to gain a view.

Below him, the highway curved its way across the hills to the east.

A copse of trees just short of the where the dirt road met the highway.

The morning sun shone off the blue of the big truck backed into the trees.

Max could feel the thump of the bass of the music the men were listening to.

Max eased his way down the hill, staying low, letting the tall grass on the edge of the wheat field hide him.

The music in the truck dimmed as a radio transmission came in.

"Zeke? You boys posted by the highway near Smith's?"

The driver grabbed a mic and replied, something Max

couldn't hear.

"Good. You boys hang sharp. That motorcycle ought to be busting out of there any second. I want to know who it is and where he's going. Could just be a kid out on his dirt bike, but somehow I don't think so. You boys follow him and if you think he looks even a little bit hinky, you take him down and get back to me, follow me?"

The driver responded, then leaned forward to set the mic back on its clip.

The music picked up again and Max used it to cover his movement as he stayed low, out of view of the mirrors. He drew even with the passenger's side door.

The windows of the pickup were open and the Death Metal the men were listening to felt like an assault. The music fed off the same energy as the men—delight in evil and pain. A desire to inflict suffering and glory in others' agony.

Max closed his eyes to let the evil wash over him, reached deep for the center of calm in his soul.

When he opened his eyes, there was a clear translucence to his vision and the sense that time had slowed.

He stood and yanked the passenger's side door open with his right hand and used the momentum to drive a hard straight left into the passenger's chin. The man's eyes barely had time to widen before they rolled up in his head and he slumped, unconscious.

Max pulled the man's body from the cab and launched himself in.

The driver's hand moved for a pistol lying on the seat, but Max was in the cab and into his face before the man could grab hold of it.

Max tucked his chin and drove the crown of his skull into the driver's face, shattering his nose and occipital bones, caving in his face.

The driver raised his hands in distress, and Max planted himself as well as he was able and drove a right hook into the man's chin.

Out like a light.

Max dragged the driver out the passenger's side door and dumped him next to his still unconscious buddy.

Max returned to the truck, grabbed the pistol—a behemoth: Smith and Wesson .44 revolver. He nodded approval and stuck the pistol into his belt at the small of his back. A quick search of the glove compartment turned up a roll of duct tape, pliers, a box of ammo for the .44 and a tin of white crystals—crystal meth, Max guessed.

One of the men groaned.

Max exited the truck with the duct tape and pistol.

The passenger groaned again.

Max looked down the road to the oak tree where he'd parked his bike.

He toed the passenger and the man sat up and put his hands to his head.

"What happened?" the man asked.

Max pulled out the pistol and poked the man in the face with it, hard.

"Stand up," Max said.

The man's eyes cleared and he focused on Max.

"Who the fuck are you?" he asked.

Max pulled back the hammer on the big gun.

"I said stand up," he repeated.

The man's lips pursed as if to reply and Max lashed out, a lightning-fast backhand with the barrel of the pistol, splitting open the man's cheek and cracking the bones underneath.

"Ah, fuck!" the man yelled.

"I'm not going to tell you again," Max said.

The man's eyes drifted left, and Max saw movement out of the corner of his eye.

The driver, still groggy and off-balance, was coming in for Max.

Max kicked the driver in the chin, knocking him onto his back, never taking his eyes off the passenger.

Max gestured with the pistol, and the man stood.

"You're a dead man," the passenger said.

"Heard that one before," Max said. He pointed toward the tree with the barrel of the pistol.

"Move," he said.

The passenger started walking toward the tree, swaying slightly.

Max walked him around to the backside of the tree.

"On your knees," he said.

The man started to say something, and Max shook his head.

The man kneeled.

"Hands on top of your head," Max said.

The man complied.

Max lowered the hammer of the pistol and set it on the ground, then pulled out the roll of duct tape.

The man started to say something and Max planted a foot between his shoulder blades in a sliding rear kick that slammed him face first into the dirt.

Max pulled the man's hands behind his back, duct taped them together with a triple wrap, then dragged him to the tree, pulled him up by the hair, and set him down again, seated against the base of the tree.

"You're a dead motherfucker," the man said.

Max nodded, then used the duct tape to strap the man to the tree, another triple wrap holding him tight. Then he wrapped the man's feet together.

"Dead motherfucker," the man said.

"Mm-hmm," Max nodded, then pulled off a strip of tape and wrapped it all the way around the man's head, sealing his mouth.

"That's enough out of you," Max said. "You piss me off, I'll break your nose and let you drown in your own blood, got it?"

The man glared at Max, then nodded.

"Good, glad we're clear," Max said.

Max went back and found the driver still unconscious. He looked pretty bad.

"Live by the sword..." Max muttered.

He dragged the man to the tree, duct-taped his hands behind his back, sat him up, taped him to the tree, taped his feet, but left his mouth untaped—he was bleeding badly from the nose and mouth, his face a shattered mess. Max walked around the other side of the tree to check his work.

Perfect. While the duct tape was visible, it wasn't glaringly obvious, and from the road side of the tree, nothing was visible of either man.

Max walked back around to claim his bike.

He fired it up, then glanced down at the two men.

The driver's head lolled, the passenger glared at him, and Max gave them a quick salute.

"Ta-ta," he said.

CHAPTER TWENTY FOUR:

Raymond glanced in the rear view mirror.

The cop car that had picked him up at the fork just out of town was still on his tail.

Monte. Always been a dipshit, always been tight with the Bannisters.

Shouldn't have flipped off Curry.

Mary Jane stirred in her sleep.

"Shh," Raymond murmured. "Everything's OK. You just sleep, Mary Jane."

Raymond passed the "Welcome to Paluma" sign and slowed as he entered town.

Monte slowed as well, but inched closer to Raymond's truck.

Best to act as if he really were on a run to Paluma for supplies.

Raymond let habit take over as he wheeled his truck through the streets to the big Costco at the edge of town.

Monte stayed with him all the way.

Raymond pulled into the giant parking lot and cruised the rows of cars, looking for a single space between two cars. Three rows from the big doors of the entrance, he found a spot between a panel truck and a Humvee.

Raymond leaned over and fumbled with the glove box.

"Mary Jane," Raymond whispered. "Wake up."

Mary Jane's eyes snapped open and she moved to sit up.

"Stay down!" Raymond hissed, laying a gentle hand on her to keep her still. "We're in Paluma. One of Bannister's cops followed us all the way here. I've got to make him think I'm just here on a normal run."

Mary Jane's eyes widened and she started to tremble again.

"Shh. We can do this. Just stay calm."

Raymond pulled his .45 out of the glove box and slid it into Mary Ann's hands.

"Hold this. I want you to lie flat on the seat, and I'm going to cover you with the blanket. Stay low, and you'll be OK. But if someone opens the door and puts a hand on you, you come up shooting, understand?"

Mary Jane's trembling increased.

"Ah, crap. I know this is hard Mary Jane. I know. But I've got to get moving, or Monte's going to wonder what's taking me. Take some deep breaths, calm yourself."

Mary Jane breathed in shakily, held it, let out her breath.

"Again."

She did, and her trembling lessened.

"Got to go," Raymond said, easing his door open. As he turned to shut the door, he gave the blanket a quick shake and covered Mary Jane with it.

"Hold tight. I'll be back. You'll know it's me, 'cause I'll load the truck when I get back. If someone opens the door without loading the truck..."

Raymond closed the door, pressed the button on his key fob, and the truck beeped as the alarm armed.

Monte cruised by in the Ramsey Police car as Raymond headed for the entrance. Their eyes met, and it took all Raymond's self-control not to flip him off.

Monte turned at the end of the row, headed for the available parking spots.

"Shit," Raymond muttered. He hustled toward the entrance, grabbed a cart, flashed his Costco card at the lady at the door and headed for the liquor aisle.

Got to make it look good. Buy ten cases of whisky, five of vodka, call it good.

As he wheeled the cart toward the island of Johnny Walker

Black Label, he heard a faint bang! bang! bang! bang! bang! and people on the way in wheeled around; those on the way out paused.

Fuck!

Raymond sprinted though the confused and milling crowd into the parking lot straight for his truck.

A woman holding a child in her arms crouched behind the passenger's side wheel of her minivan looked up at him. "Don't go there! There's a crazy man with a gun!"

The words kicked Raymond into high gear. He reached for his gun, but grabbed only his hip.

Of course. It was his gun that had gone off.

A high keening sound grew louder as he approached the truck.

Bang! Bang! Bang!

Mary Jane was standing over what had to be Monte, given the Ramsey Police uniform, but it was hard to be certain: the top of his head had been blown off and his face and chest were a wet, bloody mess.

Mary Jane squeezed the trigger repeatedly, that weird keening sound coming out of her, but the .45 was empty, the slide jacked back. A huge puddle of blood was spreading out from Monte's body; her sneakers were a quarter inch deep in it. Brains and skull matter splattered the panel truck parked to the passenger's side of Raymond's pick up.

"Holy shit," Raymond said.

He took a quick glance around: a couple of heads peering out of the doors of the Costco, others emerging over the top of cars. No one near.

Raymond tried not to step in the blood, but there was no getting around it.

Mary Jane let him take the gun out of her hands, and the keening noise she was making stopped. Raymond scooped her up and slid her into the truck, slammed the door, raced around the front, bloody footprints marking his flight. He leapt into the truck, fired it up, slammed it into reverse, hit the brakes, then dropped it into first and screeched out of the parking lot, leaving a trail of rubber.

Shit, shit, shit! Going to be nearly impossible to get out of Paluma without getting nailed, he thought. *No fucking way we're getting on the Interstate in this truck and making it to Seattle.*

He headed for the northern edge of town, for the mountains.

Mary Jane sat compliantly, staring straight ahead. Raymond noticed she'd buckled her seat belt.

Raymond cut left, right, took random turns, checked his mirrors, and scanned the roads all around, looking for flashing lights. Nothing.

He slowed to the normal five over the speed limit and tried to get a grip on himself.

We're pretty much fucked, but we're not dead yet.

"Mary Jane?"

Mary Jane turned to look at him, her eyes clear, blood splatter dotting her face and the front of her shirt.

"Mary Jane, you OK?"

She blinked at him. Took a deep breath, let it out.

"I'm OK," she said. "Great, actually. That felt…really, really, good. I really hated that motherfucker."

She turned her head and watched the road ahead.

Raymond looked at Mary Jane, felt something rising in his chest, then burst out laughing.

She watched him laugh, a smile on her lips.

"We are so fucked, Mary Jane," Raymond said. He laughed some more. "But you, darling, are on the way back. You're going to make it. I can feel it."

Mary Jane cocked her head and pursed her lips.

"I watched a lot of Oprah and Dr. Phil over the years," she said.

Raymond glanced at her, hands tight on the wheel.

"I feel great. Light as a bird," she said. "What do you think Dr. Phil'd make of that?"

CHAPTER TWENTY FIVE

Old Man Bannister looked out the floor-to-ceiling wall of glass on the south side of his house, his eyes tracking the road winding through Ramsey. Bill's scorched plot of land was a mote in the corner of his eye.

His mind roared with bloody visions: men strung up naked, branding irons, whips, other toys...he was going to have his vengeance—that was for damn sure.

He sipped Hennessy from the thick crystal tumbler in his hand.

Boot heels approached on the polished wooden floor and stopped a deferential ten feet behind him.

"What?" he growled.

"News, Pops."

Mack.

He turned and looked his son over. 6' 2" tall, 250 pounds, a bit of a gut, but not bad. Thick black hair all over, his muscular forearms looked like those of a gorilla. He was still sporting a pair of black eyes from the beating he'd taken a week ago. Other than that, he looked the same as ever: square-toed steel tipped cowboy boots, plaid cowboy shirt tucked in behind that shiny silver and gold belt buckle he'd won a decade ago bull-riding at the local fair, white cowboy hat, thick black eyebrows veed down in a permanent scowl. He was doing his best to look respectful.

Old Man Bannister raised an eyebrow. "Well?"

"It's that fucking Ingersoll, Pops."

"You got tape on him at Bill's?"

"The boys haven't found the tape yet. They're raking through the ashes. They found Bill, though..."

Old Man Bannister's vision clouded red and he shook his head in an attempt to clear it.

"I want that fuckin' tape. Tell 'em to rake faster."

Mack nodded.

"Ingersoll?"

"Monte's dead. Shot down in the parking lot of the Costco in Paluma."

"Ingersoll shot him?"

"We're hearing it was a woman. But she was with Ingersoll. They peeled out of there in his truck. Looks like they're heading for the hills: north."

Old Man Bannister tightened his grip on the tumbler of Hennessey, "Bill's fuck toy."

"That'd make the most sense. Ingersoll hasn't been with a woman since Nancy Pellerman left town is what I hear, anyway."

"Who we got up in the hills up there?"

"Nobody. That's all that hippy territory. All those off-the-grid types. No interest in hookers or meth or any of it."

Old Man Bannister closed his eyes for a second, then opened them; "I know we ain't got anyone stationed up there, you dumb fuck. What I want to know is who the fuck is up there looking for Ingersoll, 'cause if there ain't someone there, I am going to tear the liver out of somebody."

Mack looked at the ground.

"Oh, fuck me. What else you got to tell me, boy?"

"We can't raise Zeke and Elroy."

"What the fuck you mean you can't raise Zeke and Elroy? They was on the east side of town, right? Checking out that motorcycle?"

"Last we heard. I checked in with them an hour ago, and they was all set up. Just got the news on Monte a second ago, and on my way in to tell you, I notified all the boys, but

Zeke and Elroy wasn't answering. I figured to send them after Ingersoll, seeing as how there wasn't nothing out east worth worrying about."

"Sounds like you got that wrong, too, you stupid piece of shit. Where the fuck is Roger?"

"Down checking on Sherman. He was gettin' tired of waitin' on the tape."

Old Man Bannister nodded.

"Let me ask you again: Who. We. Got. Up. North?"

"I was going to grab Sherman and a couple of his boys and head up right now. What I come to tell you."

Old Man Bannister's knuckles whitened as he gripped the tumbler. A daintier piece of glass would've shattered.

"Then what the fuck you still standing here for? Go, boy! Go kick Zeke and Elroy in the ass, then go kill that motherfuckin' Ingersoll and bring Bill's fuck toy back to me. I got plans for her."

Mack spun on his heels and was out the door before Old Man Bannister got the tumbler up to his mouth and tossed the rest of the cognac down his throat.

Why the fuck Great Granddaddy didn't wipe the earth of every Ingersoll on the planet when he had a chance, I'll never know, the Old Man thought.

He wiped his mouth with the back of his hand and returned his gaze to the road below. *Well, I aim to fix that. Tonight.*

CHAPTER TWENTY SIX

Max kept an eye on his mirrors, the big Kawasaki vibrating under him.

Nothing.

He kept expecting a convoy of jacked-up pickups to come roaring up behind, yahoos leaning out the windows and standing in the pickup beds, aiming shotguns at him.

Near as he could figure it, he'd crippled a big piece of Old Man Bannister's empire. He'd killed Bill, burned down his complex, rescued Mary Jane, beat the shit out of the other two boys, taken out the two idiots in the pickup at the edge of town, sent Raymond off to Seattle with Mary Jane for federal help…yup, Old Man Bannister had to be peeved.

The question was how much the Old Man knew.

He damn sure didn't know how far Max intended to go: all the way to Mexico and then some, if necessary.

Hopefully, at this point, he had no idea Raymond was involved.

His cell vibrated.

A tremor ran through him in sympathy with the vibration.

Shit. Not good news.

Max rolled onto the shoulder and pulled the phone out of his coat pocket, glanced at the screen.

Raymond, of course.

He put the phone to his ear.

Static. Wind. Road noise.

Then Raymond, "Max?"

"Yup."

"Bad news, Max."

"What happened?"

"Well, that fucking Monte followed us into Paluma, checking up on me, seeing if I really was on a supplies run, I guess..."

"And?"

"Well, when I went into the Costco to draw him off, it seems that he decided to look into the truck,"

"He's dead, isn't he?"

"Well, yeah. Mary Jane shot him. Splashed his brains all over the side of the panel truck parked next to me."

"Mary Jane."

"Yup. Right there in the parking lot of the Costco. I heard gunfire and come running out and there she is, standing right over the bloody mess that used to be Monte, emptying the rest of the clip into him. People crouching down behind cars and shit..."

"She OK?"

Raymond laughed.

Max raised his eyebrows, "Yeah?"

"Shit, Max. It was like therapy for her or something. She seems solid. As in, just what the doctor ordered, you know?"

Max nodded, "I know. Seen that kind of thing before. Taking control over the powers that had hold of you. Cathartic. 'I took by the throat the circumcised dog and smote him,' like that. So, where you headed? You got a plan?"

"Well, we sure as shit can't take the highway towards Seattle like we were...Bannisters'll have men all up and down that sucker."

"Then again, they're sure to have someone, or a bunch of someones on your tail. If not already, pretty damn quick."

"I know. I'm aiming up into the hills north of Paluma. Folks up there are either old-timers or the off-the-grid types. None of 'em would have anything to do with the Bannisters, I don't think."

"Wouldn't count on it. They're likely to at least have someone they know up there, seems to me."

"Doubt it. Different group of people up there. If anything, they'd be, like, descendants of the people who left Ramsey to get away from the Bannisters."

"You bet your life on that? 'Cause that's what you're doing. Yours and Mary Jane's."

"Haven't forgotten that for a minute, Max. Besides...there ain't any other way. Especially now that I'm this far..."

Static kicked in, drowning out Raymond.

"Raymond?" Max yelled, sticking a finger in his other ear.

Static, then, "...worry, Max. I'll be careful. Going to try to work...come back down... Mountain Loop Highway and down...."

"Raymond..."

Static, and then the click of a dropped call.

Shit.

Max stared at the road ahead, torn. Keep going? Burn down the Bannister empire, lure Old Man Bannister into a battle, take him out? Head back, try to track down Raymond and Mary Jane, help them get to Seattle?

Sweet baby Jesus, Max thought.

An image of the Blond Woman rose in his mind's eye. She smiled, calming him.

Stick to the plan. Save as many women as possible. Burn everything to the ground. Kill Old Man Bannister. Crush the beast.

Max slipped the phone back into his pocket, secured his helmet, thumbed the beast into gear, checked his mirror, and rolled onto the highway again.

I'm coming, he thought. *Just you wait, Old Man. Going to burn down everything you and yours ever stood for. Going to burn you right off the face of the earth.*

CHAPTER TWENTY SEVEN

Men with jeans tucked into rubber boots worked the ruin of Bill's rambler and barn.

A team in the house was raking it thoroughly with heavy metal-pronged rakes.

A solid clunk! and one of the team standing in what used to be Bill's living room shouted.

"Roger! I think I got it, boss!"

Roger Bannister spit into the ash flecked dirt and stalked to the man digging through the charcoal and cinders.

The man pulled his gloved hands out of the mess, a sturdy metal container between them.

The container was blackened by the fire, smeared with soot and greasy-looking, but it was intact. A fire box.

Roger nodded.

"That looks like it, all right. Good job, Bobby Joe."

Roger took the box from Bobby Joe, tucked it under an arm, and strolled back to his pickup, pulling out his cell phone as he walked. He thumbed a preset number, brought the phone to his ear.

"Pops. Got the box."

Roger stopped short mid-stride.

"The fuck you say? Zeke and Elroy aren't answering?"

Roger listened for a minute, nodded a few times.

"All right. I'm on the way up to see you now, Pops. Have Mack bring those missing boys up to your place soon as he finds them. See you in a few."

Roger thumbed off the call, stood for a minute tapping the phone against his teeth, thinking.

No way Ingersoll had anything to do with Zeke and Elroy missing. Monte'd had Ingersoll in his sights the same time the call came in about someone heading east and Zeke and Elroy got sent out.

None of this made any sense. Raymond Ingersoll had been sitting pretty in his shitty little bar, quiet, at terms with his station in life. No fucking way he'd suddenly gone rogue, killed Bill, burned down his house, rescued that bitch Bill'd been keeping for twenty years, and booked out of town.

No way.

There had to be another factor in there. Another someone.

Well. The answer might just be under his arm.

Bill hopped into the truck, started it up, stomped on it and peeled out onto the road heading for the Old Man's.

Mack cut the tape holding Zeke against the tree and eased him onto the ground.

He was still breathing, but shallowly. As Mack laid his head down, Zeke gagged and gurgled.

"Shit, Mack. He's gonna drown on his blood, like that," said the bearded giant of a man next to him.

"Maybe we ought to let him," Mack replied. But he pulled Zeke back up against the tree, stepped away and turned his attention to Elroy, still gagged and taped.

Mack flicked his knife, severing the tape holding Elroy's gag in place, and gouging Elroy's face in the process.

Elroy shook his head in an attempt to loosen the gag, but the tape wouldn't shake loose.

Mack stepped in closer and slashed the tape holding Elroy's wrists, only missing inflicting damage by Elroy's quick lurch to bring his taped hands into the pathway of the knife so that only the tape was severed.

Elroy pulled his hands apart, ripped the tape from his face and spit a bloody wad onto the ground.

"Fuckin' hell, Mack. Cut me a little more, why don't you?"

Mack's eyes narrowed and he stepped in with the knife.

"Not a bad idea. What the fuck happened to you guys?"

Elroy looked down at his feet, dug in his pocket for a knife, got it out and cut the tape holding his feet. He held the knife ready as he staggered to his feet.

"Some fucking biker dude ambushed us. We was sitting there in the truck, like you told us to, waiting to see who come up the road and all of a sudden, this guy was at the truck. Out of nowhere, man. We never stood a chance."

Zeke gagged again and Mack turned.

"Sherman. He going to croak or what?"

"Don't think so, boss. He's pretty fucked up, but if we keep him upright, he ought to be all right."

Mack folded his knife and stuck in into its pouch on his belt.

"All right, boys. You know what to do. Sherman, get things sorted and meet me up at the Old Man's ASAP, got it?"

"You got it, boss. I'll get Zeke to the hospital, then me and Elroy will come back and take care of the truck, get those slashed tires swapped out."

"Just get Zeke to the hospital, then up to Pop's." Mack turned to Elroy. "You take care of the truck. I want that thing fixed like yesterday, got me?"

Elroy met Mack's eyes, then looked down.

"Got it, boss."

Mack hopped in his truck, turned it around, and headed back to town. Sherman and Elroy watched him go.

"That fucking Mack's getting to be too much," Elroy said, raising a handkerchief to his cheek to wipe at the blood streaming from the cut Mack had left.

Sherman grabbed Elroy by the lapels of his denim jacket and pulled him in tight, lifting Elroy up on his tip toes.

"You got one thing right. Mack is too fucking much. For you. You and Zeke fucked up, Elroy. If I was you, I'd keep that yap of mine shut, before Mack or someone else decides to shut it permanently, understand?"

Elroy waved his hands in circles of appeasement.

"Just talking, Sherman. Nothing to it, you understand. No need to worry about me, you know that."

Sherman gathered the lapels of Elroy's coat tight in his hands and lifted the man off his feet. He looked deep into Elroy's eyes, then relaxed and set him on his feet.

"Don't you worry, none, Elroy. I know you. Now let's get moving."

Sherman leaned down, pulled Zeke to his feet and together he and Elroy got Zeke into Sherman's truck and headed back into town, a plume of rising dust marking their passage.

CHAPTER TWENTY EIGHT

Roger wiped his boots carefully at the door of the Old Man's house, then let himself in.

The Old Man was standing at the floor to ceiling window in his den, surveying the land below, tumbler of whisky in his hand.

Roger hesitated for a moment, gauging his father's drunkenness—surviving an encounter with the Old Man depended on the accuracy of this—then stepped in.

"Pops," he said.

The Old Man didn't turn around.

"You got it, then?"

Roger put the firebox down on the table in the center of the room. Cleaned, it shone a dull red.

The Old Man turned around, regarded the box.

"Well, get on with it," he said.

With practiced hands, Roger opened the protective box and extracted the Night Guard digital recorder. Bill had been a mean SOB, and tight with his money, but he'd liked his toys —all kinds—and he'd gone all in with his security system. Five grand worth of cameras and recording equipment had watched over his place. The cameras were enabled with night vision and recorded a sharp 1080p. Sharp enough to enlarge photos for license plates. Sure as shit sharp enough to capture facial imagery.

Roger strolled over to the Old Man's desk and paused, digital recorder in his hands.

The Old Man waved him on, giving him permission.

The Old Man's computer system was good. Not top of the line, but then again, he wasn't a gamer or much of a computer guy. About all he used it for was porn and news, and he demanded all the accounting stuff be sent to him so he could keep an eye on it.

Roger sat at the Old Man's desk and brought up the files from the digital recorder.

"All right, Pops. Let's see what we can see."

Max sat on his bike at the outskirts of Mountain Cleft. According to the ledgers, the Bannisters ran a hotel there, Hotel 29. From what Max could make out, it looked like women were kept on the premises. Slaves.

Mountain Cleft sat on the plain at the foot of the mountains to the north. Population 640, according to the sign. That seemed too small to finance a Bannister enterprise, but then again, the Bannisters weren't above making a couple of hundred bucks in a dirt shack in a vineyard, and there were several farms and orchards around, not to mention a military base within an hour's drive.

Max raised the binoculars to his eyes and looked over Hotel 29 one more time. White stucco with brick-red trim and one of those clay-tiled roofs. Two stories, with an underground parking garage, by the looks of it. No guards that he could see.

He ignored the clamoring in the back of his head. Imagery pushing to get to the forefront of his consciousness. The emotional tenor of the imagery was clear: vicious, brutal, sadistic, bloody—pain and suffering and death. He was getting better now at holding the visions off, but it required effort.

Yet...something important was trying to come through. Something...

Women...girls, really. The sun coming through drawn curtains in a darkened room, an intolerable sense of oppression and imprisonment. The sun silhouetted the bars keeping the girls inside.

Max raised the binos again, scanned what he could see of the building. No bars on any windows, but the sense of imprisonment and despair was definitely emanating from the hotel. The holding cell must be on the backside, then.

Max took a deep breath, slipped the binos into his saddlebag, cranked up the big bike and headed in.

Roger clicked rapidly through the file system, digging down into the most recent folders.

The most recent file was smaller than the others. Looked as if the recording cycle'd been interrupted...

Roger clicked on it.

A sixteen-grid video screen popped up. Total surveillance of Bill's compound. The time stamp showed 8:00PM on the night of the fire.

Roger could see Bill kicked back in his chair, watching a game on TV, apparently, the side table next to his chair filled with empty bottles. Looked as if Bill was about six beers into his night.

Roger looked away, swallowed. Bill had been a SOB, but he was his brother. And now he was a charred, burnt crisp. Roger's lips tightened and he made a silent vow: *whoever did this has to die.*

Mary Jane was curled on her cot down in the shelter, flipping through a magazine.

Bill's handyman and general worthless hang-about, Clay, was at the bar in the living room, pouring himself a stiff-looking drink.

All normal and good.

Roger hit the fast-forward button, watched Bill drink in jerky motions, get up and piss a couple of times, Clay head back to bed. Bill pounded a few more beers, went to bed around midnight. The house dark and quiet. Then, just around 3:00AM, a flicker and all the cams went black for a second, then came up in the greenish hue of night vision.

Roger sat up and rewound the tape to 2:50AM. He leaned in,

focusing on the cams outside, looking for movement.

There! Out by the gate.

A motorcycle, headlight out, rolled up to the side of the gate right where the power lines crossed over to Bill's spread. The rider pulled something off the back of his bike, held a finger up as if to test for wind, then watched two...*balloons!*...rise and hit the wires. They bobbled for a second, then a flash and descending sparks. The compound slipped into darkness.

Roger watched the man by the motorcycle. No movement. He was waiting to see if anyone responded.

Roger hit fast forward, one click's worth to 1.5X speed, another click for 2X, then 4X, then clicked back to regular motion as the man moved to the fence, tossed something onto it, then threw a pack over the fence, clambered after it and moved into the compound.

As the man skulked past Bill's house and moved for the playpen, he walked straight toward the camera stationed above the door of the barn. Roger waited until the man was perfectly framed in the shot, then with a few clicks of the mouse, isolated the image and pulled it up to full screen.

"Pops!" Roger called.

Old Man Bannister walked over and stood behind Roger.

Roger heard the clink of ice cubes as the Old Man took another drink.

The Old Man gestured with his tumbler, "That's the dirt bag?"

"Looks like it. This is the first clear shot I got of him. Parked a motorcycle out on the road, climbed the fence, looks to be on his way into the playpen."

"You ever seen him?" the Old Man asked.

Roger shook his head, "Nope. Nobody I recognize. Bill liked to party, have a few boys over, but I've met all of them, and this guy," Roger stuck a finger on the man's face, "ain't one of them. Never seen him."

"Let's see it, then. All of it."

"You sure, Pops?"

"Roll the goddamn tape, or whatever the hell you call it," the Old Man growled.

Roger clicked back to the sixteen-screen grid and the two of them watched the tape. Cameras blacked out one by one as the fire spread and then the final frames all cut at once as the fire ate away enough of the architecture of the system to stop the recording.

Max cruised by Hotel 29 without looking. From the corner of his eye, the hotel looked dead. He considered simply pulling into it and asking for a room, but the idea of checking into one of those rooms made his skin crawl.

The office sat on the roadside, the entrance to the parking garage a dark hole into the basement. No one on duty he could see.

The town of Mountain Cleft didn't offer much. A post office, a couple of bars, a general store, a couple of gas stations, a restaurant diner.

He was taking on a building with an unknown number of targets and victims. From the ledgers, he gathered there were three guys on the payroll, but he was unsure how many of them might be there. Who controlled the women? Could just one guy do that? Or would all three be needed?

Max pulled into the diner.

Best to fuel up, think things over.

Roger clicked on the image, starting the video as the camera captured Clay coming into the frame, then being dropped with a high kick by the man standing in the shadows, Mary Jane at his feet.

A sharp intake of collective breath as Sherman, Mack, Elroy and the others watched the man stomp Clay to death.

The Old Man silenced them with a glance.

Roger clicked again, exiting that video, and pulled up the one from the living room cam.

They watched the man beat Bill, exit, come back and pour

gas over everything, exit again, and then the flames leaping into the room, enveloping Bill, Bill twisting and screaming in the fire. They watched until the image was obscured by the fire and Roger clicked the mouse once more, pulling up video of the man helping Mary Jane out of the compound, firing up his bike, and heading out the road.

Roger clicked a final time, pulling up the full-frame image of the man as he approached the playpen/barn.

"That's the son-of-a-bitch got the drop on me and Zeke!" Elroy said.

The Old Man set his glass down on his desk, hard. His movements were deliberate, though Roger detected just the touch of a tremor there. Not age—rage. The Old Man was three-quarters drunk, but, as always, in complete control of himself.

"We," the Old Man said, "are going to hunt this piece of shit down. And then, we are going to bring him down to Red Rock. We are going to keep him there. Theon Greyjoy is going to be a lion in comparison by the time we get done with him."

"Theon…?" Elroy said.

The Old Man silenced him with a stare.

"We are going to play with him on a daily basis until he dies of old age," the Old Man said. "We are going to do things to him that no one has ever dreamed of. We are going to take him to the edge of death over and over and over again, but we aren't going to let him die until I say he dies. And if I die of old age before that, Roger is going to keep at it until this piece of shit finally dies, a gray, withered worm with nothing human left in him. We are going to find out who and what is precious to him and we are going to torture it to death over the course of years in front of him."

The Old Man let that sit for a minute, then nodded at Roger.

"We don't know how, but we know this piece of shit is connected with Ingersoll," Roger said.

Sherman chuffed with surprise.

"Yep. Ingersoll had Mary Jane with him in his truck. Monte followed him all the way to Paluma, where they stopped in at Costco, probably trying to fool Monte into letting them be. We're not sure exactly what happened there, but Monte is dead. Ingersoll, or Mary Jane, we're not sure, blew his head off in the parking lot. Literally."

"Holy shit!" Sherman said. "Ingersoll...?"

The Old Man looked hard at Sherman, and Sherman shut his mouth and looked at the floor.

"Billy and his boys are on the way back with a new shipment," Roger said. "They are a long ways out, yet, but they are coming. Danny and his group are almost here. Sherman..." Roger looked up and met Sherman's eyes.

"You and Elroy are going to chase Ingersoll. Last we know, he was heading into the mountains north of Paluma. We'll send a couple of Danny's boys after you, but we need you to at least get a handle on where that son of a bitch is taking Bill's fuck toy. If you catch 'em..."

Old Man Bannister interrupted.

"You can kill Ingersoll, but I want that bitch alive."

Roger let that sit a minute, then continued.

"They were headed north on the 1 last we heard. Not much up that way, hillbillies and hippies, mostly. No place to stop in and hide out, 'less they're planning on camping. Just head up there fast and see what you can see."

"Yes, sir." Sherman said. "Um, sir?"

Roger nodded.

"What about them Paluma cops? That's got to be a mess over there."

"They know this is family business. Monte was one of ours. They know better than to mess in family business," Roger said. "And Sherman?"

"Boss?"

"You be careful. Ingersoll is no slouch. He's had training. Take 'em by surprise, best you can, and blitz 'em. No fucking around, just hammer them down."

Sherman nodded, and he and Elroy headed out of the room.

"Shit for brains," Old Man Bannister muttered as they exited.

"They better do some good up there. That Elroy is more trouble than he's worth."

"They ought to be able to handle this, Roger said. "Sherman is good. He's big, he's smart, and he can move damn fast for a big man. He'll get the drop on them, he catches up. He'll be smart enough to find 'em, too."

"What you got on this mystery man?"

"Bike was too far off, even with the 1080p cams, to get the license. But it was a big-ass bike. As for the mystery man—he's the one run in on me out at the orchard. Sure as shit. I aim to..."

"He's the prick suckered me at the diner," Mack said, pointing at the monitor, which Roger had returned to the full-frame shot of Max. "Fucking sucker punched me, or I'd've spread his ass in a thin layer over the parking lot."

Mack's man, Ralph, bit his lip.

Roger caught that, winked at him, then turned his attention to Mack.

"We'll be handing him over to you, soon enough," Roger said. "We know he's headed east. He must've jumped on the highway right there where we had Zeke and Elroy stationed. There ain't a lot out that way, and we have people all along that road. We'll catch him."

Mack flexed his massive hands, cracked his knuckles.

"Mack, I want you and Ralph to head out that way, lickety-split," Roger said. Just head east as fast as you can go. We'll call when we hear something to direct you. We'll send Danny and a couple of his boys out that way, too, to cover more area, soon as they get here."

The sound of big tires skidding on gravel and dirt announced the arrival of Danny.

"Well, here he is now. You head out, Mack. Me and Pops going to watch this video show one more time with Danny and his boys, and then we're going to war."

Mack turned to go.

"Ralph," Roger said. "This son of a bitch got the drop on me, Mack, Zeke and Elroy, killed Bill and Clay, stole Bill's fuck toy and is off and running...."

"Don't have to tell me, Boss. I'm planning on going full nuclear with him, takin' no chances."

The Old Man growled, "But bring 'im back alive, damn it. I don't care if he's barely alive, we'll get him fixed up to play with, but he'd better be alive. Or I'll put you in his place."

Ralph put on his big black hat, met the Old Man's eyes, nodded respectfully, "Yes, sir," then turned and followed Mack out the door, brushing past Danny and his crew on their way in.

"Danny!" Roger said. "You and the boys come in. Got something to show you."

Max closed the ledger on the table in front of him, tossed back the last of his coffee, and reached for the check.

Prepare for three guys. He closed his eyes and played it out. *Hit the office, take out anyone there, do a door-to-door, clear the place out, and on to the next. Leave a trail of burning hotels, massage parlors, and bars so bright the Bannisters couldn't miss it.*

CHAPTER TWENTY NINE

There!

Finally, a gas station. Needle on "E", Raymond signaled and pulled over to fill the truck.

"Hold tight, Mary Jane," Raymond said. "Got to get us some gas."

"That's good. I need to pee," Mary Jane said.

The gas station was old enough to hold serious retro allure: an ancient Pegasus crowned the roof of the cover over the gas pumps, the pumps themselves old-school with the rotating numbers rather than a digital readout.

Raymond swung the truck around so he was facing the road and eased up to the farthest pump from the store.

Mary Jane popped out to find a restroom.

Raymond pulled the nozzle out of its resting place, flipped up the reset handle, and watched with amusement as the old-school readout clicked to 000.00.

He was watching the readout, listening to the clicks as the price climbed, when a brawny old geezer wearing coveralls with "Al" embroidered above his shirt pocket, ambled over from the office.

"Howdy," the old guy said.

"Hey," Raymond answered.

"You and the lady friend headed up to Canada?"

Raymond stared at him, thinking.

"Nope," he finally answered. "Just a bit of a cruise. Might stop in at a campgrounds or something, get some peace and quiet."

The old guy scratched his chin, the stubble making a loud rasping noise.

"Seems to me, you might need some of that. Peace and quiet, I mean."

The handle of the nozzle clicked off as the tank filled.

Alarm spread through Raymond like a fever.

"What are you trying to tell me, old man?" Raymond asked.

The old guy held up his hands, "Don't get your hackles up," he said. He looked over his shoulder to see if the woman was out of the restroom yet. "It's just...news travels fast, these parts."

Raymond holstered the nozzle in the pump and turned to face Al square. He rolled his head and the bones in his neck popped.

"What news?"

The old man gave another glance around, then leaned in.

"You're the one. You're the guy shot that cop down in Paluma."

Raymond's first impulse was to drop the old guy, but he bit it down.

"Got me confused with someone else, Al," he said.

"Name's not Al. That was my dad. Wear this for sentimental reasons. Name's Guy. Guy Pearce."

"Got me confused with someone else, Guy," Raymond said.

"I don't think so," Guy said.

Mary Jane exited the restroom at the side of the station and stopped, reading the tension between the two men. She slipped the .45 out of her waistband.

Raymond caught her eyes, tried to give her a discrete shake of the head.

"No question about it, son," Guy said.

Mary Jane slid closer, taking care not to make noise on the gravel. She held the .45 in two hands, ready to bring it up and fire.

"Like I said, Guy. You're confused."

Guy cackled and shook his head.

"No, not hardly. The woman you're with shot down a cop in the parking lot of Costco back in Paluma. You hit the 1 straight out of town and haven't stopped running since. You slipped through all them tiny towns climbing up here into the mountains without stopping and about now, you are totally out of gas, aren't you? We figured you'd either stop here, or at Dave's place fifty miles down the road toward Paluma."

"We?"

The garage door ratcheted up behind Mary Jane.

She spun and began to raise the .45 into a firing stance as four men holding shotguns stepped out. Another came out of the office, also holding a shotgun, flanking her.

"Best you put that gun down, missy," Al said. "We don't want no trouble."

Mary Jane turned and brought the .45 to bear on Guy's face.

"You're going to have to kill me," she said. "No way I'm going back. No fucking way. You all put your guns down, or I'll shoot the old guy in the face."

"Relax, missy," Guy said. "Boys, lower your weapons. We don't want any confusion here."

Guy turned toward Raymond, relaxed and easy.

"Thing is," Guy said. "That cop weren't no cop. Not really. Name was Monte MacFarland, and he was one of Karl Bannister's crew."

Guy spit on the ground as if to get the taste of Bannister's name out of his mouth.

"Anyone kills himself a Bannister is a friend of ours, Raymond," Guy said.

He turned to face Mary Jane.

"Put the gun away, missy. We're friends. We want to help."

The man in the motel office lay on the floor, blood leaking out of his nose, mouth, and ears. He made a little bubbling noise as his chest rose and fell.

Max stepped out the door and moved along the face of the motel. He held the door in his head slightly open, listening, feeling...and shuddering as imagery poured in. The same savage imagery he'd been assaulted with since the beginning of this thing.

Yea, though I walk through the valley of the shadow of death, I will fear no evil....

The evil that haunted Hotel 29 was the classic variety of lust tied to the infliction of pain—the highest level of pain possible. Women as meat puppets made to suffer and perform. Hollow men filled with a red black spirit that capered and gibbered with glee with each scream of agony, each spasm of pain—a spirit held in ecstatic thrall by a body bucking in pain.

He hadn't meant to beat on the guy in the office quite so hard, but the imagery that poured off the man...his soul given over to the demons that infested him....

Max neared the end of the first floor. All the rooms on the floor empty of the living, yet populated with the echoes of the women who had suffered there and the men who had reveled in their suffering.

He climbed the stairwell at the end of the walkway, and looped back onto the second floor, the stairwell leading him into a dim corridor—a wall of doors on both sides.

The imagery in Max's head crested and he stopped, brought both hands to his temples.

Worse than the imagery was the siren call of the violence. The evil spirit beckoned, a carny side-show barker, invited Max to allow it in.

Max closed his eyes to shut it out.

Got to get a handle on that.

It had been this spirit, as much as his outrage at the man in the office's history that had led to the savage beating Max had put on him, he realized. He wasn't simply in physical peril; his soul was teetering on the brink of disaster—he could be seduced into the same lust for the infliction of pain and suffering as the men he was so "righteously" beating down. Had been, in fact. He'd killed Bill and his handyman with a dark joy and satisfaction. He'd nearly killed one of the men in the truck, may have killed him, in fact. He'd hurt the man downstairs far worse than he'd intended to....

Getting a fix on the image of the blond woman was becoming harder, and Max had the feeling that if he lost her, he'd lose himself. Eyes closed, he remembered himself back into the clearing on the mountain, pictured her, imagined her hands, her eyes.

Calmed somewhat, Max opened his eyes.

The dim hallway beckoned, and he answered, light on his feet, hands up, ready.

Danny, a compact man with the build of a wrestler, stood in the study with his fists balled at his sides.

"Dead man. Going to find that motherfucker, string 'im up..."

"No, you are not!" Old Man Bannister bellowed. "He's mine! What you are going to do is find that son of a bitch, bundle him up, and bring him down to Red Rock and get him ready for me."

Danny raised his eyes to meet the Old Man's gaze, nodded obediently, then returned his eyes to the toes of his boots.

"You can hurt him," the Old Man said. "You can hurt him bad. But I don't want him crippled. I definitely don't want him dead. I want him..."

"Red Rock," Danny said. "You want us to bring him to the outfit in Red Rock."

A spirit of anticipation mixed with fear and awe filled him. The Bannisters had dozens of hotels and massage parlors, brought women to a score of miserable little hovels around the farming circuit, but Red Rock was the pinnacle. Red Rock was a fully equipped chamber of horrors. A sprawling complex on a ranch with a security fence enclosing its 22 acres, a couple dozen cottages filled with every device imaginable, medical facilities, ovens for disposal....

"You got that right," the Old Man said. "You get this son of a bitch there, no matter what shape, we'll fix 'im up, and get to work. Like I told the boys, we're going work on this bastard for a lifetime. He's going be a work of art. Going make a new creature out of him."

Danny nodded, envisioning it. A grin split his face into halves.

"Where do we start?"

Raymond and Mary Jane sat in chairs at a table in a room in back of Guy's garage. A large room, with a pool table, dart board, several small tables and a little bar at the back. Couches against the wall where the men with Guy lounged. Gun racks, home again to the shotguns the men had carried. Comfortable, like the social hall of a men's club. Coffee steamed in mugs in front of them.

"Heard about Monte going down in Paluma probably before you were out of town," Guy said. "You know how it is in these parts. Got a call you all hit the 1, from then on, just a matter of guys checking in as you drove past. Knew it was you, Raymond, and that fit: your family been crosswise with the Bannisters for a century, after all. But, you, missy—holy shit. Mary Jane Crawford. Holy shit..."

Mary Jane brought the coffee mug to her mouth, cupping it in both hands. Sipped. Set the cup back down, stared into the rising steam.

"Twenty years," she whispered. "My God...."

Mary Jane looked up and met Guy's eyes.

"How many of you are there?" she asked. "Because the Bannisters are legion. Literally. They've got people strung out from here down to Mexico. They're in with the Mexican cartels. They have got reach and power like you couldn't imagine."

Guy kept his eyes steady on Mary Jane's.

"You got enough guys to take on that?" she asked. "Because the Bannisters cannot be allowed to live, to exist. They got to be burned out, exterminated like the disease they are."

Raymond reached a hand out, cupped Mary Jane's. "We got a plan, Mary Jane. We're going to get over to Seattle, get the Feds in..."

"Fuck the Feds and the horse they rode in on," Mary Jane said. "They ain't going to be able to do shit. Bannisters own this part of the country and everyone in it. Feds come in, they'll be talking to Bannister cops, Bannister 'witnesses,' Bannister Bannister Bannister!"

She jerked her hand loose and slammed a fist on the table.

"We got to go right to the head of the beast and slay it."

Raymond looked at Guy, then at Mary Jane, then around the room at the men seated on the couches against the wall.

"We had a plan," Raymond said. "We've got a guy out there, Max. He's on a mission to destroy the Bannisters, got quite a start...."

"He's the one burned down Bill Bannister's spread, yeah?" Guy asked.

Raymond nodded. "I imagine Max could use a little help." He turned to look at Mary Jane. "But Mary Jane. We got to get the Feds in. Got to get some law enforcement on this. We got to at least try."

"And end up getting jailed or handed over to the Bannisters? No thank you!"

"We can..."

Guy raised a calming hand.

"Hold on, you two. Maybe we can work something out. We know some people in law enforcement. We have a handle on what the Bannisters are up to. Been working on it for a long while. Maybe now's the time...."

Max reached the end of the corridor. Two rooms in the middle had men in them: he could hear the grunts and cries as they took their pleasure.

But the two rooms at the end of the hallway drew him. The weight of the oppression and despair seeping out of those rooms was overwhelming.

Max stood, poised, uncertain. Two women were in pain, for certain, though he sensed no imminent threat of death or serious physical harm. And these two rooms....

Decision made, Max stepped forward, bringing his rear leg up and out for a front kick he placed right next to the door handle.

Wham! The door rattled in its frame and bent a little, but did not give.

Holy crap, Max thought. *These are security doors, practically prison-level doors.*

He backed off, gave a hopping step and brought his rear leg up again, placing it precisely where he had before.

The door bent a little more, opening just a crack. Max felt, more than heard, the panic of several women in the dim room behind the door.

A prison. Had to be a dozen women crammed into these rooms...Max flashed on the guy in the office downstairs. He's enough to handle this many women? Alone?

The door in his head cracked open and imagery poured in from all over the hotel, nearly overwhelming him.

Countless numbers of women had been tortured, beaten and raped here. Maybe hundreds. A few had been murdered, and their faces and endings crowded into Max's head. Max pushed aside the imagery, fighting against the overwhelming mass of it, the numbers....

A spike of alarm rang through him, and he crouched and spun as he felt the approach of the Presence. A shot echoed down the corridor, and the zzzzzz! of a bullet passed over him where his head had been a split-second before.

A man was charging down the hallway toward him, a big revolver in his hand. Wearing only boxers and cowboy boots, an erection still tenting the boxers, the man fired again.

Time went liquid and slow, and Max moved easily through it. He rolled, pushed off the wall, and came up in a fluid movement with a right uppercut to the man's chin, grabbing the wrist of his gun hand with the other. The man's knees buckled, then held, and Max felt a door behind him open, the hot flash of another in the grip of the Presence behind him.

Max pulled the first man's wrist down onto his shoulder, hard, and the man squeezed the trigger.

The roar of the gun was deafening, and Max brought up a right elbow hard against the man's temple. This time, his knees buckled completely and he went limp.

Max let him fall, grabbing the revolver by the barrel and spinning with it, bringing the butt of the gun around in a vicious arc that caught the man behind him just above his left ear.

Both the man's hands were clutching at a bloody wound spurting blood from his right upper chest, so the pistol butt caught him clean and he went down in a heap.

Senses on fire, Max opened the door in his head fully and fought through the imagery desperately, scanning the environment for imminent threat.

There was none.

In each of the rooms with open doors, a young Latina was pulling on a nightgown. Max sensed the women in the rooms down the hallway milling in panic. The two men lay at his feet, both out cold, the one Max had elbowed flat on his back, the other face down, a pool of blood spreading out from underneath him.

Max glanced into the room nearest him, saw fear in the eyes of the young Latina as she backed into a corner.

Max stuck the gun under his belt in the small of his back, and raised his hands in a calming gesture. "It's OK," he said to the young woman. "I'm here to help. Relax."

Her eyes showed fear and uncertainty. And a tiny glimmer of hope.

She couldn't have been more than 15.

Max's eyes were drawn to a pair of jeans in a heap on the floor, a huge key ring attached to the belt.

Ahah.

He stepped in, put a boot on the belt and broke the key ring tether off the belt, raised another calming hand toward the young woman, moved into the hallway, looked both ways, then headed down to the end of the corridor.

CHAPTER THIRTY

Roger Bannister sat at the Old Man's desk, working the phones, the Internet, and the radio. Elroy and Sherman had reached Paluma and were heading up the 1 into the mountains. So far, nothing. Danny and his boys were headed east, hoping to come up to the motorcycle man. Billy and his group had obtained the new shipment, crossed the border and were in North Texas, on the way.

Roger had a long list of names and places, and he was working his way down it, checking them off as he went.

"That's right," Roger said into the phone. Medium-sized dude on a big motorcycle. Saddle bags. Jeans and boots, black leather jacket. I sent you a pic, check your email."

Roger sat bolt upright.

"The hell! When? All right. You get that pic out to the diner and check up on that. Danny and his boys are about two, three hours out, but if you can get a handle on this before they get there, I promise you, the Old Man will be mighty grateful to you. Mighty grateful."

Roger clicked off the line, shouted to the door towards the den where the Old Man sat, staring out the window, nursing his whisky.

"Might have 'im, Pops!"

A rustle and squeak of leather as the Old Man lowered the footrest and pushed off the chair. Then he was standing in the doorway.

"Where?"

"Mountain Cleft. Brandon says he heard a guy matching the description stopped in the diner there, sat for an hour or so, working his way through some big accounting-looking kind of books, then got up and headed back into town. Couple of hours ago."

"Mountain Cleft," the Old Man said. "Hotel 29, there. They notice anything? Maybe we'll get lucky, that piece of shit'll check in there."

Roger moved his finger down the list, "They're next on my list. Was just getting ready to call 'em."

"Well, get on it, boy. Get on it!"

Roger dialed.

Guy was working his own list.

"Started this back in the day of the listserve," he said. "Loose group of folks, all pushed out of Ramsey by the Bannisters and their like. Started as a local news kind of thing with an emphasis on the going ons in Ramsey, Aston, that area. Kept adding to it as folks had kids, kids grew up, like that. We got people on this list spread out all over the country now."

Guy did some more typing, Raymond peering over his shoulder.

Mary Jane lay curled up on a couch, asleep, her chest rising and falling softly.

Raymond cradled his coffee mug, sipped at the lukewarm coffee, then padded over to the coffee machine for a warm up.

"Letting folks know about Bill Bannister and Mary Jane," Guy said.

Raymond froze mid-pour.

"You let that out, and the Bannisters hear about it, they'll be coming even harder for her. They're going to want to bury her as deep as they can, make damn sure no one can ever prove a thing."

"Shit, Raymond. You don't think the Bannisters aren't already coming as hard as they can? From what you told me, your buddy has killed Bill, freed Mary Jane, burned Bill's whole compound down, roughed up the other two brothers, and is setting out to burn the whole Bannister enterprise out of business. I'd say they're coming about as hard as they can. I'd say Roger Bannister is rallying the troops and sending 'em out as we speak."

"But...Mary Jane," Raymond said, topping up his coffee.

"Mary Jane will spark some action, son," Guy said. "Folks remember her. Most folks figured Bill had something to do with her disappearance, and when both her Papa, and then her Mama died, folks were even more sure. Hearing about Mary Jane is going to light a fire, get folks moving, you'll see."

Raymond ran a hand through his hair. "Ah, geez. I suppose. Just feels so...exposed, I guess."

"We're going to war, son. Get used to that feeling." Guy rubbed his chin, then went back to typing. "Can't believe we're finally doing something. After all these years." He slapped the desk. "Damn, this feels good! Can't believe it took us so long."

Raymond looked at Guy, then over at Mary Jane, then sipped his coffee. Nodded.

"You're right about that," he said. "It does feel good."

Max stood in the office of Hotel 29, looking around. He'd had to kick the one door in, and his hip was sore from that, but he'd bent it so out of whack the key wouldn't turn the locks. The other door opened easily.

Now he had another problem. Fifteen women and no place to put them. He'd found a van in the basement parking garage, probably the very one that'd transported them here, but no keys. Dude on the floor was still bubbling, and the pool of blood under him had grown considerably, but nothing too large, nothing to indicate he might bleed out entirely.

Max stepped carefully over the blood and scanned the key rack.

Nothing that looked like van keys.

Drawers of the desk filled with papers and cards and pens and whatnot, office detritus.

No keys.

The guy on the floors snuffled, and Max turned his head to look at him, saw he had one of those big key rings on a spooling cord attached to his belt.

Bingo.

He edged to one side of the man, doing his best to keep his boots out of the blood, reached down and pulled the spool and keychain off his belt.

Yes, indeed. An old Ford key, almost certainly the one for the van downstairs.

Max turned to go get the women, and found the young Latina from the first room standing in the doorway, watching him.

Max stopped and looked at her. Seventeen, eighteen at the most. A beautiful young woman just in the first flush of maturity. His heart sank at the thought of how she'd been treated, all that she'd seen in her young life. The natural flush of her skin was pushing through yellowing bruising on the side of her face.

"I go with you," she said.

"I don't think that'll work out, young lady. But you can help me, if you want."

"I go with you. You are good man."

"I suppose in comparison to what you've seen.... But no, I really need your help here, miss...?"

She caught his questioning look.

"Rosita."

"Rosita," Max said. It fit. She was a beautiful flower, just coming into full bloom.

"Rosita," Max said again. "I'm Max. Look, Rosita. Here's the thing. I'm on that motorcycle out front." Max raised his chin, indicating the motorcycle, visible though the office window. "And there isn't room or time to take you along. Plus, I'm expecting a pile of bad men to come after me. I expect they are already on the way. You can't stay with me."

Rosita's eyes flashed determination.

Uh-oh, thought Max. *This could be a problem.*

The phone rang, startling both of them.

It was one of those multi-line hotel desk phones. *Unknown*

Caller, followed by a phone number flashed on the panel.

A strong sense of the Presence flooded Max.

Bannisters.

His eyes still on Rosita's, he picked up the phone, held it to his ear.

"Floyd? This is..." said the voice on the phone.

"Roger Bannister," Max finished. "Floyd can't come to the phone right now, Roger. Neither can either of the other two pieces of shit you got here."

Silence.

Then: "Who the fuck are you?"

"I'm the one coming for you, Roger. I'm coming for all of you."

"You're a dead man is what you are."

Back in Ramsey, in the house up on the hill, Roger looked up to see the Old Man leaning over him, reaching his hand out for the phone. He handed it to him.

In the office of Hotel 29, Max grinned.

"Been hearing that a lot, lately," he said.

"What you going to be hearing is the sound of your own screams, boy," said the Old Man.

"Karl? Is that you? I'll be damned. Just the man I'm looking for."

"You ain't looking too hard, are you? Everybody knows where to find me. And now, I know where to find you, you piece of shit."

The Old Man placed the phone in its cradle, terminating the conversation.

Max heard the phone click, cutting off his response.

He put the phone down and turned his full attention to Rosita.

"Rosita. They're coming for us. Right now. We've got maybe five, ten minutes. I need you to round up all the women upstairs and get them into the van as fast as you can. Tell them the bad men are coming. Get them moving."

Rosita was out the door and running down the hallway

before Max cleared the desk on his way to the parking garage to retrieve the van.

Fear punched Brandon in the gut as he raced for the door, phone in one hand, already dialing his crew. Whoever this guy way, he'd already put a real hurt on the Bannisters, and by the sounds of it, had done the same out at Hotel 29.

Brandon didn't much like a fair fight. And with only two guys left on his crew, and figuring in how this mystery man had taken out the three men at the 29, this was much too close to a fair fight for his liking.

He hit the road in his big Ford F-250, tires squealing and aimed the truck down the road for Hotel 29. The other two were on the way, but he was worried that he'd be the first on the scene. And no way was he taking this guy on alone.

He opened the glove compartment as he drove and eased out the big .44 Smith and Wesson, laid it on the seat next to him, then reached back to the gun rack for the sawed-off 12-gauge and set that beside it.

Loaded for bear.

Max had the van running and was herding the women into it.

"Who can drive? Which one of you can drive?" he asked. He mimed steering.

"Conchita can drive," said Rosita, appearing at Max's side. She pointed at a slender woman in her early 20s with a crooked nose from what looked to be a fresh break, just the faintest yellowing under both eyes.

"Conchita?" Max asked, locking eyes with her.

She froze, one hand on the sliding door of the van.

"I need you to drive, sweetheart. Slide up front and take the wheel."

Panic flared in her eyes, and Rosita rattled off some soothing, yet commanding-sounding patter in Spanish and Conchita ducked her head and slid forward into the driver's seat.

Max came around to the driver's door as the rest of the women squeezed into the van and Rosita slammed the door.

"Conchita? You go that way," Max said, indicating back toward Ramsey. "They won't be coming from that way yet, I don't think."

Once again, Rosita appeared at his side. She translated Max's message and Conchita rattled off some scared-sounding response.

"She's scared," Rosita said.

"Don't doubt it," Max said. "Tell her just to go to the first rest stop out of town. That's about twenty miles. Pull in there, park behind the bathrooms so she's not visible from the road. Tell her to wait there until dark, then drive back this way, cut through town and take them all home."

"Home?" Rosita asked.

Max and Rosita looked at one another.

"Mexico," Max said. "Isn't that where she's from?"

"Mexico is a big place, Max. We're from all over Mexico."

Max flapped his hands in frustration. "Well, tell her to get moving. That is, if she doesn't want to go back to that," he said, indicating the hotel, "or something worse."

Rosita started translating again, and Max gave her a gentle push.

"Climb in," Max said. "You've got to get moving. Now!"

Rosita ignored him, slapped the side of the van, and Conchita put the van in gear and lumbered onto the road headed back toward Ramsey.

"What the hell?" Max said. "You need to be in that van!"

Rosita shook her head, "No room, Max. And I go with you. I told you."

Frustrated and out of time, Max nodded, handed his helmet to Rosita, jumped on his bike and cranked it up.

Rosita climbed on behind him.

Just as Max angled the bike for a quick 180, heading east out of town, something zinged over his head like a monstrous bumblebee. A blue Ford F-250 headed straight for him, the driver leaning out the window with a cannon of a pistol aimed right at Max.

Time slowed as Max slipped into the zone. He braked hard, bringing the bike to a stop, planted both feet, reached behind him to pull the pistol from his belt, and brought it up and put two bullets through the windshield before the driver had time to pull the trigger again.

A splash of red inside the vehicle, and the truck veered and accelerated, hood rising up as the driver's foot came down hard on the gas. The big truck slipped past Max and Rosita, missing them by inches, and smashed into the office, obliterating the wall and half-disappearing inside before it came to a stop. The rear wheels continued spinning on the gravel, spitting rocks and dirt as the engine screamed.

Max slipped the pistol back into his belt, gunned the bike and put it back on the road. Rosita wrapped both her arms around his waist and held on.

Max felt his phone vibrating in his coat pocket, but all his attention was focused on getting out of town. Alone, he'd head straight for the next Bannister outpost, but with Rosita... things got complicated.

A sense of the presence overtook Max, and he swerved wildly and braked. Another big Ford pickup raced through the spot he'd just occupied, veered as the driver realized his mistake, bumped a wheel up on the sidewalk, changed direction again and crashed into a light pole, the force of the truck buckling it, bringing it down across the road.

"Duck!" Max yelled, and crouching, gunned the bike under the V of the light pole next to the truck and out into the road ahead. He glanced into his rear-view mirror to see the driver struggling to get out of the truck, hitting the sidewalk on his knees and raising a gun.

Max dodged left as he saw the puff of smoke from the gun barrel and sensed the bullet pass by on his right. A couple of quick left and right moves and he was around the corner and out of sight of the truck.

On high alert, and moving fast within the slowed flow of time, Max scanned the side streets and road ahead. He was already at the outskirts of Mountain Cleft with nothing but open road and plains ahead, mountains on each side. Nowhere to hide, really.

Max gunned the engine, hit a steady 120, and settled in, alert.

CHAPTER THIRTY ONE

"Try again," Mary Jane said.

"Max would answer if he could," Raymond said. "He's probably driving, didn't notice the phone."

"Exactly," Mary Jane said. "So, try again."

At the computer, Guy sat bolt upright.

"Holy shit!" he said.

Raymond and Mary Jane turned to him.

"Something's up in Mountain Cleft," Guy explained, planting a thick forefinger on the computer monitor, pointing out a message on his blog.

"Brandon Farrell, one of Bannister's crew in Mountain Cleft, crashed his truck into the side of Hotel 29—a Bannister place. One of his guys apparently crashed on the road on the way there, then fired a few shots at a guy and a girl on a motorcycle."

Raymond and Mary Jane looked at each other.

"A girl?"

Raymond rubbed a hand across his face.

"He saved someone," Mary Jane said. "Just like he saved me." She began to tear up, got a hold of herself.

"Call him again, Raymond! He's in trouble!"

Raymond punched the number.

Max glanced in the rear-view as he felt the phone buzz in his pocket again. The road was clear behind, and other than a couple of semis pulling loads headed his way, clear ahead. He opened himself, seeking out the presence, felt nothing, then let the bike slow to 60 and pulled the phone out.

"Raymond?"

"Max! You OK?"

"I'm fine. Pushing down the highway, trying to put some distance between me and Mountain Cleft. Raymond...," Max paused. "Uh, I've got a complication."

"I know. You picked up a girl back there, didn't you? Saved her out of that hotel?"

Max's adrenaline spiked.

"How do you know that?"

"Long story. Max, we found some people."

Max checked the road ahead again, his mirrors, then pulled to a stop beside the road.

"What people, Raymond?" he said.

"We're way up north of Paluma," Raymond said. "Found a guy who's part of a whole circle of anti-Bannister folks. People whose families moved out of Ramsey once the Bannisters took hold. Good people."

Max closed his eyes, tried to get a sense of the situation. An image of the blond woman came readily to mind.

She smiled at him.

"OK," Max said. "So?"

"So," Raymond said, "they've got a whole network. Dude here named Guy just got info about what went down in Mountain Cleft. He's already put word out about Mary Jane, and everyone, of course, knew about Bill..."

Max looked back over his shoulder, then at the road ahead, his sense of unease growing. "Raymond, I've got to get moving. They're coming for me."

"That's why I'm calling, Max! We can help!"

"Max?" A new voice. Gruff, older.

"Who's this?"

"Name's Guy. Now listen to me, Max. We got people right there, not far from you. Where you at, exactly?"

Max closed his eyes, opened the door all the way, tried to feel Guy out through the phone. From across the plains and down the mountainside, flickerings of suffering poked at him, people who'd died in road accidents, hunting accidents, murder. His sense of Guy grew—a ball of light, traces of darkness—but clear of the presence.

"I'd say I'm about ten miles east of Mountain Cleft," Max said. "There's nothing but plains ahead of me and the road is a straight line. Feeling pretty exposed. Hope like hell Bannisters don't have any aircraft."

"Nothing that'd get to you yet," Guy said. "Look, Max. You want to pull a 180 and head back toward town, about a mile or so. You'll see a dirt road on your right. Look for the power lines. Head up that road until you come to a little copse of trees. There's a farm there, and a ranch. You get there, I'll have someone ready. Someone to help."

Max felt the presence nearing.

Too close.

He decided.

"I'm on it. Call you back," he said, thumbing off the call, and thrusting the phone back into his pocket.

"Hold on!" he called to Rosita.

He gunned the engine, spinning the back tire, sliding the bike around in a half-donut. As the tire gripped the road, he and Rosita shot ahead, aiming for the power lines he could see in the distance.

Karl Bannister tossed back a slug of whisky, rattled the ice in his glass, held it out for a refill.

The little Latina in the French maid outfit stepped forward, whisky decanter in hand, and freshened his glass with a couple of inches.

Karl swirled the whisky and ice, and continued to pace the room.

"God damn," he said. "We've got that motherfucker. There ain't no way out of Mountain Cleft. Roger! How far are Danny and his crew?"

Roger leaned against the wall, gazing out the window. He

unfolded his arms, looked down at the phone in his hand, thumbed a quick text.

"Just a minute, Pops," he said.

The Old Man stopped pacing and turned to face Roger.

"OK, Kane just texted me their location. About twenty minutes away."

The Old Man grunted. "What about Billy and his boys?"

Roger returned his attention to his phone, held up a finger, then replied; "Wilder says they're into Oklahoma now."

"You tell 'em to step on it, boy."

"Will do, Pops. But remember they've got to be careful with the cargo they're carrying. Can't afford any scrutiny."

"I fucking well know that. But they can do 70 and not stop for pee breaks and they can get their fucking asses up here in 48 hours."

Roger knew better than to argue with the Old Man. "Yes, sir," he said, thumbing a text to Wilder.

Old Man pissed. ASAP.

Max slowed as he approached the copse of trees about a mile from the road. A dust trail rose behind him like a tail. *Easy to see from the road or the air. Bannisters know they're looking for a guy on a motorcycle. Hope these people are ready for some heavy action...*

He geared the bike down, slowed to about 35 mph as the trees above blocked out the sky. Rosita tightened her arms around his waist.

He leaned through a forty-five degree turn to find a huge bearded man in overalls, a dirty white T-shirt, and a straw cowboy hat standing in the road with an AR-15 held ready across his chest, muzzle down, stock up. The man squared up as Max geared down again and brought the bike to a halt ten feet away.

Max concentrated on the giant, jolted as imagery washed over him: visions of light, and a sense of an invisible multitude of...*what, exactly?* Max wasn't ready to call them angels, but there was a purity to the man and the...*things*...that swarmed around him. Max turned his head left and right as he sensed more men in the woods. One by one, six more men stepped out of the woods. Each holding an AR-15. They were of a type: about 5' 10", maybe 170 or so. Slender, wiry guys.

The giant stepped forward, nodded pleasantly at Max.

"Name's Dallas," he said. "You must be Max."

Max rolled his head, the bones in his neck crackling. "That's right. I hope you boys know what you're stepping into. I got some bad guys coming after me. Feels like they're almost here."

Dallas lowered his weapon and scratched his chin through the massive beard.

"Well, we ain't out here to play. Let's get you and the little lady there squared away. You drive up the road a piece, it opens up into a farm. Park the bike back behind the barn by the hay bales."

Dallas keyed the mic of a radio attached to the strap of his overalls. "Dean?"

A crackle and a response, "Boss?"

"Two on the way. And a bike to hide."

"Roger that, boss."

Dallas stepped aside and waved Max through.

Max toed the bike into gear, easing past Dallas and the others, sensing movement all around him, and a firmness, a solidity to the place that calmed him.

Maybe, he thought, *just maybe, we'll get through this.*

CHAPTER THIRTY TWO

Danny stood outside Hotel 29 looking at the devastation the truck had caused. Brick, glass, splintered wood, gravel and dirt spread out in a half-moon pattern around the truck. Smoke drifted out the hole in the wall of the office from the overheated engine.

"Yep," he said into his phone. "One dead in the office. He got squashed all to hell when the truck run him over. Brandon's in his truck here, shot to shit, blood all over the truck, the truck half into the office. Got another dead up on the second floor in the hallway, bled out from a gun wound. The other one is beat to shit, but he's coming around. Looks like both guys upstairs got caught with their pants down. Dipping into the merchandise."

On the other end of the phone, Roger looked up at the Old Man.

"You tell him to leave two guys to clean up as best they can and to head east after this mystery man," the Old Man said. "At the very least find out where he went. We're going to rain hellfire on him."

"You catch that?" Roger spoke into the phone.

"Got it," Danny said. "I'm on it."

"Grab Phillip from the diner. He crashed his truck going after this guy. Martin's out on the road heading east, looking for any sign. Coordinate with him," Roger said.

"Yes, sir," Danny said. He turned toward the men standing with him to get things moving.

"And Danny?" Roger said.

"Yes, boss?"

"Don't forget—we really want this guy alive. You can fuck him up some, but not too bad. No paralysis, no permanent brain damage, nothing permanent at all. We plan to have him with us a good long while."

"Yes, sir," Danny said. "I ain't forgot. Plan on having a turn or three at him myself."

"Good. Then we're all on the same page here."

"Indeed we are, sir," Danny said.

He thumbed off the call to get things moving.

Max drove out of the tunnel of trees and into a big clearing. A farmhouse with a white picket fence stood in the middle, a big barn-like structure off to one side, a corral with horses to the other. Chickens squawked and pecked at the dirt. They scattered as Max followed the dirt lane to the barn, where yet another man holding an AR waited. The man lifted his chin in greeting, then turned and walked around behind the barn.

Max followed.

Two more men waited behind the barn, next to a stack of hay bales. The stack had been partially taken down, and a big iron door hinged up from the earth where the hay bales had stood.

Max parked next to the hole the door revealed, killed the bike and clambered off. Rosita removed the helmet and climbed off and stood next to him.

The man who'd greeted them out front held out a hand.

"Name's Dean," he said. "This here's Kane, and this's Big John."

The two men nodded at Max and Rosita.

"Max," Max said. "And Rosita."

"All right," Dean said. "First thing's first. Let's roll that crotch rocket down into the bunker."

Max peered into the hole and saw a set of stairs bordered by a ramp. He couldn't see past the stairs, but he got a sense the 'bunker,' was enormous, far bigger than the one he'd rescued Mary Jane from.

"How deep is that thing?" he asked.

"Goes down twenty feet," Dean replied. "About 2500 square feet of space. You can roll the bike down the ramp. You'll see a couple of four-wheelers down there, tucked up against the wall next to some boxes. Tuck your bike in there with them."

Max climbed back onto the bike and rolled it up to the edge. Rosita moved to climb on, and he waved her off.

"You wait here, Rosita. You'll be fine," he said.

Doubt mixed with alarm in her eyes, but she nodded and stood to one side.

Max rolled the bike over the edge and disappeared down the hole.

"Rosita, is it?" Dean said. "Soon as he gets back up, we'll all go back to the house and get you squared away. Don't you worry none, we got this."

Rosita eyed the three men, each with an AR, each looking fit are ready.

She allowed herself to relax a little, but kept an eye on the hole, waiting for Max.

Martin sat in his truck by the side of the road, just out of town. The occasional car swept by, lots of semis, not much else. He was pissed off and a little scared. He'd missed all the commotion at Hotel 29, hadn't seen this motorcycle guy at all, and now he was posted out here.

This wasn't what he'd signed up for. All he'd wanted was a little pussy now and then. A party. Fuck this going to war shit.

He picked up his binoculars and peered at the road ahead.

The way he figured it the guy was long gone. No use being out here.

Safe that way, at least.

At the very limit of the range of his vision, a tiny dot of yet another semi lumbered towards him. Nothing else on the road.

Something even tinier veered off the main road. It was too

small for Martin to see what it was, but it raised a dust plume.

Headed for that survivalist's compound. Dallas Something-or-other.

Martin watched the dust plume rise as it headed for the compound.

Had to be a motorcycle, he figured. But it'd been headed in town from the East.

Probably nothing.

Still, Old Man Bannister was hot and bothered, and this mystery asshole had killed Brandon and at least a few of the other boys. Martin himself didn't feel one way or the other about it. Mostly, he just wanted to go home, whack off, watch some TV, but...better safe than sorry. Especially with the Bannisters.

Most especially with the Bannisters.

He picked up his phone.

CHAPTER THIRTY THREE

Max and Rosita sat at the big circular table in the dining room at the back of the farmhouse. A huge picture window framed a backyard of apple trees, cherry trees, a vegetable garden as big as a baseball diamond, and a well-kept yard. Daisies dotted the field; sunflowers bordered it.

A dirt lane ran along the line of sunflowers, curled back behind the yard, then split off into three separate lanes that disappeared into the trees behind.

"Nice set up you have here," Max said.

Dallas nodded, sipped from his coffee.

"We've been at it a while. My family moved out here from Ramsey about a hundred years ago," he said.

Dean sat to the right of Dallas, and another man, Kane, Max thought his name was, stood in the doorway with his AR.

Max opened himself up again, trying to get a feeling for what he'd driven into.Something markedly different about Dallas. Flashes and sprinkles of light swarmed around him. The same kind of light that emanated from the Blond Woman. The things Max had wanted to call "angels" but couldn't quite bring himself to.

Max sensed a sizable population on the compound. A village community. Most folks had an aura like Raymond's: a solid sense of light and good, minimal streaks of darkness.

None of the people out here would harm him or Rosita, Max figured. And if they had to bring force to bear, they wouldn't revel in it.

But they clearly wouldn't shrink from it, either.

They were trained and ready.

The question was…for what?

Elroy and Sherman slowed as the truck climbed into the mountains north of Paluma. Last anyone had seen Ingersoll and Bill's fuck-toy, they'd been up this way.

Not a word since.

Sherman fidgeted with his lucky silver dollar, rubbing his thumb across the face of it, feeling the ridges of the sides, inspecting the line of copper showing through the edge.

"They're up here somewhere," he said. "I can feel it. Hiding out."

Elroy snorted, then winced and his eyes teared. His nose hurt like hell.

"I'd like to kill somebody about now," he said. "Wish they'd sent me after that motherfucker on the motorcycle."

Sherman looked over at him, a smirk growing.

"No, you don't. He kicked the shit out of both you and Zeke, Elroy. You'd be pissing yourself if Roger sent you out that way."

Elroy's knuckles whitened as he gripped the wheel.

"You don't think I want pay back?" he asked. "You don't think I'd stick my gun up his ass and watch him swell up when I pulled the trigger?"

"Oh, I think you'd do all that and more, Elroy," Sherman said. "Once he was safely tied up and all. Face it, you're chicken shit."

A flash of rage ran through Elroy and he considered shooting Sherman in the face. Well, maybe in the back, low down in the spine when he got out of the truck. Make him try to crawl for a while, play with him, like.

Sherman laughed.

"You piece of shit," he said. "You're thinking about coming at me right now. Sure as shit, I can see it on your face. But you're too fucking chicken to come at me. You know how bad I'd kick your ass. Listen to me, though, little Elroy,"

Sherman leaned in close enough to make Elroy lean back

against his window. "You better think again. You try some chicken shit bushwhack on me, I'm gonna tear your fucking arms off and shove them up your ass. And you know sure as shit..."

Elroy gripped the wheel even tighter as they flashed by a gas station.

Something parked out back, just the corner visible. A flash of green and white.

Elroy slowed as they hit the corner and the gas station disappeared behind them.

"Hold on, asshole," he said to Sherman. "There was something behind that gas station back there. I just got a peek at it, you being in my face and all."

Sherman straightened and turned around.

Road and trees and mountains and valleys.

"Gas station?" he said.

"Yep. Ancient one. Had one of them winged horses on top, like from the old days. Could've been Ingersoll's truck."

"No fuckin' way, Elroy. You're making shit up."

"I'm telling you, Sherman. I got a feeling about this."

"You got a feeling." Sherman said.

"If it is, and we miss it..." Elroy said.

Sherman considered that.

"Whip a Uey, first chance. We better go back and look," he said.

Roger Bannister picked up the phone. He and the Old Man sat in the den, looking out over the plains and farmland below, Bill's burned compound a black spot at the corner of his vision, tugging his eye away from the rest of the view.

"Yeah?" he said.

He nodded a few times.

"Got it. Get the low-down from Marty, then get back to me. Worth checking out, I suppose."

He put the phone down and turned to the Old Man.

Karl Bannister sat in his captain's chair at the head of the table, feet up, big mug of coffee steaming in his hands. A little drunker than he wanted to be, he'd switched for now. Had to have a clear head. Things were coming together.

"That was Danny. He says one of the guys we have out at Mountain Cleft spotted what might be a motorcycle."

The Old Man's jaw clenched. "Might be? What the fuck they bothering us with this 'might be,' shit?"

"Well, Pops, the deal is, this 'might be' motorcycle turned off the road and headed out to Dallas Krell's place. That big compound his granddaddy set up? That whole survivalist bullshit thing?"

The Old Man grunted.

"Yeah?" he said.

"Yeah. Thing is, the 'might be' motorcycle was heading back towards town, not away from it, so Marty doesn't think it's the guy, but..."

"But the little chicken shit is covering his ass, just in case," the Old Man said, nodding. "Best send someone out that way to check, I guess. Danny going in?"

"Him and two of his boys are parked outside of town with Marty, considering. They're checking in. Thinking of waiting on the two Danny left behind to clean up at the 29. Krell's got quite the set up out there."

"Tell 'em to send one man in. A scout. One of Danny's crew. Somebody no one around there would recognize. Check it out. Then get out and call back."

"I'm on it," Roger said, picking up the phone.

"And Roger?" the Old Man said.

Roger paused.

"Tell 'im he'd better not fuck up. Not if he knows what's good for 'im."

Dallas looked up as one of his men came strolling in.

"Got a couple of trucks just sitting by the road out there, a mile or so down. One of 'em's that Marty asshole," the man said.

Dallas grunted. "Figures. Bannisters going to be all lit up looking for this guy. And her," he said, looking at Rosita.

"They'll be looking for that van, too," Max said.

"Where'd you say you sent them?" Dallas asked.

"I didn't," Max said. "Told them to lay low until night, then head out."

"Uh-huh," Dallas said. "Might work."

He stood and strolled to the front of the room to look out the front window.

"Got Max's bike put away? Hay bales back, all that?" he asked.

"Yep. Pulled one of the four-wheelers out, too, ran over his tracks a couple of times, parked it back in front of the barn."

Dallas looked at the window again, peering up the road at the barn.

"Uh-huh," he said. "Good thinking,"

He strolled back into the room, hands in his pockets.

"Dean, Kane," he said. "Let's get things back to normal. You all get everyone working again. Keep Forrest out front, guard duty. One team ready with the ARs, but out of sight. Everyone else, side arms only."

Dean and Kane stood. Dean raised his coffee cup, drained it, then walked over to the sink, rinsed his cup and put it in the dishwasher. He and the man who'd come in left.

Dallas turned to Max and Rosita.

"I'm going to put you two upstairs for now," he said. "Stay away from the windows out front. No one's getting into this house without my say-so. Kane will show you the way."

Kane rinsed his cup, put it away, then turned to face Max and Rosita, who stood.

"This way," Kane said.

Dallas reached out a hand the size of a dinner plate and put it on Max's shoulder.

"We've got this. Like I said, no one's coming in that I don't invite in. You've got nothing to worry about right now."

Max nodded. "Appreciate it, Dallas. Sorry for the trouble.

We'll be out of your way soon as all this dies down."

Dallas smiled.

"Wouldn't have it any other way. An enemy of the Bannisters is a friend of mine. We'll talk this thing out later."

Rosita reached out and grabbed Max's hand.

Max looked at her, realized how scared she was.

"It'll be OK, Rosita," he said. "You'll see."

Rosita nodded at him, trying to put on a brave face, but her lips trembled and the alarm was clear in her eyes.

Max followed Kane out the room and up the stairs, leading Rosita by the hand.

Roger and Karl Bannister stood at the big table, a map spread out in front of them.

"The compound's right here," Roger said, poking a finger at the map. "About ten miles out of Mountain Cleft. I looked it up on Google Earth, but about all you can see is a big farm house, a barn and a couple of sheds. Garden. A couple of trucks. You can see some dirt roads heading up this way," he poked at the map some more, "but that's about it. Lots of trees."

The Old Man rubbed his chin. "Krells been out there a hundred years, I bet," he said. "That's a fair amount of time to build things up."

"Yeah, but who knows what they're thinking," Roger said. "Looks to me like they're trying to make themselves self-sufficient. They got fields and livestock. Big barn to store shit in. Wouldn't surprise me if they built a bunker or two out there."

"Right-wing nuts? Building for the end of the world?" Old Man Bannister said. "Well, we should hear back from Danny pretty soon. We'll see what he has to say."

Roger's phone rang.

"Speak of the devil," Roger said.

He looked at his phone.

"Strike that," he said. "It's Sherman."

He raised the phone to his ear.

"Hello? Sherman? What you got?" Roger asked.

He gripped the phone tighter.

"All right! Good work, man! You two stay put. Try to keep an eye on things, I'll get some guys up there as quick as I can."

He paused a minute. Listened.

"Just be sure you don't lose them. You understand? Or it's your ass," Roger said.

He put the phone down and looked up at the Old Man.

"Sherman and Elroy think they found Ingersoll and Bill's fuck-toy," he said. He moved to a different section of the map, traced the road up north out of Paluma. "Think they saw Ingersoll's truck out behind a gas station up here."

The Old Man took a sip of his coffee, grimaced.

"Damn it all to hell. We ain't got anyone near them. Think we can send them two in to handle it?"

Roger looked at the Old Man, considering.

"Suppose we can send them in, like a blitz attack. Take everyone there by surprise. That might work."

"That Elroy is an idiot. Probably shit himself just thinking about it," the Old Man said.

"Maybe," Roger said, "but Sherman is as solid a guy as we got. With him watching over Elroy, running the show...."

"Maybe," the Old Man said. "Meanwhile, let's see who we can send out that way. It's time to rally all the fucking troops. We're going to war, son. We need every man. Pull guys out of Red Rock, pull 'em off duty at the toy palaces and off the road. We need men up with Sherman and Elroy, we need men out with Danny and his boys, and we may need men all down the line. Where's Billy and them?"

"Colorado by now, I'd bet," Roger said.

"Get a hold of them. Tell 'em to hustle," the Old Man said.

Roger picked up the phone again.

Danny hopped into his truck and eased onto the main road, his eyes on the power lines that snaked off the main road and back toward Krell's compound. Just a quick recon. In and out.

See if there was anything to see.

He hoped so.

He was itching to hammer someone. Seeing the mess at Hotel 29, watching the video of the mystery man at Bill's compound, Danny was more than ready to do some hammering.

He turned left off the main road, felt his tires hit dirt, heard the scrunch as they found traction.

He kept his eyes on the tree line ahead, scanning the perimeter, looking for men. The dirt road itself was well trafficked, though he could make out some tracks. There *were* smaller wheel tracks...could be a motorcycle.

Danny's heart bumped a bit as he considered coming face to face with the mystery man.

He slowed as he entered the trees, reached for his piece, thought better of it. Krell and his group were unlikely to ambush a stranger. But if that stranger had a pistol in his hand...different story.

The dirt road snaked through the copse of trees and opened up into a sizable compound. Very similar to Bill's actually, Danny thought. It occurred to him that killing everyone here and burning it to the ground would be a nice start at pay back. Most especially if the mystery man was here.

A man hoeing the big vegetable garden behind the farm house looked up at the sound of the truck, shouldered his hoe, and ambled towards Danny.

Big guy. Bigger than Sherman. Huge beard like Sherman.

Danny's heart bumped up a little faster.

Might be, he'd get a little action.

Max put his hand to the bridge of his nose and squeezed lightly, trying to contain the flood of imagery and emotion that roiled through him.

Before he'd heard the tires of the truck on the road, he'd felt the man coming. This was a guy as consumed by the evil force as any. Max saw faces contorted in agony, felt as much as heard the meaty snap of bones breaking, and that terrible, clawing lust for pain and domination, the desire to rape and maim and kill, the capering glee of an evil man as he watched the life flicker out in the eyes of his victim.

He squeezed harder, took a deep breath.

Whoever was in that truck was a very bad man.

Max fought the impulse to confront the man, and as the desire to hurt him grew, he realized that once again, the Presence had gotten its hooks into him. Not deeply, but enough to stir him, to make thinking difficult. His desire to hurt this guy, to make him pay for the death and pain and misery he had authored nearly overwhelmed him.

I will make him pay, Max thought. *But not right now.*

He conjured an image of the Blond Woman, recalling her face and voice, the feeling in his spirit as he'd talked with her, the peace.

Her light met the red darkness of the Presence and drove it from him.

Max pulled himself back to the moment and was surprised to feel a hand on his arm.

Rosita, hand on his arm, was looking at him with alarm.

"Max?" she whispered.

Max shook his head to clear it, tried on a smile.

"It's OK, Rosita," he said. "Just a bad moment. Whoever is out there is a bad man. But it'll be OK."

Elroy trudged down the side of the 1, irritated. *Who the fuck did Sherman think he was, ordering him around like a grunt? Like a nobody?* "Walk down the road like you've been hitch-hiking,' Sherman had said. 'Get a look. Get back to me.'

He'd tried to tell Sherman it'd make more sense for him to go, seeing as Elroy's face was all busted up. Anyone driving by would notice that, he'd told Sherman.

But no, the big idiot was too good to do the scouting. Had to be the boss man.

I'll get him, Elroy thought. *One day....*

He shuffled through the gravel at the roadside as he rounded a corner and the gas station came into view.

Sure enough, one of those old winged horses crowned the gas station. Elroy hadn't seen one of those since he was a kid, and then they'd been retro. *This place must be 100 years old,* Elroy thought.

The left rear corner of a truck was just visible behind the gas station.

Elroy stopped.

Could be, he thought. *Can't tell for sure, but it looks right.*

He rubbed his chin, thinking, looked both ways across the road, then skittered to the other side.

Sherman had told him just to walk by and give it a look. To keep going.

Fuck him.

Elroy ambled toward the back of the gas station, hands in his pockets, harmless-looking, he hoped.

The little pocket pistol he gripped in his right hand gave him courage.

Fuck Sherman, fuck Ingersoll, and fuck this, he thought.

Dallas kept himself loose but ready as he strolled toward the truck that had stopped by the white picket fence in front of the house.

A man leaned out the window, narrow-faced, dark, hair with long bangs combed over to one side, five o-clock shadow. Rat faced, something cunning and furtive in the man that Dallas didn't like.

"Howdy," the man called.

Dallas couldn't see the man's right hand. He nodded and came to a stop five feet away from the truck, left hand on the handle of his hoe, right hovering near the knife on his belt.

"Do for ya?" Dallas asked.

"Got a bit turned around," the man said. "Was hoping you could straighten me out."

The man's beady little eyes darted around the compound,

taking it all in. Dallas could see him cataloging it: the layout, the four-wheeler in front of the barn, the road, the farm house, trying to see in to the windows.

This was no lost little lamb.

Dallas had ditched his radio before he came out, and now he felt its absence. The man in the truck was as dangerous as a viper.

His concern must've communicated itself; the big barn door squeaked open, and Dean and Kane stepped out, wiping their hands on rags like they'd been working on something.

They spread out, triangulating the man in the truck.

A new look came into the man's eyes. A click of understanding, a flash of amusement, of...triumph?

Dean and Kane stood casual, but ready.

"On my way to Paluma," the man said. "But got turned around."

Dallas angled himself a bit closer to the man, light on his feet, ready to whip the hoe around. *Paluma?* The guy was definitely messing with him.

"I'll say," he said. "First thing you want to do is to turn this around, get back on the main road. Then turn right. Drive straight through town, keep going. Stay on the road heading west. In about 150 miles or so, you'll see signs for Ramsey. Keep going through there, another hour or so, then you'll come up on Paluma."

The two men stared at one another, feeling each other out.

The rat-faced man's eyes darted to Dean and Kane, back to Dallas.

Dallas took a grip on the handle of his hoe, sensed Dean and Kane poised on the edge of action.

Danny was amused. *Fucking Krell. Fucking idiot. Had to be him, the way Marty'd described him—big-ass man with a beard.*

Be entertaining to set Sherman loose on him, Danny thought. *Kind of like a dog fight. Put the two of 'em in a pit and let 'em go at one another.*

Danny's right hand inched its way towards his gun.

Or, I could just blow him away here and now, take down his two compadres here, find that fuckin' mystery man and bring him back to the Old Man.

The mystery man was here, Danny was certain. He could feel the motherfucker.

Danny caught movement out of the corner of his eye.

Two men emerged from the trees, one on either side of the road behind him. Each with an AR held ready, muzzle down, stock up and close to the shoulder.

Or not, he thought. *Not now, anyway. But I'll be back to play. You can count on that boys.*

"Well then," Danny said. "I guess I'll just be on my way. Much obliged."

Dallas watched the truck disappear down the lane into the trees.

"He'll be back," Dean said.

Dallas took a long, hard look around the compound. Everything normal. Nothing out of place. No sign of Max, Rosita, or the motorcycle. But an image of the man's face stayed bright in his mind. The feral look, the cunning intelligence, the quick furtive glances, the way he'd kept his right hand out of sight.

But most of all the feel of the man. A darkness poured off of him that was horrible.

"I expect you're right," Dallas said. "We'll be ready."

Elroy stepped around the corner of the garage to the back.

Ingersoll's truck. Sure as shit.

Got ya, motherfucker, he thought.

"Help you?" A voice behind him.

Elroy spun, bringing the little .380 out of his pocket as he turned.

A powerful hand grabbed his wrist, turned his arm up and back, had him raising up on his toes in pain, trying to take some of the torque off the wrist lock.

As he raised up on his toes, the grizzled guy in coveralls who had a hold of him brought a huge bony elbow down and crossways across his temple and everything went black.

Sherman sat in his truck.

It'd been twenty minutes. About ten too long.

Stupid motherfucker, he thought. *All he had to do was stroll by the garage, stroll back, report. How could he fuck that up?*

He fired up the truck, put it in gear and eased back onto the road.

He looked hard at the gas station as he passed.

No truck visible behind the gas station. Nothing unusual. Just an old guy in coveralls, walking into the open bay of the garage.

Sherman cruised down the road until he was out of sight of the garage and pulled over.

No Elroy.

He'd flat disappeared.

So far as Sherman could see, there was only one place he might've disappeared.

He picked up the phone and dialed Roger.

CHAPTER THIRTY FOUR

Dallas sat at the big table in the back room. Fifteen men sat around the table with him, not counting Max. Rosita was at Max's side.

"It's going down," Dallas said. "A hundred years in the coming, and it's going down now."

A rumble of exclamation worked its way around the table.

"We didn't ask for this, but then neither did our families back in the day."

He looked around the table, met each man's eye, then nodded to himself, satisfied. These were strong men. They were ready.

"We've been out here a long time," Dallas said. "We've built a community. We are self-sufficient; we need nothing from nobody. We've got livestock, fields, and homes. Many of us have worked with the teams—we got SEALs and Rangers and Marines. We've trained, and we're well organized. We've got wives and kids to protect and build a future with. We're not letting anyone threaten that—most especially no way we're letting *Bannisters* threaten that."

Nods of agreement. A couple of fists pounded the table. The energy level in the room kicked up a notch.

Wives and kids? Max thought. *No.*

Rosita had a hand on his arm again.

The energy that roiled through the room was clean and pure. None of the lust for pain and domination that so colored the Bannisters' world. No sense of the Presence. The energy here was a counterbalance to the Presence. Just as strong, just as determined, just as relentless, only driven with an entirely different fuel.

For the first time, Max got the feeling he might get out of this alive. And that the world was worth saving. That there really were good people out there.

And yet...he was the one who was bringing down Bannister wrath on these people, loosing the Presence in their midst.

No.

"Now hold on, everybody," Max said. "They may be coming, but I aim to take a little heat off of this thing for you."

Heads turned. All eyes on him.

Rosita dropped her arm and sat back.

"Look," Max said. "The whole reason trouble's coming is because I brought it to your doorstep."

"Max," Dallas said.

Max raised a hand.

"Hear me out," he said. "Whoever and whatever is coming is coming because they're after me. I've put a real hurt on the Bannisters, and..."

Laughter.

"I'll say you did," one man called out.

"Damn straight," another said.

Max pushed through.

"I put a real hurt on them. I beat the shit out of a few of 'em, I set some girls free, killed Bill, the guy living with him, pulled Mary Jane out of there, and burned Bill's compound to the ground."

He paused. The room was silent, all eyes still on him.

"So long as there is a Bannister left alive, they're coming for me. And that's OK. That's the plan. But you all have women and kids here. You're building a future here."

Max looked around the table. His turn now to meet every eye.

"And there's no way in hell I am going to put all that in a war zone. Not if I have a way to take some of the heat off this thing."

Max leaned forward.

"The minute I set fire to Bill Bannister's compound, I knew they'd be coming. And I knew I couldn't take 'em on alone and that I'd have to keep moving, do a lot of hit and run. 'Cause I also knew just how big this Bannister thing is. How evil. And I aim to take the whole damn thing down."

"We're with you!" Big John cried.

"Bannisters are legion," Max said. "Bannisters have an army. The way you take out an army is you spread it out thin, scatter it, then attack the pieces. You don't take the whole damn army on."

"Big John is right," Dallas said. "We are with you. You aren't fighting this alone anymore."

"And I appreciate that," Max said. "More than you can imagine. For the first time, I can see light at the end of the tunnel. Maybe. Maybe we can do this thing. But I think my plan is still the best plan."

Dallas leaned back and crossed his arms. Several of the men did so as well, their united posture expressing resistance and a desire to be a part of this fight.

"Look," Max said. "I have a list of all their properties and businesses. They spread clear across the country. The Bannisters have grown tentacles that reach down into Mexico.

He looked at Rosita, then turned his attention back to the men; "My plan is to move down the line of Bannister businesses. To burn down every single one. To leave a trail of fire that the Bannisters couldn't miss. I want them to have an easy time figuring out exactly what I'm doing."

Men nodded and shifted in their seats.

"I'm going to need help, and I'm going to need you. And for that to work, there's no way I can let you all take on the full force of the Bannisters. No doubt some will come, but if I lead them away before they get here, they'll split their forces. They might even leave you alone."

Another rumble of exclamation worked its way around the table as the men mulled this over.

"I aim to head down the road to the next nasty little Bannister enterprise. They've got a massage parlor/bar down in Greencreek, tiny little town. Look to have about ten women there. Maybe three guys running the whole show. Something I can take care of pretty easily. Let me get moving on that."

"Greencreek's about an hour away," Dallas said. "The Bannisters'll have eyes all over that road."

He scratched his chin through his big beard, "But if we run you up through the village in back, that road climbs up the mountain and comes in behind Greencreek as a little dirt road. Take you two hours, but they might not be expecting you that way. Or..." Dallas scratched his chin some more. "You could take a van. They're looking for a motorcycle. Might not pay much attention to a van."

Max considered it, then stood.

"Let's get going."

Dallas waved him down.

"Soon enough. Got to think this through first, Max." He nodded at Rosita, raised his eyebrows. "Got to debrief you, get a plan on. Like I said, you aren't in this alone anymore."

CHAPTER THIRTY FIVE

Dallas handed the ledgers back to Max.

"So then. It's settled," he said.

"Settled," Max said. A feeling of *wrongness* ran through him. He knew he needed help, couldn't do this all alone, but it felt... *wrong*. Like it should be just him. He shook his head.

"What?" Dallas said.

"Just feels wrong, is all," Max said.

Dallas snorted.

"What's wrong, Max is the idea that you can take on the whole Bannister clan all by your lonesome. They've ruled this area for over a hundred years. Those ledgers we just got done copying show how deep and wide their reach is. They got judges, cops, mayors, border guards, hell—entire cities. And you think you're going to take them down alone? Get real, Max."

Put like that, it did sound pretty stupid, but Max's gut would not let him rest.

"I'm putting you all at risk," he said. "Your wives and children. It's not right."

"What's not right is standing by and letting this shit happen," Dallas said.

He put a meaty hand on Max's shoulder and turned Max square to him, put his other hand up on the other shoulder.

"Good people have stood by too long," Dallas said. "That's what's allowed this monster to grow. And we *need* to be part of this, Max. You don't understand. Bannisters have been a cancer in this region forever, and we've all felt the pain of it. Each of us has history with them. A reckoning is past due."

Max closed his eyes and took a breath. Opened himself up. Let his sense loose, the door open.

The knot in his gut clenched, then relaxed.

He took another deep breath, opened his eyes.

From one of the trees outside, a woman hung, eyes open, face distorted, bloated tongue lolling out of her mouth. It was hard to tell, but Max figured her to be in her twenties. Once pretty, now hideous—face purple black and bloated. Dressed in ranch gear: cowboy boots, jeans, plaid shirt with a red bandanna around her neck, twisted into the rope.

"Hasn't been easy out here, has it?" Max said, his eyes on the woman.

The intensity of Max's gaze turned Dallas to look out the window.

Nothing.

"Nope," he said, turning back to Max. "But we've made a life out of it. A life under a dark shadow, though. One that's always hovered over us, an unspoken, evil little secret."

"Let us help you, Max. You need this. We need this."

Max nodded.

"She'll be safe with us," Dean said.

Max sighed and stroked the seat of his motorcycle.

"Think of it as your way of saying you'll be back," Dean said.

Max's phone rang and he turned away from the motorcycle and headed for the barn door.

"Hello? Max said.

"Max? Raymond. We got a situation here...."

Elroy looked like hell warmed over, shit on, slapped around, then set on fire. He had two bad black eyes, a swollen nose, and a split eyebrow with a fresh scab pointing out the spot where Guy had elbowed him into unconsciousness.

A little puddle of puke in his lap.

"Yep," Raymond said into the phone. "Most definitely. I know good ol' Elroy here personally. Always thought he was a piece of shit."

On the other end of the line, Max tapped the phone to his teeth, thinking. He and Dean stood in the barn, at the foot of the Ford Transit.

"How many guys you got up there?" he asked.

Raymond chuckled and looked around the room.

"Well," he said. "We've got Guy, the guy that runs this place. Six others, right here. Plenty of guns and ammo. And this whole garage was made to withstand a nuclear blast, looks like. Two-foot high raised foundation, inch and a half-thick siding held together with steel plates."

"Bannisters will be coming," Max said.

"No shit," Raymond said. "This gas station is the only place within two miles. Elroy here says it's him and Sherman. So Sherman's out there."

"Any chance of taking him down before he gets word out?" Max asked.

Dean said something into the mic clipped to his shoulder, and clapped Max on the shoulder, getting him moving back toward the farm house.

"Doubt it," Raymond answered. "I'd bet Sherman's already called for troops. Cell reception is great up here; Guy has a cell phone antenna just behind his garage. So we're getting ready."

Max and Dean reached the back porch.

Max stopped.

"Raymond," he said. "You keep Mary Jane safe. You hear me?"

"First priority, Max. First priority."

"Anyplace to put her? Keep her safe?"

"Guy's bringing in some more men. We might have a chance to slip Mary Jane out of here, get her hidden somewhere."

Mary Jane punched Raymond in the shoulder, hard.

"Ow!" Raymond said.

He met Mary Jane's eyes.

"Might be easier said than done getting her out of here,

though," he said. "She wants a piece of these guys worse than any of us. Took two guys to keep her from clawing Elroy's eyes out."

Max nodded, sighed.

"I know you'll do your best, Raymond," he said.

He and Dean stepped through the door. Dallas and the others stood in the room, waiting.

"Keep me up to date," Max said.

"Will do, buddy," Raymond said.

"And Raymond?"

"Yeah?"

"You be careful, you hear?"

"Careful as I can be," Raymond said. "You, too, you crazy bastard."

Max grinned and put his phone away, then turned to face the room.

Old Man Bannister cackled. It was an odd sound, coming from him, a sound like a witch out of an old movie.

"Hot damn!" he said. "Got 'em all! Mystery man out there by Mountain Cleft, Ingersoll and Bill's fuck toy isolated up there on the mountain. Going to clean house!"

Roger sat calmly as the Old Man cackled and rubbed his hands together.

"This calls for a drink!" the Old Man said, snapping his fingers.

The girl in the French Maid outfit materialized with three fingers of whisky in a thick crystal tumbler, placed it into the Old Man's hand and faded back against the wall, trying to stay out of sight.

"We got some logistics to work out, Pops," Roger said.

"Logistics," the Old Man snorted. "It's always 'logistics' and shit like that with you. What we need to do, son, is just march the fuck in and take what's ours. Those people are *mine* and I aim to have them."

Outside, the plains glowed pink in the light of the setting

sun. Streetlights began to pop on, lights winking on in windows of the houses in the town below.

"We will, Pops," Roger said. "We got them. Just a matter of scooping them up."

"Then let's get the fuck on with it!" the Old Man roared, tossing back a finger of whisky.

"Let's rub that Ingersoll out of this world, bring that bitch back, and most of all, get that fucking mystery man where he belongs and get down to business."

"We will, Pops. But we don't want to blow it by rushing in. Krell's got a big setup there. Danny figures he's got at least six guys, and he spotted a couple of them with ARs. With just Danny, Marty and a couple of boys out there right now, it would be risky to go in."

"Not if you go in hard and fast in the middle of the night!" the Old Man said. "Like that, like that...," the Old Man gripped his tumbler, faltering for a moment. He tossed back another finger of whisky and his eyes teared. "Like that motherfucker who snuck into Bill's and ambushed him. One man did all that, Roger. One. We got four."

Roger eyed the Old Man carefully. He'd been on coffee for a couple of hours, but had been drinking pretty steady up to that. The whisky he'd just put down, combined with the emotion and the length of the day were wearing on him. He was right on the line between melancholy and rage.

Roger placed a gentle hand on his father's shoulder.

"Dad. Believe me: I want these motherfuckers as bad as you do. And we will have them. Listen to me one minute."

He led the Old Man to the La-Z-Boy in front of the big picture window, eased him into it and sat himself in the chair next to him.

"Billy and his boys are into Nevada. They've been taking shifts driving and sleeping. They can drop off the shipment at Red Rock, arm up, grab a few more guys, and be into Mountain Cleft by tomorrow night."

The Old Man rubbed his chin, thinking. He tossed back the

last of his whisky, held the empty tumbler out.

The girl in the French Maid outfit was there in seconds with a fresh tumbler. She took the empty one and turned, but the Old Man laid a hand on her bare ass, stopping her.

"You," he said. "Hold on."

He ran his hand over her ass, around front, and grabbed her crotch, hard, making her wince and bend with the pain.

The Old Man set his tumbler carefully into the cup holder and pulled the girl in the French Maid outfit closer.

"Mmm," he said. A light came on his eyes. "Maybe you got a point, son."

The girl in the French Maid outfit bit her lip as the Old Man maneuvered her into position.

"On your knees, bitch," he commanded.

Roger smiled and stood.

"Good. So we're set. We'll hit Mountain Cleft tomorrow."

The Old Man paused in his play and rolled his head to look up at Roger.

"Sherman's in place?"

Roger nodded.

Mack and Warren there?

"Just about."

"Sherman sure nobody left that gas station?"

"Pretty sure, Pops. It's just him keeping an eye on things until Mack and Warren get there, so he can only cover one direction, but he's pretty sure."

"Remember. Full blitz. Three AM."

The girl in the French Maid outfit cried out as the Old Man played.

"Roger?" the Old Man said.

"Yeah, Pops?" Roger said.

"I want to wake up to see Ingersoll's head. On a platter. Got me? Then I want to hear you got Bill's fuck toy secured at Red Rock."

"You know it, Pops."

The Old Man nodded, returned his attention to the girl,

waved Roger away.

Max faced the room.

Counting Dean and Dallas, there were fifteen men in the room beside himself.

"They know where Raymond and Mary Jane are," he said. "Raymond tells me they grabbed up a guy named Elroy out behind the garage, checking out Raymond's truck."

The men looked at one another, shifted on their feet.

"My guess is they'll hit the gas station tonight. They don't know how many men they are facing, any of that. All they really know is that there's an old guy who runs the garage, Raymond and Mary Jane. It's a garage, after all, so that would explain having all those cars there."

Dallas stepped forward.

"We could send Timmy and his squad," he said. "It'd take 'em about four hours. But that'd put them there before midnight."

Max rolled his head, thinking.

"According to Raymond, they've got him and six guys up there. They're ready. They're not as well trained as you guys, but the Bannisters probably aren't planning on facing a prepared force. Tactics and planning don't seem to be their style, they're more of the smash and grab types."

Timmy stepped forward. He was a regular-looking guy. Five ten, 170 pounds, wiry, light on his feet.

"We could be up there by 11:30," he said. "I'd take Marcus, Tyler, and Socrates, set up a perimeter. We could close in on them before they even get to the garage."

Dallas faced Max.

"Max?"

Max looked around the room, counting.

"I don't think they'll hit this place tonight," he said. "But they might. And I have no idea how many men they might send in."

He looked around again, mentally subtracting Timmy and his crew from the men there.

"You'd have to move fast, and get back here as fast as you can. Without Timmy and his crew, you're down to 11 guys. What if the Bannisters hit tonight? What if they really bring it?"

Dallas grinned.

"Max. There are four more guys out there. Posted as sentries. We've got closed-circuit surveillance, motion detectors, and heat sensors set up around the perimeter. Bannisters would have to send in full battalion to have any hope of taking us.

Max closed his eyes, opened up, tried to get a feel for the way things might go.

Stirrings of ghosts in the general area, most noticeably the woman hanging from the tree out back. A sense of longing like a mist across the plains. No sense of the Presence, but then, no sense of an answer, either. His "gift" didn't include foresight.

Max opened his eyes, sighed.

"Go," he said to Timmy. "Go now, go fast, and get set up. If you can get there before midnight, you'll probably be in time, but we can be sure Bannisters are riding hard and fast to get there."

Timmy looked to Dallas, who nodded. He and three other men clumped from the room and headed up to the barn.

Max watched them go, passing by the woman swaying from the rope in the tree.

"Who was it hanged herself out there?" he asked.

Dallas startled, looked hard at Max.

"Say what?" he said.

Max looked Dallas in the eyes.

"I asked you who it was that hanged herself out there—from that tree," he pointed at the woman as her body twirled slowly one direction until the torque built up in the rope, then the other as the rope unwound itself.

"How...?" Dallas said.

"I told you," Max said. "I see things. Somebody hanged herself from that tree. I've got no idea when or why, but I can see her."

Dallas grimaced.

"My great grandma," he said. "First generation out here. Story goes she'd been raped by the Bannisters and just could not get over it. Never made the adjustment. Put her kids to bed one night, slipped out back, climbed the tree and hung herself."

Max watched her sway.

"One more reason to put the Bannisters down for good," Dallas said.

"Then, let's get on with it," said Max.

CHAPTER THIRTY SIX

Raymond answered his phone.

"Max?" he said.

"Who else?"

"What's up, partner?"

"I'm on the road for Greencreek," Max said. "Alone. Was not easy getting Rosita to stay with Krell and his group, but we finally talked her into it."

"All right," Raymond said. "We're set up here. Got two guys posted outside with shotguns and pistols, the rest of us holed up in here. Nobody's getting in."

"Good," Max said. "I gave Timmy and them your number. They ought to be there in another..." he glanced at the clock on the dash, "three hours or so. Timmy figures about 11:30. Make sure you guys communicate. It'd screw everything up if you get into a firefight with each other."

"Relax," Raymond said. "He already called. Said pretty much the same thing you just did. We're all good up here."

"OK," Max said. "Be careful, Raymond. Keep Mary Jane safe."

"You know it," Raymond said. "And Max?"

"Yeah?"

"You be careful, too."

"Absolutely. I'll talk to you soon."

Max hung up, his eyes scanning the road ahead, his mirrors for the road behind.

A figure rose up in the cabin behind him, and Max swerved.

"What the hell?" he said, reaching for the pistol at his side.

"Max! Don't shoot me!"

Rosita moved forward and slid into the passenger's seat beside him.

"Damn it, Rosita!" Max said. "I thought we'd settled this!"

"Max," she said. "There's a truck back behind you. He's been there since you got on the main road."

Max checked his mirrors.

Danny watched the brake lights on the big Ford Transit flash, the van swerve, then steady itself.

Interesting, he thought. *Something in the road? Nerves?*

The Ford resumed its previous pace of 69 miles per hour.

Posted on the main road outside Krell's compound, he'd watched the van roll down the little dirt road, signal left, and turn onto the main road and head east. Something about the van had grabbed him, a gut feeling that he needed to follow it.

Marty had whinnied like a little girl about only having three guys, but Danny had pointed out that all they had to do was keep an eye on things and wait for the troops to arrive.

After an hour of following the van's steady pace, he'd only grown more certain. A buzz of excitement coursed through him as he considered forcing the van off the road.

The right turn signal on the van began flashing.

Rest stop.

Ah, Danny thought, his excitement growing. *Here we go.*

He reached for the TEC-9 next to him and slowed.

Mack Bannister hunched over the wheel, peering into the darkness.

Streetlights were nonexistent on the windy mountain road, the fog line faded, reflectors marking curves rare.

"We should be coming up on Sherman any minute," Warren said from the passenger seat.

The Ford 250 rumbled and shook as a curve in the road took Mack by surprise and he muscled the truck around it.

"Holy shit, this road is fuckin' hairy," Mack said.

Warren fiddled with the weapon in his hands.

"Just get us there, boss. We got work to do."

The road straightened out, and a truck parked on the

shoulder halfway down the straightaway flashed its lights.

"Bingo," Mack said.

Roger sat at the Old Man's desk, staring at the phone.

He picked it up to call Mack, then set it down again.

Stupid motherfucker is going to blow it, I can just feel it, he thought.

Roger stood, yawned, leaned into a good stretch, and thought about hitting the sack.

He grabbed his phone and ambled towards the guest room he normally bunked in when he stayed over at the Old Man's.

Better rest up, he thought. *Shit is going down tomorrow.*

CHAPTER THIRTY SEVEN

Billy, Jack, Wilder and Bobby sat alert as the big rig rumbled through the gates of Red Rock. The red adobe-looking material of the compound spread out over 10 acres of landscaped desert. Armed guards held each side of the gate open, then rolled the gate shut as they passed.

"We got to offload and get moving," Billy said.

Wilder nodded from his place in the passenger's seat and gripped the handle of the cattle prod he used to move the cargo around.

Wilder enjoyed the cattle prod.

Billy guided the truck through the compound, aiming it at the loading dock of the big building at the very rear of the compound.

A tall smokestack, like that of a smelter, belched smoke from the smaller building just off to the side of the big building.

Wilder sniffed the air.

"Been busy out here," Wilder said. "To be in need of a burning."

Jack and Bobby chuckled from the seats in the back.

Billy fingered the thick scar that ran from the top of his right cheekbone to the tip of his chin. Had to be careful with the cargo, he thought. Never know what they might come up with.

A dark red cloud of rage built inside him.

Fucking bitches.

His cock throbbed as he imagined all that he was going to do, breaking these bitches in.

But no, he had to get going. Raid some fucking hillbilly's little hippy compound looking for some dickweed that had the boss shitting his pants.

Red rage nearly blinded him, and he bit it back, calming himself.

Soon enough, he thought.

His thoughts turned to Bill. His buddy. It'd been Big Bill and Little Billy all his life. This dickweed had killed Bill. *Unacceptable.*

Play later, he thought. *Unload the cargo, find this fucking dickweed, get him back here, and take gameplay to a whole new level. That's the ticket.*

Billy wheeled the truck around in a practiced arc and backed into the loading dock.

All four doors of the cab flapped open as the men exited the vehicle and walked around to the loading dock to begin.

Max eased the Ford off the main road and followed the signage around the back of the rest stop towards the rest rooms.

He found a spot off in the shadows and backed into it, facing the entrance.

A bad man was coming.

Max could feel the gibbering Presence as the man neared.

He figured the man would take the split in the road for big rigs, then try to use the cover of the bathrooms and the brush to ease around and take Max and Rosita by surprise.

"Here's the deal, Rosita," he said. "You sit here in the cab like you're waiting on me to get out of the restroom. Nice and visible."

Rosita nodded, gripping the sawed-off 12 gauge Max had given her.

"I'm going to get out," Max said. "Set up off to the side over here. Wait and see. Don't worry, Rosita, I've got you covered."

Rosita's small hands looked like little bony spiders on the shotgun.

"I'm OK," Rosita said. "He come here, I kill him."

"Don't jump the gun, Rosita," Max said.

"What? Jump the gun?" Rosita said.

"An expression. What I mean is, don't shoot. Not unless you absolutely have to. Got me?"

Rosita's eyes narrowed as she thought of all the men she'd seen, and the way they'd treated her. She nodded, but her finger eased around the trigger guard and caressed the trigger.

"Yes, Max. I won't shoot. Unless I have to."

Max gave her a hard look, unconvinced. A cold rage poured off of her.

Going to have to get a hold of this guy fast, before Rosita gets a chance to take him out, he thought.

He considered taking the gun from her, but no way he was going to leave her defenseless—not after all she'd suffered.

Not that she'd have let him take it, anyway.

Danny fought with himself as he eased off the main road onto the lane leading back to the rest stop. Part of him wanted to ease around to the other side of the rest stop, park behind a big rig, sneak out, and take down whoever was in the van. Another part of him clamored to stomp on the gas, race into the other side of the rest stop and ram the van.

The excitement was buzzing through him and he felt almost as high as he did when he stepped into the play shed on Bill's compound, or was given a rare opportunity to party down at Red Rock.

The thought that Bill's playpen had been burned down was a dagger in his chest. The excitement he felt shifted into a red, burning rage.

He stomped down on the gas pedal and aimed the truck into the rest stop.

Mack, Sherman, and Warren huddled in the cab of Mack's truck.

"So, you didn't get a good look at the gas station?" Mack

asked.

"That's not what I said, Boss," Sherman replied. "What I said was I drove by a couple times, and couldn't see Ingersoll's truck. Didn't see anyone around, either. One time, I saw an old guy in coveralls walking into the garage, but that was it. No one in the office. There's an extension off the office, though—pretty good-sized room in back. Might be where the old guy lives."

"No sign of Elroy. Or of Ingersoll, or the bitch," Mack said.

The three of them sat in silence for a minute.

"Roger figures a 3:00AM raid is the way to go," Warren said. He watched Mack carefully, only too aware of the explosiveness of his temper.

"Fuck Roger," Mack said. "I'm not sitting out here for another..." he glanced at his watch, "three and a half hours waiting. Fuck that noise. I say we hit the place now."

Warren and Sherman glanced at one another, uneasy. They both knew better than to argue with Mack, but they also knew the price they'd pay if they failed.

"Boss," Warren said, "let's just give it another hour or two, at least. Make sure the old guy's had time to bunk down. If Elroy's in there, we'll get him. And if Ingersoll and Bill's fuck toy are there, we'll get them, too. Better if they're all asleep, you know?"

"Fuck that," Mack said. "Fuck this waiting bullshit."

He started up the truck.

"We're going straight in," he said. "I'm going to ram that fucking garage, and we'll bust into the place and kill anybody tries to stop us. Look around. Nobody out here. Not a single car has passed us. It's go time, damn it."

Warren and Sherman exchanged glances again.

"OK, Boss," Warren said. "Let's just take both trucks, though. Just in case your truck gets too fucked up ramming into the garage."

"This thing is a fucking tank. You know how much steel you've welded on to it. I could knock over a fucking tractor with it," Mack said.

"I know, Boss. Just in case. We don't want to get stuck there on foot."

"Fuck you, Warren. You little pussy. Get out. Take Sherman's truck. Me and him will hit the fucking garage without you."

"Ah, Boss," Warren said. "It's my truck. Let me drive it."

"Fuck the both of you," Mack said.

He leaned across the two men and opened the passenger side door.

"Get the fuck out, then," he said.

Sherman popped out of the truck and jogged over to his as Mack punched the accelerator and whipped the truck around, back toward the gas station, the door snagging Sherman's jacket and tearing it as it slammed shut.

Fucking idiot, Sherman thought. He imagined Old Man Bannister's face if they failed and shivered.

God damn it, he thought. *Fucking hell.*

He hopped into his truck, fired it up and screeched down the road after Mack and Warren.

Timmy put the phone in his pocket as the gas station came into view. Raymond had told him they'd set up two guards, so he flashed his lights to let them know he was on the way in.

Just then, a big Ford 250 came roaring in from the other direction.

Son of a bitch is really moving, Timmy thought.

Alarm ran through him as he realized the truck was crossing the center line and aiming itself toward the garage.

Holy shit, Timmy thought.

He stomped down on the accelerator of Chevy Silverado he was driving.

"Hold on!" he yelled.

Marcus, Tyler, and Socrates braced themselves as their truck leaped forward to meet the other.

Danny slewed through the curves and hit the parking area

at fifty miles per hour. He spotted the Transit in the far corner and grinned.

"Got you, motherfucker!"

Max heard the whine of an engine pushing as hard as it could and whipped around to see the big Ford 250 swerve into the parking area and make a bead for the van.

The Presence was alive in the cab of the Ford: an unmistakable mix of rage and glee and murderous intent.

Time slowed as he reached around for the pistol in his waistband, and brought it to bear on the Ford.

Max squeezed off a shot at the windshield of the Ford, and the big truck swerved right at him. He stood his ground and aimed for the driver's side tire and squeezed off another shot, the truck now twenty yards from him and closing fast.

The tire exploded and Max watched in relief as the metal rim of the tire bit into the pavement, spitting sparks as it gripped. The truck tilted, swerved to his right, rolled once, twice, came up on the passenger's side and skidded to the edge of the parking lot, sparks and smoke marking its trail.

Mack Bannister was zeroed in on the garage door.

From the corner of his eye, he saw headlights looming.

"Look out!" Warren yelled.

Mack gripped the wheel harder and stomped the gas all the way to the floor.

The headlights grew and just as his wheels hit the pavement under the apron over the gas pumps, the Chevy smashed straight into his door with a terrific crunch and a blasting impact that tore him loose from the wheel.

Before he could right the truck, it was off to the side of the garage, off the pavement, and into the dirt.

Mack's head rang and spots danced before his eyes. His left arm hung dead in place as he fought to get back behind the wheel. Warren was pushing him upright, off of his lap where he'd landed.

Trees loomed in the windshield and then danced crazily as the truck plunged off of the garage lot and bounced across the rough ground to fly off the hill into the valley below.

Danny had been all grin and game going into the lot, and then things had gone crazy. The windshield spidered in front of him, a bullet zinging though the air and burning a groove in his scalp just over his right ear.

Then the truck had swerved and tumbled and he was on a merry go round, bouncing around the cab to come to rest against the driver's side door and a final explosion of light as his head bounced off the dash.

Things went dark and fuzzy, a burning in his head ramping up the rage and confusion building inside him.

He was dimly aware of the passenger door creaking open and a head poking in.

Timmy fought to control the Silverado as it rebounded off of the Ford. The big crew cab pickup shuddered and slid sideways on the pavement, its wheels smoking. All four wheels grabbed at the same time, and the Silverado hunched for a moment like a sprinter at the starting line, then all four wheels left the ground and the big Chevy pickup hopped ten feet to the left and planted itself, rocked up on to the driver's side, the wheels on the passenger's side lifting off the ground. The angle increased and Timmy thought for sure the truck was going to roll, but the world stopped tilting at about forty-five degrees, hung there for a moment, then banged back down into place.

Steam filled his vision as armed men swarmed the truck, shouting and pointing weapons at him and the others.

Max wrenched the passenger's side door open, clambered up, stood on the side of the truck, and looked down into the cab.

The man who'd been out at the compound was crumpled against the driver's door below him.

The man groaned, wiped blood from his eyes, and looked up

at him, his brow dark with blood. He spotted Max and grinned.

"It IS you, motherfucker!" the man muttered.

His right hand clabbered around the cab, looking for something—a weapon, most likely.

The hand closed and came up and Max found himself looking down the barrel of a mighty big pistol.

Max hopped off the side of the truck into the cab and aimed himself straight at the man.

He kicked the pistol to the side as it fired, the bullet zzzzing off into the air above him as he landed with both boots on the man's chest.

Air wheezed out of the man and his eyes bugged. His hands opened involuntarily and the pistol clattered off the door underneath the man.

"Got one thing right, you little weasel," Max said. "It IS me."

Max raised his foot and brought his boot door hard, stomping the man's face, pounding the back of his head off the truck door. He felt a satisfying crunch as bone and cartilage gave way. The man slumped.

Max squatted down, retrieved the pistol and began going quickly through the man's pockets.

CHAPTER THIRTY EIGHT

Sherman idled toward the gas station, lights off.

Mack's truck had sailed off the edge of the lot and disappeared.

No way Sherman was heading back to Aston. This was not news to bring the Old Man. Not if he wanted to keep all his parts.

Despair washed over him.

At least eight men converged on the Chevy Silverado that sat smoking at the edge of the lot. There was a lot of shouting and gesturing with guns.

Standing on the edge of the crowd, leaning forward, fixated on the Silverado stood a woman with long brown hair in jeans and a plaid shirt.

Bill's fuck toy.

Sherman couldn't believe it.

Maybe.

Maybe if he could bring her back, the Old Man wouldn't kill him. Maybe he'd understand what an impulsive fuck up Mack was and that Sherman had done all that could be done.

Sherman eased along the road, closing in on the gas station.

Max sat behind the wheel of the Transit, going through the rat-faced man's wallet.

Danny David, 37, 5' 10", 170 pounds, 4123 12th Ave. NE., Ramsey.

Should have a little skull and crossbones sticker, he thought. *Something to identify him for what he is.*

Max stared at the driver's license.

The man was unconscious, but Max hadn't put a real beating on him. He'd raised his boot to stomp him some more, but the necessary malice and rage were not there. The man deserved to die a miserable death—over and over—for what he had done. But killing him here and now didn't feel right.

Imagery of the atrocities the Bannisters committed—for fun—clamored in his head. Visions of the scene in the shack at the orchard mixed with those of the barn filled with S&M toys at Bill's and the sight of Mary Jane in the bunker.

He remembered the Blond Woman in the clearing on the mountain.

Choice, he thought... *Free will. At what point, in giving over your will, have you lost control?*

Most of the Bannister clan were no more than gibbering monkeys, really. Mean apes fixated on pain and suffering, sex and death, everything so mixed up in the red cloud of the Presence that life was one long rage and lust-filled dance driven by...*what?*

"Max?" Rosita asked.

She placed a hand on his arm.

Max shook his head to clear it of the visions pressing on him.

People were heading for the wrecked Ford, drawn to investigate.

Time to move.

Timmy and the others sat in the Silverado, hands in the air.

"It's me!" Timmy yelled. "From Krell's!"

More shouting outside, but the guns wavered, and some of them lowered.

The men outside advanced toward the truck.

From the corner of his eyes, Timmy saw a pickup, lights off, ease to a gentle stop on the road, a bearded giant clamber out and come around the truck to advance towards the group.

The giant moved quickly towards the woman standing at the rear of the crowd.

No one noticed him.

Timmy watched as the man raised an arm, something dangling from his hand, then brought it down viciously, slamming the woman in the back of the head.

Timmy ejected himself from the truck.

The men gathered round erupted in a chorus of yells; "Hands up!" "Freeze!" "Don't fucking move!"

"Bannisters!" Timmy yelled. "Turn around, you idiots!"

The bearded man caught the woman as she collapsed, turned, tossed her roughly into the back of his pickup, and sprinted to the driver's side and hopped in the truck.

The woman had to be Mary Jane, Timmy realized.

He pointed, yelling; "Some asshole just grabbed Mary Jane!"

Timmy pushed though the crowd, bringing up his Glock as the truck tires screeched and it sped down the road.

Finally, understanding washed through the crowd.

"Mary Jane!" Raymond howled.

He brought up his shotgun and emptied it at the cab of the speeding truck.

Timmy emptied his Glock amidst the cacophony of eight men firing weapons as fast as they could

Bullet holes frosted the rear windshield and sparked off the tailgate and steel bumper, the left rear light shattered and winked out, and the truck was gone.

Sherman hunched over the wheel of the Ford, using both lanes as he wound his way back down the mountain.

He risked a glance in the rear view mirror.

Nothing.

He was a little worried about Bill's fuck toy, but not badly.

Like Mack's truck, this one had been modified and solidified. It was a solid chunk of reinforced steel, a weapon itself. While the windows were not bulletproof, the body was. Little chance any those bullets had penetrated.

If he was going to survive this without finding himself strapped to one of the Bannisters' toys in Red Rock, he'd have to bring Mary Jane in alive.

Technically, he should really head back and try to snatch up Ingersoll as well, if he wanted any level of certainty, but that was insane.

The road curved sharply, a flimsy guard rail the only thing between him and a sheer drop of hundreds of feet.

Sherman braked and fought the wheel as his bumper scraped off the guard rail, the lights of Paluma winking far off in the distance.

The truck swerved, then came back under his control.

Sherman wiped sweat from his brow, shot another look into the rear view, then stomped down on the accelerator again, aiming the truck for Aston.

Max slowed as the sign for Greencreek appeared on the roadside. Someone had spray-painted a big white X over the 350 population count, and written 342 next to it.

Up ahead, streetlights marked off the town: a single Main Street, a couple of residential streets, and a line of huge silos out at the edge of town.

A low roil of malice hovered over the little town. Meanness.

"Rosita," Max said. "Wake up."

Rosita yawned and stretched, rubbed her eyes and blinked, instantly alert.

"We're here," she said. Flat, not a question.

She reached for the shotgun by her side.

Max glanced over, gestured with his right hand, a put-it-down motion.

"Hold steady, girl. This is a one-man job. You got that just in case, you understand? You are to sit in the van and wait for me to get back."

Rosita shot a glance at Max, her dark eyes flashing in the reflection of the streetlights as they drove through town.

"More bad men," Rosita said. "Best to kill them all."

Max grinned. "Maybe," he said. "But no way I'm taking a chance of trading your life for three of theirs. Or 340 of them.

You're worth about a thousand of these Bannister types." He thought for a minute, "No, I take that back. A Bannister life is worth about exactly zero, so you're worth more than all of them and then some."

Max scanned the streets of the town as they drove, looking for the combination bar/massage parlor indicated in the Bannister ledgers. A place called The Play Box.

The streets were empty and glistened from a recent rain shower, nothing moving.

He spotted a bar on Main Street and slowed. The sign read simply "Bar." He kept moving.

A spike of alarm flared in Max's head.

He'd gotten better at controlling the vision. He could open and shut the door at will, manage not to let the phenomena overwhelm him, but he suddenly realized he *needed* to keep the door open a little, letting this "gift" of his remain vigilant, keeping him informed.

"Get down!" Max hissed, putting a hand on Rosita's shoulder, pushing her down.

Someone had eyes on them, and that someone was a very bad man indeed.

Winter Young watched the Ford van roll past his car parked in the alley behind the bar. Roger Bannister had passed word on down the line to be alert, to post guards, to look for this mystery man the Bannisters were hunting.

Winter might not know a lot of things, but one thing he did know, absolutely, was that you did. Not. Fuck. With. Bannisters. Not. They said jump, you said how high, that kind of thing.

This had to be the guy.

Three o'clock in the morning, nothing moving but this shiny new van. A van Winter had never seen in town.

Winter picked up the phone, held down the button, "Call Play Box," he said.

The phone rang in his ear as he eased the car into gear. The van turned a corner and disappeared.

Max took in the whole scene. He had an overview, an image of the town in his head that came from more than his eyes and having looked at the map. The man who'd opened the door in his head was moving now, coming up behind.

"Rosita," Max said. "You get down in the back. Get your back up against a wall so you can cover both the rear and the front doors, got me?"

Rosita picked up the shotgun and slid between the seats into the back.

"Hold on" Max said.

He brought the van to a stop.

"Anyone opens a door, shoot them," Max said. "If it's me, I'll let you know."

He slid out of the van and slipped across the yard of a dilapidated old house and eased his back up against the front wall.

Calm spread through him as he entered his combat state. His vision sharpened, the granularity of the sidewalk popping, the peeling paint on the siding on the houses sharp, the light mist that softened the edges and contours of the buildings. Lights out in all the houses, just the headlights and taillights of his van illuminating this stretch of residential street.

The men in these houses were dreaming dark, violent dreams. The women, what there were of them, slept fitfully and frightened. Their claustrophobia and sense of helplessness angered Max.

Max had his back to the wall of the house on the corner when a police car turned the corner and braked abruptly.

Winter jammed his foot down on the brake.

What the hell?

The big Ford van idled in the middle of the street, exhaust rising in the night air to blur the red taillights.

He sat for a moment, disconcerted. His body tingled, a

biological "Danger" sign flashing through him.

The ringing of the phone in his ear stopped as someone picked up.

Death metal poured through the speaker against his ear, a woman's anguished cry, the sound of heavy laughter in the background.

"Yeah?" a voice grumbled.

"Someone's here," Winter said. "Hold on a minute."

He set the phone down on the seat beside him and picked up his pistol.

Eyes locked on the van, Winter eased open the door of the cruiser and stepped into the street, his boots unnaturally loud on the asphalt.

Max watched the man get out of the police cruiser and stand, gun in hand.

The man crouched and began to step cautiously toward the van.

Max noticed the tremor of the barrel of the gun and grinned.

Got that right, he thought. *You need to be afraid. Very afraid.*

Max eased up on the man, careful not to make a sound.

The man turned, bringing the gun around, and Max used his forward momentum to jump into the air and deliver a right bicycle kick directly to the side of his neck where the man's spine joined his skull.

The man dropped into the street in a crumpled heap as Max landed on his feet next to him.

Max leaned down and picked up the man's pistol.

Standard looking Glock. 9mm.

Max shoved the pistol into his belt and grabbed the cop by the lapels of his jacket and dragged him quickly out of the street and rolled him up against the side of the house he'd ambushed him from.

He felt stirring in the house and paused.

Whoever it was settled back into sleep.

Back at the cop car, Max spotted the phone on the seat.

He picked it up and held it to his ear.

Death metal music, or whatever they called it.

Max's gut clenched as he felt, more than heard, the cries of a woman in pain, followed by thick, guttural laughter.

"Winter! What the fuck is going on," said a voice on the phone.

The voice raised the hairs on the back of Max's neck. Another soul completely ruled by the Presence. A man filled with hatred and malice. A man who had centered his whole existence on causing others pain. Because he enjoyed it. Lived for it.

"Winter can't come to the phone right now," Max said. "But don't worry. I'll be seeing you soon, bring you up to speed."

Max clicked off the phone.

Billy supervised as Wilder cracked open the doors to the big container.

Stale air tainted with the scent of human shit washed over Wilder and Jack as they pulled the doors open.

Ten women lay on the floor of the container.

Minimal effort had been made to accommodate them: a five-gallon bucket served as their toilet, a stack of heavy wool blankets their beds. The women had been tossed in and left to their own devices.

They'd arranged the blankets and pulled the bucket to the far end of the container.

Now, the women lay scattered around. Several sat up and rubbed their eyes as the lights of the loading bay reached in and the men shone flashlights around.

"Get up, you lazy bitches!" Wilder yelled.

He pressed the button on his cattle prod to emphasize his words.

The crackling voltage sat most of the women upright. The majority of them had tasted the sting of the prod and were unwilling to risk it again.

"I said, up!" Wilder yelled, stepping in and zapping the

woman closest to him.

She cried out, and leapt to her feet.

Wilder laughed with a high, hysterical-sounding cackle.

"That's more like it!" he said. "Move!"

Nine of the ten women stood, wavering uncertainly, not wanting to pass too close to Wilder.

The tenth, a woman who'd chosen to nestle against the side of the container about halfway back, stayed buried in her blanket.

Jack and Bobby started yelling at the women.

"Move, you cunts!"

"Forward!"

"Ándele!"

Billy stepped forward.

"Jack, you ignorant shit. That Speedy Gonzales shit ain't Mexican," he said.

"Rapido!" Billy said.

The women stiffened at the sight of Billy. They lined up obediently and exited single file as Billy pointed them toward the open loading door of the big building the truck was backed up to.

Wilder reached the tenth woman, leaned down, and gave her a long zap with the prod, giggling.

"Hoo-ah!" Wilder yelled, zapping the woman again.

The woman twitched, but otherwise didn't move.

"This one likes it!" Wilder yelled. "I'm going to play with this one first!"

He zapped her again, and the woman twitched.

Billy watched carefully from the end of the truck.

Zap her all you want, you stupid asshole, he thought. *That one's dead.* He'd seen enough dead women to know their bodies might twitch under the stimulation of electricity, but that was not an indicator of life. The way this one was twitching left no doubt.

Billy counted the days in his head. *Loaded 'em up down in Tenancingo, drove 'em up around Mexico City, hit the border,*

Texas...hmm, four days, tops? How could one have died already?

He looked around the container. Empty plastic water bottles littered the floor. They'd left a case of water back there... appeared as if the women had drank it all. Billy tried to do the math: 24 bottles of water, 10 women, five days.... He waved a hand in frustration. Should've been enough, he thought.

A new thought struck him. *Maybe, these women had fought over the water. Maybe the dead one had lost out...*the idea excited him.

Damn! Maybe get some cat fights out of this group. Fuck yeah, give a couple of 'em knives or something, starve 'em another couple days, put 'em down in the arena with some food laid out, tell 'em only the survivor got the food...fuck yeah.

Billy did some more calculating. That'd only leave seven for the real fun, though. Huh. He'd have to float the idea to Mack. Mack'd be up for some sport like that.

Billy was drawn out of his reverie by Wilder going apeshit.

He was kicking the body and screaming at it, punctuating each kick with a work.

"I. Said. Get. The. Fuck. Up. You. Cunt."

"Hey!" Billy yelled.

Wilder kicked the woman a couple more times.

"Wilder!" Billy roared.

Wilder stopped his foot mid-kick. Nobody ignored Billy. Even Mack was careful around him.

Wilder turned, faced Billy.

"What?" he said.

"That one's dead, you stupid piece of shit," Billy said. "Pick her up and get her over to the burn room. Looks like they're cleaning up after a party. You won't have to fire the whole thing up or nothing, just add her to the pile."

Wilder looked down at the body at his feet.

His prodding and kicking had worked the blanket off of the woman, a frail-looking young woman, though maybe woman was pushing it a little far—she was likely about 14.

Her face had caved in where he'd kicked her, nose pushed off to one side, but no blood leaked from her, no bruising.

Damn. Dead as shit, all right.

"Aw, shit," Wilder said. "I thought I found me the perfect playmate."

"Only if you like 'em dead," Billy said.

They both knew men who did.

"Naw, I like a little zip out 'em," Wilder said. "Shit."

He slipped the cattle prod into a holster on his belt and leaned down, picked up the tiny woman with ease, tossed her over his shoulder and headed for the burn room.

"And Wilder," Billy said as Wilder shouldered past him, "you just drop her off, get the others settled and head back. We're heading straight out, got that? Got to make the drive up to Mountain Cleft lickety-split, got it?"

"Aw, Boss," Wilder moaned. "Seriously? We been in that fucking truck for days. We done everything we're supposed to. We should be having some play time now."

Billy reached out and grabbed a hank of Wilder's hair and spun him around to face him.

"I already told you all that, you dumb shit. And I don't like repeating myself. You drop that bitch off on the pile, round up Jack and Bobby and meet me at the parking lot. You all make sure to gear up proper, too. We're going to be hitting a place with Marty and Danny and some others tonight, and we got a nine-hour drive ahead of us."

Wilder's mouth moved like he was going to complain, but then he caught sight of the rage in Billy's eyes.

Whoops, he thought. *How the fuck did I miss that?*

"Yes, sir," he said. "Right away, sir. Sorry, sir."

Billy let go of his grip on Wilder's hair and patted him on the face.

"Atta boy," he said. "Now, get!"

Wilder shuffled as quickly as he could out of Billy's sight and towards the burn room.

Sherman pulled off onto the shoulder at a deserted spot on

the road. He checked his mirrors one more time, then turned his attention forward and scanned the horizon for lights.

Nothing.

Good.

He popped out of the truck, a roll of duct tape in his hands.

He leaned over into the bed of the truck to check on Bill's fuck toy just as she leapt up at him, a hammer in her hand.

She swung wildly at him, catching him with a glancing blow off the temple that staggered him. He felt warm blood gush down the side of his face and wet his collar.

"God damn it," he roared.

The bitch took another swing at him, and he got a hand up to block it just before it cracked down onto his skull.

Pain shot up the length of his arm into his shoulder.

"You going to die now, bitch," he yelled.

She was crouched in the bed of the pickup, hammer in one hand, the other out for balance.

Sherman jigged one way, then the other, and with a quick step vaulted himself into the back of the pickup.

He'd had to place both hands onto the rail of the pickup bed to haul his bulk up and over, and the bitch took advantage of that to leap in with another mighty swing.

Sherman managed to slide his head out of the path of the hammer just in time as it slid down his face, breaking the skin, twanging off of his jaw, down to catch his collar bone a glancing blow that hurt like hell.

But he was in the bed of the pickup with her now, and he had momentum going.

He used that to bring up his right arm, his left not entirely cooperative after the crack to the collar bone, and he got his hand deep into the bitch's hair, a solid grip.

He kept moving forward, using his bulk and strength, taking her off her feet and up and down in an arc that slammed her head into the rear windows of the truck, adding another spiderweb pattern of cracks to the bullet holes.

The safety glass sagged in a little in the shape of her head and she went limp.

Sherman let her slump down into a crumpled fetal position and raised his fist to scream into the sky.

A dot of headlights on the horizon.

Sherman leapt back into the road, blood obscuring his vision, and swept the road with his eyes, looking for his duct tape.

Raymond walked into the big room at the back of Guy's garage and sat down.

Timmy and Marcus had taken Raymond's truck to look for Mary Jane, their big Silverado out of commission temporarily.

He and Chad, one of Guy's men, had taken Chad's truck and followed Timmy and Marcus. They'd split at the first fork in the road, Timmy and Marcus going down the mountain, the idea being whoever had snatched Mary Jane was aiming at taking her back to the Bannisters, while he and Chad had run all the side roads on the off chance the guy had had to hole up for a while, lick his wounds, work on the truck, hide…whatever.

No luck.

Guy had wheeled the Silverado into the garage and gotten to work on it. Nearly three hours later it was ready to go.

The rest of Guy's men had fanned out, heading up the mountain.

Tyler and Socrates had down-climbed the slope behind the garage to check on the truck that'd rammed them to start this whole disaster.

They'd found one man dead in the cab of the truck, his head split open, blood all over the cab.

They'd left him there, figuring the truck was well out of sight of the road and far enough down the hillside it was unlikely to be discovered anytime soon.

Socrates had found a blood trail, and he and Tyler were tracking that down.

Raymond looked around the room.

The men were all returning now, heads hung in defeat.

Just Timmy and Marcus on the road, Tyler and Socrates in the woods below.

Raymond grimaced, the taste in his mouth horrible.

The taste of loss.

CHAPTER THIRTY NINE

Max juggled the phones in his hands, his and the cop's. Rosita sat on the seat next to him, tense and ready.

"Max?" she said.

Max juggled the phones some more.

"Got to get moving," Max said. "They're expecting me."

The door in his head open, all senses on alert, Max had a bead on The Play Box. He could feel the men there, their minds pulsing and squirming with hideous desires and passions. They were jazzed, ready—and angry as hell.

Good, Max thought. *They'll be easy to draw out.*

"Rosita," Max said. "Can you drive?"

Rosita looked at him like he were an idiot.

"Of course, I can drive," she said.

"I got an idea how to draw these guys out," Max said.

Mack blundered through the brush and with a last lunge of energy broke through to find himself on a well-maintained trail.

His left arm hung useless; dried blood crusted on his face, his shirt stiff with it. Every muscle ached and he was as tired as he'd ever been.

An animal sense, a lust for survival, drove him forward.

He could feel predators on his trail.

He had to keep moving.

One step after another.

"Just put one foot in front of the other," he croaked to himself, the song from the children's Christmas cartoon suddenly bright in his mind, "and soon you'll be walking out the door...."

"Right here," Socrates said, "look."

Tyler shook his head.

"I don't see it," he said.

Socrates knelt by the patch of grass he'd indicated.

"Look," Socrates repeated. "The grass is bent back, like something big moved through it this way."

Tyler pointed at another batch of the tall grass, "It is there, too."

Socrates shook his head in irritation.

"It's not the same," he said. "Look at the way the dew is wiped off on this side, that's from somebody or something pushing through here. It's got to be him."

"We've been following this asshat for two hours," Tyler said. "I think we've lost him. No way he'd stay ahead of us. He's hurt. And we haven't seen any blood for the last thirty minutes."

"That's because he finally stopped bleeding," Socrates said. "I guarantee you we're close. Just hang in there. We'll get him."

Tyler threw up his hands.

"One more hour, OK? If we don't catch up to him by then, we aren't going to, anyway. He didn't have that big of a lead on us."

Socrates nodded and stood.

"Then let's get a move on," he said.

Raymond stared at the phone in his hand.

He should call Max.

He really should.

The idea of telling Max they'd lost Mary Jane was too much, though.

But he really should know.

Max eased his way through the field of tall grass outside of The Play Box.

It looked as if it had once been an office for the company that ran the silos, a low roofed log cabin style building set off to one side of a row of giant silos by the train tracks,

Those logs are good cover, Max thought.

He raised his night vision binoculars and scoped the place from his vantage point.

A thin, disused trail ran through the field to the door at the rear of the building.

A couple of pickups stood in the gravel lot out front.

The front had an old-style facade that stuck up above the roof line.

Decent place to plant a sniper.

He scoped the area carefully.

He didn't see anyone, but then again, the binos were not infrared, and a man might be able to hide in the shadows.

Max scoped the whole area again, carefully, looking for any detail that might give away an ambush.

He picked up the cop's phone and punched in his number.

Rosita picked up on the first ring.

"I'm in place," Max said. "Going to give it ten more minutes, then it's a go. You remember what to do?"

"Aim the cop car at the door of the place," Rosita said. "Flip on the siren, get out, put that brick on the gas pedal, get down, aim the shotgun at anybody that comes my way."

"That's my girl," Max said. "Don't hesitate. If anyone sticks his head out that door, let 'em have it."

"I will," Rosita said.

Max heard cold certainty in her voice, had no doubt anyone who stuck his head out the door would get a face full of double-ought buckshot.

He raised the binoculars and scoped the cabin some more, watching the shadow above the facade carefully.

Mack trudged down the trail.

He'd stuck his left hand into his coat pocket, a half-assed sling, but his arm still swung sloppy and loose with his gait. Each swing hurt like a motherfucker.

That stupid song from the cartoon echoed in his head and

he envisioned himself kicking the living shit out of someone. Anyone.

No. That asshole from outside the diner, the one way before all of this started. The Mystery Man.

Mack tried to fix the man's face in his mind, wrap a fantasy of torture and pain and misery around his image. He began to envision ever more elaborate tortures, more exquisite pain.

He smiled, and his step lightened a bit.

Going to get through this, he thought.

It's going to be all right.

CHAPTER FORTY

Raymond sighed.

He picked up the phone.

Put it back down.

Picked it up again.

Dialed Max.

Rosita sat in the car, staring at the door of The Play Box.

Hatred pulsed through her.

More of those...creatures. *Cucuy*.

Rosita stuck the car in drive, grabbed the shotgun, flipped on the siren to the cop car as Max had shown her to, then stepped out of the car, the grass of the field soft under her feet, the siren cutting rudely through the night air.

She leaned in, walking at pace, and set the brick she and Max had found against the gas pedal.

The car picked up speed and she let it roll ahead, siren whooping. The car picked up more speed and its wheels crunched audibly as the car left the field and gripped the gravel of the lot.

Rosita hit the ground and lay flat, shotgun pointed ahead, grass high on each side of her, hidden from view, a lioness in ambush.

The door of The Play Box burst open and a man stepped out holding something big and bulky in front of him.

The siren sent a jolt through Max, even though he'd been expecting it.

He watched Rosita take cover and breathed a sigh of relief as she disappeared into the grass.

Light spilled out of the bar to join the light from the headlights spotlighting the bar entrance.

A big man stepped into the light, lit up as if he were on stage, and raised something surprisingly large in front of him.

The thing spit fire and erupted with a deafening brrrrrrrrrrrraaaaaatttttttt of automatic gunfire.

Max's body leapt into combat mode. His vision sharpened and the sound dimmed—the experience tinged with an underwater quality.

Max rose into a crouch and sprinted to the rear door.

Sparks blossomed all over the cop car, the windshield frosted and sagged in, the headlights popped and went dark. The car slowed.

Then Max was out of sight and to the back of the bar.

A security door. Every bit as solid and unbreakable as those he'd found back in Hotel 29 in Mountain Cleft.

Max pulled up the crowbar he'd brought along, pleased with himself for thinking of it and at the same time in mortal panic that Rosita was possibly dying out front while he messed around with the door.

A security plate welded to the door covered the door jamb where the bolt joined the door.

Max forced the crowbar under the plate as the siren out front warbled and died.

Rosita!

With a sudden, rapid move, Max put all of his strength into a wrenching jerk and was rewarded with the security plate bending back enough to allow him to see the deadbolt and door latch peeking through, gleaming brassily in the moonlit night.

He inserted the tip of the crowbar between the door and jamb just as he heard another quick bllllaaaattt of automatic fire answered by the roar of a shotgun out front.

Rosita covered her head with her arms and lay as flat as possible.

Bullets zinged over her head and dirt splattered around her

as the bullets from the machine gun chewed up the ground around her.

The heavy sound of the machine gun reverberated in her guts; the impact of the bullets on the cop car loud, rapid-fire banging over the noise of the siren.

The engine of the cop car coughed, chugged, and died. The siren blipped then cut short.

Silence.

Rosita raised her head to look.

A man stood silhouetted in the faint light coming from the doorway of the bar, smoke all around him.

He held the big gun crossways across his body, ready to bring it up at any movement.

Rosita aimed the shotgun at center mass.

The man stepped forward in a crouch, angled to one side of the cop car.

He turned his head as he scanned the parking lot and its environs, then flipped his attention back to the car.

The phone in Rosita's pocket rang.

In one fluid movement, the man brought up the bulky machine gun and turned, spraying bullets.

Rosita pulled the trigger and the shotgun roared and kicked her solidly in the shoulder.

Max burst into the back room of The Play Box.

He blinked his eyes against the sight that greeted him, trying to separate what was real and immediate from the past carnage that littered the place.

The first assault was the stench—a slaughterhouse on a hot day.

The back room was dimly lit with a single red bulb that hung from the ceiling. Max's boots scuffed on the hard dirt floor.

Max dropped his hands to his side and tried to breathe through his mouth.

A score of naked women hung from chains on the ceiling, some with their arms behind their backs, their arms rotated through to impossible positions, bent at impossible angles, others with their hands straight up. The blood on them looked black in the red light.

Other women were affixed to frightful looking contraptions that littered the room. The paraphernalia of hell: gynecological-looking tables with women strapped in, their legs buckled into stirrups and spread wide, something that looked like a medieval rack, and a few other pieces that Max could not make sense of.

Max blinked and tried to clear his vision, pushing the door in his head as close to shut as he could, desperately trying to separate ghostly vision from living reality.

Most of the hanging women dimmed, but two remained sharp and clear. And moving.

One lay on the table in stirrups—alive, but not moving.

The others were immobile, a horrible 3-D tableaux that had become the imagery of Max's life since the arrival of the gift.

Max berated himself, *get a move on, asshole*.

He let the crowbar he'd been gripping tightly in his left hand fall to the dirt floor with a dim thud, brought the cop's pistol up in a two-handed grip and moved to the door of the back room.

He opened himself again and let his senses feel out the room ahead.

A nasty snarl of red rage and malice filled the room. Max felt at least two men in there, but sensed they were moving for the entrance, getting ready to join the assault out front.

Max reached down with his left hand and tested the door.

Unlocked.

He eased it open a sliver, peered into the room ahead.

A standard-looking bar: pool table, bar up against the wall with stools in front, a couple of booths.

Not a big room.

Two men holding what looked to be machine guns edged toward the open front door, framing a moonlit view of the gravel lot beyond.

Max slipped into the room, and was upon them before they

had taken two steps.

He flipped the pistol around to grip the barrel and brought it down squarely on the back of the head of the man to his left, using the swing of his arm to lean into a kick to the rear leg of the man to the right.

The man on the left crumpled in a heap, his gun clattering to the floor.

The man on the right tilted back and swung in quarter circle clockwise as his leg was chopped out from underneath him, the muzzle of his gun arcing skyward. He squeezed the trigger and bullets tore into the door jamb and ceiling. Bits of plaster and wood filled the air.

Max dropped the pistol and leaned in and grabbed the body of the machine gun with his left hand, pulling the man toward him. As the man turned and staggered toward him, Max caught him with a vicious right elbow to the temple and the man went down on a knee.

Max ripped the gun from the man, raised it high and brought the stock down, aiming at the spot where blood spurted from the man's temple.

Another shotgun blast sounded out front.

The man fell forward and lay still. Max stepped over him and into the lot, bringing the gun to bear.

Rosita stood over the giant in the parking lot, her legs spread to brace herself as she jacked another round into the chamber of the 12 gauge.

She'd watched the man drop from the first blast of the gun and flail on the ground like a wounded bird. He'd been scrabbling for his gun, and in the act of bringing it around toward her when she'd fired a second shot.

This one had caught him just under the chin and ripped off a fair piece of his face, but the man had kept moving as Rosita reached him and squared herself.

A figure moved though the doorway and Rosita raised the shotgun and fired blindly.

Max saw the gun raise and dove backwards into the bar as wood splintered off of the door jamb, momentarily blinding him.

The brrrrrraaaatttt! of automatic fire had him back on his feet blinking desperately to see as he stumbled over the man in the doorway back into the lot.

"Rosita!" he yelled, "it's me! Don't shoot!"

Rosita watched the man dive back into the bar and chambered another round as the man at her feet clenched his gun and it erupted.

Her vision whited out from the muzzle flash so close to her face, a searing red agony blossomed as something dug a groove around the side of her head.

She squeezed the trigger as she fell, the shotgun leaping in her hands.

Max watched Rosita tumble to one side, the shotgun erupting in her hands, the buckshot blasting into the man's head and exploding it like a pumpkin.

"No!!" Max yelled, racing forward. "Rosita!"

Rosita crumpled to the side of what was left of the man on the ground and lay still.

Every step sent a shiver of pain through Mack's arm. Hand tucked into his coat pocket, the arm flopped like a noodle, each centimeter of movement a jolt of fire and pain.

Mack stuck his right hand in his other coat pocket to balance the swing, maybe slow it some, and puzzled over something hard in the pocket.

Cards?

No.

Box of some kind.

Mack stopped dead in the trail and pulled the thing out.

He stared at it dumbly.

It finally dawned on him.

My phone! he thought.

Damn! I can call someone! Get some help.

He stared at the phone some more, tried to think.

Damn. Must've hit my head harder than I thought.

His mind flashed back to sailing off the edge of the lot back at the gas station.

He and Warren bouncing around in the cab and a burst of stars and blackness and pain.

And...*Sherman.*

Wait a minute.

Where the fuck was Sherman?

Sherman wiped blood from his eyes and tried to keep the truck in its lane.

The bitch had really done a number on him with the hammer.

He considered pulling to the side of the road again, beating on her a little bit.

It'd make him feel better.

Then he remembered the Old Man. Roger.

They had been very clear: kill Ingersoll. Bring back his head. It was OK to hurt the bitch, but not too bad. She had to come back alive and intact. the Old Man was going to make her into one of his projects.

Sherman glanced back over his shoulder into the bed of the truck.

Hard to tell if the bitch was even alive back there; she was just a lump in the dark.

Sherman glanced back at the dash.

Shit.

Going to have to get off the road, or at the very least get cleaned up and get her covered before light.

The phone in his pocket buzzed and vibrated, startling him enough that the truck swerved completely out of its lane before he got it back under control.

Get your shit together, asshole.

He pulled his phone out, mind racing.

If it was Roger....

What could he say?

He glanced down at the phone.

Mack.

Holy fuck.

Mack?

Sherman raised the phone to his ear, kept his eyes on the road.

Max lifted Rosita and raced to the Ford.

He lay her gently down in the back, then climbed in and pulled the First Aid kit down off its brackets.

As he cleaned the blood off of her face and head, she moaned.

"Max?" she said.

Max's heart leapt in his chest.

"Rosita! Thank God!"

Rosita moved to sit, but Max laid a gentle hand on her and eased her back.

"You stay still a while, you hear?" Max said. "Looks like you got your head creased by a bullet. You've got a concussion, at the very least."

He looked into her eyes.

They were clear and lucid.

No stranger to head injury, Max was uncertain.

"Rosita," Max said. "Do you know where you are?"

Rosita blinked, kept her eyes on Max's.

"We are in Greencreek," she said. "We are at the bar..."

She gasped and bolted to sit.

Max gently pushed her back down again.

"Shh," Max said. "I got you. Relax."

"No!" Rosita said, struggling to sit.

"Yes," Max said.

"No! Max! The women! Les *chamacas*."

Alarm bumped Max's heart.

How could he have forgotten?

"Oh, shit," Max said. "There are three of them back there."

"Go! Max! Now! You have to hurry!"

Max nodded.

"OK," he said. "Let's get you situated, then we'll go."

He helped her to the front seat and got her buckled in, then slid behind the wheel.

"You going to be OK?" he said.

She made a face, waved at him.

Max looked at her, hard.

He flashed on the two women hanging from chains in the back room of The Play Box, then stuck the Ford in gear and stomped on the gas, tires kicking up dirt and grass as he crossed the field toward The Play Box.

"Yeah?" Sherman grunted into the phone. He braced himself.

Either Mack had somehow survived that tumble off the side of the hill or those assholes at the garage had gotten his phone.

Either way, this was not going to be the easiest phone call he'd ever taken.

His eyes played over the landscape, looking for refuge, a place to pull over. He'd been driving in the general direction of Aston, his only thought moving forward, and now the reality of his situation crashed over him.

"Sherman!"

A disquieting set of emotions washed over him: relief, confusion, and a solid jolt of sheer panic.

Oh fuck, he thought. *I left the Old Man's son behind. Mack. Meanest son-of-a-bitch ever.*

Sherman cleared his throat.

"Mack! What the fuck? Where? How?"

Max hit the gravel lot of The Play Box at forty miles per hour. He braked hard and swung the wheel to his right, spraying dirt and gravel through the open front door, and bringing the rear end of the truck sliding around to come to stop parallel with the building.

He leapt out the door and was hit by a wave of red rage.

Oh shit. Somebody's awake.

Cursing himself for not taking time to incapacitate the men at the door more thoroughly, Max dove in headfirst, threw himself into a front roll.

As he cleared the door, he saw the one he'd given the elbow smash to standing groggily, muttering to himself and clawing at the big machine gun. The other man lay crumpled where he'd dropped after taking the pistol butt to the back of his head.

Max rolled to his feet and launched himself at the one fumbling with the machine gun and tackled him, sending the machine gun spinning off into a corner. He quickly gained a full mount on the befuddled monster and rained blows down on him until he felt him go limp.

Then Max was on his feet, a final soccer kick to the head to make sure and through the door into the back.

He blinked his eyes and shook himself to fight the onslaught.

So. Many. Women.

He shuddered.

How long had this place been in business? How well supported?

An icy shard of fear ran through him. Too many women had suffered and died here. Far too many. No way this place was a secret.

The whole town must know about this place.

Which means, the whole town will be moving, maybe is moving now. There'd been an awful lot of noise generated over the last hour.

Max turned first to the woman hanging from the ceiling with her arms behind her back. She twisted slowly one direction, then the other, limp and dangling.

Yet...alive. Barely.

Max scanned the room frantically, looking for something to stand on, to release the woman, found a blood-crusted chair with manacles on the arms and legs, dragged it over, climbed it and carefully lifted the woman up and over his shoulder, then reached up and eased the chain off its hook.

Back through the front room, sliding open the side door to the van, easing the woman onto the floor.

He paused as red fingers of malice flared in his brain.

Men were coming.

Rosita watched him from the front seat.

"Rosita!" Max gestured at the bloody mess that had been the man in the lot. "Get his gun, get back into the van and aim at in the direction of the road. Any car that comes, let 'em have it."

Rosita's brow furrowed, "Have it? Give them the gun?"

Max stopped mid-turn.

"No, dear. Shoot them."

He looked at her again.

He'd cleaned the blood from her face and her eyes still appeared clear, the cold determination in them he'd seen before.

She climbed out of the van to retrieve the gun and he turned back into the bar.

The second hanging woman moaned as Max lifted her off the hook and carried her back through the front. He leaned down and collected the two machine guns on his way. He lay the woman beside the other in the van, and placed the machine guns behind the driver's seat. Rosita was back in her seat, the window down, gun barrel resting on the window sill, aimed at the road. She had to scoot back in the big bucket seat for her position to work, but she was a small woman, and she looked to be ready.

The woman strapped down to the table was awake and waiting.

"Who are you?" she asked.

"I'm here to get you out," Max said. "Let's move."

The shackles that held her down were primitive, but effective, U-shaped bolts of metal closed off with a kind of a pin on a hinge and a spring that had notches on it, allowing the pin to tighten down. The release mechanism was a little bar that gave Max some trouble. These things weren't meant to come off easily; they were designed to crush and brutalize.

The woman moaned in pain as Max finally released the first shackle on her wrist.

Brrrrrrrraaaaattttt!

Oh, shit. They were coming.

Now that he'd gotten it figured, the other three shackles gave him little trouble, but it was clear the way the woman reacted that bones had been broken holding her down. Bruises covered her, long bloody slices where someone had cut her, and peculiar little inflamed-looking marks that Max realized had been made with some kind of pliers....

A naked man standing over her, reaching out with the pliers, grabbing a pinch of flesh, twisting and pulling and laughing like hell as the woman screamed, obviously aroused by her pain, reaching out again...

Brrrrraaattt!

Max pulled himself back into the moment and lifted the woman from the table.

Out front, a truck had veered off the road and rolled into the field, its windshield frosted and opaque, the driver's side door open.

A man lay face down next to the truck, a shotgun by him.

Max eased the final woman into the van, slid the door shut, leapt into the driver's seat and gunned the van, spinning the rear wheels around in an arc to face the road.

Headlights flared in his eyes as two trucks raced toward him, brights on.

"Rosita! Get your head down!" Max yelled.

He ducked low, reached behind him, pulled up a machine gun and levered it out the window to face the trucks.

Light flashed from one of the trucks as someone fired on him.

A bullet skimmed off the driver's side door, sparking in the night, and Max had a bead on the shooter. He pulled the trigger on the gun, surprised by the way the gun jumped on him, almost losing it, bringing it back down to rake the windshield as the truck approached.

It veered off the road and crashed into a power pole.

The truck behind it angled off, trying to pull some kind of a flanking maneuver, but the driver hadn't really thought it through and all he'd done was open up his side. Max let the gun loose on it, punching holes all along the side, through the fenders, the driver's side door, both wheels exploding.

The truck bobbed to one side, back again as the driver fought to control it, then rolled over and slid into the field on its roof, dust rising into the night sky.

Max brought the hammer down and the van leapt forward, chewing up the dirt road to bite into asphalt as they gained the edge of town and shot towards the main road ahead.

Roger Bannister snapped out of sleep.

Disoriented, he sat up in bed, checked his surroundings.

The Old Man's place.

His phone buzzed again, the vibration spinning it a little on the bedside table.

Sherman.

It was just about 3:00AM.

Roger had little respect for the intellect of most of the crew, but Sherman was different. As smart as he was big.

He picked up the phone.

"Sherman," Roger said.

"Boss?"

The line crackled and warbled with distance, but even so, the fear in Sherman's voice sent an icy barb of dread down Roger's spine.

He swung his feet around and put them on the floor.

"What is it?" he said.

"Ah, hell, Roger. Everything went to shit."

Roger hung his head.

"Shit. What'd Mack do?" he said.

Sherman related the attack on the gas station and disastrous outcome, highlighting the fact he'd pulled Mary Jane off the tarmac right from under the assholes there, and that Mack was alive.

"So where the fuck is Mack, exactly?" Roger asked.

"That's part of the problem," Sherman said. "He up on one of the trails on the mountain there, probably the one up to Lake Berlin, but he's not sure. He also thinks someone's on his tail, but he's not so sure about that, either."

Roger stood and walked out into the Old Man's den.

"You're going to have to go back and get him," he said.

"But, Roger! They'll be crawling all over those hills. And what about Mary Jane?"

"Fuck," Roger said.

He scratched himself, looked out over the lights of Ramsey below.

"Tell you what," Roger said. "Let me make a few calls. I'll send someone out to pick up Mary Jane, bring you a new truck. And some back up."

"Yes, boss," Sherman said.

"Find a good place to hole up. There's a turn off just before the rest stop at the mile marker outside of Paluma," Roger said. "Leads down a dirt road to a little wood shack at the outside of a field. You know the one. We bring girls out there sometimes, for Novakovich's workers."

"I'll be there, boss," Sherman said.

Roger hung up, looked down at his phone to dial Danny.

The floor creaked, and he spun around, startled.

The Old Man stood there in his boxers, arms akimbo, staring at him.

For a 70-year-old guy, he still carried some muscle and was far from harmless.

His voice was low and dangerous.

"Tell me," the Old Man said.

CHAPTER FORTY ONE

Socrates led Tyler through the bushes onto the trail. He gestured at some splintered branches and Tyler nodded.

"Fresh," Socrates said. "Look how the pith hasn't had time to discolor."

"Pith?"

Socrates grinned. "The soft inner tissue of the branch."

"Pith. Huh. I remember that as in pithing frogs in lab."

"Yup, that's another meaning. We're right on top of him."

Socrates pulled out his phone, tapped Guy's contact icon, and raised the phone to his ear.

"Guy? We tracked this son of a bitch to a trail. Followed him along the bottom of the valley where he crashed, alongside a riverbed, then up an incline to a plateau, through a few scattered trees, cut through some heavy brush, and finally broke out into a trail. Google puts us about four miles up the mountain from you."

He waited. Nodded a few times.

"He's headed back down the mountain, which makes sense. He's hurt and now that he's on a trail, he's going to want to follow the path of least resistance. Send a couple of your guys out to the trailhead and tell 'em to walk up it. If we're right, we'll meet along the trail. We'll come in on both sides of this asshole."

Socrates put the phone back into his pocket. Looked at Tyler.

"We've got him," he said.

Rosita held up Max's phone.

"Dallas," she said.

Max grabbed the phone.

"Dallas!" he said. "We've got a problem. I've got three hurt women here and they need help. I'm headed south on the 195, about ten miles out of Greencreek."

Max paused and listened.

"Yep. Things got hot there and we had to hit the road running, didn't have time to set fire to the place like I wanted to. Still, the Bannisters can't fail to notice."

He listened some more.

"A junction? Just before a place called Freedom?"

Max nodded.

"OK. I'll let you know."

He handed the phone back to Rosita, checked his mirrors, and put his foot down.

"Should be at a hospital in ten minutes," he said. "We'll be in and out of there as fast as we can and hope to God a little place like that doesn't have any cops on duty in the ER."

Rosita braced herself as the van leapt forward, the speedometer nearing triple digits.

Raymond was disconcerted. He'd finally called Max, and... nothing. *What the hell*?

He took a deep breath, picked up the phone again.

He really had to let Max know about Mary Jane.

And Mack.

The whole shit storm.

The Old Man and Roger sat across from one another at the big meeting table in the den. The lights remained off, but there was enough ambient light over the stove top in the kitchen for them to see one another.

"Danny's not answering," Roger said. "We've got to assume he's down, somehow. Marty and them are still posted outside of Krell's compound, and they say Danny took off following some van that split out of the compound there. He had a feeling it was our number-one asshole, and went after him. Left the others to watch the compound, make sure."

The Old Man said nothing.

"Mack's fucked up, but moving. He's on a trail up the mountain. Looking over a map of the area, I'm thinking he's got to be on that trail that goes up to Lake Berlin."

The Old Man said nothing.

"Sherman recovered Bill's fuck toy, and is holed up at that shack on Novakovich's outside Paluma."

"That bitch is MINE," the Old Man said.

Roger nodded.

"You bet, Pops. All yours. No problem. I sent a team out to meet Sherman and grab her. They'll take her down to Red Rock and get her all set up for you. Sherman's all fucked up, and his truck is shot to shit, so they'll bring up another truck and then go get Mack."

Silence.

"Billy and Wilder and his boys are on the road, but still about seven hours away. They're ready for war."

"Call Danny again," the Old Man said.

Roger knew better than to argue. He lifted the phone and punched in Danny's number, keeping his eyes on the Old Man.

The phone in Danny's pocket buzzed.

He shook his head and opened his eyes to see concerned-looking eyes peering down at him.

What the fuck?

He sat up and the world rocked as his head exploded in agony.

Hands reached out to push him back down.

He knocked them away angrily, brought his hands up to his temples as they throbbed and the world swam before him.

Gradually, things stopped spinning and he oriented himself.

Rest stop.

Oh. Yeah. Saw the van, went for it, something...rolled the truck...the asshole!

"Shit," Danny said. He tried to stand, lost his balance, had to sit down.

The phone is his pocket buzzed some more.

"Mister?" said a voice.

Danny's vision came back into focus. Four people had gathered around him. He was on the grass in the picnic area. His truck sat on its side about ten yards from him.

"Don't worry, Mister," one of the men said. "We called 911. They'll be here soon."

"Shit," Danny said. He fought his way to his feet and stood, swaying. "Don't need no 911, damn it."

The men around him glanced at one another. The one doing the talking stepped forward.

"Beg to differ, mister. You climbed out of that truck then fell off the side and knocked yourself out on the pavement. You been out at least 30 minutes now."

Thirty minutes? Fuck.

The phone in his pocket buzzed again.

"Can't do 911," Danny said.

The buzzing in his pocket again.

Phone.

He pulled it out and looked at it.

Through the spider-webbed glass, the caller ID was clear: Roger.

"Oh, fuck," Danny said. He waved the little knot of men away and wandered to a table and sat down.

The men looked at one another again, but gave him his distance.

Marcus slowed as the lights of Paluma twinkled ahead.

"Damn it," he said. "If we ain't got him yet, we're not going to."

Timmy nodded from the passenger seat.

"Son of a bitch got away," he said. He slapped the dash in frustration.

Marcus hit the turn signal and pulled off the main road at a mile marker, just out of town.

"Let me turn around," he said. "You call Guy and give them

the score. We'll drive back there, decide what to do next."

Timmy glanced down at his phone, dialed, brought it to his ear and waited for it to connect.

Marcus punched the accelerator in frustration, and the big Silverado zipped down the dirt road, raising a tail of dust behind it.

The junction off 195 came into view and Max slowed.

"Look for signs for a hospital," he said.

He and Rosita leaned forward to scan the road ahead.

"There!" Rosita said.

"Good," Max said. "Hospital's supposed to be right off the 195 here. We'll be in and out as fast as we can."

Rosita settled back into her seat as Max slowed for the off ramp.

Raymond took a deep breath and punched Max's number one more time.

Please answer, buddy. Please.

Dread of delivering the news had shifted to dread that Max wouldn't answer. Would never answer again, in fact. Visions of Max, bloody and lifeless, swam before Raymond's eyes.

Ring tone.

"Hello?"

A woman's voice.

What the hell?

"Rosita?" Raymond said. "What the hell? Are you with Max?"

Max's voice came on the line.

"Raymond? What is it?"

Sherman had pulled the pick up around the side of the shack in the lee of the road and parked where he could keep an eye out for reinforcements. His head and shoulder hurt like hell.

He glanced back in the bed of the pick up again.

The bitch was alive. That was all that mattered.

He fingered the rifle sitting on his lap.

Damn, it'd be good to put a bullet in her knee, watch her writhe a little. Maybe pour some gasoline into the wound. No, Draino. That was the ticket. He'd pour a bottle of that shit onto the wound. A tablespoon at a time.

Lights bounced down the road approaching him.

He tightened his grip on his weapon.

Didn't look like one of the Bannister trucks.

Who in the hell?

Max eased the van to the side of the road.

"Say that again," he said.

Raymond told him about the attack, the truck going off the side, big bearded guy snatching Mary Jane, Marcus and Timmy setting off in pursuit, Socrates and Tyler on the tail of the survivor of the truck.

Max closed his eyes and rested his head against the wheel.

"You got to be shitting me," he said. "You guys lost Mary Jane."

Max pictured Mary Jane in the bunker, the barn at Bill's, the twisted faces of men in the grip of the Presence taking their pleasure....

It almost brought him to tears.

He sat up.

"No word from Marcus and Timmy?"

"Nothing good," Raymond said.

"Call 'em," Max said. "Tell 'em to keep going. Whoever grabbed Mary Jane is going to be heading back to the Bannisters. See if someone can't set up a lookout on Old Man Bannister's place."

He hung up and put the van in drive, aimed it down the road toward the hospital.

Marcus eased off the gas as a shack at the end of the road came into view. There was a clearing there with space to whip the truck around and head back.

Timmy's phone rang.

"Hello?" he said.

Marcus reached the clearing and swung the truck around.

A truck at the side of the shack.

Something not right...

"Timmy! Get down!" Marcus yelled.

Gunfire erupted out of the truck. Bullets pinged off of the Silverado. The passenger window shattered.

Marcus punched down on the gas, the truck bouncing across the rough ridges of a plowed field. The wheel wrenched in his hands as a tire exploded and the truck lurched to one side and dug itself into the field, stuck.

"Out, out, out!" Marcus yelled, but Timmy was already out and in a position of cover behind the truck, his AR aimed back across the field toward the truck behind the shack, firing in patterns of three.

"Marcus!" he yelled. "That's him!"

Marcus took a position next to Timmy.

"No shit," he said.

Marcus fired a short burst at the cab of the truck as its back wheels spun and the truck jumped forward, heading up the dirt road.

Timmy joined, and they both fired into the cab as the truck slipped out of sight and up the road.

"Damn it!" Marcus yelled.

He and Timmy took off across the field at a tangent to the head of the road, hoping to cut off the truck before it reached the main road.

Sherman was frantic. He'd reopened the wound above his eyebrow with all the bouncing around, his left arm hurt like a son of a bitch, and now he had a point of fire spreading out from the trapezius on his right side.

Son of a bitch.

He needed to call Roger, tell him what was up, but it was all he could do to handle the truck.

The main road came into view and he hammered down the accelerator.

The wheels spun on the dirt, then screeched as they caught the pavement. The truck raised up a bit, swung way over the center line, swerved, came back into the lane and gradually straightened out as Sherman pointed it towards Paluma.

Little flashes of light behind him informed him they were still shooting, but nothing touched him.

God damn it.

He kept the pedal to the metal as the outskirts of Paluma rose up around him, slid around a couple of corners, slowed, found an alley and parked behind a garage.

God damn it.

Sherman fumbled for his phone.

Mack paused.

Something behind him.

He froze, all senses alert, listening.

There!

A boot scrape.

They were almost on him.

He scanned the trail frantically, looking for a place to hide.

Not much cover. The trail led through an alpine forest, plenty of space between the trees, very little brush.

A big tree at a bend in the trail.

Mack tiptoed to the tree and slipped behind it.

He reached for his gun.

Gone.

Fucking hell.

Mack squatted, swaying a little from the pain and exhaustion, his useless left arm unbalancing him.

He pawed around his ankle, came up with the little .38 he kept in an ankle holster. The boys used to tease him about it being a bitch's gun, or had until he'd gotten pissed off one night and crippled one who'd gotten a little too lippy.

We'll see who's a bitch now, he thought.

Max swung the van into the circle drive in front of the

entrance to the ER.

He leapt out as the van came to a rest, slid the door open, and gently lifted the woman he'd found hanging with her hands behind her back.

She looked horrible: limbs twisted at impossible angles, face puffy and discolored, one eye swollen completely shut, burn marks and cuts scoring her naked body.

Max stepped through the doors as they slid open and set her on a gurney sitting empty against the wall.

Another gurney sat at its head, and Max slipped back outside for the next woman.

As he set her down on the only remaining gurney a nurse approached rapidly, her soft shoes making no noise on the hard stone floor.

"Horrible fire, outside of town," Max said.

The nurse's hands came up to her mouth as the women on the gurneys came into view.

"Oh, my God!" the nurse murmured.

She moved quickly to the side of the first woman Max had brought in, her hands fluttering about helplessly before her training took over and she began a more careful inspection.

Max returned with the last woman and eased her into a padded chair in the lobby. The woman's blood discolored the thick beige arms of the chair.

"This was no fire," the nurse said.

She grabbed a walkie talkie clipped to her belt.

"Security to the ER," she said. "And a full trauma team. Call in Dr. Gruender and Dr. Martin. We're going to need everybody."

She turned to address Max, but he was already gone. The taillights of the van winked red as he hit the road in front of the hospital, turned right and disappeared.

CHAPTER FORTY TWO

"At the rest stop just outside of Greencreek, but I got to get out of here," Danny said into the phone.

"Was it him?" Roger asked.

"Yeah. It was our mystery man, all right. Fuckin' ambushed me, or I would've had him."

He glanced around the rest stop.

The men who'd been helping him had formed a little knot, conferring.

"They fuckin' called 911. Cops'll be here any minute."

A pause and then, "We got Winter, up in Greencreek," Roger said. "911 is likely to come out of the hospital down by Freedom; it'll take 'em probably 40 minutes to get there. I need to call Winter anyway, just in case the asshole is heading that way."

"Better fuckin' hurry, man," Danny said.

"Excuse me?" Roger said.

Danny's vision sharpened, and his heart bumped. You *never* wanted to be on the wrong side of Roger when his voice went flat like that.

"I'm sorry boss. I'm all fucked up here. Forgot myself."

A deep breath sounded down the line.

"You sit tight, you hear me? Nothing else stupid."

"No, sir. Nothing else."

Danny put the phone in his coat pocket and leaned forward, sweat sticking the shirt to his back.

Roger was pissed in that quiet way he got.

Danny's heart bumped a couple of times, rattled his chest.

He wasn't so sure he wanted this Winter guy to find him. Not so sure at all.

Boots on the hard dirt. Two sets.

Mack hunkered behind the tree he'd chosen.

The men were almost on him. If he timed this just right, he'd take care of both of them and be on his way.

Roger'd have someone up to the trailhead within a couple of hours. He'd be back home by breakfast time.

He gripped the little .38 in his right hand, wiped sweat from his brow with his sleeve.

Stung like a son of a bitch, all the little cuts and shit on his face.

Now!

He burst out from his position, gun up and firing.

Timmy caught the movement off to his left and behind.

Ambush.

"Marcus!" he yelled, pushing Marcus' shoulder and diving off to one side.

Marcus rolled with the push, heard and felt a bullet go zizzing by his ear as he hit the ground, bringing his legs up in a scissor kick to sweep the gunman's legs out from under him.

The man came down like a sack of lead, and hit the hard dirt of the trail with an audible thump. He bellowed like a cow that'd been tipped in a field, and the gun flew out of his hand.

Marcus rolled some more and launched himself at the man, scrambled on top of him, and brought down a couple of hard rights hands.

The man bucked and struggled briefly, then sagged.

Marcus grabbed the man's hands and pinned them together.

He could hear bone on bone grind somewhere as he did so, the sound of a badly fractured arm or shoulder. The man under him twitched, but did not otherwise react.

"Timmy!" Marcus called. "You OK?"

Timmy rose up beside him.

"I'm good." He reached a hand up to his ear. "Fucker shot the tip of my earlobe off, though."

He reached over and toed the man on the ground.

"He don't look so good, does he?" Timmy asked.

Blood bubbled out of the man's nose, his face a mess of abrasions and bruises. His shoulder looked awkward, even lying on the ground.

"Dangerous little snake, isn't he?" Marcus said.

He eased off the downed man and did a quick pat down, relieving him of his phone and wallet.

He opened the wallet and started going through it.

"Hot damn," he said.

Timmy raised his eyebrows.

"We got ourselves Mack Bannister," Marcus said.

"The Bully himself!" Timmy said.

"Indeed."

"Finally got us a break here," Marcus said.

The cop's phone buzzed in Max's pocket, startling him. He'd forgotten all about it.

He and Rosita were parked in an RV park on the outskirts of Freedom.

Max felt pinned down, helpless.

Mary Jane was back in Bannister hands and Max had drawn a whole community of good people into this fight.

The plan had been to keep moving forward. Down the line. Taking out Bannister motels, massage parlors, bars, nasty little farm set ups like the one he'd met Roger at...just keep moving, painting a line of fire, get the Bannisters spread out and after him....

And then what?

Put an end to it. An end to it all: the Bannisters, the Presence, the reign of evil tainting the land...

How? And would it work? Would it free him of the ghastly visions? Would all the unhappy dead finally leave him in peace?

Would...

He pushed the questions aside as the phone buzzed again.

He pulled it out of his pocket and looked at the screen.

The caller ID read, "Roger."

"Huh," Max grunted.

Rosita stirred in the seat beside him, asleep. Her hands, palms together, formed a rest for her cheek against the cushy leather seat in its full-back reclining position.

She was beautiful.

He answered the phone, "Yeah?"

"Winter! Round up the boys and a couple of trucks. I need you out at the rest stop north of town, fast as you can get there."

Max grinned.

"Winter can't come to the phone right now," he said, a curious sense of déjà vu coloring his night.

Max could feel the jolt all the way down the line.

"You," Roger said, his voice quiet and flat.

"Name's Max," Max said.

"Your name's shit," Roger said. "We're going to make a play-toy out of you. Name's going to be Gimp, maybe Dickless, maybe..."

"How's the head, Roger? Last time I saw you, you weren't doing so well."

Silence.

"Ribs? Ribs take a long time to heal. Seems like I cracked a few."

"That's it," Roger said in a quiet, flat voice. "Laugh it up. Enjoy yourself. Won't be long now before I have you bent over a rack, spine just about bust, taking my pleasure with you. Not long at all."

A click and a beep as the line went dead.

A chill worked its way up Max's spine and he set the phone down on the dash, keeping a wary eye on it, as if it might leap up and bite him.

Roger looked across at the Old Man.

Dressed in crisp Levi 501s, plaid shirt tucked in behind a big and polished rodeo champion belt buckle, he looked every inch the rancher he was. The lines etched into his face painted a picture of a harsh man with a temper, a cruel streak.

The Old Man sipped from the mug of coffee he held in his hands.

"The asshole has Winter's phone," he said.

Roger nodded. "Said his name's Max."

"Max," The Old Man said. "Huh. Not for long."

"That's what I told him."

"I heard you," the Old Man said. "Better call The Play Box, though I expect you'll find Asshole's been through there."

"He can't be too far from there, then," Roger said. "Billy and them are heading right his way. Still hours out, but that puts the asshole between Billy and the guys we got posted outside of Krell's. We could maybe close in on him, if we send everyone after him."

The Old Man stood and walked to the window.

The horizon was almost visible as the night stood on the edge of dawn, sunrise an hour off or less.

"Lot of road. Unlikely to catch him that way," the Old Man said.

He held the mug of coffee in both hands, the warmth easing the ache in them. He'd broken his hands numerous times over the years, all in the name of having a good time, but the price he paid was a constant ache, sort of a low-level arthritis.

"Nope," the Old Man said. "That ain't likely to work. What we need is to draw him in. And we got the bait."

Marcus and Timmy struggled down the trail with Mack. He was a huge man, and only half conscious. His feet snagged on rocks and roots, and he'd stagger and almost fall, wailing in pain as the bones in his shoulder ground into one another with each jolt.

"Keep moving, you asshole," Marcus said, prodding him.

Mack moved as if to punch, then winced from the pain.

"Serves you right, idiot," Timmy said.

They turned a corner and the trail opened up into a parking lot.

The trailhead. Finally.

As they moved into the lot, a van flashed its lights.

Marcus and Timmy aimed Mack at the van and shuffled him across the lot.

Sherman sighed in relief.

Two big pickups rumbled down the alley.

The troops had arrived.

One truck pulled in ahead of him, lights blinding, the other swung around behind.

Men climbed out of the trucks.

Sherman held his hands up, shielding himself from the headlights.

"Turn those fuckin' lights off," he said.

The men flanked his truck: two on the driver's side, two on the passenger.

"You look like shit," said one, leaning in the window to look Sherman up and down. "Bitch do all that to you?"

"The fuck's wrong with you?" Sherman said. "I been shot at all night long. I been..."

"Yeah, we heard," said the one leaning up against the truck. He straightened, and his arm came up. The others stepped away. At the end of his arm a long silver pistol gleamed in the glow from the street light at the end of the alley. The muzzle flashed and a tremendous boom! reverberated off the buildings around them. Sherman's head exploded like a pumpkin tossed out of a speeding car.

"Damn!" the man said. "I always get a kick out of that."

He holstered his pistol and vaulted over the side of Sherman's truck into the truck bed.

Mary Jane squirmed and rolled in the back. Duct tape bound

her arms tightly behind her back, wrapped her ankles and knees together, a final long strip around her mouth. Her eyes were round and large. Rage, pain, helplessness, and fear poured off of her. She rolled to her back and raised her legs, bending them at the knees, aiming to kick the men in the truck.

One of the men laughed.

"Got some fight in her, this one," he said.

"You see how fucked up Sherman was?" another said.

The first man laughed again as he maneuvered into a position to make a grab at Mary Jane. "Got to admire that," he said. "Me, I like 'em with a little fire in 'em."

The other man snorted as he jumped into the truck and leaned down to grab Mary Jane by the legs.

"Like 'em on fire, you mean," he said, grunting as Mary Jane bucked and kicked.

"Looks like he at least got her trussed up proper," the first said.

"Yep."

They handed the twisting, bucking, frantic Mary Jane over the side to the other two men who carried her over to one of the trucks.

The first man vaulted back over the side and moved quickly to the truck blocking Sherman's in and opened the door, then leaned the passenger seat forward.

The two carrying Mary Jane tossed her into the space behind the seat like she were a duffel bag, and the first man returned the passenger seat to its position.

The four men squared up.

"Albert, you run this bitch down to Red Rock," the first man said. "Don't stop on the way. You got plenty of gas. The Old Man don't want no fuck ups, clear?"

Albert looked over his shoulder at the bloody mess in Sherman's cab.

"Crystal," he said.

He walked to the driver's side and hopped in.

"Good luck getting Mack back," Albert said.

"Luck ain't got nothing to do with it," the first man said. He pulled his pistol out of its holster, jacked the magazine out and thumbed in a bullet.

He slammed the full magazine back into the pistol, and Albert eased the truck down the alley and turned towards the main road.

The three men climbed into the other truck, swung it around Sherman's, and followed.

Max pulled the ledgers out and opened them.

Mountain Cleft, Greencreek.

Check and check.

Hangman. Jackpot. Wells. A dozen others, most of them smaller—two to three men operations by the looks of things—then: Red Rock.

Based on the ledger, Red Rock had a crew of up to twenty men working there. Utility bills like those of an industrial plant.

Max ran a finger down the pages of the ledger and paused as the aura that presaged his "gift" swelled and he felt the weight of the dead pressing in on him.

Finger stuck on the page, Max closed his eyes.

The all-too-familiar circus of pain and death paraded across the closed lids of his eyes. The stench of blood and guts. The buzz of flies...the number of women that had died at the hands of these men was staggering.

A gentle hand reached out and brushed tears he hadn't known he'd shed from his cheeks.

He opened his eyes to see Rosita leaning in, concern on her face.

He reached up and gently moved her hand back to its place by her side.

"Don't worry any, Rosita," he said. "I'm fine. Just tired, is all."

"You need some sleep," Rosita said. "Dawn is not far away. Let's find someplace."

Max straightened, then fired up the van and put it into gear.

"We'd better put some more distance between us and the hospital," he said. "I'm sure they've got police and state troopers on this by now."

"Even better reason to find a place and wait," Rosita said.

"Maybe," Max said.

The van rolled off the RV lot and onto the street.

Max headed east—visions of Red Rock dancing in his head.

Danny put the phone back in his pocket.

So, the asshole had run through Greencreek as easily as he'd run through Hotel 29. As easily as he'd taken down Bill Bannister. As easily as he'd beat the living hell out of both Roger and Mack Bannister.

Holy shit, Danny thought. *Maybe I'd better just get me the fuck out of this party*.

He cocked his head as he considered it.

On the other hand, there were certain perks the Bannisters provided that you just couldn't get anywhere else. Sure, he could head out on his own, find his own game...but it wouldn't be the same. And he wouldn't have Bannister protection.

Also, he wanted a little payback. Old Man Bannister would give him a day with the asshole, eventually.

Danny took a look around the rest stop.

A beautiful huge Dodge pickup gleamed in a parking space in front of the Men's Toilet.

Danny hitched up his pants and strolled back over to the knot of men eyeing him warily.

Danny pointed at the truck.

"Which of you owns that fine piece of automobile?" Danny asked.

The men looked at each other.

Danny saw a flash of fear in the eyes of the younger guy, a sturdy-looking buck in a cowboy hat and jeans.

He grinned at the man and pulled his pistol out.

"I need to get moving now," Danny said. "Ease your keys out nice and easy and toss them to me."

A sudden movement to his side.

Danny spun that way, squeezing the trigger as he moved.

The 9mm bullet caught the man square in the face. His momentum carried him forward and dropped him at Danny's feet.

The remaining three had gone white and each had his hands raised in alarm and surrender.

"I am not fucking around here," Danny said. "I told you I need to get moving. Now toss me them fucking keys."

The side door on the van in the parking lot at the trailhead slid open.

Marcus and Timmy pushed Mack toward the dark opening.

Mack bucked and reared back with his head, attempting to head butt Marcus.

Marcus simply leaned out of the way and allowed his movement to twist Mack's arm in a way that ground the shoulder bones against one another.

Mack cried out and fell to his knees in agony.

"Just a big pussy, isn't he?" Timmy said.

Mack glared up at them, tears and murder in his eyes.

"You two are going to die," he said. "Real slow. I'm going to take care of it personally."

Marcus looked at him a second, considering, then kicked him square in the solar plexus, bending him over.

He and Timmy each grabbed Mack by an arm and tossed him into the back of the waiting van.

"Maybe," Marcus said. "Maybe not."

They climbed in after Mack, nodded at the two men in the van, and took up position watching over Mack as one of the men slid the door shut and the other started up the van.

The tires crunched over the gravel lot as the van left the trailhead, then went quiet as the van reached the 1 and headed back up the mountain towards the gas station.

CHAPTER FORTY THREE

Dallas Krell stirred in his sleep.

His phone on the night stand next to his bed vibrated again.

Marcus reporting in.

4:00 AM.

Dallas sat up and grabbed the phone, slid his feet over the side, and let them hit the floor.

"Dallas," he said.

Marcus related the evening's events.

"So," Dallas said. "We're in a war."

"Like it or not," Marcus said.

Dallas nodded, only half aware Marcus couldn't see him.

"You figure they'll be hitting the compound?" Dallas asked.

"Maybe, maybe not," Marcus said. "According to Raymond, Max busted up a place down in Greencreek. Took out the local Sheriff—a Bannister man. Winter something-or-other. Also had a run in with a Bannister man at the rest stop just outside of Greencreek. So…if the Bannisters are after him, maybe that's the way they'll run."

"And maybe not," Dallas said. "Old Man Bannister's never been known for letting things slip or going half-assed about anything. Best to be ready for them."

"We've got four teams ready," Marcus said. "Perimeter wire, DFPs. Shit, I say 'bring it.'"

Dallas stood.

"You're right," he said. "Let's put this long, sordid mess to an end. Tell you what. Don't let them hold Mack up there. If

Old Man Bannister's got any sense, he'll send up a team of real killers to get him back."

"Ah," Marcus said. "Bring him to the compound."

"Exactly," Dallas said. "And we'll see what we can see."

"I'll put it to them," Marcus said. "I expect they'll be happy to be rid of him. Truth be told, though they're looking tough and mean, I think they're shitting their pants a little bit."

Dallas put the phone down and moved out of the room.

Time to get to work.

Max's eyes moved from the road ahead, to the side roads off the freeway, to the driver's side mirror, the rear view mirror, the passenger side mirror then back forward again. He opened the door to his "gift" enough to keep his awareness tingling.

An old Chevy Bel Air convertible lay on its side as the Ford flashed by. The driver was impaled on the steering column, a woman in a red dress (!) halfway through the windshield, the skin peeled off her face and neck, a splash of blood over the whole front of the car like a gigantic impressionist painting.

Max's eyes continued their careful scan of the environment.

Nobody ahead worth worrying about.

Nobody coming up behind.

Max felt Red Rock pulling him forward like a maelstrom sucking him into its vortex.

And that was OK.

One way or another, he was ready.

He glanced over at Rosita, sleeping in the passenger's seat beside him.

Just one problem to take care of before he got there.

He let his mind run over the list of Bannister properties.

Probably best to take out a few more, let the Bannisters know he was still coming, and coming hard. Might take some of the pressure off of Raymond and Dallas.

The road ahead of him blurred as ghosts of Bannister victims rose in his mind's eye. The first hotel, back in Aston. The farm where he'd confronted Roger. The horror show at Bill

Bannister's.

So many women.

The van swerved and Max forced himself back into the moment.

Rosita stirred in her sleep, turned her back to Max and settled in again.

It's coming, Max thought.

He could feel it in his gut.

All of it. Coming to a head.

La raison d'être for my gift.

Good, he thought.

Finally.

The rising sun pinkened the sky and laid its paintbrush across the long stretch of fields that disappeared into the horizon. *Such a peaceful, pastoral setting*, Raymond thought. *Who would have thought the evil to be found here*?

He sat in the passenger seat of the van, Timmy and Marcus in back, watching over Mack, tied and trussed on the floor. Chad's fingers drummed on the steering wheel as the lights of Paluma twinkled behind them.

Chad steered the van towards Ramsey, headed on through to Mountain Cleft and Krell's compound. He glanced over his shoulder at a thump of boot heels on the thinly carpeted metal floor, and a wild grunt.

Mack was acting up again. Given his penchant for ropes and other devices, he didn't seem to much care for being on the receiving end of things.

Marcus reached over with the toe of his boot and nudged Mack in the shoulder, causing him to kick and bellow once more.

"You keep acting up, I'm going to have to knock you out," Marcus said.

Mack kicked viciously at him with both feet, his legs taped together.

Marcus moved out of the way, and he and Timmy effortlessly rolled Mack over onto his belly.

Mack's muffled scream rose over the road noise, died down, rose again as Marcus and Timmy quickly hog-tied his feet to his ankles.

"That was stupid, Mack," Marcus said, regaining his seat.

He leaned down and grabbed Mack by the hair, lifting his face enough that their eyes met.

Murder and pain poured out of Mack's eyes.

"This is where you ought to be conserving your energy," Marcus counseled. "You got a long road ahead of you."

He dropped Mack's head, his face twanging off the floor, then wiped his hand off on Mack's jacket.

"Greasy motherfucker," Marcus said.

Raymond turned his attention back to the road and fished his phone out of his pocket.

"You got Mack?" Max asked.

Max guided the Ford down a dusty two-lane road toward the town of Hangman. He'd decided to leave another message for the Bannisters. He was tired as hell, but figured he had one more stop in him before he put up somewhere to rest.

Rosita sat alert in the passenger seat, apparently enjoying the beauty of the sun rising over the fields ahead.

"We're on the way to Krell's now," Raymond said. "Socrates and Tyler are trailing us, and Guy's out front."

"I'd step on it if I were you," Max said. In the back of his mind he could feel the red Presence, the countryside alive with evil, the Bannister crew thrashing about like a pack of sharks in heavily chummed water.

"I expect Bannisters'll have every man on alert, looking for anything they can find. I plan on leaving them another message pretty quick here, ought to disperse their attention a little bit, but there's no way they're not watching every single car, truck, train, van, and carrier pigeon heading through their territory."

Raymond glanced around the van, looked ahead to spot Guy's truck, checked the side mirror to see Tyler behind the wheel, Socrates slumped in sleep against the passenger window behind him.

"I think we're good," Raymond said.

"Best stay ready," Max said.

Max leaned left as the road curved and rose up a hill. At the crest of the hill, the vista below opened up and Hangman spread out below.

Much like Greencreek, Hangman was a tiny town built around a set of silos and a railway line. It'd see quite a lot of action around harvest time, Max figured, farmers bringing all the grain in, trains taking it away, but that'd leave the bulk of the year, for, well, he wasn't quite sure what.

One thing was clear: the red Presence was alive and kicking around here. He could feel its tentacles waving, looking for something tasty.

That was all right, too, he figured. He planned on meeting them head on.

And quick.

Roger and the Old Man sat at the big table in the den. The sun was halfway up on the horizon, and the table was crowded with men. Two women dressed up like sexy French maids served them platters of sausage, bacon and eggs, toast, pancakes, pitchers of coffee. Normally the men would be joking around, slapping some ass, pinching a nipple here and there, but the mood today was somber and glowering.

They were going to war.

The Old Man set his coffee mug down with a bang.

Every man at the table froze; the Old Man had 100% attention.

"We got a big day ahead," the Old Man said. "Roger has team assignments for all of you."

The Old Man picked up his fork, speared a sausage link, waved it at the men.

"Roger's going to bring every one of you up to speed. I don't have to tell you your asses are on the line. You either get this son-of-a-bitch, or I'll sell your ass to somebody who wants to play with it, you catch my meaning."

The men stiffened. Once, a man had defied a direct order from the Old Man. Story was, The Old Man had broken him down over a month's time down at Red Rock. Devoted himself to seeing just how far he could take things without pushing them over the edge, then had sold the broken man to a certain —demon—down in South America with a taste for badly broken toys. Story went that the man was still used as an entertainment piece at special parties.

The Old Man put the sausage link in his mouth and chewed, his eyes roving over the men in front of him.

Satisfied, he swallowed, picked up his coffee mug, took a drink, then held it out for a refill.

A pretty young Latina took it from his hand and was filling it before the Old Man had time to blink.

She set it down carefully on the coaster at the Old Man's setting.

The Old Man reached out, stroked her bare ass, then stood.

"You men get to work."

He grabbed his coffee and strode from the room.

All attention turned to Roger, who sipped his coffee, then cleared his throat.

"All right," he said. "Let's get this show on the road."

Dallas sat at the big table in his great room and looked at the men assembled in front of him.

Plates were cleaned of food and each man had coffee in front of him. The mood was tense and expectant, but excited. Every man in the room had suffered under the Bannisters' iron grip one way or another. Each man stared into the steam rising from his mug, playing back memories of abuse and grief: fathers beaten and broken, sisters fondled or worse, businesses burned or extorted, the dismal cloud of the Bannister presence.

"I don't have to tell you men what kind of evil is coming," Dallas said. "You've all lived it, and you know it, or you wouldn't be out here with us."

He stood.

"One thing's certain," Dallas said. "No one's taking this compound." He paused for emphasis. "It'd take a trained battalion to take this place, with air support."

The men grinned.

"We have lookouts on all roads leading in already. Some of you will be spelling them on a regular basis until this is over. We are loading up the perimeter wire with Claymores. We have patrols. DFPs in place. The bunkers are stocked and ready. The women and children have drilled and know what to do. We are survivors. We will prevail!"

Men thumped the table and hooted support.

Dallas raised a thick finger. "But that don't mean we can get cocky." He looked around the table and met each man's gaze. "Bannisters got numbers. Truth is, we got no idea just how many they got. Once we get Mack across the wire and in here… they'll be coming. They'll keep coming. They ain't likely to forget him or give up. This will be war."

The men quieted.

"But like I said, no one is taking this compound. We will survive."

Dallas sipped his coffee.

"But we're going to have to fight for it. As far as we are concerned, this is the war to end all wars. This is where we take back our patch of country, where we put down pure evil, where good prevails."

Dallas leaned down and tapped his laptop, bringing it to life. The big LED screen on the wall showed a detailed layout of the compound. Areas were color coded for teams and bunkers, the perimeter a bright red line with little yellow "danger" triangles where the Claymores were positioned.

He tapped his laptop a few more times and windows

appeared on the screen, each showing the view of a security camera: a view in each direction where the road leading to the compound met the main road passing by; another two cameras covering a 180 degree arc of the road leading up the mountain just past the wire perimeter at the other end of the compound; a cam from the barn; others from the bunkers—dozens of cams.

"We are secure," Dallas said.

He stood and folded his arms across his chest.

"Gentlemen," he said. "Let's keep it that way. Do not let your guard down. Do not relax. Do not forget they are coming. Do not forget who they are and what they are capable of. Do not forget who we are and what we stand for. Think on your wives and kids. Think on your parents and grandparents. Think on the future: what we do here today, and in the days coming, determines all of our fates."

He bowed his head; "Lord, watch over us this day. Guide us. Show us the way. Your will be done, amen."

The men echoed, "Amen," then stood as a group, cleared their plates and mugs and filed through the kitchen on the way out the door, to take up their positions.

Danny fishtailed the big Dodge pickup through the corners into Greencreek. The big beast ran like a dream and he was pleased with it, a little sad that he'd have to part with it so soon, but there was no driving this thing around, not for long. The men he'd left standing back at the rest stop were likely giving out the license plate and his description at the very moment.

He'd considered killing them all, in for a penny, in for a pound, all that, but truth was, he wasn't sure he'd have been able to get them all down if they rushed him. The likelihood of them rushing had seemed remote, but not so remote it was worth gambling his freedom on.

The big engine roared as he punched it, sliding the rear end around the curve that put him on the main road through town headed straight for The Play Box.

He raced through the streets in the dawn light, the sky rosy and pink, the silos down the hill ahead still silhouetted and dark, the fields leading to them tinged golden as sunlight touched the tips of the wheat.

A big man stood in the parking lot of The Play Box, hands on his hips, watching as other men scurried about picking detritus off the lot, tossing it into the bed of a pick up that kept pace.

The big man spun, and a pistol was in his hand, aimed straight at Danny.

He was wearing a cop uniform.

Danny slammed the brakes on, the truck digging grooves in the gravel lot, and raised his hands.

"Woah, woah!" he yelled. He kept his hands visible and nodded at the big man, who approached the pickup cautiously, both hands on his weapon, the barrel steady as a rock.

Danny could see the size of the bore as he approached. Thing was at least a .44 if not a full-on Desert Eagle .50.

"Winter!" Danny called.

The tip of the pistol bobbled as Winter straightened and narrowed his eyes, trying to identify who he was dealing with.

"It's me, Danny," Danny said. "Roger sent me."

Danny stepped cautiously out of the truck and faced Winter.

The big man had a lump on his forehead and the look of a man pissed off enough to kill someone just to ease the pressure.

Which described Winter's mood exactly.

A backhoe rumbled around the corner and headed their way.

"Danny?" Winter asked.

"Don't be fucking stupid," Danny said. "Who the fuck else would it be?"

The backhoe came closer, and Winter holstered his gun.

The driver leaned over and yelled at Winter, "Dug a nice deep hole out in the grounds out back by the others. Everything's neat and tidy."

Winter nodded at the man and waved him on.

The backhoe lumbered away.

"You might want to be calling him back," Danny said. "We got to hide this truck."

Winter eyeballed the truck and Danny balefully.

"The fuck you say? That's one hell of a hole."

"Exactly," Danny said. "The sooner the better in fact."

Winter whistled, a startlingly loud shriek that pierced through the rumble of the backhoe. The driver stopped, stuck his head out and peered back.

Winter waved him back.

"Come on," Danny said. "We got lots to do."

Winter sighed and nodded.

Raymond sat straight and tense in his seat as the road led into Aston. A gentle morning light lit the town and it gleamed and sparkled like a movie maker's image of quintessential small-town America. A curious mix of emotions ran through him: nostalgia, anger, comfort, shame, despair, and rage. Nostalgia for his past and ancestry, growing up here; anger for what the Bannisters had done to his town; shame for having lost Mary Jane; despair about getting her back; a growing rage coloring it all. He wanted Mary Jane back. He wanted his town back. He wanted the Bannisters dead and gone.

Chad downshifted and they followed Guy's pickup into town. Marcus and Timmy kept careful watch over Mack, who seemed unconscious or asleep at the moment.

Tyler and Socrates were both straight and alert in the pickup behind.

Sun winked off the picture window of Old Man Bannister's place up on the hill.

Raymond saw a number of trucks parked up there.

A gathering.

They drove quietly through the deserted streets of Aston, nothing moving except their cars.

A flash on the hill drew Raymond's eye back to the Bannister compound. Men were climbing into the trucks, their side mirrors catching the sun and reflecting it back toward town.

"Let's get moving," Raymond said.

Chad nodded and bumped his speed up a little as did the others.

Trucks circled around the Bannister lot, filed onto the single lane leading down the hill toward town.

Raymond rubbed the back of his hand across his brow and it came back wet with sweat. He glanced back at Marcus and Timmy, saw both of them watching the trucks heading down the hill.

The Bannister motel came up on Raymond's right.

Then Mack was on his feet, bellowing like a bull, making a rush for the side door. He got his back up against it, hands on the latch and had clicked the door open and slid it back, daylight pouring through it, as Marcus and Timmy each grabbed an arm and threw him back to the floor. The van rocked with their weight, bouncing Raymond up and down in his seat.

Marcus landed on Mack, spinning him around, face to the floor, and got a knee in the square of his back as Timmy slammed the door shut.

Raymond looked into the office of the motel as they passed and met the geezer behind the counter's eyes. He saw recognition flash across the old guy's face.

"Move, move, move!" Raymond yelled.

The convoy picked up speed and Raymond turned his head to see the geezer in the motel pick up the phone.

CHAPTER FORTY FOUR

Chris, Tony, and Hedges glanced around the gas station.

The windows were dark. Other than one car up on the lift in the garage bay, empty.

The men split up and circled the building, checking doors and windows.

The one who'd shot Sherman pulled out his big pistol, a gleaming silver Desert Eagle, a full .50 calibre behemoth and caressed it.

The other two looked at one another nervously.

"Nothing?" the man asked.

"Place is empty, Hedges," the taller one of the two said.

"That's some fine detecting, there, Chris. Fine detecting," Hedges said.

Tony, a solidly-built type with thick black hair on his muscled forearms, pointed to the edge of the gravel lot.

"Something went off there," he said.

Hedges eyeballed the first man, then slid his gaze over to the third.

"Now there's some detecting, Tony. Let's go take a look see," he said.

The three men walked over to the edge and peered down the steep incline.

Loose, unstable dirt and rock led down a thousand feet to level out where some evergreens bordered a creek that wound its way through the valley below.

A truck-sized slide of dirt and debris cut a swath to the

underside of a pickup truck, slammed up against the trees.

"Lookee what we found," Hedges said.

He looked meaningfully at the two men.

"Well, hop to it," he said.

The heavily muscled one, Tony, shrugged.

The two stood for a second, mentally carving a trail down the slide then stepped over the edge.

Hedges watched them slip and slide their way down the first hundred yards or so then turned his attention to the gas station.

Had to be something worth mentioning to the boss in there.

Max paused for a moment, exhausted.

Two men lay beaten and unconscious at his feet.

A third was strapped into a chair, glowering at him through the blood that streamed down his face from a split eyebrow.

"So," Max said. He glanced around at the implements lining the walls, the tables with stirrups and straps, the chains hanging from the ceiling. "No women here."

The man in the chair attempted to spit at Max. A bloody wad of spit and mucus landed in his lap.

"I thought we were past all that," Max said.

He reached out with the pistol in his hand and poked the man's eyebrow with the barrel. The man twitched away, and the sight on the tip of the barrel dug in and ripped the cut there open further, more blood cascading down his face.

"That was stupid," Max said.

He wiped the barrel off carefully on the man's shirt.

The man turned his head back and met Max's gaze.

"You're a dead man," he said. "Your body's going to be hanging from one of them chains before nightfall."

Max laughed.

"Been hearing that a lot lately," he said.

He poked the man in the solar plexus with the barrel, hard enough to knock the air out of him. The man leaned forward as far as the straps would let him.

Max closed his eyes for a moment, opened himself up.

The place was another horror show. As hardened to it as Max had become, the women's faces tore a place in his soul that he figured would never heal.

None of them were still alive. All here were ghosts. Dozens of them.

Through the open back door, Max could see the train tracks that led to a platform by the silos.

Same set up as back in Greencreek.

Women on trains.

A loading dock.

Transfer.

That made for a lot of women.

Max sighed, then picked up the red jerry jug of gasoline next to him and continued his work, carefully spreading an even layer around the concrete floor of the building.

Satisfied, he backed out to the door, where he'd set a propane torch.

The wind whistled through the open front door, both doors creating a breezeway.

Max stepped into the lee of the front door, sparked a lighter and lit the propane torch, then set it carefully down on the floor in the path of the front door.

"You got one chance," Max said. "If you can get yourself over here before the wind knocks this torch over, you might not burn to death."

Max grinned.

"Good luck," he said.

The phone rang and Roger picked it up.

"Hello?"

He stiffened and gripped the phone.

"You're sure?" he said.

Roger crossed the floor to the window and stared down at the town below.

A line of pickups wound down the Bannister driveway

towards town.

At the edge of town a pickup hit the main road out of town and sped off, followed tightly by a van and another pickup.

"Good work, Slim."

Roger thumbed off the call, scrolled quickly though Contacts and dialed a number.

"Curry!" Roger said. "Ingersoll just passed through town! White van! Every man on this! Step on it!"

Dust rose behind the lead truck heading down the hill as Curry punched it. The back end swiveled around the curves and a puff of smoke rose as the tires spun and caught the asphalt road in town.

The other trucks followed suit and soon a convoy was smoking down the road after Ingersoll.

"They'll be heading for Krell's." the Old Man had moved right up behind Roger in the silent way he had, startling Roger badly.

The Old Man huffed out a chuckle.

"Call Marty, whoever else Danny set out there. Tell 'im to swing his truck around and watch the road coming in, be ready to ambush that van. Slim get a make and model on it?"

"I didn't ask," Roger said.

The Old Man looked at him.

"On it," Roger said, putting the phone to his ear.

Raymond watched as the speedometer rose: 70, 80, 90, 95, 100....

They were tearing down the road, which was straight as a ruler for the most part. Good for speed, bad for evasive tactics.

Guy's white pickup ahead bounced and shimmied on the road. It was an older model, and 100 was top speed.

The landscape flashed by as Raymond scrambled to think of a way out.

Socrates bounced in the seat as the pickup went over an irregularity in the road at 100 miles an hour, his phone rubbing against his ear.

"Just outside of Ramsey," he said. "And we're pretty sure they're hot on our tail."

"Haven't seen 'em, yet?" Dallas asked.

"Nope, but Raymond says the old guy who recognized him at the Bannister motel went straight for the phone. Won't be long."

"Unlikely you'll make it all the way here without them catching you," Dallas said.

"That's what I was thinking," Socrates said.

"Tell you what," Dallas said. "Get everyone to take the back way. Head up the hills, circle back down and around, enter down through the residential compound."

"They'll be on us way before that," Socrates said.

"Good" Dallas said. "Here's what you're going to do...."

Mahler, a thin man with a worn face and tobacco-stained teeth, wrapped a hand around the strap up high beside the passenger door. He reached into his jacket pocket with the other and answered his phone.

"Yeah?"

He listened a minute, then broke into a grin.

"Yeah! We're on it!"

He turned to Guy, who had a white-knuckled grip on the steering wheel, trying to control the shimmy of the old vehicle as it strained to hold speed.

"You know that turn off that heads up to Cougar Mountain?"

Guy nodded.

"Aim for it," Mahler said.

Guy risked a look at Mahler.

"Back roads," Mahler said.

Mahler dialed Raymond.

Curry led the pack as it roared out of Ramsey.

Six pickup trucks in a tight line screaming down the road.

In each, men fingered weapons as imagery of blood and gunfire played over and over in their minds.

Several of the men felt the stirrings of arousal as they fondled their guns.

The mood was hot and ready.

Just about time to play.

Danny and Winter sat in the little police station in Greencreek.

Winter held an ice pack to the lump on his head, the swelling already down.

Danny had brought him up to speed and now Winter had a very specific target for his rage: a piece of shit named Max.

Winter pressed the button to release the magazine cartridge out of his Desert Eagle, thumbed out the big bullets into a pile on his desk, then reloaded it carefully and slid the cartridge back into the gun. He fished around in the drawer of the desk he was at and pulled out more cartridges, a couple of boxes of bullets and started loading bullets into the cartridges.

Danny picked up his phone, scrolled through it, pressed a number, then held the phone to his ear.

"Billy? Danny. Where the fuck you guys at?"

Billy eyed the odometer and the road ahead.

"I'd say about 40 miles out of Wells. Where are you?"

"Greencreek. Sitting here with the Sheriff hisself, Winter Young."

Billy chuckled.

"Crazy son-of-a-bitch, isn't he?"

"We'll see," Danny said. "Right now, he's a pissed off son-of-a-bitch. Our asshole came through here, took down The Play Box, got the women out, killed a couple of guys, and is gone."

A rush of rage so deep the copper taste of adrenaline filled his mouth flooded through Billy.

"God damn it," he said. "How the fuck? What...?"

"He's out on the road, headed your way, we figure," Danny said.

"What's he driving?"

"Some kind of a big white van," Danny said. "I trailed it all the way from Krell's down to the rest stop out of town where I got ambushed."

"So why the fuck are you calling me, Danny?"

"Roger called. We got shit going down all up and down the line and the Old Man's organizing the troops. Here's what he's got in mind for you…"

Hedges stood in the office of the gas station, the shattered door behind him.

Nothing much. A table with some magazines on it, chairs, coffee maker, rack with slots for bills on the wall behind the counter, hooks for keys, etc.

Hedges moved through the office into what looked like an alcove behind, came to a door.

Not bothering to see if it were locked or not, Hedges pulled up his Desert Eagle, raised a boot and kicked the door open.

Early morning light came through the windows in back to dimly illuminate the room: pool table, darts on the wall, couches, booths, a couch…

Something moved on the couch.

Hedges angled in, alert and ready, gun in both hands.

A man on the couch. Beat to shit by the looks of it. Trussed up.

As he drew near, the man's eyes widened and he shrunk back into the cushions of the couch.

He attempted to yell something, but the duct tape over his mouth muffled it.

Hedges took a look around the room, leaned down, checked under the table, slipped to one side of the room and back, then holstered his gun.

He strode up to the man on the couch and ripped the tape off his mouth, skin coming with it, little dots of blood showing.

"Ow, fuck!" the man yelled.

Hedges poked the man in the sternum with his boot.

"Who the fuck are you?" he asked.

The man's eyes darted about the room as if seeking the

answer there.

"Let me clear things up for you," Hedges said. "Roger sent me and my team up here to take care of things. Where's Mack?"

"Ah, Thank God!" the man on the couch cried. "They took Mack off somewhere. Heading for some compound, I think."

Hedges considered the man in front of him.

"Who're you?" he said again.

"Elroy! Roger sent me and Sherman up this way. Then Mack and Warren showed up. That's when all hell broke loose."

Hedges phone vibrated in his pocket.

He put it to his ear.

"Yeah?"

"Slim spotted Ingersoll in a van heading past the motel in Aston about ten minutes ago," Roger said. "What you got?"

Hedges considered the man on the couch again.

"Got some good ol' boy named Elroy trussed up here on a couch in a back room of the gas station. Got Chris and Tony down the side of the hill checking out what looks to be Mack's truck at the bottom of the slide. Got Albert taking Bill's fuck toy down to Red Rock for some R&R, but you know that part."

"What's the word on Mack?"

Hedges phone clicked: an incoming call. He glanced at it.

"Give me one second, boss. Chris is calling in. They must be down at the truck by now."

Hedges clicked over to the other call.

"What?"

"Dead man in the truck," Chris said. "Passenger's side. Head splattered open, hard to say what he looks like. Wallet in his pocket has a license for a Warren something or other."

"Hold on," Hedges said.

He clicked back to Roger and relayed the message.

"That's Mack's right-hand man," Roger said. "Where the fuck is Mack?"

"Good ol' boy Elroy here says they took him somewhere, aiming at some compound, he thinks."

Hedges felt the electricity crackle through the line: Roger

was excited.

"Hot damn! That's what Ingersoll's doing! He's bringing Mack to Krell's! We got him!"

"What you want me to do here, then?" Hedges asked.

"I'll leave that up to you," Roger said. "That's what I sent you for. You've got good judgment, and you clean things up nice."

Hedges pictured Sherman splattered all over the inside of his truck.

"In a manner of speaking," he said.

"Once you're done up there, head back," Roger said. "We got every man in the area after Ingersoll already. Now that we know he's got Mack, we're focusing all our attention on this. Soon as we get Mack back, we'll mobilize for the asshole. I got a couple of teams on him, too. Figure we ought to have him in hand by nightfall."

Hedges' stomach dropped a little in disappointment. He'd really wanted in on that.

"I'll be there quick as I can," he said.

He turned and walked back toward the door to the office.

"Hey! What about me?" Elroy called.

"Oh, yeah," Hedges said. "Almost forgot."

He pulled the Desert Eagle out of his holster and turned back toward Elroy.

"Always get a kick out of this," he said, raising his gun.

CHAPTER FORTY FIVE

The gates of Red Rock rose up in the sunlight, black against the red rock all around.

Albert glanced over the back of the seat.

Mary Jane lay immobile, eyes closed. She'd kicked around intermittently during the long drive, but for the last hour or two had gone silent. She appeared to be breathing.

Albert drove slowly towards the gates.

An armed man lit by the rising sun stood on each side of the big iron gates. The one on the driver's side advanced slowly, hands on his weapon while the other took up a position on the passenger's side.

Albert clicked a button and rolled down the window.

"Hands where I can see 'em," the guard on his side barked.

"Take 'er easy," Albert said, bringing his hands up to 10 and 2 on the wheel. "I got valuable cargo here."

The guard eased up, peered into the truck, shot a glance into the truck bed.

His rifle snapped up and a red dot appeared on Albert's forehead, another on his temple as the other guard sighted in on him.

"Easy, easy," Albert said. "Holy Shit. I've got the bitch Old Man Bannister is hot after, she's trussed up behind the seat."

"Step out of the truck," the guard ordered. "Slow. And keep your hands where I can see them at all times."

"Going to have to lower one to open the door," Albert said.

"Keep 'em on the wheel. Grip it so tightly I can see the strain," the guard said.

Albert complied and the guard reached out a hand and pulled open the door, his other hand steady on the stock of his weapon, finger over the trigger. The red dot on Albert's forehead barely bobbled.

"Now put your hands behind your head and step out," the guard said.

"Got to release the seat belt," Albert said.

"Go slow."

Albert released the catch and stepped out of the vehicle, his hands together on the back of his neck.

"You boys need to chill the fuck out," he said.

The one on the driver's side never took his eyes off of Albert.

"Check it out," he said to the other guard.

Albert considered. He was almost close enough to snap the gun up and away, pound this asshole a little bit, teach him a lesson. He angled a bit to bring the other guard into his sight.

"Freeze!" the first guard barked.

Albert froze.

The second guard was once again targeting him. Albert was sure he could feel the red dots on his forehead.

There would be some payback for this.

Billy, Wilder, Jack, and Bobby stood grouped together over the hood of the big truck. The sun lay low on the horizon, and a low breeze kicked over the grit on the blacktop where they'd pulled off the main road. No other cars were in sight. Billy had his iPad out, a PDF map of the area was on the screen. Red dots, triangles and stars dotted the map all the way down the state and into the next: Mountain Cleft, Greencreek, Hangman, Jackpot, Wells...

"Don't have to tell you what these mean," Billy said. "So far, our boy been hitting mainly dots. Don't' know if he's lucky or what, but mostly small operations. Biggest he's hit is Hotel 29 here." His finger came down on the map at Mountain Cleft, marked by a triangle.

"Greencreek's a small operation, so are most of the others, 'till we hit Red Rock." He indicated the big red star that marked Red Rock.

"He's only hit a few places, but then he ain't got so far down the road yet," Billy said.

"He's working his way down the line, ain't he?" Wilder said. "Stupid fuck. All we got to do is set up an ambush, like at Wells," he jerked a thumb backwards the way they had come, "or up to Jackpot," he nodded his head in the direction they were heading.

Billy eyed Wilder coldly. Wilder froze, then relaxed as Billy nodded, slow and deliberate.

"That's what Roger figures, too," he said. "Asshole grabbed some ledgers out of Bill's. Knows the operations. So...we got Danny and Winter coming down from Greencreek, and us coming up. That puts our asshole straight in the middle."

Wilder nodded.

"Hangman's next after Greencreek," Jack put in.

"Shouldn't we boogie down there?" Bobby asked.

"That's part of why we're stopped here," Billy said. "Roger ain't been able to raise anyone down in Hangman, so he sent Danny and Winter down to check. We're going to sit here and keep our eyes peeled for any white vans that head our way."

"We know he's in a white van?" Jack asked.

Billy nodded. "Danny followed a white van out of Krell's down the road a piece. Followed it into the rest stop just shy of Greencreek. Got ambushed there, and by the time he worked his way back out to Greencreek, it was all over. Winter's the only one standing from that operation. One dead, one in the hospital, the women gone. Asshole brought them to the hospital in Freedom. Shit load of cop activity there, too much for us to control."

"Make and model?" Jack asked.

"Danny doesn't know. Not much of a car guy, I guess," Billy said.

Wilder snorted. "More of pincers and pliers kind of guy," he said.

The men grinned at one another.

"Always liked me a pincers and pliers guy," Wilder said. "You can drag things on for days, like that, you're careful."

A knot of excitement grew in the men.

"We got to get this fuck," Wilder said. "Been on the fucking road too long, time to play."

Billy's hand snatched Wilder by the Adam's apple and pulled him in tight.

Wilder's face went bright red, then white as he gagged. His hands flapped and he moved as if to draw his gun, then thought better of it.

"One more stupid thing out of your mouth," Billy said, "and I'll have Jack and Bobby digging a hole, you got me?"

Billy squeezed a little for emphasis.

Tears rolled down Wilder's face. He raised his hands helplessly, tried to nod.

Billy shoved Wilder away.

Wilder went to his knees.

Jack and Bobby looked down on him.

Billy leaned down and got in Wilder's face.

"I ain't going to say it again, Wilder. This is twice I've had to redirect you, and it's getting tiresome. You're going to do your fucking job, you're going to shut your fucking mouth, and you're going to complain about nothing. You follow me?"

He stared hard into Wilder's face.

Defiance flared in Wilder's eyes, then died as terror took its place as he realized he was an eye blink away from death.

He nodded meekly, and tried to rasp out an apology, but his damaged voice box would form no words.

Billy grinned.

"Atta boy," he said, clapping Wilder on the shoulder. "I like you better mute like that."

Billy nodded at the truck and the four men climbed in.

Billy gave a sharp look as Wilder headed for the rear seats, directing him to the passenger seat up front and Jack to sit behind him.

"No fucking snakes behind me," he said.

Max stopped for a minute, closed his eyes, rotated his head to crack his neck, then opened his eyes and holstered the .44 S&W he'd taken off one of the men back in the shack behind him.

The wind whistled through the open door of the shack and the grunts of the man in the chair made their way out into the lot.

Gravel crunched under his feet and he moved toward the van.

Rosita sat in the passenger seat, erect, eyes wide and lucid, shotgun between her legs, barrel up, pointing at the ceiling.

Their eyes met.

Max looked at her.

Big eyes, eyebrows with a natural curve that needed no accentuation, thick eyelashes, smooth, skin, still yellowing from some bruising, but otherwise perfect. A vision.

He felt the connection between them in his chest, a deep hollow longing and powerful attraction.

He shook his head to clear it. Blinked and looked away.

No. This poor girl had had enough of men to last her a lifetime, he figured. Last thing she needed was that kind of attention....

She couldn't be more than 18. A crime twice over.

He stepped around to the driver's side, pulled open the door and climbed in, the van settling the tiniest bit with his weight.

He scooted forward and pulled the holster off his belt—too big and clunky to drive with. Better to have it on the console between them.

Rosita reached for his hand.

"Now, we rest," she said.

Max felt electricity shoot from her hand up his arm and zap him in the chest. He gave her hand a squeeze, then started up the van and wheeled it around toward the highway.

"Might be smart to hole up a bit," he said.

He glanced in the rear view mirror just in time to see the

wind swing the door shut, and a whoomph! of flame blast it open again.

Max reached out and patted Rosita on the shoulder, then put both hands on the wheel and headed south.

"That's it," Mahler said, pointing at the small dirt road ahead.

The van carrying Raymond and the others was tight on their rear, Tyler and Socrates right behind.

As yet, nothing was in the rear view behind them, but no one had any doubt pursuit was hot and heavy.

Guy signaled and downshifted, the pickup rising up on its shocks as the engine screamed. He took the turn at 70, rear end of the pickup slewing around the corner, the other cars right behind.

Dust rose into the air, a big rooster tail of an arrow pointing their way.

Which was fine. All part of the plan.

Curry had the pedal to the floor, death metal screaming over the engine, a solid grip on the wheel and his eyes fixed on the horizon.

A couple of miles ahead he spotted the dust rising from a small convey of vehicles that had hit the turn off to Cougar Mountain.

He laughed and pounded the horn on the big Dodge Ram in time with the music.

"Going to have us a par-ty!" he yelled.

The man next to him checked the clip in his rifle, pulled out his revolver, clicked out the cylinder and spun it, then slapped it back in.

"Got that right," he said.

Curry stuck a hand out the window and waved with a round-em-up motion to the line of trucks behind him, then pointed at the turnoff.

He hit the turnoff at 80, the pickup sliding clear off the road and into the field, nearly tipping before he fought it back in line and edged it up onto the dirt road.

His passenger glanced at him, grim-faced, but knowing better than to criticize. Checked his guns again.

Curry slammed the truck down the road into the cloud of dust, hot in pursuit, a sexual excitement growing in him as he anticipated the blood ahead.

Winter guided the cop car up over the ridge to see Hangman open up below. Nearly identical to Greencreek: small little town with a main street, a few businesses off of it, a bar, houses, the big silos by the rail line, and…next to the silos, just off the loading dock, one building ablaze.

"Holy fuck," Danny said. "The son of a bitch been here already."

Winter punched it and the cop car flew down the hill toward town.

"Let's see what we can see," he said. "Maybe the asshole's still down there."

Hedges glanced into the rear view. Red and blue lights behind him, inching forward.

He glanced down at the speedometer, the needle wavering at 110.

"What the fuck?" he said.

Tony looked over his shoulder.

"Huh," he said. "Lights are State Trooper, not local."

Hedges pounded the wheel.

"We haven't got time for this," he said.

He scanned the road ahead, looking for some kind of cover, an off-road, anything.

This stretch of highway between Paluma and Ramsey was straight and relatively barren: wheat fields to the left, wheat fields to the right, wheat fields ahead. Hedges considered plowing into a field, heading for a side road, then rejected the possibility.

"Tony, get down low. Chris, you sit up high. We're going to take this motherfucker down and get moving."

Tony slid down in his seat and pulled out his pistol.

Chris looked in the rearview mirror, then at Hedges.

"Risky, boss. And he could be one of us," he said.

Hedges tapped the brake lights and aimed the truck at a wide spot in the road, "Maybe, maybe not. We're not real long on Troopers, more on locals."

"If he's one of us, and we smoke him, there'll be hell to pay with the Old Man," Chris said.

"If we don't and he's not, there'll be hell to pay," Tony said as he squeezed his bulk down to the floor and twisted himself around to cover the driver's side.

"He'll most likely come to the passenger side out here," Hedges instructed. "Less likely of getting creamed by a passing motorist."

Tony swiveled his bulk, grunting.

Hedges pulled the truck over and came to a stop. He reached up and switched the domed light to its off position.

"Tell you what," he said. "I'm going to pop out and have a parley with him. Chris, you keep an eye on the mirror. I'm going to wave at him all big and friendly, that'll distract him enough to miss Tony slipping out the side door, if you're quick enough about it."

Hedges popped out of the truck and slammed the door.

His boots were loud on the grit of the road as the Trooper's car came to a stop twenty feet behind the truck.

A loud click and the Trooper's bullhorn; "Driver! Stop right there! Put your hands over your head!"

"Well, I guess he's got Officer Friendly's attention all right," Chris said. He leaned over and popped the latch, allowing Tony to slip out the door, then pulled it shut again.

More bullhorn; "Passenger! Hands where I can see them! Slide out the door and exit the vehicle!"

Chris slid out the driver's side door and faced the Trooper.

"What do you think?" he said to Hedges.

"I think we smoke this asshole, that's what I think," Hedges said.

"Both of you! Interlace your fingers and put your hands behind your heads."

Hedges complied, Chris following suit.

Tony inched his way toward the rear of the truck, belly crawling. He stayed as far out of the line of sight of the Trooper as he could, but the truck was jacked up and on big wheels, so there wasn't as much cover as would be optimal.

He saw Hedges and Chris go to their knees.

He reached the rear wheel of the truck, and peered out from underneath.

The Trooper sat behind the wheel of his vehicle, lights on, mic in his hand.

Tony sighted in on the Trooper carefully, and squeezed off three shots.

The Trooper's windshield frosted and a tight group of three holes formed a triangle in front of the Trooper's face. The engine roared to full RPMs. Hedges and Chris were on their feet, guns out and pumping lead into the Trooper's car.

Tony rolled out from under the truck and approached the Trooper's car as the shooting stopped.

The inside of the Trooper's car was a riot of blood, brains and bits of bone. The combined fire had pretty much obliterated the man's head. The man's hat lay to one side, bits of skull and brain still in it.

"Get the lights," Hedges said over the roar of the engine.

Chris popped open the driver's side door, keyed off the engine, its roar dying abruptly. He flipped switches randomly until the lights died.

The three men stood for a moment in the silence, staring at their handiwork.

"Most likely not one of us," Tony said, after a pause.

"Most likely," Chris agreed.

"Well, we'll find out, one way or another," Hedges said.

Hedges looked both ways.

Wheat fields, and in the distance, from each direction, traffic.

"We got to get moving, boys," he said. "These cops all have dash cams now, too. We got to ditch this truck and keep moving. And we have to move now."

The three men took a last look at the Trooper, then Chris slammed the car door and they walked quickly back to their truck and climbed in.

Hedges stomped on the gas and the rear wheels spun, spitting rocks and dirt into the windshield of the Trooper's car.

In seconds, it was a tiny dot on the horizon and Aston was coming into view.

CHAPTER FORTY SIX

The dirt road was uneven with deep ruts cut into it over years of traffic. Everyone was buckled in tight. Marcus and Timmy watched over the bouncing Mack on the floor of the truck.

Mack never stopped raving, though the duct tape over his mouth made it impossible to tell just what he was raving about.

Timmy leaned in and yelled over the noise of the engine and the jouncing springs of the van; "Hope it hurts, asshole. You're the one that put us on this road."

Mack's eyes rolled like a rabid dog's and he looked to be baring his teeth under the duct tape.

"Leave him be," Marcus said. "Stay ready."

Timmy leaned back in his seat and popped the clip out of his AR, looked at it, slid the bolt back an inch to be sure one was in the chamber, then reseated the magazine, and double-checked the safety was on.

Marcus watched him.

"Just like old times, yeah?"

Timmy grinned. "Damn close. Was a step hotter over there, but yeah."

"Be ready," Marcus said.

"Born ready," Timmy replied.

The two grinned at one another.

Socrates raised an arm and pointed.

"There's the dogleg up ahead," he said.

The dirt road hit a hard right-angle turn around a copse of trees as it gained altitude and steepened, climbing out of the wheat fields and into the forested hillside.

Up ahead, Guy slid through the corner, drifting his rear wheels around the bend, followed by Chad and the boys in the van.

Tyler slid the Silverado into the corner and sideways across the road, coming to a stop twenty yards from the road. The trees stood between them and the road, shielding them from sight.

The van idled ahead as Timmy and Marcus popped out and trotted over to join them, weapons held across their chests in the ready position.

Marcus raised an arm, and Chad hit the gas. In seconds, the van disappeared down the road.

The faint roar of truck engines rose from the road below.

Getting louder.

Marcus nodded at the Silverado.

"Four-man ambush at the dogleg. Take positions and dig in as well as you can. Wait for my signal. Fall back to the truck as necessary."

The men sprinted down the road, fanning out, each taking a corner at the dogleg with a clear view of the road rising from the fields below.

Max slid the door open to the van and climbed in with paper towels and some cleaning fluid they'd bought at the convenience store where they were parked.

It stood on a lonely stretch of road between Hangman and Jackpot, a middle-of-nowhere oasis of alcohol, cigarettes, junk food, windshield-wiper fluid, oil, and other kinds of things folks on the road needed to stock up on.

The building blocked Max's view of the road, but he figured that was a fair trade. He couldn't see out, but then again, no one could see him, either.

He pulled off a wad of paper towels and scrubbed at the blood drying on the floor. A fair amount of it had worked its way into the grooves on the metal floor, but it was coming up decently, some of it flaking away, some of it sticking stubbornly.

Rosita picked up the spray bottle of cleaning fluid and joined in.

They worked side by side for ten minutes without speaking.

Finally Max straightened up.

"That'll have to do," he said.

Rosita grabbed the used paper towels and dumped them into the garbage, came back with the vacuum nozzle.

"OK," Max said.

He climbed out and inserted all the change he had in his pockets into the coin slots to activate the vacuum.

He watched as Rosita efficiently moved through the van, first getting what she could off the floor in the back, then moving to the front seats, and finally the wheel wells as the vacuum died.

She climbed back out and holstered the vacuum nozzle in its place.

"We rest now?" she said.

Max nodded. "Just got to find us a place. We're about twenty miles out of Jackpot. I'm afraid to put in there, Bannisters'll have eyes all up and down this stretch. Which also rules out rest stops and the like. We're going to have to find a place more private and lonely to hole up."

They climbed into the Ford and Max started it up. He inched forward, gaining a clear view of the road, waited for the one car on the road to pass by and disappear towards Hangman, then eased the van on the road and headed for Jackpot.

"Keep an eye out for side roads," he said.

Rosita sat up a little straighter and smiled.

"I will," she said.

Albert popped the passenger's seat forward and leaned in to grab the bitch. She hadn't moved for a couple of hours, and he had a bad moment when the consequences of her death flashed across his mind, then he reached in and reassured himself: still warm. Breathing. He took a deep breath and pulled her out and threw her over his shoulder.

Light as a bird.

Albert looked around the compound.

Once a resort, the compound was built out of adobe-looking material with red-clay tiles for roofs. The compound spread out over 10 acres of once-landscaped grounds, with a few main buildings, a scattering of side cottages, a big warehouse-looking thing at the rear of the compound with full-sized loading docks for container trucks, and a small building with a tall chimney, like one you'd see at a smelter.

Albert debated: hospital or holding pen?

He pictured having to tell the Old Man she was dead, and sweat popped out on his forehead in the chill desert morning air. He shivered and stepped lively toward the warehouse-looking building in the back.

Winter and Danny stood in the parking lot of the Bannister play box in Hangman. Flames shot twenty feet into the air, out the doorways and windows. A smell of burnt meat and hair permeated the air, an oily unpleasant aroma that clung to the skin.

Danny wanted to shoot someone.

He glanced over at Winter.

Winter stood with his fists clenched, staring into the fire. The fire reflected in his eyes and Danny felt a shiver of fear—Winter looked demonic and unstoppable.

"That motherfucker," Danny said.

Winter kicked at the gravel, looked about.

"Got some clean up to do," he said. He pointed at two trucks in the lot. "Them's Clem and Bobby's, and Jimbo always rides with Bobby, so I'd say that's the whole crew in there. I can call in my guys, have 'em here inside an hour."

Danny nodded. "Better get on it."

He pulled his phone out of his pocket.

More bad news to relay.

Danny stared at the phone, considering. If things kept going this way and he was the one kept calling it in, the Old Man might just string him up for the medicinal value of watching him scream.

He punched the call in and raised the phone, staring into the fire, the hot flames reflected in his eyes.

Curry hooted and stomped down the accelerator. The truck roared and leaned into the climb up the hill. Death metal thundered in the cab of the truck and he sang along.

He glanced in the big side mirror to see the convoy at his tail.

Hot damn! Things was happening.

It was all well and good playing with the bitches, made life interesting, plus, let's face it, a man has to have a piece of ass now and again, but this—this was what really lit him up: Guns, fighting, the rush of a powerful beat down or placing a bullet perfectly between a man's eyes and watching him die. That was what gave life its real juice.

The truck climbed the straight road up the hill, the others falling in line behind him.

A flash at the crest of the hill alerted him.

Curry ducked as bullets punched through the windshield, and the man beside him splashed warm blood all over the cab.

Curry stayed low, held the wheel as straight as he could, grabbed his shotgun and bailed out the driver's side, rolling over and over into the tall grass that bordered the road.

The truck continued up the hill for ten feet, got a wheel off the road, stuttered and died, blocking the road ahead.

Gunfire from above: multiple bursts of three. A trained crew.

Curry looked downhill to see all five trucks behind him stopped.

Muzzle flashes. Each truck had men beside it, firing up the hill.

Low in the grass as he was, Curry couldn't see up the hill. And no way was he getting up to take a look.

A faint cry from below and one of the men crumpled beside

his truck.

More firing—from above and below.

He wanted to scream at the idiots below, firing blindly up the hill.

Windshields frosted, trucks sagged as their tires blew out, another scream of a wounded man.

Then men were running down the hill.

The last two trucks, as yet unscathed, shot dust into the air as the drivers desperately maneuvered them to turn around.

Men climbed up the bumpers and dove into the truck beds as the trucks turned and spurted down the hill.

One man flew off as the truck he was holding hit a rut and bounced. A splotch of blood appeared on another, and he fell to the road.

And then the trucks were moving fast down the hill, out of range.

Curry listened.

Just the wind whispering through the grass around him.

Roger gripped the phone.

"How the hell?" he said. "I called them. They'd been warned."

He rose and looked out the window. It took all his self-control not to heave the phone through it.

"How long ago?" he asked.

"Fire's burning real strong," Danny said. "Timbers haven't given way yet, so I'd say inside an hour."

Roger paced back to the computer, pulled up the map. "So, asshole's hit Mountain Cleft, Greencreek, stopped by the hospital in Freedom, and now Hangman. Billy's right," he said. "Our asshole is working his way down the line. Billy figures he'll aim at Jackpot next."

Danny stared into the fire. He thought he could make out the twisted form of a burned man lying on the floor in the inferno, but it could have been his imagination playing tricks on him.

"Where's Billy at?" Danny asked.

"Forty miles outside Wells, on the way in to Jackpot. Posted by the side of the road eyeballing the traffic heading his way."

Danny considered it.

"If me and Winter clear the town, make sure asshole ain't here, then set up on the road..."

"We'll have him in between you two," Roger said. "Huh. Then send some guys in from either side, checking."

"That's what I was thinking," Danny said.

"Huh," Roger said again. "Might be something. the Old Man has a plan, too."

Danny's heart bumped in his chest. the Old Man's plans were generally ballsy as hell, and involved lots of blood and guts.

Good times.

"What's he thinking?" Danny said.

"We got Mary Jane back," Roger said.

"Hot damn!" Danny said.

"The Old Man figures we can lure asshole in. Let 'im know we're fixing to play with her a bit, where we're at, and he'll come."

"He'll come, all right. But how we going to let him know?"

"Well, he's got Winter's phone, for one," Roger said.

Danny looked over at Winter, who was now standing close enough to the fire for it to redden his brow.

"Hey, Winter!" he yelled. "Call your guys and get 'em out here for clean up!"

Winter turned and looked at Danny. He had the thousand yard stare of a man far away in his thoughts.

Danny gestured with the phone.

"Your guys?" he said.

Winter shook his head, showed Danny open hands.

"Need your phone," he growled.

"Uh - huh," Danny said. He held up a hand in a wait-a-minute gesture.

"That's something," Danny said into the phone.

"You follow through with your idea," Roger said. "Set up the pinch, and I'll let you know..."

The roar of a truck engine cut through the quiet of the

Bannister den. Roger returned to the window to see a big cab pickup swing into the parking area and race around the corner out of sight.

'Shit," Roger said. "Gotta go. You sweep that town clean, get set up, call back, got me?"

"Yes, sir," Danny said.

He thumbed his phone off and stared at it a moment, then looked up into the fire.

Raymond jostled as the van barreled down the lane, springs working hard on the uneven ground.

Mack was letting out a litany of muffled complaint and invective from the back. Raymond turned sideways, and braced himself against the passenger door to get a better look at him.

The man lay securely trussed and hog tied. It looked horribly painful.

A pulse of mean satisfaction ran through Raymond.

"Nothing comes up, we'll be at Krell's inside an hour," Mahler said.

Raymond looked back through the windshield to see Guy's truck bouncing along ahead, Mahler silhouetted against the red morning sky.

"Good," Raymond said. "I'm ready."

His phone vibrated with an incoming call.

Marcus.

"Yeah?"

"Four trucks down, two fled away like the little piggies they are," Marcus said.

"Which way they head?" Raymond asked.

"Back towards Ramsey," Marcus said.

"I'll be," Raymond said. "From what I heard, I wouldn't want to run back to Old Man Bannister with my tail between my legs."

"Who says that's where they're going?" Marcus asked. "Might be bailing entirely, pulling themselves out of the fight.

Not long on courage, these types. Bullies. Not fighters."

"Maybe, maybe not," Raymond said.

A rustling of the phone.

"Three o'clock!" Marcus shouted, his voice faint over the jostling of the phone.

The roar of a shotgun and then the phone cut off.

Max eased the Ford down a narrow dirt road.

The road cleared the wheat fields on either side and opened up into hilly terrain that led down to a river that glowed pink against the morning sky. A single lane path ran alongside the river as it wound its way through the hills.

"This is nice," Rosita said.

Max looked both ways. "River runs pretty much directly north-south," he said. "We'll head south."

"Where are we going, Max?"

"We'll talk about that after we get set up," Max said. He yawned and shook his head to keep himself awake. The repeated adrenaline dumps and combat of the night had taken their toll and now his body was crying out for sleep.

A huge tree spread itself over a patch of land at a bend in the river, just fifteen yards up from the road.

Max pointed, "African conifer," he said.

Rosita stared at him.

"African conifer," he repeated. "The tree. Someone must've planted it here. Gives great shade, and with its foliage spread out like that, concealment." He studied the tree and the ground rising to meet it from the river.

"Perfect," he said.

CHAPTER FORTY SEVEN

Hedges slammed on the brakes and the truck ground to a halt under what looked like an RV shelter.

"Let me do the talking," he said.

Chris and Tony nodded.

The three men climbed out of their car.

"No weapons inside," Hedges said, throwing his TEC-9 into a case built into the console between the driver's and passenger's seat. Chris and Tony followed suit with their 9s, then all three men shucked their coats and twisted around to remove their shoulder holsters.

Hedges caressed the stock of his big Desert Eagle.

"Feel naked without it," he said.

Chris and Tony tossed their sidearms into the box.

Hedges sighed, then leaned in and gently set the pistol in its holster on top of the pile and shut the lid.

"Thought you were going to fuck it before you let go of it," Tony said.

Hedges eyed him.

The two men stared at one another.

"Thought about it," Hedges said, finally.

The three men burst into laughter then turned to the house.

"Remember," Hedges said. "I do the talking."

Mary Jane opened her eyes.

Pain roared through her head.

Bright white light. Indistinct shapes.

Am I dead? she wondered. *Finally?*

She moved to touch her face, but something was holding her back.

What?

She tried the other arm.

She could only move it a few inches.

Feet.

The same.

The room snapped into view: she lay on a hospital bed with metal rails. An IV line snaked down from the bag hanging on a stand, over the rail of the bed and into her wrist where tape held the needle in place.

Padded shackles held her wrists and ankles to the rails of the bed.

Mary Jane convulsed and screamed as memory flooded back: *standing at the roadside by the garage, a noise behind her, then blackness to wake up sick and nauseated in the back of a slowing pickup.* Furtive memories of rage and swinging...*a hammer? The joy of contact as the hammer landed, the man bellowing, and then he was on her and she was flying up and...blackness.*

Now this.

"You motherfuckers!" she screamed. "Assholes!"

Words degenerated into incoherent rage which mixed with sobs as the full weight of her situation landed on her.

"Assholes!" she sobbed.

A tall, thin man stepped into the room and studied her from the doorway.

He nodded to himself.

Mary Jane calmed herself.

Snot bubbled in her nose. Her nose stung, a familiar sharp flash of pain—she'd been punched in the nose often enough to know the feeling of having it split. And the pain of loose teeth in her mouth—the kind of pain that shot up into the orbitals if she pushed on her teeth with her tongue.

Pain announced itself from a dozen other places.

She'd taken a beating all right.

The low throb in her head conquered all.

Her stomach lurched and she turned desperately to puke.

The tall man was there, bringing up a bucket and she puked into it.

She gagged and retched for an endless moment, each spasm sending shockwaves of pain all through her: her head, her ribs, a shoulder, a big spot low down on her back. Too many places to catalog.

Finally, she fell back on the bed exhausted.

The tall man walked across the room and opened a door.

She heard the sound of him pouring her bucket of puke into a toilet.

Running water, the hollow thrum of a shower into the bucket.

The water shut off, and the tall man emerged from the room, dangling the bucket from one lanky arm, his boots loud on the tile floor.

He walked to the foot of the bed and surveyed Mary Jane.

Nodded to himself.

"Please," Mary Jane croaked. Her voice was broken and rocky. "Please, mister. Please let me go. Get me out of here."

The man set the bucket down and walked around the bed past Mary Jane.

She craned her neck to see him, but he'd stepped out of her line of vision.

She heard him fumbling with something. Tearing paper. A clink.

He reappeared next to the IV stand, a large syringe in his hand.

"No!" Mary Jane cried. She thrashed against her restraints. "No! Please!"

The tall man never looked at her. He ran a hand down the IV line to a port. He slipped the needle into the port and depressed the plunger.

"No!" Mary Jane said again.

She fought against the warm rush that ran through her body as the narcotic swept into her system.

"No." Quieter.

The thrum in her head snapped out, the various aches and sharp jabs of pain clicking off, one by one as the narcotic reached into every crevice of her body.

"No..." barely audible.

The narcotic overwhelmed her, a thick, heavy blanket of warm fuzziness that carried her away.

Marcus dove to one side of the road, seeking cover, his gun coming up as he flew through the air.

A short man, as wide as he was tall, had stepped out of the high grass by the dogleg and opened up with a shotgun.

Timmy lay flat on his back, his weapon out of reach, his arms windmilling in pain.

Gunfire chattered from each side of the road as Socrates and Tyler opened up.

The short man straightened as the bullets stitched across his torso, jittered and jerked as he fought to stay on his feet, the shotgun swinging around.

Marcus watched as the bore of the shotgun swung his way and squeezed off a shot just as the bore steadied on his own head.

The short guy's hands flew up as the bullet entered his forehead, punching a neat little hole, then went over backwards as the bullet exited the top rear of his head with a spray of blood and brains. He landed on the dirt road with an audible thump, a little puff of dust rising, then lay still.

Socrates and Tyler flanked the body, kicking the shotgun away, and Marcus turned his attention to Timmy.

Timmy was still on his back, his legs bicycling as he tried to sit up.

Marcus knelt beside him, put a gentle hand on his shoulder, held him down.

"Stay quiet," he said. "Let me see how bad this is."

Timmy grunted in pain.

"Hurts like hell," he said. Blood stained the right side of his shirt, and the center of it was torn away to reveal the Kevlar vest underneath. "Double-ought buck, heavy load, I figure."

Marcus nodded. "Looks like it. One of the pellets went wide enough to dig a hole in your shoulder, looks like."

Timmy sucked in a deep breath and composed himself.

"Going to have to get me a new shirt," he said. "And vest. Damn it."

Marcus looked at him and grinned.

"You are one hell of a bullet magnet, aren't you?"

Timmy huffed out a chuckle then groaned in pain.

"Why is it always me that catches one?" he said.

"Well, looks like once again, you're going to be fine, you freaking multiple Purple Heart asshole, you."

The men looked at one another, visions of combat in various places around the world flickering behind their eyes.

"No medals today," Timmy said.

"Nope," Marcus said.

Timmy nodded as Marcus helped him to sit up.

The men climbed to their feet and shuffled over to the big truck as Socrates and Tyler dragged the short guy's body off into the grass by the roadside.

Hedges stood in front of the big table in Old Man Bannister's den, hands clasped behind his back, head bowed. The Old Man was seated at the head of the table, a mug of coffee in front of him. Roger was at his side, also with some coffee.

Hedges eyed the steam rising from their mugs from under his furrowed brow. The coffee smelled good, and it'd been a long night.

No one had offered him or his guys any.

"Let me get this straight," Roger said. "You come up on the gas station, find Elroy all tied up there, learn about these good ol' boys grabbing up Mack, figure they're heading this way, toward Krell's. Then you shoot him in the head."

Hedges shrugged. "Struck me as a worthless motherfucker. More trouble than it was worth to patch 'im up and fit him into the truck. And we had Sherman to get, and Mary Jane."

Roger set his coffee down with a bang.

"And you shot him, too!" he roared.

Hedges shrugged again, shifted his weight on his feet.

"Sherman was one of our best guys!" Roger said.

He leaned forward, elbows on the table and squinted at Hedges and the others.

"You two," Roger said. "How the fuck do you let him do this?"

Chris and Tony looked at one another, their turn to shrug.

"Never even knew about this Elroy type," Chris said. "News to me."

"And Sherman," Tony said, "that was quick. One minute we was talking to him, and the next his brains were splattered all over the windshield."

"He'd fucked up," Hedges said. "And he was fucked up. Looked like he'd been in a war. Bleeding all over the place. Not sure he was going to make it anyway, loss of blood and all. He sure as hell was going to attract a lot of attention."

He straightened and eyed Roger, has hands still clasped behind his back. His hands ached for the feel of the checkered grip of the Desert Eagle, to bring up its heavy weight, center it on Roger's forehead, feel the beast leap in his hands and watch Roger's skullcap fly off as the .50 caliber bullet blasted his brains over the wall behind him.

Fuck you, Roger Bannister, he thought.

He let the silence sit for a minute, then said, "It's my job to clean up." He looked over at the Old Man who was sitting quietly, sipping his coffee as calm and cool as if he were watching the morning news.

"We were in a hurry. Had Mack out there somewhere, Mary Jane to take care of, and it was getting light. Sherman was going to start attracting attention, and we just wanted to get going."

He and the Old Man locked eyes.

The Old Man nodded.

"Let it go, Roger," he said. "I got a feeling there's more news to come, the way these boys tore in here and ditched their truck under the canopy out back."

The Old Man never dropped his eyes from Hedges' as he took another sip from his mug and waited.

"So?" he said. "What else?"

Now, Hedges was uncomfortable.

He shifted on his feet.

"Ran into a complication," he said. "Just outside Ramsey."

Max laid out bedrolls in the back of the van.

He'd parked tight up against the trunk of the huge tree, its branches spreading out against the roof, shielding it from the sun—and from sight.

"Taking a bit of a chance, sleeping out here," he said. "But we have to. Can't keep going like this."

Rosita laid the shotgun to her right, stretched out, pulled a blanket up over her shoulders, then curled up with a hand on the stock of the shotgun.

"Buenas noches," she said, and fell instantly asleep.

Max stretched out beside her, then propped himself up on an elbow. She lay on her left, face towards the side of the van, dainty hand resting on the shotgun.

Max reached down and gently stroked her hair behind her ear, trying to clear the puffy groove of flesh that ran across that side of her head from the bullet wound.

The wound was warm, but not overly so. She'd not given any signs of brain damage, but the possibility lingered, and as Max settled down next to her worry knotted his thoughts.

He pillowed his head with interlaced fingers and stared at the ceiling of the van.

He'd fled Thailand in the hopes of freeing himself from the nightmarish visions that crowded every corner there only to step into something far worse than what he'd left. Thailand seemed pretty restful by comparison. He could be training in the Muay Thai camp outside of Pattaya, going into town on weekends to party, and living with the mostly static ghosts of the countryside there. He could....

Max sucked in a deep breath, held it, let it out. Closed his eyes.

The meadow on the mountain came back to him. The blond woman.

There was purpose here.

Rather than simply moving through life like a fish carried by the current, he was facing the evil in the world, doing his best to conquer it and allow the light to shine.

Not that he considered himself pure or good or, anything, much. He stood on the line, a foot on the side of pain and murder, a foot on the side of the light and love. The fact that he didn't get his kicks actively torturing girls didn't set him that far apart from the Bannisters and their crowd—that standard was about as low a bar as any he'd ever heard of. And he'd let the very same presence he was combatting get its hooks into him more than once: the man outside Bill Bannister's, the one he let burn to death in Hangman, the beatings he'd dealt out lately.

He pushed the dark imagery of the past week out of his head and focused on the warm light of the clearing on the mountainside.

Warmth ran through his bones, a heaviness grew in his muscles, and he drifted off to sleep.

Rosita stirred beside him, rolled over. Pain from her injury awakened her and her eyes blinked open. She adjusted the bedding, carefully padding it to cradle her injured head, then settled down again, watched Max sleep.

In sleep, he looked peaceful, sweet. She could see the little boy he once was.

She reached out and gently rested her left hand on his chest, comforted by the rise and fall of it as he slept, then closed her eyes and let her own exhaustion take over and joined him in sleep.

Marcus helped Timmy to the truck as Socrates and Tyler

stepped back onto the road by the dogleg. He got him into the rear seat, handed him the First Aid kit, then walked out to join the others, his AR in the ready position.

The three men stood apart from one another, triangulated as they focused their attention on the road leading down the hill, then scanning their position in full 360. None of them wanted to be surprised by someone else jumping out of the grass.

"Could be one or more of 'em hiding in the grass down there, or some wounded," Socrates said.

Marcus nodded.

"Could be," he said.

"And those trucks'll catch attention," Socrates said.

"Mm, hmm," Marcus said. "There is the law to think of."

"Most of it is Bannister controlled, these parts."

Marcus nodded. "I say we leave it. Risky to head down there and try to clean up."

The three men scanned the hillside, then looked at one another.

"Hard to say how Old Man Bannister'll go with this," Socrates said.

"He might try to use the law to get us on this one," Tyler said. "Those are our 9mm bullets in those trucks and bodies."

"Possible," Marcus said. "My guess is the Old Man is going to want to keep this in-house. He's going to want to take care of this with as little fuss and notice as he can. This kind of gun battle—that's national news. He's really not going to want that kind of attention."

"If he can kill us, pin it on us, he could spin the story that way," Socrates said.

"Maybe," Marcus said. "Maybe not. And he has to kill us first." He nodded toward the truck. "Pull back. Let's get out of here."

Marcus kept his attention fixed on the road and fields downhill as Socrates and Tyler swept down the road towards the truck, alert and ready.

When they reached the truck, Socrates signaled Marcus. He

and Tyler covered Marcus as Marcus walked to the truck.

The men climbed in, and Marcus brought the truck to life and stepped down hard on the accelerator, sliding the truck around to straighten it out, on the way to Krell's.

CHAPTER FORTY EIGHT

The phone in Marcus' hand buzzed.

Marcus glanced at it, put it to his ear.

"Hey, Raymond. Sorry. Son of a bitch jumped out of the grass and got the drop on us."

"You guys OK?"

"Timmy took a double-ought pellet to the shoulder, tore some things up. Nothing too bad."

Raymond heard the rumble of the truck in the background, the squeaking of the springs as it barreled along the road. "Sounds like you guys are on the way."

"We are. We're probably something like thirty minutes behind you guys."

"Good. Then we'll see you soon. And Marcus?"

"Yeah?"

"Thanks, buddy. You saved us."

Marcus grinned. "I wouldn't get too happy about it just yet. We fended off the first wave, I expect Bannisters'll send in something a little more quality next." His grin died. "So you guys get ready. They'll be coming."

"Got it," Raymond said. "We'll hit Krell's pretty soon now."

"OK," Marcus said. "Bye."

He lowered the phone, looked at it, thumbed up Dallas' contact and pressed the button.

"Marcus!" Dallas said. "Been waiting on you. How'd it go?"

"We're good," Marcus said. "We put down four trucks on the rise leading to that dogleg, the other two turned tail and ran."

"Casualties?"

"Ol' Bullet Magnet caught a pellet in the shoulder, but seems OK."

"Timmy? Didn't Mack Bannister shoot off his earlobe, too?"

Marcus glanced up in the rearview mirror to look at Timmy in the back seat.

"Yep, he's even uglier than usual, but he'll clean up OK, I think."

"Rough night. How about Bannisters?"

"Hard to say for sure, but I think we put down three men on the hill there. Likely more wounded. Those that made it might not have a taste for this anymore, either. Possible they may just keep on driving, hide out somewhere, wait to see what happens."

"Possible, but not worth counting on," Dallas said. "We got men stationed at all the guard posts, surveillance cameras are up, and perimeter wire armed."

"Just don't shoot at us as we come in."

"Wasn't planning on it," Dallas said. "What's your ETA?"

Marcus looked over at Tyler and raised his eyebrow.

Tyler looked at the odometer, then out the window.

"Twenty, twenty-five minutes, I'd say," he said.

"See you in a half hour, Dallas," Marcus said.

"Looking forward to it," Dallas said.

Mary Jane drifted in a fuzzy warm cloud of cotton. Her heartbeat sounded in her ears, that and her breathing the only sounds in the universe.

Lub-dub, lub-dub.

Hish, hoo.

The cloud was heaven. The universe tingled and buzzed with ecstasy. Nothing mattered except the wonderful feeling that completely filled her up.

Yet something was tugging at her, moving her around, jostling her, interfering with the buzzing and the tingling and the heartbeat and the breathing.

The heartbeat picked up.

Edges of pain jabbed at her, black and jagged and ugly.

"No," she moaned.

The cloud parted, and the tall thin man stood above her.

He was tearing at her, pulling pieces of her off.

It hurt.

"No," Mary Jane said again.

The tall thin man pulled off another piece of her, white and red, strips dangling from it...*a medical dressing*?

Realization shot through Mary Jane, obliterating the warm buzz, replacing it with an icy dagger of steel. Her head throbbed with pain and the memories that came with it.

"No!" Mary Jane said.

She fought to sit up, but her body wouldn't obey. She thrashed as well as she was able. "Let me up!" she said. "Let me out of here!"

The tall thin man dropped the dressing into something out of sight. He studied Mary Jane, expressionless.

He stepped out of her line of vision toward the head of her bed.

"NO!" Mary Jane said. "No more! I want out! I want out! Let! Me! GO!"

The thin man was back, syringe in one hand, the other finding the port on the IV.

Mary Jane screamed.

The man stuck the needle into the port and depressed the plunger, his expression never changing.

He looked into Mary Jane's eyes as the drug swam up her veins and took over. Mary Jane's view of him dimmed as her eyelids drooped and the warm cotton fuzz filled her again. She fought to keep her eyes open, but they were growing heavier and heavier. Too heavy. Impossible.

The tall thin man nodded to himself, and went back to work.

"You what?" Old Man Bannister roared. The news had shattered his early morning calm and he was on his feet facing

Hedges.

"You killed a fucking State Trooper? Are you fucking crazy?"

"Couldn't risk it," Hedges said. "He popped us at 110. All them guns in the truck, whatnot. Bad scene, all around. Didn't have time, neither."

Roger's phone rang.

He looked at it.

"Mertzig," he said.

"Well, fuck," Old Man Bannister said. "At least you didn't kill Officer fucking Mertzig."

Roger hit the answer button.

"Hello?"

He listened for a minute.

"That so?" he said.

Trooper Mertzig was loud and angry, his voice audible across the room.

"Nope, can't say as I have any idea, Stan," Roger said.

A pause.

"We'll put the word out. Don't you worry. We'll get the motherfucker."

Roger looked up at the Old Man, then over at Hedges.

"Hey, Stan," Roger said. "Any chance we can keep this in house? Let us find this asshole and handle it?"

An explosion of verbiage through the phone. Roger held the phone away from his ear, waited for it to subside.

"Keep your pants on, Stan. I told you we didn't have anything to do with it. Just got a few things going on right now. Having troopers swarming the area would complicate things."

Roger nodded a few times, "A-huh, a-huh. Yeah. Got it. Don't you worry, Stan. Bannisters are all over this."

He hung up.

"A vacationing family found the trooper, guy named Schaefer. Mertzig liked him. Family's freaked out, news already has an ear on it. This thing is going to be big."

Hedges glanced at Chris and Tony.

"I'm sorry, boss," Hedges said. "There was just no way we were getting out of there otherwise. And..."

The Old Man waved him quiet.

"Shut your mouth, Hedges," he said. His voice had gone low and quiet.

His tone sent a spike of fear down the spine of every man in the room, including Roger.

The Old Man set down his coffee mug, rounded the table and stood an inch from Hedges, nose to nose.

"One: you are going to get that truck into the barn out back, pronto. Fit it into the big horse stall at the end. Get it covered with straw. Completely."

Hedges nodded, keeping his eyes on the floor.

"Two: You are going to grab a truck from the lot over there and get out of town. I wanted you in on this thing going down at Krell's, but now I need you away. You drive—legally, no getting popped this time—to Hangman. Get a hold of Danny, find out where he and Winter are, and then Danny'll have something for you to do."

Hedges bristled.

The Old Man reached out and lifted Hedges chin, bringing his eyes up.

"Danny. Will. Tell. You. What. To. Do. Got that?"

Hedges pictured sending a .50 caliber bullet through the Old Man's head. Saw the entry wound and the jet of blood, brains, and hair from the exit wound. Envisioned the Old Man dropping and flopping over on the floor, spasming as his body dealt with the abrupt departure of a major portion of its nervous system.

He smiled.

"Yes, sir." Hedges said. "Anything you say, sir."

The Old Man rotated his hand and pushed Hedges in the face, hard.

"Now," he said. "Get the fuck out of here. You fuck anything else up, and I mean anything, you'll be hanging from chains in the arena at Red Rock. You follow me?"

Hedges raised a hand, wiped his face.

Red rage pulsed through his system, but the survival instinct was stronger.

"Yes sir," he said. "Right away, sir."

He turned on his heel and marched out the door, Chris and Tony right behind him.

Roger's phone rang again.

"It's Ralph," Roger said. "They must have Mack. Good news at last."

He answered the phone.

Raymond watched as Guy drove up the dirt road and through the open gates into Krell's compound. Chad followed. A guard stood on each side of the gate, each with his AR slung in the barrel-down ready position.

He glanced back at Mack, who'd gone quiet.

A man in the yard made a round-'em-up motion with one arm and pointed up to the barn with the other. Another man stood at the barn.

As they drove by the big farm house, the screen door swung open and Dallas Krell stepped onto the porch.

Dallas watched as his men guided the truck and van around the corner of the barn and out of sight around the back.

Kane came out and stood beside him.

"What to do," Dallas said. "What to do. Moral dilemma coming up, Kane."

"That's a fact," Kane said.

Dallas took off his hat and ran his hands through his hair, then set his hat back and squared it.

"Well," he said. "Let's get on with this. Daylight's burning."

Hedges parked the backhoe in its spot by the barn, climbed down, and walked over to the truck. Tony was behind the wheel, the engine idling, Chris in the passenger seat.

"Move over," Hedges said.

Tony scooted over without a word and Hedges got behind

the wheel, threw it into Drive, stomped down on the gas and sprayed gravel and dirt as he whipped the truck down the long driveway to the street below.

It took all his self-control not to race through the city and put the pedal to the metal once he hit the road out of town.

"What's safe?" he asked.

"Safe?" Chris said.

"Like, how fast can you go before the Troopers start pulling you over?"

"Normally, I'd say 9 over," Tony said, "but with them being on high-alert and all, I'd stay close to the limit."

Hedges grunted, looked down at the speedometer, brought the truck to 73, then hit cruise control.

"God damn it," he said.

He thumped the wheel for emphasis.

"God DAMN it!"

Tony and Chris stared straight ahead.

"Be four fucking hours or better before we get to Hangman. Shit be going down at Krell's...fuck!"

"It's all good," Tony said. "The way I figure it, we're going to be the ones hunting down asshole number one."

"How do you figure that?" Hedges asked.

"Well...there'll be shit going down at Krell's. That'll eat up a lot of men. We got Danny and Winter outside Hangman, Billy and his boys outside Wells. Our boy is somewhere in between them. The Old Man wants us to talk to Danny, so..."

"So, we're the best team he's got and he knows it," Hedges said, sitting up straighter. "Yeah...an old-fashioned coon hunt. That's the ticket."

Hedges eyes lit up.

"Fuck, yeah. We'll track this son of a bitch down and deliver him to the Old Man, be back in no time. Yeah."

Hedges moved to stomp down on the accelerator, caught himself, sighed, then settled in for the long drive ahead.

Max turned over, felt a warm hand on his chest.

His eyes snapped open.

The ceiling of the van swam into view.

Where?

He looked over, saw Rosita sleeping peacefully next to him.

Ah. On the road. Outside Hangman.

Max disengaged himself from Rosita gently, then climbed into the driver's seat with the ledgers.

He pulled out a map and traced his path: Ramsey, Mountain Cleft, Greencreek, Freedom, Hangman, now this little hideout beside the river.

His finger moved on down the map: Jackpot, Wells, a dozen towns, many of them on the Bannister ledger, then the big red star: Red Rock.

They'd be expecting him to hit the next place in line, Jackpot, or maybe Wells. They'd be set up, looking for him.

Red Rock.

Bypass the whole mess in between, take out Red Rock.

At least twenty men down there, though. A big operation, judging by the ledger.

Suicide just to storm in. Especially since they'd be on alert.

Max leaned back in the seat and played various scenarios out in his head: a raid on Red Rock with Dallas and his men; storming the place on his own, middle of the night, like the operation on Bill Bannister's; setting the place on fire and sniping the men like rats as they left; scouting the place; or...

Too big. Too much.

He needed a plan. Something better than roll with it and see when he got there. That'd worked so far, but so far he'd mostly had the element of surprise and a maximum of three men to work against.

Max eased the seat back, folded his hands over his belly, and gazed through the windshield at the foliage of the big African Conifer.

Taking on Red Rock was a serious operation. Required coordination. Help.

Damn it, he thought. *This was supposed to be just me.*

He looked back at Rosita.

She hadn't moved, her hand still outstretched as if reaching for him in her sleep.

The tree filtered the soft morning light golden green as it gently outlined Rosita's features.

The bullet wound was a simple red line starting at her temple and disappearing under her hair. The puffy redness had subsided. In the golden light, her bruises faded into invisibility and she looked soft and pure. Beautiful.

He had to figure a way to get Rosita safe—away from him.

A pang ran through him and he paused, surprised at himself.

Really? What part of you doesn't understand what she's been through? How young she is? You're as bad as the Bannisters.

He pushed the rising emotion down. Squelched it.

Alone. That was what he needed. That was the way to go.

Damn, she looked beautiful though. Pure. Wonderful.

Max shook his head to clear it, closed his eyes and relaxed.

Still the mind. Don't think about it. The answers will come.

Max drifted into a dreamy pre-sleep zone listening to Rosita's quiet breathing as the light fell through the tree above him.

Roger bolted to his feet, chair skidding out from under him and crashing into the wall behind.

The Old Man froze mid-sip of coffee and raised his eyebrows at Roger.

"What the fucking hell?" Roger yelled into the phone. "You better be shitting me, Ralph."

Roger listened for a minute, his eyes pulsing with rage and frustration.

"Tell you what. You get your sorry asses back up the hill here and we'll regroup."

Roger moved to throw his phone at the wall, caught himself, slid it into his pocket.

"What'd they do?" the Old Man asked. His voice was quiet.

Conversational.

Got to give the Old Man an "A+" for calmness in the storm, Roger thought.

He knew that calm well: it was the gathering of forces before the storm broke. And when the storm broke...people died. Painful, brutal deaths, mostly.

Roger sucked in a deep breath, let it out, got a grip on his own emotions.

"Ingersoll and them went off road up the hill toward Cougar Mountain," Roger said. "Curry went chasing up the hill, wild-ass as usual, after 'em, and the whole posse followed him. According to Ralph, they were near the crest of the first hill, up by that sharp turn, when they got ambushed. All the trucks were in a straight line heading right into the fire, didn't stand a chance. First four trucks in line got hit hard. All four stuck: blown tires, dead drivers, like that. Ralph got the men together and into the last two trucks and high-tailed out of there."

The Old Man was standing at the big picture window, back to Roger. He raised his coffee cup again, sipped.

"Mmm-hmm," he said. "How many men we lose?"

"Well, Ralph says it's him, Henry, David, Twitchy, Smoker, and Rank."

"That's six. So we lost six, then?"

"Ralph doesn't think everyone else is dead. He figures they left a few wounded behind, and a couple of guys might not have made it to the trucks and are walking out."

"Left the trucks up there? Right on the road? Plain sight?"

"Yep."

"God damn it," the Old Man said. "We got to get that cleaned up. And fast. Normally, wouldn't be such a deal, but we got the Troopers to worry about now. They come across this, they'll be looking at us a hell of a lot harder than they already will. Damn it!"

The Old Man pivoted on his heel and strode back to the table. He and Roger faced each other.

"Better work the phones. Get Ralph and them back there.

Have Ralph pull trucks from where he can get them. Have Shirley's Towing get all that shit off the hill and into his lot. Tell him to send all three of his tow trucks up there, pronto. Ralph and them can sweep the area and clean it up to keep the Troopers off of it."

"We'll need more men for Krell's," Roger said.

"I know that," the Old Man snapped. He scrubbed his chin, worked his hand around behind his neck, looked at the floor.

"We're going to have to pull a team or two out of Red Rock. That'll leave Red Rock a little thin, but it's secure. Nobody's getting through the gates without our say so. Just make sure to leave enough men down there that the new shipment is handled properly. I don't want no other fiascos to complicate things."

Roger nodded.

"Call down the line for more men. And get me a map of the area Krell's compound is at. Print that Google Earth shit. We'll hit them so fucking hard they won't know what happened. Going to turn that whole compound into a smoking hole in the woods. Going to look like a fucking meteor smashed into it."

The Old Man turned his back and strode from the room, his boots a steady, deliberate beat across the wooden floor.

Going to take it out on his girls, Roger thought. *Good. Keep him off of me for right now.*

Roger moved back to the computer and got to work.

CHAPTER FORTY NINE

Sunlight poured through the windows of the big room in Krell's farmhouse.

Men crowded around the table, filled the couches and easy chairs.

"Mack's secure?" Dallas asked.

Kane nodded at him.

"Absolutely. Got him in the bunker. Two-man guard. Widrigs patched him up, then hit him up with a dose of pain killers. I wouldn't say he's happy, but he's manageable."

Dallas turned his attention to Dean.

"Perimeter's secure?"

"Absolutely," Dean said. "Men posted at all the guard spots, cameras up and running, perimeter wire armed. A rabbit's not crossing our line without our knowing about it."

Dallas looked out at the men in front of him.

"It comes down to this," Dallas said. "All our work, all our building, everything we've done for most of our lives comes down to today."

The men leaned forward. Fire in their eyes.

"All of us moved out here to get away from it all. From civilization and its craziness. From all the bullshit. We wanted pure lives for our families. We wanted to be self-sustaining. Independent."

Rumbles of agreement.

"Some of our families moved out here more or less chased away by the Bannisters." He paused as men acknowledged that.

"Some of us came out here to build a community. Some of us came out here for the independence. All of us are proud of what we've built. All of us are devoted. All of us have families."

Dallas moved through the room, meeting men's eyes, resting a hand on a man's shoulder for a moment, moving on.

He stepped to the center of the room and raised his hands.

"All of this," he gestured out the window, "is in jeopardy. Everything. Our land, our crops, our families, our lives."

He dropped his arms.

"Our souls, too. We are going to win this war. We are going to defend what is ours. No one is taking that from us."

Rumbles of approval swept the room.

Dallas raised a hand.

"But we will not descend to the Bannister's level. We will not become animals."

He turned to Kane.

"We need information from Mack, and he's a bartering chip, if it comes to that. But we are not going to hurt him. Got that?"

Kane met Dallas' eyes. Dipped his chin in acknowledgement.

"We are the good guys in this fight," Dallas said. "And it's important that we stay that way. If we sink to the Bannister level, even if we win, we lose."

He looked around the room and waited for that to sink in.

"Now," he said. "Is the time. Now is the day. Now is a turning point. Now is when we make this place and our lives here secure. Inviolable. Now."

The room was silent and still.

"Let's get out there. And let's remember what we're fighting for. Go."

The men stood as a group.

Dallas moved to the front door and shook every man's hand on the way out, looked him in the eyes, and clapped him on the shoulder.

"Remember," he said. "We're the good guys here. Remember that."

Max startled awake as Rosita moved into the passenger's seat beside him.

The sun was high.

His stomach growled.

He stretched in the seat, arms over his head, twisting around to get the kinks out of his back.

Rosita watched him, quiet and calm.

"How's your head?" Max asked.

"Better," Rosita said. "I'm good."

Max leaned over and lifted her hair away with the back of his hand, peered at the wound.

Still an angry red line, but very little puffiness.

"Keep putting that ointment on it," he said. "Looks pretty good."

Her skin was warm and smooth under his fingertips. A surge of desire ran through him.

Rosita's eyes met his. He read acceptance there. An invitation.

He pulled his hand away.

"Better get moving," he said.

Max climbed out of the van, walked around, slid the side door open and pulled out his camping stove, some of the freeze-dried bacon and eggs they'd stocked up on at Krell's, and got to work.

Rosita watched his every move, her eyes gentle and alight.

"Hedges! You ornery motherfucker!" Winter crowed.

Hedges and Winter stood an arm's length from one another, in between the two trucks pulled off to the side of the road just out of Hangman.

The long road divided the countryside down the middle all the way to the horizon. A few tiny dots of cars aside, the road was empty, wheatfields green on each side.

"How long's it been?" Hedges asked. "A couple of years?"

Winter scrubbed his chin, let his eyes scan the horizon.

"I reckon so," he said. "Last time was that operation down by the border. Little disagreement between the Old Man and his little Mexican buddy."

Hedges laughed. "Holy shit. That was a wild one."

He pulled out his Desert Eagle, held it flat on his palm. "That's where I learned to appreciate the power of this little beauty. Still got yours?"

Winter grinned and pulled out his own and displayed it.

"Twins," Winter said.

Both weapons were in perfect condition, white matte finish gleaming in the noon sun.

Hedges stroked his weapon, then holstered it and studied Winter.

"So," he said. "You've seen our man?"

Winter grimaced and shoved his pistol back into its place in his shoulder holster.

"Wouldn't say 'seen him,' exactly," he said.

Hedges nodded. "That's how you got that knot on your head?"

Winter dipped his head. "Precisely. Came to up against the side of a house in town. Last I remember is this van, just idling in the middle of the street, driver's side door wide open, exhaust..." His eyes dimmed in memory, and his jaw tightened.

"I get up and puke a couple of times, look up, and my car's gone. Knew exactly what happened. Got my crew out there, but it was too late."

Hedges reached out and put a hand on Winter's shoulder.

"Don't you worry none, Winter. We'll get him. Danny says we've got him pinched in. You hold the line here, me and Chris and Tony will sniff him out and haul him in. But before we do...."

The two men grinned at one another.

"Hey!" Danny yelled from his truck. "You two going to start kissing or are we getting on with this?"

A flash of rage sparked in Hedges' eyes.

Winter's grin widened.

"Heard tell you been playing with that gun a lot lately. Danny says the Old Man's pissed about Sherman. Best not take out Danny. Not just yet, anyway."

"Little rat bastard," Hedges said. "Always did want to have a run at him."

"All good things come to those who wait," Winter said.

"Stop googly-eyeing each other and get on with it," Danny called.

The two men gave each other a last slap on the shoulder.

"Good things," Hedges said.

Winter tipped a finger to his bruised brow in salute.

The two separated, each to his own truck.

Hedges climbed into his, jammed it into gear and hit the road, tires screeching, smoke rising in a big blue cloud, and then he was gone.

"Asshole," Danny said, conversationally. "You two good buddies, or what?"

Winter kept his head straight, watching Hedges' truck disappear into the horizon line. "Something like that," he said, watching Danny out of the corner of his eye.

He does kind of look like a rat, Winter thought.

Old Man Bannister wiped sweat from his forehead, took a deep breath and let it out.

He'd gone a little rough on the girl, messed her up a bit more than he meant to, but it'd been an aggravating day.

The maid lay bent over backwards on a kind of a rack/wheel contraption he'd built himself. He'd cranked it tight enough to hear her vertebrae pop, then spread her out nice and accessible and played himself out.

The girl was out cold. All her joints looked in place, though, and he was pretty sure he hadn't broken anything. Well, anything serious, at least. She'd be pretty sore for a while. He grinned, thinking of the subtle contortions of pain she'd wear on her face, trying to serve him for the next week or so.

The Old Man grabbed a towel, wiped some of the blood off of himself, then reached over and pulled the release on the mechanism. The chains rattled as the tension bled out of the system, and the maid's body contracted a little, leaving her rounded over the arch of the wheel.

The Old Man padded across the floor to his bathroom suite. He hit a button to one side of the door and waited.

"Yes, sir?" Another of his maids.

"Clean up," the Old Man said into the intercom.

"Right away, sir."

The Old Man stepped into the bathroom, the world back in some tiny semblance of the way it should be.

A nice long shower, and he could get to work setting things straight.

CHAPTER FIFTY

Max and Rosita rumbled over the bumpy dirt road that ran alongside the river. It was more of a track than a road, but it kept them away from prying eyes and led in the general direction Max wanted to go.

It was a beautiful day out, the green of the fields darkening into the maturity of crops about to enter their prime.

He glanced over at Rosita. Her skin had the same kind of glow to it—the fresh smoothness of a young woman about to blossom into the full maturity of womanhood. The fading yellow bruises couldn't tarnish that.

"Rosita," Max started.

She turned to him.

How to tell her?

"Rosita," Max tried again. "I'm going to have to let you off pretty soon."

"Let me off?' Rosita said. Alarm flared in her eyes. "What are you talking about, Max? There's nothing out here."

"No, no, no," Max said, waving his hand in dismissal. "That's not what I mean. I mean..." Another glance. "Things are going to get really nasty really fast. It's going to get more dangerous. I don't want you to get hurt, so..."

"*Hurt*? I've already been *hurt*, Max. There is nothing you can drive me into that is any worse than what I have already seen. And endured. When I was new..."

Rosita turned her head to watch the fields as the van worked its way down the road.

"When I was new," she said, "I was a favorite. They did... things. I thought I was going to die. I thought I had died. Many times. And now? With you? This is life, Max. This is freedom.

This is me living by my choice."

"But," Max said. "You're so young. You have so much life ahead of you. I want you to have the fullest life possible. A life filled with joy and laughter and children—if that's what you want."

Rosita laughed, a terrible, hard laugh that didn't fit with her youth and beauty.

"They stole my youth, Max. And I'm older than you think. How old do you think I am, anyway?"

Max studied her. The delicate features. The smooth skin of youth, the sense of the skin barely able to contain the vitality and muscle straining to grow. The shininess of her hair. The breasts full and tight.

"You can't be more than 17, maybe 18," Max said.

Rosita laughed again, this time more of a true laugh.

"I'm 22, Max. I was 18 when that bastard José courted me, persuaded me to follow him...and sold me to the cartel in Tenancingo. I am not the little girl you think I am."

Max blinked, taking in the new information.

"That's not the point. The point is you deserve a full life. I will not be responsible for leading you into the kind of danger I'm walking into. I will not be responsible for causing you any more pain. I will not..."

Rosita reached out and put her hand over Max's mouth.

"You will not deny me my freedom, Max," Rosita said. "Never again do I want a man deciding for me what my life should be. Can you understand that? Never again. I would rather die a thousand deaths than to have my freedom taken from me again."

Max brought the van to a stop.

A light breeze rippled the crops in the field, blew through the cab, lifted the hair from Rosita's face.

"I chose you, Max. I chose to get into this truck with you. That was the first choice I made with the freedom you gave me, and that is the choice I will continue with."

Max moved to say something, but Rosita stopped him with a

look.

"Those men stole from me," she said. "They stole my youth. I may never have a family. Children. The laughter you speak of. But I will have my..." she faltered for the word. "Not revenge, exactly. I will balance things. I cannot begin to think of making a life until I have balanced what happened to me. To my friends. To those girls that I watched die. I cannot think of such a thing until things have been set right."

She looked back out the windshield at the road ahead.

"Maybe not even then," she said. "But those things are for later. Now there is only..." she gestured at the road ahead.

Max looked at her. Saw the iron will. The resolute determination. And the pain.

He turned back, put both hands on the wheel, and eased the van forward.

Dallas, Kane, and Big John stood over a glaring Mack.

Mack was handcuffed to a bed. He'd been washed, bandaged up, and put into clean clothes.

Dallas raised an eyebrow at Widrigs.

"So?" Dallas said.

"Well, he'd dislocated his shoulder, and I put it back in. He didn't like that much, but it'll be OK. Mostly a bunch of bruises and things. Nasty knot on the side of his head. I figure he has a concussion, but that'll be OK, too."

Dallas stepped in to inspect Mack.

Mack was wearing a big olive-green T-shirt that said 'Property of USMC' and clean boxers.

"We're not going to hurt you any," Dallas said. "But we're not ready to let you go, either. We figure your Old Man will be coming for you pretty soon, so we're saving you for that, right now."

"The Old Man is going to destroy you," Mack growled. "He's going to come in here and kill every last one of you. Slowly. And I'm going to watch."

"Maybe," Dallas said. "Maybe not. The way I see it, you are

useful to this operation in one of two ways."

"I ain't helping you in one of any ways," Mack said. "Go fuck yourself."

"One," Dallas said; "We let the Old Man know we've got his little boy safe and sound and that if he comes storming in like the maniac he is, he's likely to kill him."

"Oh, he'll come," Mack said. "Count on it. He's not going to worry too much about how it all goes down just so long as he burns it all down when he's done. He'll expect me to fend for myself and to make it out on my own, once shit starts going down. And I will. Believe it. And then..."

"Two," Dallas said. "the Old Man got Mary Jane back. I'm fixing to give him a call and offer you up in exchange."

Mack hooted. "Ha! So Sherman got that bitch back! Hah! No way in hell the Old Man is letting her loose again. He'll have that bitch down in Red Rock before the day is done. Won't be nothing left of her but ash, I expect."

Dallas nodded. "Well, we'll see about that, Mack. We'll see. Meantime, you stay comfortable."

Dallas pulled Mack's phone out of his pocket, scrolled through his contacts. "I'm guessing 'Old Bastard' is the Old Man?" He scrolled through some more. "Lots of numbers in here, Mack. I'm bettin' we get to work on these, all kinds of interesting things going to pop up."

Mack laughed. "Fuck you, Krell. Not like you're going to be able to do anything. You're already up to your neck in shit. You'll be dead by tomorrow. Fucking hippy asshole. Should have killed you and your family years ago. Should've killed all you fucks. Should've...."

Dallas looked at Kane and Big John.

They shrugged and looked back at him.

Mack continued to rave; "I'll be skull fucking you by tomorrow morning. This place is going to burn, the Old Man will..."

"Good work, Doc," Dallas said. "Looks like Mack is back to himself again. We'll keep a guard down here with you. 'Til then, Big John will watch over him."

"Big John? Big John can suck my cock," Mack said. "In fact, he may as well get some practice in right now. By tomorrow..."

"Kind of sad, in a way," Dallas said to Kane. "Such a one-track mind. What a waste."

"You're a waste, you hippy-ass piece of shit! But not for long! By tomorrow..."

Dallas and Kane walked out of the room, across the bunker floor and up the stairs into the open air behind the barn.

"Red Rock? Did you catch that?" Dallas said.

"Indeed," Kane said.

"Get on that. Find the place. Call Max and tell him. He can scout it out for us and once we take care of whatever the Old Man sends our way, we'll clean up and send Marcus and his crew down to help, a couple of the others, too."

"I'm on it," Kane said. "Anything else?"

"Might get some useful information off of Mack's phone," Dallas said. "Get everything: names and accounts behind these numbers, best you can. See what we can see. I expect he's right about the Old Man coming in strong, but it isn't going to be as quick as he thinks, not after Marcus and his team took out that posse chasing after them. It's going to take the Old Man some time and effort to pull together enough guys to attack this compound. In the meantime, let's see what we get. I might have another chat with young Mack, and then I'll call up his daddy and see what he has to say."

Kane took the phone from Dallas.

"I'm on it. I can do that, check out this 'Red Rock,' and monitor the cameras and crews at the same time."

"Do that," Dallas said. "I'm thinking we might have to get a little more proactive on this one. So get me that info as quick as you can."

Kane nodded and walked up the path back toward the bunker.

Dallas watched him go, then turned to survey the compound.

The sunflowers tracked the sun across the sky, and Dallas glanced up.

Daylight was burning. Time to move.

Ralph watched as Shirley winched the last of the trucks up onto his tow truck. It'd been a bitch, maneuvering the big tow truck around on the narrow lane without getting it bogged down in the soft ground on either side, but they'd done it. A total of three bodies had been located and thrown into the backs of the trucks, the last Curry's, found off to the side of the road by the sharp turn off at the crest of the hill.

"Curry must've given them a run for their money," Ralph said.

The tall, rail thin man next to him drew deeply on his cigarette, pinched between his thumb and forefinger and nodded, hissing out smoke.

"Reckon so," he said. "Never was short on balls, Curry."

Ralph shook his head.

"Unbelievable," he said. "Bill and his place, Mountain Cleft, Greencreek, Hangman. Roger at Osbakken's farm. Took down Mack outside the diner that morning." He shook his head again, "and now this."

He watched as the tow truck lumbered down the hill, bouncing on the rough road, then pulled onto the main road and slowly geared up, headed back to Aston and the tow yard.

"Asshole's got allies. Dallas Krell and his crew."

Roger kicked a rock and watched it tumble down the gravel road, veer right and go into the weeds.

"You've seen this asshole," the tall thin man said. He took another deep drag on his cigarette, then dropped it, grinding it out with the toe of his cowboy boot. "What'd you think?"

"That morning outside The Spotted Owl? Shit," Ralph said. "It was something to see, all right. I stepped out the door, and there was Mack, flat on his back and angry as hell about it. At the time, I just figured it was Mack being an asshole, bitten off more than he could chew. Was kind of pissed at him, matter of fact. Had a lot to get done, and he's fucking around getting in a fight outside a diner in the morning like that? Knew he'd picked that fight; he'd been looking for an excuse to kick the shit out of someone."

The tall man nodded. "Yep, seen 'im do shit like that a thousand times." He pulled a pack of cigarettes from his shirt pocket and shook one out, then offered the pack to Ralph.

Ralph waved it away, leaned back into a stretch, then started walking back down the hill toward his truck.

"Son of a bitch moved like lightning," he said. "Mack rushed him and then Mack was flat on his back, down and out. Dennis took a poke at him, and this asshole just stepped in and head butted him flush. Fucked him up good."

"Why didn't you fuck *him* up?" the tall man asked, taking a few quick steps to catch up and walk down the hill beside Ralph.

"Honestly? I figured Mack deserved it, and I was kind of pissed at him. Dennis tried to sucker punch the asshole and he'd just defended himself."

Ralph stopped and turned to face the man.

"Smokes, you keep that to yourself, you hear me? Mack's going to be on the warpath once we get him back. If we don't have something to occupy him, he'll go after one of us, just for the hell of it."

Smokes nodded. "Don't you worry none, Ralph. I got your back on this. I always got your back. You know that."

Ralph nodded. "I know," he said. "Crazy times. Crazy fucking times."

"Ah, don't get too worked up about it," Smokes said. "We been through shit before. the Old Man always comes out on top."

Ralph took a deep breath, his eyes focused inwardly, then looked back at Smokes.

"We'll see. Got a hinky feeling about this one, Smokes. This asshole has dropped the Bannisters as easy as one-two-three. Shut down all them little operations. Pretty much all by himself. And now we got Krell and his group to think about."

"Aw, relax, hoss," Smokes said. "We got this. We always do. Now come on, let's get back and get ready. Five will get you ten the Old Man has us move in on Krell's tonight."

"You're right about that," Ralph said. "Better rest up a bit before we go in. Going to be a crazy night."

The two men walked side by side to Ralph's truck, climbed in, and drove away, dust rising behind them.

Hedges checked his mirrors, slowed, then brought his truck around in a U-turn to pull in behind the big Silverado.

They'd covered the road carefully between Hangman and Billy's truck, all three of them alert and ready. Itching for a fight. But there'd been no sign of a van, white or otherwise.

"Hell," Hedges said. "Asshole must've pulled off somewhere. We're going to have to go back, scout the likely roads he might've taken."

He banged the steering wheel with the heel of his hand.

"God damn it to hell," he said. "I want this asshole so bad I can taste it."

Tony put a hand on his shoulder.

"Don't you worry none. He didn't get past us or Billy. Or Winter. We'll get him. Just a matter of time."

Hedges looked up at the sky. The sun was edging toward the horizon on its way down.

"Ain't got that much daylight left, damn it," he said. "Going to get harder in the dark."

"We'll get him," Tony said again.

Hedges sighed and opened the door, climbed out of the truck.

"Going to check in with Billy and his boys. Then we'll get on with it."

Tony and Chris watched as Hedges walked around the side of the big Silverado parked ahead. The driver's hand came out the window and Hedges clasped it.

"Think we'll get him?" Tony asked.

"We always do," Chris said.

Roger hung up the phone, then turned and studied the satellite shots of Krell's compound. He'd pulled two teams from Red Rock: Wolff and his boys and Barry and his. He'd gotten Bakke on the line, told him he needed them choppered up to the Bannister compound with all their gear. Spendy, but worth it. Bakke said he'd be in the air in less than an hour, which put them at Bannister's in three and half hours or so. It'd be tight, but doable.

If he had a plan. *If* the boys could execute. *If* Krell didn't have too many men and gear ready.

He needed the element of surprise.

He studied the satellite shots some more.

He followed the narrow dirt road into the trees, then out a quarter mile later at what was probably a gate. Nice little layout there: big farmhouse, a barn, huge vegetable garden, some trees, dirt lane snaked around the big yard branched into the trees behind....

Roger squinted. He zoomed in on a spot, but the resolution was poor. This far out from civilization, it didn't appear Google was all that concerned with razor-sharp detail. Everything got unreadably fuzzy. Roger zoomed out to maximum clarity.

Looked to be something under those trees in an area about a quarter mile up from the field.

Houses?

Huh.

Further back, up the hill toward the mountain, another dirt lane.

Roger followed it with his finger.

Holy shit, he thought. *How could I have missed that?*

His finger traced the road to the spot where Curry and the rest had been ambushed.

Of course.

Roger sat back in his chair and stared at the ceiling.

A team on the gate, maybe two, spread down the fence.

A couple of teams on the back road coming in.

Get Bakke to drop a team right in the middle of the compound. It'd probably take a gun to his head, but he'd do it.

Holy shit, Roger thought again.

This will work.

CHAPTER FIFTY ONE

Max eased the van down the dry river bed in all-wheel drive, then climbed the shoulder out of the river bed toward the desert plain. He'd followed the river into Nevada, under the big Interstate and out into the desert. The desert floor was hard-packed, easy driving.

The GPS on his phone had been outside the zone of cell coverage since shortly after he'd crossed under the Interstate, but judging by mileage and what the map had showed him of the river's path, he figured he was into Utah by now.

About an hour out of Red Rock. If he were careful, he'd creep up on it at dusk.

Take a look and see what he could see.

The springs of the van jounced as the van crept over the lip of the shoulder and onto the desert floor. Ahead, he could see a mountain line on the horizon: Red Rock was nestled right up against it, somewhere.

Problem was, it was a wide-open plain and anyone would see the van from miles away.

Max checked his cell phone again.

No coverage.

If he angled west, he'd run into the road that skirted the hills, ran along the desert. The way it snaked around the base of the mountains, it might just hide him from view.

Might. He headed due west.

Only one way to find out.

Albert sat up. He'd fallen asleep waiting to hear back from Hedges. It hadn't even been twenty-four hours, so he wasn't too worried, but whatever was going down, he wanted in on it.

Boots clomped down the passageway outside his room.

More boots.

What in the hell?

Albert swung his feet over the side of the bed, put on his own boots and stepped into the hallway, narrowly missing getting body checked by four men making a bead for the weapons locker.

Albert stepped into line behind the men and followed them down.

Wolff had already opened the security door and the locker swarmed with men.

Two full teams: Wolff's and Barry's.

All ten men were wearing flak jackets and webbing. Fully geared up.

The men pulled weapons off the racks, checked magazines, grabbed boxes of ammo.

"What's going on?" Albert asked.

"Roger called," Wolff said. "He wants two teams ready. He's going to chopper us up to the Old Man's. Something big going down tonight. Don't know anything else."

Albert stepped out of the way as men began to file out of the room, brushing past him.

"He didn't say what was going on?"

Wolff stopped and stared at Albert.

"He didn't. And I didn't ask."

The men looked at one another.

"With you and Barry and your guys both gone, that don't leave many guys here to hold the fort."

Wolff slapped the wall of the weapons locker.

"This place is secure as a prison. Nobody's getting in."

Albert grinned. "There's that," he said.

"Roger said you're in charge for now. All you got to do is make sure them bitches don't get out or die on us. They're going to have to sit here a while longer while whatever the hell it is the Old Man's got going gets settled. I'll let Wade and the others know. Shouldn't be too much trouble, just those nine in the holding pens, plus the one you brought in. Doc'll stay here with you, make sure the one you brought in gets better. Besides him and Wade, you'll have Page, Holt, and Hill."

Albert rubbed his chin. "Plus me, that's six guys. I suppose that'll do. Any idea how long you'll be gone?"

"No idea at all," Wolff said. He glanced at his watch. "Chopper's supposed to be here in about fifteen."

He slapped Albert on the shoulder.

"Be seeing you, hoss."

Albert tipped his chin in farewell.

Interesting, Albert thought. *Just me and the weak ones. I'll be able to do pretty much anything I feel like.*

A pulse of excitement ran through him.

And I feel like...having some fun.

Kane sat in front of a bank of monitors at a huge command-post of a desk in the bunker.

Krell's men had opened the bunker up fully, and Raymond was amazed. It was a high-tech wonderland—a survivalist's wet dream.

"We're not part of the black-helicopter-one-world-order crowd," Kane said as he played with his keyboard. Images shifted and zoomed: with the touch of a finger, Kane could zoom in on any spot in the compound.

"But I'll tell you what: we paid close attention to Ruby Ridge. That happened not far from here. We paid attention to Waco. To the Dakota pipeline deal. Way things are going in this country, won't be too much longer 'til they'll be coming after people like us; people who don't buy all the crazy bullshit they are trying to shove down our throats."

"You do know the one thing in common with all of those incidents, right?" Raymond said.

Kane looked up from his monitors.

"The Feds won. Every time."

Kane grinned. "Oh. I get it. You think we're crazy enough to think we can take on the Feds?" He shook his head. "Nope. We got no illusions. We noticed what happened to the Weavers. What happened to all those people down in Waco. But if the Feds—or anyone else—come for us; we'll dictate the terms. And if they force it, we'll die for what we believe."

"What *do* you believe?" Raymond asked.

"That a man has a right to live free. That a man has the right to believe what he wants to believe. That this country is the best country in the world."

"That doesn't seem too controversial," Raymond said.

"Been reading the papers?" Kane asked.

He waved his hand in dismissal.

"All that's by the by. We live our own lives out here. We got crops and animals and we need no one. We got Internet businesses and plenty of money; some of us were investment types before they got sick of all the greed and corruption. And truth be told, we're not worried about the Feds. Not yet, anyway. We just want a place where we can live in peace and raise our kids away from the madness of what's going on out there."

Raymond leaned in to examine the screens.

"Speaking of what's going on out there...you've really got a camera on every piece of the property?"

"Pretty much. We believe in privacy, so not much in the way of indoors. Just a couple of the main spots: the great room down at the farmhouse, meeting places, like that."

Raymond pointed at a monitor showing a stretch of fence through the trees.

"Where's that?"

Kane fiddled with the keyboard and a map popped up on the monitor next to the one Raymond was pointing at. A red dot pulsed on the map.

"Three hundred yards west along the fence from the main gate," he said.

Raymond pointed at a little rectangular box stuck into the ground with what looked like little metal legs. "Is that what I think it is?"

"Yes, my friend, that is a Claymore mine," Kane said. "That'll clear a path in a sixty-degree arc for about fifty yards; kill anything within 100 feet."

Raymond squinted, then pointed.

"They look to go all the way up along the fence. How many of them do you have?"

"Standard deployment, about six per 100 yards, close enough to have overlapping fire zones, not so close that setting one off will start a chain reaction and blow them all."

Still leaning into the monitor, Raymond poked at a couple of spots.

"Looks like you got tripwires set up," he said. "Remote detonation as well?

"Indeed," Kane said. "I can trip them from here, and we've rigged them so defensive teams can trip them from position once they've set up."

"I don't see anyone," Raymond said.

"You're not supposed to. And it'll take the Bannisters some time to regroup and come after us, and we expect them to come at night, if they come."

"Won't that mess with your surveillance?"

Kane toggled a menu and pointed.

"Night vision," Raymond said. "Holy shit. You guys are set up better here than any post I've been on."

Kane raised his eyes. "Where might that have been?"

Raymond met his gaze. "Iraq. Afghanistan. I did two tours. Marines."

"Well. Semper Fi, Marine!"

"Uh-huh. What were you?"

"Most of us were SEALS. Been all over. A couple of Army Rangers. Some regular army, infantry. Just about all of us have served. Like I said, we love this country. We believe in it. Not many places where you can live free in this world."

"Free...with Claymores and high-tech toys," Raymond said. "Where the hell do you even get Claymores?"

Kane grinned.

"Walmart."

Raymond looked at Kane in astonishment, and then both men burst into laughter.

Men crowded the table in Old Man Bannister's den. Ralph and his crew sat with their backs to the window, Roger sat at the head, and Old Man Bannister stood like a rock off to one side. In total twelve men, not counting Roger and the Old Man.

The sound of a chopper in the distance.

The sound grew as the chopper advanced towards the compound.

Roger cocked an ear. "Excellent," he said, checking his watch. "They made good time. We can get this started."

He handed a stack of folders to Ralph. "Take one, pass it down. Set one at each place at the table." He gestured at the eleven empty chairs around the table.

The chopper roared overhead, deafening, pitch rising, then leveled off, hovering, pitch lowering as it set down in the lot outside. The engine shut off.

A minute later Wolff walked through the door, Barry and the others behind.

"Excellent," Roger said again. "This is all coming together real nice."

The two teams from Red Rock took their seat.

A big, soft looking guy, bald with a fringe of hair and a massive nose ambled over and sat next to Roger.

"Roger," he said.

"Bakke," Roger said.

"A little night flying, as I understand it."

"Yep. We got a mighty big operation going on here. Good to have you on board."

Bakke grimaced. "Just how big we talking?"

Roger waved at the group, grown to twenty-three men.

"You're looking at it," he said.

Roger stood.

"Let's get this show on the road," he said. "Open up your

folders and we'll start with the map."

Each man opened his folder, face grim.

No backing out now.

Go time.

Raymond pointed to another monitor.

"What's with the pin marks on this map?"

"Every city in the USA named Red Rock," Kane said.

"Why?"

"Mack slipped and gave us the name. Said that's where they'd take Mary Jane."

Raymond straightened up.

"Holy shit—you know where Mary Jane is?"

"We think so." Kane toggled a few things and the map zoomed in. He pointed. "We got three Red Rocks within a twenty-four hour drive from the gas station where they snatched Mary Jane. Here, here, and here."

Raymond looked. Utah, New Mexico, and Arizona.

"The two most likely look to be Utah and Arizona." A few more keystroke commands. The map zoomed in tighter to the Red Rock in Utah revealing a tiny town nestled up against a mountain range. Looked to house about a hundred people, if that.

"Look here," Kane said. He zoomed tighter, to the point of pixilation. A compound tucked up tight against a steep drop on the mountain, pushed back into the V formed by two mountains coming together.

"Looks like a secure compound, doesn't it?" Kane said.

Raymond stroked his chin. "It does. Damn."

Kane leaned back and toggled up the Red Rock in Arizona.

Bigger. At least a hundred thousand people.

"That Red Rock is a tourist town" Kane said. "I've gone over it in a tight grid search, found nothing like that compound in Utah." A few more clicks. "Red Rock, New Mexico, is another big town. Smack in the middle of a desert. There are some really isolated places on its outskirts, so it's a possible. Couldn't find anything like what we see in Utah, though. "Plus, it's longer than an overnight drive to get there. The way Mack was talking, they'd have Mary Jane at Red Rock by now."

"Utah, then," Raymond said.

"That's what I'm thinking," Kane said.

"What are we going to do about it?" Raymond asked.

"Right now?" Kane said. "Nothing. We got the Bannisters to deal with. Once we settle that?" He swiveled his chair to look at Raymond. "Plenty."

CHAPTER FIFTY TWO

Hedges steered the Silverado down the little dirt lane that ran alongside the river. He'd taken the side road on a hunch—the first likely looking turnoff outside of Hangman—and as he drove he felt certainty tighten his gut.

"You two be ready," he said. "I got a feeling about this."

Chris grinned. "Born ready, hoss. And you know it."

Tony caressed the handguard of his weapon.

Hedges rounded a corner, spotted a huge tree, pointed.

"Hello," he said. "What's that?"

He stopped the truck near the tree.

"Lookee here," he said. "Tire tracks leading up to the tree." He leaned over the wheel, examined the ground in the fading light. "Turn around marks." He maneuvered the truck and hit the lights. In the bright glare the dirt ridges formed by the tire tracks sharpened. "Those are damn fresh," Hedges said. "Look how sharp them ridges are."

"Fresh as hell," Chris said. He sat up higher. "Looks like we got ourselves a trail, hoss."

"Sure as hell," Hedges said. "Told you I had a feeling about this."

Hedges aimed the truck back down the lane.

"Eyes peeled, assholes," he said. "We got a party to get to."

Max slowed the van to a crawl.

"What is it?" Rosita asked.

Max raised a hand and pinched the skin on the ridge of his nose between his eyes.

The air was electric. He grimaced and held the door in his mind closed.

"We're on it," he said.

"On what, Max?"

"Red Rock. Right around the corner. And it's a bad place, Rosita. I can feel it pushing at me already."

Max took a deep breath, centered himself. Turned his mind to the Blond Woman. Let peace fill the roiling gap in his gut. He turned off the headlights, eased the van into gear and rolled around the corner.

Red Rock sprang into view. The town was edged in deep shadow by the setting sun. A scattering of trailers, containers off of trucks, and ranch houses, dotted with a few larger elaborate homes spread over the hilly plain. Low brush edged in the town and homes, holding the dirt down. A wind swirled through town, kicking up little dust devils. Lights in some of the homes.

At the extreme west end of the town, tucked tight into the V of two mountains, little red lights topped a tall fence with what looked to be a security gate.

Max pointed. "Bingo," he said.

He pulled the van to the side of the road.

The air pulsed with the Red Presence. It was like he'd stepped into an electrified pool of water. His whole body vibrated with it.

"This is it," he said.

Imagery pounded at the door in his mind.

He held it shut.

"We got to get a better look at the place," he said. "Figure out how to get in there, take it."

Rosita turned and put her back against the passenger's side door.

"Alone?" she said. "Are you willing to die? For nothing?"

Max looked at her blankly.

"Die? Yeah. For nothing? No. To take down the Bannisters? Free the women they're holding? Put an end to this evil empire of theirs? Absolutely."

"Max," Rosita said. "You go in there alone, you will die. And you will help no one. You will die for nothing."

"Maybe, maybe not," Max said. "Let's get a better look."

As he moved to put the van into gear, the phone in his pocket buzzed, startling him.

"Forgot about that," he said, pulling the phone out and looking at it.

He looked at Rosita.

"Raymond," he said.

He put the phone to his ear.

"Yeah? What's up, Raymond?"

Marcus toggled the switch on his goggles and the area lit up with the greenish glow peculiar to night vision.

He clicked the transmit button on the shoulder mic of his two-way radio. "Check," he said. "Timmy?"

"Copy," Timmy's voice was clear and sharp in Marcus' earphone. "All equipment operating, team in place, over."

"Socrates?"

"Copy, loud and clear."

And on down the line.

Every team in position. Night vision and radios working.

"Kane?"

"Copy. Loud and clear. Time to settle in, teams. Get comfortable, over."

Marcus eased his back against the tree and looked around. He was fifty yards behind the line of Claymores with his team. He scanned the fence line and the Claymores. Looked up to where he knew the next team was, 300 yards up the hill. Even with his night vision, they were invisible.

"All teams," Marcus said into his mic. "All teams: settle in. Stay alert, over."

Each team: "Copy."

Marcus clicked off his night vision and relaxed. His ears were in tune with the surroundings: the gentle whisper of the night breeze through the grass and trees. The occasional pop of a tree adjusting to the cooling temperature of the night after the hot day. Rustling through the brush of small creatures. As he relaxed and opened himself, he could make out the breathing of his men.

Ready.

Images of a hundred patrols played in his head: Iraq. Afghanistan. Desert patrols. City patrols. Mountains. Bare hills. He'd seen it all.

His body tingled, a tiny current powering him. It'd been a long time since he'd engaged in combat. The warrior in him welcomed it.

Bring it, he thought. *Let's get it on.*

And over with.

Raymond sat with Guy, Chad, and Mahler in the trees on the backside of the compound. Kane and Dallas had plotted out the teams, spreading them around the perimeter, with Kane and Dallas at the command center in the bunker, Dean, Big John, and Forrest up at the farmhouse with the backup communications center and video.

He figured Dallas had put him back here as the back position was least likely to take any heat, and thus had less chance of messing up the operation of their teams.

He toggled his night vision goggles and looked up and down the line.

He could see neither team on his flank, and the feeling of being alone grew.

He looked down at the detonating device for the Claymores on his section of fence. Part of him wanted to click it, just to see if it worked.

He resisted the urge.

Marcus' voice came through the earphone in his ear.

"All teams, settle in. Stay alert, over."

Raymond clicked the mic.

"Copy. Over," he said.

He clicked off the night vision and raised the apparatus out of the way. As his eyes settled, he could make out the sharp ridge line of the hills above him, a black silhouette against the night sky. The stars brightened. This far away from any civilization the sky was packed with their glow and shimmer.

He played over the conversation with Max in his head. Max was going to try to hit Red Rock by himself. *Suicide.* He silently wished for the Bannisters to attack, to get it over with. Max needed help. Mary Jane needed help. They needed to get Marcus and Socrates' teams down there. Raymond needed to get down there.

Max had said he was within sight of Red Rock. He was planning on raiding the place, and torching it.

And Raymond was hundreds of miles away, sitting in the dark woods.

Come on, you son of a bitches, he thought. *Let's get this over with.*

He looked up the line of the fence toward the mountain, then down the other way.

It was a beautiful night.

He took a look at the men dug in around him, then returned his gaze to the stars.

Mary Jane struggled against her chains. She was hanging from the ceiling, arms stretched overhead. Her hands had long gone numb and it felt as if her shoulders were being pulled out of their sockets. She shook and kicked her legs, rattling the chains. She tried to take hold of the chains, pull herself up, but her hands would not obey her. She tried to swing herself, then to make her hands small to pull them through the manacles. The pain in her wrists was intense, growing sharp and bright as the sun…

Her eyes snapped open, and she was in a bed, strapped down. A bare gray room, three empty beds. She tried to pull her hands free and pain shot through her wrists, up her arms to her spine. She cried out.

"Heh, heh, heh."

A man at the foot of her bed. A big man, silhouetted against the open door. Something familiar about him.

"Having some bad dreams, bitch?" he said. "Ain't that a shame. 'Cause whatever you were dreaming, we got worse in store for you."

The man stepped to the head of the bed and Mary Jane recognized him. The one from the truck. He reached out a hand for her. She bared her teeth and lunged at him, catching a pinch of skin as he tried to pull his hand away. She bit down and felt her teeth connect through his tissue, tasted his blood. She turned her head and spit the piece of skin to the side.

The man howled.

"Ahh! You fucking bitch! I'm going to finish you for that!"

He moved to step forward, when someone above Mary Jane's head cleared his throat.

The man stopped.

"Doc!" the man cried. "Fucking bitch, bit me. You know we don't allow that. She needs to learn."

The tall thin man who had been changing Mary Jane's dressings and filling her with drugs stepped into view at the side of her bed.

"This one's special, Albert. You know that. You shouldn't even be in here."

"I am in charge!" Albert said. "Barry and Wolff's teams are out. That leaves me, Wade and his boys...and you. You listen to me, Doc."

"Maybe so," Doc said. "But I still have to answer to the Old Man. And Roger made it very clear. The Old Man has a special interest in this one. He considers her his private property."

The tall man stepped closer to Albert, leaned down to look him in the eyes.

"She fucked you up and you want to hurt her, I get that," he said. "And now she bit you and we don't allow that. I get that, too. But here's the thing, Albert—she belongs to the Old Man. I suspect if I were to let Roger know you'd even been in here, fucking with her...."

The tall thin man let his words hang in the air, and Albert took a step back.

Albert shook his hand in pain. "This fucking bitch. She fucking hit me with a hammer. Fucked up my shoulder. Just about fuckin' knocked me out. Barely got her in control. Almost got me fuckin' caught out there...."

Mary Jane laughed.

"Poor little Albert!" she said. "Can't even defend himself against a big, bad woman. You are so pathetic! You're a weak little man. A worm!"

Albert lunged for her, but the thin man was stronger than he looked and he pushed Albert back.

"You get out of here, Albert. If you have to, take one of the new ones and start training her. Just make sure you don't hurt her too bad. We're due to ship them out after training and we're already one down."

Albert glared down at Mary Jane.

"Could you at least shoot her up with some of the special?" he asked.

The tall thin man paused, turned, and looked at Mary Jane.

A gleam in his eyes.

Mary Jane sensed a hunger growing in the man.

The tall thin man shook himself like a dog—a gesture that sent terror coursing through Mary Jane's body—the man was barely in control of himself.

She was facing two wild animals, and she was the one tied down.

The man's hand shot out and he pushed Albert in the chest, then walked him to the door.

"Maybe," he said. "Maybe just a taste. But not now, Albert. Go away. I got to think about it. The Old Man...."

Albert stood framed in the doorway, then turned and was gone.

The tall man stood there for a long moment, gazing down at Mary Jane, the hunger in him naked. His arms were trembling with it. He was panting like a dog. Fighting for control.

Mary Jane carefully looked away from him, tried to make herself invisible as possible. She had no idea what "the special" was. The Bannisters had used a pharmacopeia of drugs on her when she was housed in the compound, and she'd never heard of "the special."

She wanted no part of it.

As she waited, head averted, she heard the man step out of the room and close the door.

"Oh, God," she whispered. "Help me, please. I can't take much more of this."

She closed her eyes and waited.

Marcus' eyes snapped open. A low rumbling on the horizon, moving fast. He reached for his shoulder mic.

"Everybody. This is Marcus. Alert. I repeat. Alert. We have a chopper coming in, low and fast. Repeat. We have a chopper coming in low and fast. Alert. Over."

"Marcus. This is Kane. Situation? Over."

"Chopper. Coming along the ridgeline. Low. Coming fast. Over."

"All teams. This is Kane. Lock and load. Repeat. This is Kane. Lock and load. Over."

Each team called in its receipt of the message.

Marcus snapped his night vision goggles down and the fence lit up.

Nothing.

The growing roar of the chopper vibrated inside him.

Choppers had always meant reinforcements or a ride home. Or he was coming in on one. He'd never been on the receiving end of an incoming chopper.

So this is what that feels like, he thought.

It was terrifying.

Who would have thought the Bannisters would get their hands on a chopper?

At 3:00AM, there was no doubt who was in that chopper.

As the chopper neared, he picked out the distinctive double whop of a two-bladed chopper.

"All teams. This is Marcus. It's a big one. Repeat. A big one.

Expect multiple teams. Over."

The chopper roared overhead, momentarily blacking out the sky. It was moving fast, headed for the center of the compound, its prop wash causing the little branches on the trees to flail.

"All teams. This is Kane. We have trucks moving in on the gate. Repeat. Trucks moving in on the gate. Engage. Repeat. Engage. Over."

A quick stutter of fire down by the road leading in to the compound. The characteristic blaaat! of automatic fire returning.

The gunfire at the gate heated up.

"North teams. This is Kane. North teams. We have trucks moving in on the back road. Repeat. Trucks moving in on the back road. Engage. Repeat. Engage."

Gunfire to the north.

The sound of the chopper roared as if flared over the farmhouse.

"Marcus. Socrates. This is Kane. Marcus. Socrates. Pull your teams to the farmhouse. We are under attack. Pull your teams to the farmhouse. Engage. Over."

Marcus picked up his gear and ran back toward the farmhouse. He could hear his men behind him. The sound of men moving through the brush to the west told him Socrates and his team were rolling, too.

The whop! whop! whop! of the chopper dimmed as it lowered its bulk to the ground.

Gunfire from the farmhouse.

Gunfire from the barn.

The chopper was caught in a crossfire.

As Marcus burst into the clearing with his team, he motioned for them to take position. His men quickly set up in attack formation.

"Pick your targets!" Marcus yelled into the shoulder mic. "Fire!"

Men poured out of the chopper, fast and low. They moved in

trained coordination, and Marcus' gut clenched.

Damn.

He followed the lead man with the muzzle of his AR as the group split into two teams. He fired a quick three-shot burst, center mass, and the man went down, then rolled off and took cover.

"They've got vests!" Marcus yelled. "Adjust for the vests!"

Marcus loosed several rounds at the figure on the ground. The man had rolled out of the initial line of fire and adjusted himself to present the smallest target.

He hadn't counted on night vision.

Marcus slowed himself, sighted carefully, and squeezed off three shots.

The figure jittered and went still.

One down.

CHAPTER FIFTY THREE

Max wove his way through the roads of Red Rock toward the security gate at the west of town.

The town couldn't have housed more than about a hundred people.

Not much movement.

Lights in some windows. The blue glow of TVs in a few.

As he drove by a ranch-style house, a man headed for an ancient-looking shed in the back yard stopped and stared.

A tangle of bodies rested at the foot of the stairs to the shed. Bloodied, with limbs twisted into impossible positions. Faces blackened and swollen. One woman's legs had been spread so far apart and pulled up and over her head so violently there was no doubt the bones had been pulled out of both hip sockets.

But the little clothing the victims wore was early 19th century.

Ghosts.

Max sensed more of them about, hundreds—more than a century's worth.

His gut roiled as he realized that this town had been a center for the Red Presence since its inception.

He rolled the van down the street and around a corner, away from the man in his yard and the tangle of ghosts at the foot of the container.

A few more turns through the streets, and he was within sight of the fence.

The road curved around the last house and its bare dirt yard, thirty yards from the fence, then ran parallel the length of the fence. The land was flat and bare, the only other house on the street set in a copse of trees at the far corner.

The steel fence stood ten feet high, with razor wire along its top. Insulators anchored wire set about six inches apart that ran the length of the fence from ground level to the coiled razor wire along the top. Max imagined he could feel the voltage crackling through the wires. As he drew even with the big security gate set dead center, he studied it. Thick steel bars set into a metal groove embedded in the concrete that anchored the entire fence line.

Someone had put some serious work into that fence.

And, according to Raymond, that fence stood between him and Mary Jane.

Rage and anxiety, worry and murder coursed through Max's veins.

He had to get her out of there.

A guard shack was set off to one side of the fence. Simple wood construction, normal-looking windows.

The shack was dark and appeared unmanned.

The road turned sharply as it approached the end of the fence. The thick red rock of the steep hillside anchored the fence, the slope comprising half of the V that housed the compound. Max slowed for the corner and studied the rock.

Vertical red rock, a slight overhang five feet above the fence, then straightening out to tower a hundred feet above.

As his headlights swept the fence and rock wall behind it, Max spotted a dark line zig-zagging its way up the rock, next to the fence. It angled up and over the fence and disappeared at the lip of the overhang.

Doable, Max thought.

The van crunched down the dirt streets as Max searched for a safe place to settle in and prepare.

Hedges kept his eyes on the trail down the dry river bed,

creeping along in all-wheel drive, then climbed the shoulder out of the river onto a desert plain. He'd followed the trail into Nevada, under the big Interstate and out into the desert.

As the truck climbed on to the big plain of the desert, Hedges oriented himself.

Utah.

Hedges laughed.

No doubt about it. Asshole was heading for Red Rock.

"What's so funny?" Chris said.

"I told you we was going to party," Hedges said. "Look where we're at." He gestured at the desert plain.

Chris and Tony looked around, then they too started to laugh.

"Fuck me," Tony said. "He's heading for Red Rock."

"Call Roger," Hedges said. "Tell him they need to prepare one of the party rooms at Red Rock. He's going to want to throw his new guest a welcome party."

Hedges stomped down on the accelerator and the truck rocketed across the flat plain.

No need to track the asshole now.

Just had to get ready to welcome him to Red Rock.

Raymond stood with his team just outside the gate under the dark bulk of the mountain above. Three trucks stood abandoned in a cluster, draped across the road at odd angles, doors open, bullet holes pocking their sides and frosting their windshields.

"Holy shit," he said.

Six men lay dead at his feet.

Forrest walked among them, toeing them with his boot, checking for response, two of his men covering them with their ARs.

Raymond kept his finger straight, along the lower receiver, just above the trigger. His night vision goggles were in place, and he swept his area of the fence and the field outside it, looking for the ones that got away.

"Uh, Forrest," Raymond said. "The fence still armed?"

Forrest toed another body, rolling it over onto its face.

"Yup," he said. "Make damn sure you don't touch it. You'll get us all blown up. Kane said to leave it that way until we've found the stragglers, or cleared the area."

"Holy shit," Raymond said again. His head swam. The combat and the bodies seemed surreal, dreamlike. The familiarity of the tension and release, the solid reality of blood and death flipped a thousand switches in his system, ones he'd thought he'd left behind forever.

Gunfire down the hill, at the farmhouse, by the sound of it.

All the men froze, listening.

"All teams. This is Kane. All teams. Area inside the perimeter secured. Repeat. Area inside the perimeter secured. Hold your positions and stay alert. Repeat. Hold your positions and stay alert, over."

Forrest reached for his shoulder mic. "Kane. This is Forrest. Copy that. Repeat. Copy that. Over."

He looked at the men spread along the fence line.

"Raymond," Forrest said. "You and your team space out along the fence down the hill toward the compound. Put thirty yards between each of you. Be damn sure not to touch that fence, you hear?"

"Got it," Raymond said.

"Keep your eyes peeled. We don't know how many got away, but I'm guessing at least three. They're most likely still running, but if they aren't they're setting up an ambush."

"Yes, sir. Will do," Raymond said.

Forrest gestured to his team and the men spaced themselves out and began walking up the line of the fence.

Dallas Krell looked over the mess in the yard.

The big helicopter had put down right in the middle of the vegetable garden, destroying the spinach. He still held out hope for the potatoes and carrots, but the spinach and peas were definitely ruined, damn it all to hell.

He turned his head back toward the silent helicopter and the bodies laid out in the field next to it in neat rows.

Eight dead.

Two men were trussed and blindfolded, under guard.

And the big softy—the pilot—stood between Big John and another guard. He'd already puked once, and looked about to again. Tremors ran down his arms, vibrated his shoulders. His hands were shaking.

That one'll talk, Dallas thought. *That one will do whatever I need him to.*

He motioned to Big John, took him to one side.

"Move Mack. Put him back in one of the storage lockers. Give him a bucket and water, a chair and a blanket. A bible. Then get that big softy over there strapped into the chair downstairs. We're going to have a run at him, see what he can tell us."

Big John grinned at him. "Ten-four, good buddy. I'm on it." He looked around the compound, his smile disappearing. "Some serious shit went down tonight, boss. How much more we got to wade through, you think? Or is this the end of it?"

Dallas stuck his hands in his back pockets and leaned into a stretch, paused to admire the canopy of stars, then looked back to Big John.

"Ever hear of a Bannister folding?"

Big John shook his head.

"Me, either. We got a ways to go, I figure. And then there's the law to consider. I'd like to keep this between just us and the Bannisters, but with all this..." Dallas gestured at the bodies and captives, "I don't see how. The only thing keeping this on the down low is that the Bannisters got a lot to hide."

Big John pointed at the captives.

"Them?"

"Same treatment as Mack. Storage lockers. Chairs, blankets, buckets and bibles." Dallas grinned. "Got kind of a ring to it, don't you think? 'Blankets, buckets, and bibles?' Maybe we could open us up some kind of B&B, what do you think?"

Big John shook his head and smiled.

"Don't figure it's going to be so popular with our guests here. I'm guessing one-star reviews."

Dallas laughed and clapped Big John on the shoulder.

"You're a good man, John. Don't you worry too much; we'll get this all sorted out."

Dallas watched Big John talk to the man watching over the pilot, then take charge of the prisoners and walk them up toward the barn.

Yep, he thought, *we'll get this sorted. One way or another.*

I hope.

Ralph angled his way down the hill, toward the road below. He stepped carefully, trying hard to make as little noise as possible. It was difficult, using only the starlight to guide him. He couldn't risk a light, though. He didn't think Krell's group was following him, but they might be.

What a clusterfuck, he thought. *Drove right into an ambush. Got lit up before we even breached the back gate.*

He'd exchanged calls with Wolff and Smokes just before each of their teams went in.

Wolff had clicked off just as the helicopter cleared the fence, Smokes shortly after when his team hit the main gate.

Then the night had lit up and he found himself running for his life.

God damn survivalist hippies. Fucking loaded up with firepower and organized, too. And they was waiting for us. God damn it all to hell.

He pulled the phone out of his pocket and looked at it.

Roger was going to be unhappy.

Roger was going to be very unhappy.

And the Old Man....

Ralph wasn't sure he wanted to see that.

Bannisters had a way of killing the messenger, every now and then.

Avenues of escape crowded his mind as he continued his traverse of the hill, the road not far below.

There was that old high school buddy that'd settled in Alaska. Kept asking him to come up.

Relatives along the coast.

Enough money stashed to make an overseas run, maybe. But what then?

Alaska sounded pretty good.

His feet hit the hard packed dirt and gravel on the shoulder and Ralph looked left, right, then up at the stars.

What to do. What. To. Do.

Gotta make a decision here.

He made a quick mental inventory of all he had on him, then took a step.

North.

Hedges was on the phone.

"I'm telling you, Winter. He's headed for Red Rock. Stupid motherfucker. We get in there and get set up, all we have to do is wait. He'll walk right in and bam! Party time!"

Winter's bass chuckle warmed Hedges' heart.

"Hot damn!" Winter said. "You told the boss, yet?"

"Nope," Hedges said. "Was thinking I'd get him all packaged and ready for delivery, then give Roger a jingle."

"Better call now," Winter said. "They're as hopped up as I've ever seen them. If they think you're fucking with them...."

"I ain't 'fucking' with them. I'm doing my job."

"Yeah, the way you see it. Don't believe that is how Roger will perceive it. Call him."

"Aw, Winter. Don't get your panties in a bunch. Get in that fucking truck and get down here in time to party!"

"Nope. Don't believe I'm going to do that. You call Roger. Then call me back, and then I'll come on down."

"Jesus, Winter. What's gotten into you? You were never slow to party before. All them days down on the border? Fucking party we had down there?"

"That was different. We were in a war. They was happy so long as we were taking down them Mexicans. All that partying is what eventually brought the Mexicans back to the table and got things sorted."

"I can't believe this," Hedges said. "OK. Fine. I'll fucking call Roger and his fucking Big Daddy and get you your hall pass dismissing you from fucking class so you can come on down. I can't believe what a pussy you're being about this."

Winter's voice deepened. "Hedges. Best watch your mouth, brother. I'm telling you for your own good. Unless you want to be hanging from chains somewhere, or bent over a wheel, or tied to a pole and left out for a calf, shit like that."

"Ah, fuck that," Hedges said. But his mind filled with pictures of a party—guy tied to a pole, naked, starved calf let loose. Hedges had laughed his head off then, but the idea of being the guy tied to that pole....

"All right already," Hedges said. "I'll call Roger and let him and Big Daddy know."

"Atta boy," Winter said. "Get back to me."

Hedges clicked off and handed the phone to Chris.

"Call Roger. Let 'im know what's what."

The scattered lights of Red Rock appeared on the horizon. Hedges glanced down at the speedometer, 80 mph over the flat desert floor. Twenty minutes, at most.

Coming for you, asshole, he thought. *Going to party soon.*

Roger slammed the phone down on the table.

"God damn it!" he roared. "God damn it all to hell!"

"None of them?" the Old Man asked. "Not one?"

"Talked to Barry, Wolff, Ralph, Smokes, and the others just before they went in. It was all coordinated. Perfect. They all hit the compound at the same fuckin' time. Front gate. Back gate. Helicopter down by the farm house. Three o'clock in the fucking morning. We should *own* that place by now."

"But we don't."

The Old Man's voice had slipped into the quiet growl of command. That quiet growl had sentenced men and women to death. Shot fear through the gut of the most hardened men on the team.

Right now, it reassured Roger.

Things were definitely going to shit, but the Old Man was still the Old Man.

He would find a way. Roger was sure of it.

CHAPTER FIFTY FOUR

Max backed the van into what appeared to be an RV shelter. With the van all the way in, Max figured it was just about invisible from the road. The farmhouse whose land the shelter sat on was dark and appeared empty. Thick dust lay on the front porch, pushed up into little hills against the wall. The siding was plain wood, splintered in places, the exposed wood as gray and weathered as the original siding.

"Max," Rosita said. "I have a bad feeling about this. You are crazy to go in there alone."

"I have to," Max said. "You heard Raymond. They got Mary Jane in there. I can't let them have Mary Jane again."

Rosita pulled out her little rosary, draped the beads over her hand, the crucifix in her palm, rubbed the image of Mary with her thumb.

"If you go in there and they capture you, you will not get Mary Jane out, and they will torture you for months, Max. Months."

She closed her eyes as she remembered her handler. The one that'd gotten crosswise with Mack. They'd pulled him into what they called the "arena," a big pit with a steel fence around it, risers encircling it, like a rodeo, she'd thought. A fire pit burned in the center, various metal rods and pincers stuck into it, handles out, tips glowing red hot. A wheel-like device. A rack. Chains dangling from a sort of gallows-looking thing. A chair with stirrups and clamps for spread legs. A portable car battery charger. A stainless steel table with a variety of sex toys and clamps and whips and things she couldn't make out. They'd led the man into the center of that place....

Rosita opened her eyes to find a blurry Max studying her.

Tears rolled down her cheeks.

"They made you watch something, didn't they?" he said. "And it was someone close to you."

Rosita barked out a bitter laugh. "Close to me? No. *Hijo de la chingada* was the one who brought us north. Who delivered us to these monsters. When they began, I was pleased to see him suffer. But then, it went on and on...and...." Rosita looked down at the rosary in her hand.

"It was too much. He screamed and cried like a little girl. And they laughed. All of them. They laughed and threw their cigars at him. Some of them went down into the pit to help..."

"Pit?"

Rosita wiped the tears from her eyes, decision made.

"Yes. They called it the 'arena,' and it is where they had their 'shows.' In that big building at the back, next to their, what do you call it? *Crematorio....*"

Max reached out and gently tilted Rosita's chin to look her in the face.

"Here?" he said. "You've been here?"

Rosita nodded.

"This is where they took us first. This is where we received our 'training.' We rode up in the back of a truck, all the way from Tenancingo. At first, I thought things were going to be OK. They fed us and a doctor checked us out. I thought...." She shook her head at her naiveté. "But then the 'training,' began. We had to watch when 'discipline' was necessary. It was horrible. I've tried to put it out of my head. Over and over, I have tried, but the memories, they always come back. They wake me up in the middle of the night, they..."

Rosita closed her mouth. Tears ran down her face; her shoulders shook.

Max drew her close and held her as tenderly as he would a newborn.

"Shh. Rosita, honey. It'll be OK. I promise, you, sweetheart. It'll be just fine. I've got you. They aren't ever going to lay a hand on you or anyone close to you again, I swear that to you."

"You cannot go in there alone, Max." Rosita's words were muffled, her face against his chest. Max felt her warm tears soaking through his shirt.

"Shhh," he said. "Don't you worry. I've got this. I've got a plan. You'll see. I promise."

Dallas sat across from the pilot and studied him.

The man pooled into the chair like a big bag of water. He was trembling and snot ran down his nose. Puke stained his shirt.

"You don't strike me as the Bannister type," Dallas said. "Does he, Big John?"

Big John walked around behind the man and put his meaty hands on his shoulders.

"No, indeed. He does not," Big John said. "A factor in his favor, as I see it, Mr. Krell."

"I'd have to agree with that," Dallas said. "A factor in his favor, indeed."

Dallas leaned forward and tapped the man on his knee.

"Let's start easy, shall we?" he said. "What's your name, son?"

"Bakke," the man said. "Kevin Bakke."

He made a visible effort to control his shaking. A shudder ran through his body.

"Look here, Kevin," said Dallas. "We are not the Bannisters. We don't treat people like the Bannisters do. You can relax."

He stepped forward and leaned down, put his face close.

Bakke flinched and turned his face away.

Dallas stood up and exchanged looks with Big John.

"Here's what I need to know, Kevin," Dallas said. "How many men Bannister got left to send in? Or did he blow his whole wad?"

"I don't know," Bakke said. His voice was low and trembly. "I'm just a pilot. Roger had me fly ten guys up from Red Rock to his place and then here..."

Dallas stepped up close this time, got nose to nose with Bakke.

"Ten armed 'guys.' Ten 'guys' you knew had automatic weapons. What'd you think they were going to do out here at 3:00AM? Rabbit hunt?"

Bakke's eyes widened. His mouth opened and closed.

"I...I...I...."

Dallas thumped a thick meaty finger into Bakke's sternum.

"Yes, YOU," he roared. "You dropped off two teams of trained killers right into my backyard. Literally. While others were banging at my front and back gates. YOU did that."

Dallas ground his forehead into Bakke's sweaty, greasy forehead, pushing him back in the chair hard enough to lift the front two legs off the ground.

"You ruined my spinach," he growled. "My peas."

Big John leaned over and put a hand on Dallas' shoulder.

Dallas stood up, crossed his arms and looked down at Bakke.

"This Red Rock," he said. "How long it take to fly there in your rig?"

"Clear," Raymond said into his shoulder mic. "Repeat. Area is clear. We swept all the way down the fence to the cliff on the east border. Over."

"This is Kane. Repeat. This is Kane to Raymond. Over."

"Copy. Over."

"Check the Claymores and cameras along the line. Meet up with Forrest at the gate. Secure the gate, then head back to the compound, over."

"Copy, Kane. Will do. Over."

"All teams. This is Kane. Repeat. All teams. This is Kane. Check the fence line, the Claymores and cameras. Repeat. Check the fence line, the Claymores and cameras. Then return to the compound, over."

One by one, each team reported back to Kane.

They had not lost a single man, nor taken any injuries.

The battle was over.

But not the war.

Max stuck his fingers into the crack over the top of the fence, twisted his hand to wedge it in firmly, then pulled himself up and over.

The crack worked its way crosswise through the red rock surrounding the compound, and Max followed it another five feet past the fence.

He could see the big building in the back with its truck-loading docks and raised square of what had to be the 'arena,' probably originally a theater, nestled up against the V of the two mountains coming together. A tall, cylindrical chimney thrust out of a small building next to the big one in back.

The compound was more complicated than Rosita had indicated: A scattering of six adobe cottages on either side of a larger, two-storied central building. A long, low building between the cottages and the big building in the rear. Twenty feet behind the guard shack off to the left, a pool with a wet bar up against the south wall of red rock. What looked to be disused tennis courts.

Wind kicked little dust devils through the compound. Max watched one snake around the side of the central building and disappear.

He looked down at the ground, studied the wall to which he clung.

Enough holds to down climb far enough to jump; he'd get down without breaking an ankle. But coming back up and over the same way would be a problem.

In for a penny, in for a pound.

He worked his way down the wall to where the holds petered out, then let go and dropped the final ten feet to the desert floor.

The ground was hard-packed red dirt.

Max paused and listened.

Just the wind whistling through the steel fence. The rustle and scratch of a tumbleweed off a ways in the desert.

Max braced himself and opened the door in his head a crack.

Imagery poured in, dragging along a wave of emotions that knocked the wind out of him. What Max had taken to thinking of as The Red Presence gibbered and capered in demonic glee: Grendel on a lark; Cain pounding his brother's head in with a rock and raising his arms to the heavens in victory, flushed with the hot satisfaction of the lust to kill sated.

Blood lust and sexual desire mixed in an unholy cocktail that twisted his mind. The Red Presence echoed the rage he carried, amplified it—a siren call to violence. Vivid, clear imagery of suffering women coupled with the spiritual current flowing into him: Tied, trussed, hanged, bent over devices frontwards and backwards, spread wide open, beaten, stabbed, burned, electrocuted, raped, strangled, crippled, bones sticking out through flesh, penises and enormous sex toys shoved into various offices and wounds...

And running through it all an unholy glee: a crazed, frenzied spirit for whom inflicting pain and suffering, bringing another to the point of death and beyond—in the most agonizing way possible—was ambrosia. The ultimate drug. Pleasure beyond which any mortal could aspire to.

Max took a deep breath and forced the inner door mostly shut, leaving just enough sense to alert him of danger in immediate, human form.

The sense compelled him towards the big building in the back.

That was where Rosita had said the women were first delivered. Where the doctor checked them over. Fully equipped hospital facilities.

Mary Jane had to have gotten banged up and beaten down in her recapture. From what Raymond had said about how she'd been at that Costco back in Paluma and later... she was never going down easy again in her life.

So: the hospital.

That was where he had to go.

He rose to his feet and moved silently along the wall of rock, angling around the tennis courts and cottages, heading for the big building in the back.

The Old Man stood at the window, looking down over the lights of town and across the plains westward into the darkness.

He ticked over the possibilities in his mind: call in teams from along the line, stage another attack. Call Krell and set some kind of trap for him. Set fire to the whole compound. Get the Mexicans to send up some teams to help.

A tiny shiver ran through him.

The Mexicans wouldn't stop with Krell. They'd run right through his whole operation, take over the pipeline he had built. Shit. Take over the whole shebang. Drugs, women, farm, the whole string from Mexico to Aston.

He imagined Barrera's men running loose…

Sweet mother of God.

Those killers were indiscriminate. No sense of subtlety.

They come up, there are going to be heads in the street, bodies stacked in town. No going back.

But what if I get them to just send up a couple teams? Or a single assassin? One who'd get the job done?

The Old Man stood at the window picking at the thing in his mind.

Going to have to make a decision, he thought.

And quick.

Roger leaned back, feet on the table, a mug of coffee in both hands, and watched the Old Man—a silhouette against the sky, like a statue of an old-time cowboy.

Well, cowboy, he ain't, Roger thought.

He knew the Old Man's mind was going a mile a minute, but he also knew the range of possibility available to them.

It boiled down to call in the Mexicans, set a trap of some kind and take Krell and the others out that way, or run. Take the cash stashed in various places, get out. Out of the area, out of the country, gone. Someplace where money afforded the kinds of pleasures a man had grown accustomed to.

Roger favored the idea. SE Asia had an appeal. Money went a long way over there. Most places had law that was friendly to financial negotiation. He'd heard good things about Cambodia. Places in Thailand. Some in Vietnam. Even places in mainland China.

Mexico had its appeal, but Bannisters had history there, and the fucking Mexicans would show up and take everything. They'd torture the shit out of them for days, make sure they'd squeezed every penny out of them possible, then toss their carcasses out in the desert somewhere.

Nope. Not Mexico.

Roger didn't favor the idea of calling them in to help.

Could just relocate the whole shebang down in Red Rock. Run everything from there.

The idea of leaving Mack behind dug at him, though. Even if the stupid motherfucker had dug his own grave.

But it wouldn't do to leave him there with Krell.

He eyed his father at the window.

"Pops?"

The Old Man turned to face him.

"Yeah?"

"What you want to do with Winter and Billy and them? We still ain't told them. Just told Hedges to find that asshole and call back."

"I notice Hedges ain't called back yet," the Old Man said.

"Which means either he hasn't found the asshole, or..."

He let the possibility hang in the air.

The Old Man walked slowly across the floor, his boots loud on the wood, poured himself a coffee, then turned and regarded Roger.

"I don't figure asshole got Hedges and his group. Them boys got the luck of the devil on their side. Shot a State Trooper and got away with it, looks like. Mertzig figures it was us, but he ain't about to stick his neck out, what we got on him, but, hell."

He sipped his coffee and peered at Roger over the brim of the mug, then lowered it and moved to sit next to his son, put his legs up on the table, and settled the coffee mug in both hands on his belly. He leaned back and looked into the dark night.

"If Hedges is right, asshole is thinking of moving on Red Rock. Dumb as bag of rocks, obviously."

"Maybe. Motherfucker's got something on the ball, though. He's moved through us like we were nothing. So far as I can tell, he ain't got a scratch on him."

They Old Man grinned in the dark.

"Well…just gives us a nice clean canvas to paint on, don't it?" He chuckled, a light in his eyes.

"Have Hedges and his crew go in to Red Rock and set up," the Old Man said, "If this asshole really is coming, let him come. Tell Hedges to get ready to welcome him."

"OK. That might work. What about Winter and Danny, Billy and his boys?"

"Take 'em 'til noon to get there, I figure. Same or longer to get up here. Send 'em all down to join Hedges. Red Rock is too close to empty as it is. We pulled all our best boys…"

The Old Man's voice cracked, and Roger glanced over at him, surprised and alarmed.

"God damn it to hell," the Old Man whispered. "God *damn* it."

The Old Man took a sip of coffee, cleared his throat.

"We can't let Mack down," he said. "Them hippy asshole survivalist motherfuckers are obviously a little better prepared than we figured," he said.

He went silent again.

"God damn it. Damn it."

He drummed his fingers on the rim of the coffee mug.

"There's the Mexicans…" Roger ventured.

The Old Man glanced at him. Sharp like.

Roger held his gaze.

"We both know what happens we let them wolves loose in the chicken house," the Old Man said.

"They got teams, though. Military. Hardest men I ever seen."

"Exactly. We let them in, they cut right through us like

butter, take it all over, maybe don't even bother to go in and get Mack out for us."

"We could contract a team or two…."

The Old Man took in a deep breath and let it out slowly.

"Well, we ain't leaving Mack there. One way or another, we're putting that situation to rest," the Old Man said. "God damn it. Damn it all to hell."

Dallas was back in the great room at the farmhouse, the teams at tables littered with empty plates and dishes. The smell of bacon and coffee filled the room.

The men had been up all night, and though exhausted, they were alert.

"So we put them all down without losing a single man. Without a scratch, in fact," Dallas said. "We were ready for them, we were organized, we had the firepower, and…we got lucky."

Men nodded in agreement. Sipped their coffee, eyes unfocused as they ran the night through their heads.

"What comes next depends on a lot of things," Dallas continued. "What move Old Man Bannister makes next. What we do with Mack and the two others. Whether or not the law gets involved."

Kane stood beside Dallas and looked over the men.

"We got to prepare for all eventualities," Kane said. "But there's something we got to do first, before everything else and it is key to the whole business."

He looked at Dallas, and Dallas nodded.

"There's a place called Red Rock, down in Utah," Kane began.

CHAPTER FIFTY FIVE

Max pressed his back up against the big building, gripped the MP5 in his hands.

It'd taken him thirty minutes to work his way past the cottages and other buildings. He'd taken time to get a feel for them—and he was 98% sure they were empty. No sense of anyone there—no Red Presence, no suffering in real time. Echoes of both filled every square millimeter of the compound, though. The place was steeped in blood and pain and suffering and lust and sadism and evil glee, but at present, mostly deserted.

Max didn't figure things would stay that way for long.

The big building pulsed with the Red Presence. So much suffering and death had happened there it had infused every atom in the building.

Max stared at the little building off to the side with the huge smokestack and shuddered.

Best not to think about that right now.

He ran over the floor plan of the building behind him in his head.

It was incomplete, but Rosita had a good knowledge of the rooms she'd been in, and a sense of the full floor plan she'd sketched out as well as she could.

The blast of a horn sent ice shooting through his veins. Every hair on his body stood.

Max spun around, toward the gate, and saw headlights shining on the other side.

A wave of menace poured off the truck.

Three men...

The horn sounded again, echoing off the red rock, bouncing

back seemingly amplified.

A door down the building, past the truck loading dock, burst open and a man stepped out clumsily, buckling his pants and staggered down the stairs to the hard-packed dirt, headed for the gate.

"Hold your horses," he yelled. "I'm coming, assholes."

Max's heart was moving his ribs an inch with each pulse.

He could take the man out, but that'd end up in full view of the truck and the men in it.

He crouched low and watched the man finish buckling up, set his hat straight and disappear around the corner of one of the cottages as he approached the gate.

He waited until the man reappeared between him and the truck, then slipped quietly up onto the loading dock and strolled to the door the man had exited, counting on the buildings to conceal him as the man at the gate distracted the men in the truck.

He took a deep breath, put a hand on the doorknob and twisted.

The door opened.

Max slipped into the building, heart slowing, vision getting that clear, underwater quality as he prepared for combat.

It was time.

Raymond held a hand strap as the helicopter chopped its way through the tail end of the night. He looked out the window to watch the desert whip by beneath him.

The pilot had said it was a three-hour flight to Red Rock; there was less than an hour to go.

Raymond looked around the helicopter. Men lined the seats against the wall, four to a side with Marcus sitting in the copilot's seat, AR in his lap, keeping a weather eye on Bakke.

Timmy, Tyler and Socrates sat on one side of him, comfortable and at ease. Ready.

Big John, Forrest, Chad and Dean lined the seats on his side.

The red glow of the instrumentation in the cockpit cast a

surreal light across the men, their faces in shadow, mostly.

Raymond's gut tightened with the familiar feel of flying into danger. He thought he'd left all that behind, had settled into life as a bartender back home, the horrors of war and violent death a distant chapter in his life.

He thought of Mary Jane. The grim facts of her life. The Bannisters.

He thought about Red Rock. It sounded like the deepest pit of hell. A playground for demons.

He thought of Mary Jane again, laughing in the truck as they climbed the hills into the mountains outside Paluma.

He'd rather die than let the Bannisters have their way with her.

He remembered the Mary Jane of high school. Smart, sassy, sexy. She'd been a couple of years older than him, the prettiest girl in school. Way too smart for Bill Bannister. Everyone had expected great things of her. There had been a light and a charm about her, a strength and a sense of specialness. Things happened for her.

And then there was Bill Bannister.

Even then that asshole had inspired fear. Nobody messed with him as he bullied his way through high school. Mr. Turner, the PE teacher and wrestling coach had tried to put a stop to some of the bullying when Bill was a sophomore. And then Mr. Turner was just...gone. His departure ended the reign of the Ramsey Bulldogs over the wrestling world, a big deal in that part of the state, and Bill had gained a new swagger and menace as he stalked the hallways. Teachers were afraid of him. The principal avoided meeting his eyes.

And then, Mary Jane had disappeared.

An elbow to the ribs brought Raymond out of his reverie.

He looked over to see Timmy gesturing out the round window between them.

Raymond turned his head.

A ridgeline, black against the starry sky. A few twinkling lights on the desert floor. Tiny red lights in a line connecting the dark mass of rock where it formed a V at the extreme western edge of the collection of houses, cottages, trailers, and containers that formed the little town.

Red Rock.

Hedges leaned over the wheel and banged his hand down on the horn again- a Wolo Bad Boy Air Horn he'd installed himself —triple the decibel level of a normal horn.

"Son of a bitch!" he said. "Where's the fuckin' guard? Security ought to be all over us by now!"

"Chill," Tony said. "Roger told us they pulled nearly everybody out. Sent 'em into the Krell compound."

Hedges laughed. "Lot of fuckin' good that did. Lost every last motherfucker, didn't they?"

Chris and Tony exchanged looks.

"What the fuck's gotten into you, Hedges?" Tony asked. "Vegas was in that group. Dylan. Miller. Seal. Wolff, for fuck's sake."

Hedges slammed his palm against the horn again.

"I don't give a fuck. You can't take out a bunch of hippies living in the woods, you're no good to me anyway. Fuck 'em."

A familiar figure staggered into the glare of the headlights, waving his hands at the truck in a cease-and-desist way.

"Albert," Hedges said. "About half drunk, by the look of it."

He banged the horn some more.

Albert stopped, squinting into the headlights. Then he raised both hands, middle fingers up.

Hedges blasted him with the Wolo Bad Boy.

Albert raised his hands up and down in a jabbing, fuck-you motion, then turned and walked away.

"Motherfucker!" Hedges yelled.

Albert walked to the edge of the first building and turned to head towards the back of the compound.

Hedges leaped out of the car and approached the fence, careful not to touch it. He cupped his hands and raised them to his mouth.

"Albert! You low-life motherfucker! Get your ass back here and open the gate, or I'll string you up by your nuts and let you hang there 'til the Old Man gets here!"

Albert stopped mid step. Turned.

"Hedges?" he called. "That you? The Old Man? What?"

Hedges dropped his hands to his hips.

"Of course it's me, you stupid asshole. Who'd you expect? Mother Teresa?"

Albert approached the gate.

"Mother Teresa's dead," he said.

"So will you be if you don't open this gate in about five seconds," Hedges said.

"Hold your horses, I'm getting on it. Holy shit, Hedges. How was I supposed to know it was you?"

"Just open the fuckin' gate, asshole, and let us in."

Albert disappeared into the guard shack.

"What was that about the Old Man?" he called.

A sharp, electric snap, a clack of a metal release, the quiet hum of a small electric motor, and the gate opened, clattering on its rails.

Hedges climbed into the truck.

"I'll tell you all about it," he called back. "But first we got to get ready for a party. Company's coming."

"Company?" Albert stood half in, half out of the guard shack, a hand inside on the controls.

"Let's get back to the party house, and I'll tell you all about it," Hedges said.

Albert stabbed a button, and the gate rattled closed behind the truck. He climbed in, and nodded at Chris and Tony. Hedges stepped on the accelerator and wove his way through the buildings towards the big one in back.

The Old Man sat, feet on the table, and played with the phone in his lap.

The wall of glass that looked down upon his kingdom revealed only stars in the black night sky.

He could feel it all slipping away.

Grief and loss ran through him. His baby boy, Bill—the one he'd groomed and trained and poured all his energy into. The one who'd been ready to take over the kingdom. Expand it.

Dead.

Mack, his problem child—stupid little shit got himself grabbed up by these hippy assholes.

Anger moved in to replace the grief; rage pulsed in his temples.

Kill them all.

Kill the entire clan of hippy assholes. Burn the place down. Scorched earth.

Find that asshole that'd taken out Bill. String him up. Torture Mary Jane to death in front of him, but take time with it. A month or two.

But how?

Barry's team, Wolff's team: gone. Ralph and the others—dead or running.

The assholes! The worthless, weak assholes!

He needed hard men. Men who wouldn't run from a few deaths. Men who could look into the face of carnage and chaos and grin. Men who would walk right through the gates of hell and take it to the devil himself.

He flipped his phone over again, checked the time.

Too early to call Don Barrera.

Max shut the door and leaned back against it. He swung the Heckler & Koch MP5 around and gripped it.

His heartbeat slowed, each pulse an ocean inside him, carrying him through the world on its tide. Time slowed, the air viscous and thick, sound sharp yet gentle at the same time, clear as a bell and yet somehow separate, distant.

The Red Presence was a million bees buzzing in his ears, a million mosquitoes driving their needles into him. His skin crawled, his head swam, his vision blurred, then sharpened as he fought to maintain control.

Screams and wails, sighs of despair, sobs, and noises he'd never heard humans make.

His heart picked up speed, hammering him in the ribs, driving breath from him.

Deep laughter, cackles, the quickened breath of men nearing orgasm, growls of satisfaction, peals of giggles mixed with the cries of agony and sobbing.

Putrid, slaughterhouse-in-high-summer stench...

The phone in his pocket buzzed, startling him, sending his heartbeat racing even higher.

Max focused on an image of the Blond Woman. His heartbeat slowed. He closed the door in his head some more and that shut down the worst of the cacophony surrounding him.

He pulled out his phone and checked it.

A text from Raymond.

30 mins out.

Max blinked the world back into place, turned and checked the door behind him.

A heavy steel security door, with bolts and brackets. It'd take a breaching charge to open.

He texted back: *Truck at gate. Full team inside. Be ready.*

He flipped the deadbolts on the door, lowered the crossbar into place.

He closed his eyes, picturing the floor plan Rosita had sketched for him.

The doorway had opened into a cavernous room, mostly empty save a few pallets stacked with something under canvas, the truck loading doors down.

Max moved to the loading doors, secured the latches holding them down, then stepped carefully toward the back of the big room.

A hallway led further into the bowels of the building.

According to Rosita, the hallway branched: left was where the women were held when they arrived, with the medical facilities and holding pens. To the right, the hallway branched again: The branch to the left led to what Rosita had called the Arena. She had never been down the hallway to the right, but suspected it contained rooms for the men, maybe some storage.

Max entered the hallway, gun up and ready in his right hand, left held out for balance and defense. It'd all be close-quarters work in here.

He came to the first fork in the hallway, opened the door in his head a crack.

He winced as a wave of imagery assaulted him, blinked it away, then scanned through the wave of emotion and found the women: terror, despair, and relief—they were alone and undisturbed at the moment.

To the right—a buzzing beehive of lust and desire.

Max moved down the hallway to the right.

Less than thirty minutes. He had to secure this place, take out the threat here. Then he could move on to the women, and, hopefully: Mary Jane.

Hedges pulled the truck to a sliding stop in front of the truck loading dock.

"All right," he said. "Let's arm up and get settled. I'm betting that asshole is already out there somewhere, scouting the place."

The three men popped out of the truck and climbed the stairs of the loading dock and walked to the door.

Hedges reached out a hand and gripped the knob.

"What the fuck?" he said. "Albert, you stupid son of a bitch, you locked it. Give me the key."

Albert flushed and dug in his right pocket. Then his left. He held up empty hands and shrugged at Hedges.

"I don't have the keys, Hedges. And no way I locked that motherfucker."

Hedges took a few quick steps and got into Albert's face.

"God damn it, Albert. That door would stand up to a fucking nuclear bomb. How the fuck do you leave your keys inside?"

"I swear to you, Hedges. I didn't lock that bitch. You can only lock the knob, anyway, without a key."

"Like that makes a difference, right now," Hedges said, eyeing the steel security plate welded to the door, covering the door latch.

"Should be a set of keys back in the rec room office," Chris said.

"I expect that'll be locked, too," Hedges grumbled. "Going to have to break a door, one way or the other. Fuck!"

Hedges stomped back to the truck.

Albert leaned in to Chris and Tony.

"What's up with him?" he asked.

"You haven't heard?" Chris asked.

"Heard what?"

"Barry and Wolff, Ralph and his boys, Smokes—the Old Man sent the whole crew after that hippy asshole Krell, aiming to get Mack back and teach the stupid motherfucker a lesson..."

"Yeah. Wolff told me. What about it?"

Chris and Tony exchanged glances.

"No one's answering. Looks like they're all gone."

Albert straightened up, shocked.

"All of 'em? Wolff? Barry? Really?"

Chris shrugged. "Looks like it."

"Holy shit," Albert said. "What's the Old Man going to do? Holy shit. Wolff and Barry? Shit!"

Tony looked at Hedges, opening the door to the truck, then back at Albert and Chris.

"Without them, the Old Man ain't got much left around here. Us. Winter and Danny. Billy and them boys."

"There's good ol' boys all the way down the line," Chris said.

"Yeah, but that's all they are," Tony said. "Good ol' boys. Most of 'em lazy asshole pukes with a taste for the good stuff, happy to do what the Old Man says just so long as he keeps sending 'em pussy and whatnot. They ain't worth a solid shit in a fight."

Hedges cut off the conversation by holding down the horn to the truck.

The three men huddled near the door and covered their ears, turning their backs to the barrage. The blast hurt, even with hands over ears.

Hedges paused.

"Pound on the door! Wake up them lazy fucks and get 'em to let us in!"

Chris moved to the door and hammer fisted it five or ten times. Waited. Looked back at Hedges, shrugged, hammer fisted it again.

He put an ear to the door. Listened. Straightened up again. Shrugged at Hedges another time.

"God damn it," Hedges roared. He leaned in and held the Bad Boy down, the sound filling the cavernous loading dock, echoing out across the compound and out into the desert. Loud enough to wake the dead.

Max stiffened as the sound of the horn cut through the steel and concrete to penetrate into the warren of rooms he'd come upon. He still held the MP5 in his right hand, snug against his belly, his left arm out.

Pounding at the door, faint, but audible.

At least he knew where the men from the truck were. And that they weren't finding easy ingress into the building.

Sounds of stirring from behind the closed doors.

Max slid back down the hallway, edged his way around a corner, and got his back up against the wall.

Doors opened up.

A jumble of men in the hallway.

"What the fuck is going on?"

"I don't know. Where's that fucking Albert? He was all loud and proud about being 'in charge,' he ought to be on this."

"Maybe the stupid fucker locked himself out."

"What's with the truck, though? Is that a combine cab? We got another load in? We ain't finished with this one yet."

"Go open the door and find out, why don't you?"

"You go open the fucking door. I'm tired."

"And I'm tired of you, you fuckin' pussy. Go open the door."

The sound of a quick scuffle, a slap.

"Ah, fuck! What'd you do that for?"

"I told you to go open the fucking door!"

The horn sounded again, long and loud. Whoever wanted in, really wanted in. They were leaning on the horn, and it sounded like they weren't going to let up until they got in.

"OK, OK! You didn't have to fuckin' hit me, man. I'm on it."

Feet scuffled down the hall towards Max.

A door slammed shut. Then another.

Max slipped the MP5 around on its strap behind his back.

No need.

Raymond braced himself as the copter swooped down to run along the desert floor, maybe twenty feet off the ground. A container swept by under the skids, feet away. The roof of a cottage.

The gate to the compound drew into sight.

Bakke brought the copter up and over and they were into the compound.

Raymond's headset crackled.

"All teams. This is Marcus. We have a truck in the compound. I have three men in view. Repeat. Three men in view. Over."

Each man checked his weapon, readied himself.

Bakke flared the helicopter into a hover, then settled it down behind the largest building in the midst of the cottages.

A long low building that looked like a storehouse blocked their view of the truck.

"All teams. This is Marcus. Exit locked and ready. Wait for my command. Repeat. Exit locked and ready. Wait for my command. Over."

Bakke set the copter down gently.

Marcus prodded him with the barrel of his gun, and Bakke leaned over and clicked a series of switches and the helicopter wound down. Marcus leaned over and yanked the key out of the ignition, then produced a pair of handcuffs and shackled

Bakke to the door.

"All teams. Exit. Locked and ready. Over."

The ramp at the rear of the big copter dropped down with a clunk and Raymond followed Big John out, Forrest, Chad, and Dean behind him. They fanned out, combat ready, on the port side of the chopper.

Timmy led Tyler and Socrates out and they formed up by Marcus on the starboard side.

The teams swept the area with their night vision.

"This is Big John. Our six is clear. Over."

"This is Timmy. Our six is clear. Over."

"This is Marcus. Stay alert. Spread out. We have a team of three behind that building, up against the big building in the rear. Expect more. Team Marcus will sweep the north side of the building. Team Big John the south side. Repeat. Team Marcus will sweep the north side, team Big John the south. Over."

Marcus moved to the face of the long, low building in a crouch, weapon up and ready, then along the wall to the north side of the building. His team followed, spaced ten feet apart, each man sweeping a sector with his night vision.

Big John padded silently to the building and slid along the wall to the south, Raymond ten feet behind him.

Raymond's heart hammered his chest as he turned the corner of the building. The greenish glow of the night vision kicked his senses into hyperdrive. The cottages were dark and felt empty, but he scanned each window and door carefully.

The long low building had no windows or doors on its side, just a long low slab of concrete. If anyone threw a grenade at them, the shrapnel would scatter down the line and take out every man. No one would stand a chance.

Raymond felt the hair on the back of his neck rise.

He scanned the buildings again, forcing himself to stick to his sector, trusting the other men to do their job.

Big John held up a fist and the line halted. He peered around the corner of the building, opened his fist, motioned them forward.

He disappeared around the corner.

Raymond followed.

Hedges felt a deep rumble in his gut as he leaned on the horn.

What the hell? That was a chopper. A big one, too.

He left off the horn and listened.

A chopper, winding down, back over in the direction of the rec room.

"Chris! Tony! What the hell?"

"What?" Tony called.

"A motherfuckin' chopper lands, and you don't notice?"

Chris and Tony looked at one another, brought their guns up.

"Back by the rec room!"

"Albert! Grab one of the guns outta the locker in the truck!" Hedges called.

As Albert reached into the truck, Chris and Tony formed up beside Hedges.

"That's got to be Bakke's chopper," Chris said. "Maybe they got out after all? Just didn't want to deal with the Old Man? Tell him they fucked up?"

"And come back here? Maybe," Hedges said. "Either way, best be careful. The Old Man won't be too upset if we accidentally shoot one or two of 'em. If they up and run on him, he'll be thinking about shooting them anyway. He *will* be upset if we let anybody get away."

Albert exited the truck with a gun.

"You're sure that was a chopper?" he said. "I couldn't hear shit over that horn."

"It was a fucking chopper, numnuts. Get that fuckin' weapon up and ready."

Hedges and Chris moved left, toward the long building, Tony and Albert right, the four men falling automatically into long-established patterns.

A silhouette of a crouched man appeared to the left of the building, and Hedges loosened a burst at it. The silhouette disappeared.

All four men hit the dirt, weapons up.

More silhouettes appeared on each side of the building.

The night erupted in muzzle flashes and the stuttered blaattt of small-arms fire.

Max watched the shadow of the approaching man as he neared the corner of the corridor. He pushed off the wall and stepped out into the hallway as the man turned the corner.

Max pivoted and fired a perfect right hand straight and true to the man's chin.

He dropped like a sack of lead.

Max leaned down and pulled him down the hallway, out of the way.

He moved back to his spot just around the corner and waited.

The horn continued to sound, with intermittent pounding on the door.

A door burst open, and a man's heavy steps approached.

"God damn, motherfuckin' worthless piece of shit can't answer the motherfuckin' door..."

The man stepped around the corner and into Max's shin upside his temple.

Down like a bag of rocks.

The horn stopped.

Max dragged the second man out of sight, then brought his MP5 around and slid around the corner into the corridor.

Three doors on each side of the hallway which dead-ended at a set of big steel security doors.

Two doors on the left stood ajar.

Max moved to the first one, took a breath, then pushed it open and swept into the room.

A ruffled bed. Bedside table with a pistol lying on it. An easy chair. Empty.

Max moved back into the hallway.

From outside, a short burst of automatic weapons' fire.

Max froze.

More weapons fire, this time answered.

Max stepped quickly into the second room.

Two doors burst open on the other side of the hallway.

"What's going on?"

"I don't know. Sounds like shit hit the fan."

"Let's go!"

Max peered through the crack in the door into the hallway to see two large men, their backs to him, one bald, one with a long ponytail down to his butt. Both in jeans and T-shirts. Both carrying weapons with long banana clips.

As the men hustled down the hall Max stepped out, slipping the MP5 around his back on its sling.

The one with the ponytail was in back. Max took a quick shuffle step, then launched a side kick at the crook of the man's knee, just as he put weight on it. The man's hands came up, windmilling for balance as he fell backwards. Max reached out and grabbed the man's ponytail, helping him along, guiding his head into full contact with the concrete floor. There was a sickening crunch as the bones of the man's skull met the concrete, and the man's legs spasmed as he convulsed.

Max moved forward to meet the second man as he spun at the noise behind him, raising his gun.

The bald man turned as if moving through thick liquid, slow and exaggerated.

Max stepped inside the man's arm, and got a grip on baldy's gun hand, twisting it up and away as he stepped in and brought a knee flush into the man's groin. The man's mouth opened in an O of agony, and his eyes rolled as Max took the gun from him with one hand, yanking it down and toward him, using the motion to fire a switch knee to the man's chin.

The man straightened marginally, then crumpled into a heap.

Four down. No idea how many to go.

Max paused, hands out, opened the door in his head a crack.

The Red Presence was right there, yammering at him, gibbering.

Max looked down at the two men at his feet. A surge of revulsion and rage swept through him.

They didn't deserve to live.

Max raised a boot over ponytail's face, imagined bringing it down, over and over again, the satisfying crunch of bone and flesh, the hard work of cracking the skull open, eyes popping out of their sockets, stomping down on that thick bone, using the concrete floor as an anvil, hammering the man's head flat, blood and brains splattering out...

A thick sense of glee clogged his throat, and he pulled his knee higher, ready to bring full force down, already anticipating that first eye to pop out, aiming his heel at the hollow to the side of ponytail's eye...

Hold on.

Something pulsed deep inside him where his soul lived. The part of him the blond woman had awakened. He felt a tiny click and his head cleared.

He looked down at ponytail, sprawled awkwardly on the concrete floor, legs buckled under him, wrist turned around.

Just a man.

A fucked up man, to be sure.

But that doesn't explain the unholy joy I felt just now, the lust for pain.

Max looked at the other man, this one crumpled in a heap, his forehead on the floor as if paying obeisance to Max.

Stay focused. Don't let the Red Presence get the best of you.

Focus: Mary Jane. Find Mary Jane. That's your One Thing. Get on it.

Throughout all this, the small arms fire had continued.

As Max moved to clear the other rooms, it stopped.

He cocked an ear, poised, listening.

Nothing. Just the tick of the thin vanes of metal on the baseboards in the rooms.

Max opened the door in his head and listened.

He sorted through the ghosts of more women than he wanted to count, the echoes of men in the grip of a twisted lust that made him shudder with revulsion, hunted for a sense of a living man in the here and now...*nothing close by. Something... outside? Down that other corridor where the women were?*

Max did a rapid room to room of the corridor he'd cleared. Six rooms. All six looked occupied and he'd taken down four men.

Two to go?

One outside—the one he'd locked out.

Another?

He sensed other corridors. No telling exactly how many were still here. And then there were the cottages, the other building—he was pretty sure they were empty, but were they? Had his "gift" missed someone?

He checked his phone.

No texts.

He texted Raymond, a single question mark.

He watched the screen. No bubbling ellipse to indicate a response en route, no click of "Read at...," nothing.

He waited another second, then slipped the phone back into his pocket.

The double steel door at the end of the corridor was locked. He shouldered it, tugged at the handles, then turned to go. He wasn't getting in there without the keys or a breaching charge of some kind.

He stepped over to ponytail and baldy, and gathered their weapons, then combed the rooms for more. He bundled them up, slipping two into his belt and carrying the others.

He retraced his steps back down the way he'd come to the first branch in the hallways.

Hedges rolled himself out of the way as bullets stitched into the earth where he'd been. He released the clip in his weapon, pulled another out of his back pocket as he continued rolling, bullets chasing him. He shrimped and shifted direction as he slammed the new clip into place, brought his weapon up and loosed a burst at the nearest muzzle flash. It flashed again, this time up at the sky and Hedges grinned.

Got you, motherfucker.

He scrambled back, felt his boot hit the big tire of the pickup, worked his way underneath the truck, and got the big wheel of the truck between him and incoming fire.

Albert screamed as bullets punched holes across his chest, then slumped, silent.

Chris and Tony were pinned down and Hedges watched as silhouettes flanked them.

He took careful aim at the lead silhouette, then lowered his weapon.

Chris and Tony were toast. He'd only give his position away.

Maybe, he thought, *in the heat of the fight, they won't notice one got away.*

Maybe, I can still have some fun here.

He pulled back behind the tire and scootched himself out of sight.

Maybe.

CHAPTER FIFTY SIX

Rosita sat in the van, hands gripping the steering wheel, staring into the dark. She'd heard the chopper fly low over the town, into the compound and land.

Then the sound of gunfire.

She reached over and tapped the phone Max had left her. The screen lit, displaying the last message; "Raymond in the chopper. With help. I'm good. Stay put."

The gunfire had died down at least ten minutes ago.

Still no word.

She tapped the phone again.

Nothing.

Max had been specific: Don't text. Don't call. Wait for word.

But she was tired of waiting.

What if Max was dead? What if *they* had him?

She eyed the machine gun in the passenger seat.

She'd rather die than let these *cucuy* win.

She had to get a look at what was going on.

If she drove by the gate, just for a look, that should be OK.

No harm in that.

Danny followed Billy's truck off the highway and down the loop to the road that ran along the base of the mountain headed for Red Rock.

"You suppose this asshole really is headed for Red Rock? All by hisself?"

Winter shrugged.

"Don't matter much. Boss man says go to Red Rock and wait for 'im; we go to Red Rock."

"Don't know about 'boss man.' Sounds like things didn't go

so great at Krell's."

Winter turned toward Danny, put a meaty forearm on the seat back.

"You best not count the Old Man out just yet."

"I ain't. I'm just sayin'…"

"You ain't saying nothing, Danny. You and me go back a ways. Not so far as me and Hedges, but a ways. Ever since I known you, you been solid. Don't go gettin' all squirrelly on me now."

Danny watched Billy's truck weave its way across the desert, its lights the only other ones on the desert plain, the highway out of sight behind the hills.

"But what if it's just us left? Us, Billy, and Hedges and Albert and the guys left behind at Red Rock? Roger was agitated. Barry and Wolff ain't answering."

Winter turned back to face the road, his face demonic in the red glow of the dash.

"Don't matter," he said. "We go forward. Get to Red Rock. Get ready to party. Don't recall you ever being too slow to party, son."

Danny's lips twitched into a semblance of a grin.

"I suppose we can always party," he said. "Billy and them just dropped off a shipment before they headed up, so there's that."

Winter slapped Danny on the shoulder.

"There you go. That's the Danny I know. Just drive. It'll all sort out in the end. You'll see."

Mary Jane watched the tall man step back into sight, the syringe in his hand.

Sweat beaded on his forehead and the syringe trembled, its needle twitching back and forth, a tiny pendulum.

She worked her right wrist under the sheet. She'd scraped her hand raw over the last couple of hours, but it'd been worth it.

Her hand was free.

She watched the man carefully.

He raised the hand holding the syringe, wiped a bit of drool from his chin, licked his lips, and looked at her some more.

Staring.

The blast of a horn had awakened her, and panic had kicked her in the stomach as she'd opened her eyes to find the man standing there, looking down on her.

He twitched when gunfire sounded outside, but that was all. Just this creepy, mesmerized stare. Playing with his syringe.

She could feel panic rising, but she bit it down.

That was the old Mary Jane. That woman was gone.

The new Mary Jane was going to go out fighting.

The man's eyes were a weird mix of deadness and light, like an inbred dog getting ready to attack. Whatever was going on behind those eyes wasn't good.

He stepped closer.

Mary Jane took a long, slow breath in through her nose and let it out slowly.

She didn't know precisely what was in that syringe, but every atom in her body told her it wasn't going to be pleasant.

The tall man stepped up to the railing of her bed and reached out a hand. Slowly.

A creepy, twisted smile turned up the edges of his face, his dead eyes inward looking and removed. He ran those eyes up and down Mary Jane's body, licked his lips, then leaned over and reached out with one hand to remove the sheet, the syringe coming closer...

Mary Jane exploded upwards as well as she could, her left arm still tethered to the bed.

She put all her energy and focus on the syringe hand, snapped the hand down and back and forced it up.

The syringe sunk deep into the man's neck and she leaned in, reached the plunger and depressed it.

She fell back on the bed, exhausted yet weirdly exhilarated.

The tall man straightened up and staggered back, the syringe sticking out of his neck.

His hands waved helpless circles and then he got one on the

syringe and yanked it out. His eyes rounded as he looked at the empty syringe.

"Oh, no," he said. His eyes widened some more and he shook his head back and forth. "Oh, no. No, no, no, no, no!"

He staggered back some more, looked down at Mary Jane with horror.

"What'd you go and do that for?" he asked.

His mouth twisted down in a grimace, his face screwed up, his head cocked to one side, his shoulders came up in a weird caricature of a shrug as his arms straightened and then he fell onto his back, every muscle in his body in rictus, arcing him up into a bow with just the back of his head and his heels touching the floor. His body began to vibrate and a tight grunting erk! erk! erk! escaped his lips as white froth bubbled out. His eyes squeezed shut, trickles of blood streaming out the corners down his temples as his whole body bucked and trembled, the only sounds in the room the erk! erk !erk! and the back of his head thwapping off the floor. His bowels cut loose with a ripping sound and yellow pee dripped pooled on the cement floor underneath him.

Mary Jane reached over to the handcuff that held her left arm to the bed, keeping an eye on the horror show on the floor, and frantically worked the cuff, squeezing her hand as small as possible, trying to fit it through and out. This one was tighter than the right had been, though, and all she managed to do with her frantic efforts was to send white hot bolts of pain shooting up her arm.

She collapsed back on the bed, breathing hard, her eyes rolling, searching the room desperately for something, anything, a way out.

The Old Man thumbed off the call and stared at his phone. Then he slowly put it down on the table. Stared at it some more.

Roger sat beside him.

The two stared out into the cold and dark night, the stars

aswarm on the canvas of the sky.

"Well," the Old Man said.

Roger raised a mug to his lips, the mug trembling just slightly. Sipped.

The Old Man stared out the window.

"Beautiful night," he said.

Roger nodded, unable to form words, his whole body seized with dread.

A team was on the way. Fifty-fifty chance of whether they'd do the job and leave or simply take everything they could.

One way or another, the whole thing would settle itself.

Soon.

Raymond looked down at the three bodies splayed out on the ground.

Dead, they looked like normal guys. Cowboy types. Jeans, boots, button-down shirts...normal.

Marcus and Timmy worked the three bodies quickly and efficiently, kicking their guns out of reach, checking for signs of life, pulling their wallets.

Socrates motioned to Raymond to fan out and Raymond drifted to his spot and began surveying the compound.

"We don't know how many are left here," Marcus said. "Count on there being a lot more. Stay sharp."

He turned to Raymond.

"Word from Max?"

"Oh, shit," Raymond said. "I haven't checked."

He whipped the phone out of his pocket.

Truck at gate. Full team inside. Be ready.

"Nothing since the last text."

Marcus turned to Socrates.

"Text him?"

"Tough call," Socrates said. "If he's concealed, it might give away his position."

"You don't think all the gunfire has everyone on red alert?"

"My point exactly. Whoever's left is on red alert. If Max

hasn't texted, he might not be able to. We could mess him up."

Marcus nodded.

"All right, men. Listen up. These guys were trying to get into the big building here. We'll start there, clear it, then move forward through the compound, got it?"

The men nodded.

"Take nothing for granted. Proceed as if surrounded by the enemy. For all we know, we are."

Marcus motioned them to form up.

"We cover and move. Cover and move. Sweep every inch of the area as you progress. Timmy, you take point."

Timmy gripped his weapon and scanned the area.

A bare patch of scoured red dirt about thirty feet wide and a hundred long between the long low building they'd swept around and the huge building in the back.

Bare red dirt. Nothing moving.

A big dual cab pickup nosed into a loading dock for container trucks, next to a concrete set of steps that led up to the loading platform.

Timmy looked left, right, then directly at the pickup.

Something felt off.

He scanned the area again, internal radar up.

Truck at gate. Full team inside. Be ready.

'Full team inside.' What did that mean? In his experience, a 'full team' could be anything three to four to ten men.

He looked at the dual cab truck.

Made to fit four.

He looked at the three bodies in the dirt.

"Keep alert," Timmy said. "I got a feeling there's at least one more out here."

Timmy sprinted for the concrete stairs by the pickup.

CHAPTER FIFTY SEVEN

Dallas rubbed his face, ran his fingers through his beard.

He glanced around the empty storage room, then back to the man tied to a chair in front of him. He stepped around and behind the man.

"So, you all are out of Red Rock, then. Work for the Bannisters."

The man, tightly blindfolded, swiveled his head to locate Dallas.

He nodded.

"That's good, son," Dallas said. "That's progress. What's your name again?"

"Mayo," the man said.

Dallas knew that, but he also knew that winning small concessions led to larger ones.

"So. The Old Man sent you in here to wipe us out."

Mayo stiffened in his chair.

Dallas placed a big hand on the man's shoulder, heel on the scapula, thick fingers reaching down over the clavicle and halfway to his nipple.

He squeezed.

"That's all right, son. Perfectly understandable. Just doing your job. I get that."

He squeezed some more.

"The thing is, son, you owe me now. And all I want, right now, is to know how many men you all left back there in Red Rock. What the layout is, like that. You give me all that, maybe

I can let you go."

Mayo shrugged his bony shoulders.

Thin bones, birdlike, Dallas thought.

He squeezed again.

"Thing is, son, I want to put this whole business to rest. Get it behind me. You know? And you can help me with that. Put it behind you, too."

Mayo winced against the big hand on his shoulder.

"Look. If I tell you everything I know, the Old Man'll kill me. And he won't be nice about it."

"I wouldn't worry too much about the Old Man," Dallas said. "Seems to me he shot his wad, trying to take this place out. We counted eight dead out of the copter and we've got another eight out front and six out back. That's twenty-two down. I don't know just how big an army the Old Man's got, but it can't be that many more."

Dallas walked around in front of the man and looked down at him.

"Maybe you can help me with that. You must know how many more men the Old Man can call up, yeah?"

He leaned forward and with one brutal yank tore the blindfold off of him.

"Besides, son. the Old Man's not here right now. I am. And I aim to find out what I need to know."

Max edged his way down the corridor where, according to Rosita, the women were kept.

The corridor was bare and industrial looking. Naked concrete floor. Walls covered with thick green paint. He followed the left branch out of the big loading room, ears cocked, pistol ready, alert. He sensed men outside, opened the door in his head a crack and peered in…

The Red Presence was going wild out there…but in a subdued, lesser way. Contained. Trapped. Afraid?

Max focused.

One man. Very close, too. Right up against the doors outside.

Raymond! Shit!

Max focused carefully on the area around him.

Another man filled with the Red Presence, but this one was... damaged. Something badly awry—an animal thrashing and confusion and agony—agony on a new level of being, agony itself the thing alive and thrashing.

But again...just one.

Nothing of immediate threat. Nothing on the move right now...and then: the one outside the doors flashed with tension and animus and...opportunity.

Max whipped his phone out of his pocket, checked it for texts from Raymond.

Nothing.

He slipped the MP5 on its lanyard back over his shoulder and quickly tapped out a message: *Ambush! Near the loading dock! Ambush!*

The Red Presence pulsed and squeezed and Max heard the spatter of small arms fire right outside the door, a scream of pain, and then a steady drumming of fire, bullets spacking off the thick metal loading door, divoting little pockets out of the concrete walls.

Max looked back over his shoulder at the door.

Whatever was happening out there was going to take care of itself.

One left inside.

Max stepped forward again, this time moving quickly.

He opened the door in his head again, seeking...

There! Down the corridor, to the right.

The pulsing, writhing sense of the Red Presence. A man in agony, mindless with it.

Rosita drove the dark streets of Red Rock, her headlights the only illumination. No streetlights, the houses she passed dark. She turned a corner and came head to head with the long steel fence at the edge of town, pulsing with electricity and menace, a solid line demarcating the end of town and the compound

Max had entered.

Lights far back, at the far edge of the compound. Movement.

Rosita drove the road parallel to the fence, heart pounding, alert.

Max!

A man crossed in front of the light at the back of the compound, hunched, weapon in his arms, ready.

Mierda!

Rosita banged her hand down on the steering wheel in frustration. She had to do something to help. No way could she let these *cucuy* take Max. No way could she let them win.

She stopped the van by the gate.

Looked out the window.

Buildings blocked her view, light and movement beyond them. Out of sight.

Max had texted her men were coming.

Was that them?

Should she honk the horn? Text? Announce herself in some way?

What if those were cucuy *swarming the building?*

What if Max was overrun?

What if the men coming to help had not arrived?

No. That had to be them. She'd heard the chopper swoop through town and into the compound. Max had texted her that was the help.

Had they won? Were the cucuy *defeated?*

She had to know.

She turned and grabbed the machine gun off the passenger seat, stepped out of the van, and approached the gate.

Hedges tensed as the man sprinted across the open dirt. He could take him down, easy, but then he'd be announcing his position.

These guys were no amateurs. Cover and move. Cover and move. No bunching up.

Hedges' thoughts raced.

He'd driven the pickup nose in to the loading docks.

Which meant the gas tank was on the far side from the guy behind the concrete stairs. The side Hedges was hiding under.

Damn.

Still, his best shot at a diversion, getting out.

He scrunched his way around the front tire on the driver's side, keeping it between him and the stairs and the long low building where the team had set up, covering their guy.

Hedges took a deep breath.

Nothing to do but go for it.

He pulled the little .38 he carried in an ankle holster out, aimed carefully, squeezed one off.

Tink!

Gas began pouring out of the hole he'd punched through the tank.

Guy behind the stairs shouting.

Hedges holstered the pistol and scrambled back, pulled out his Zippo, flicked it open.

Timing was critical. He had to move with the explosion, all eyes drawn to it involuntarily, no way to ignore something like that.

He listened to the gas pouring out.

Plenty.

Time to move.

He thumbed the little wheel, sparking the flint, igniting the butane-soaked wick, and tossed the Zippo toward the growing pool of gas with a single fluid motion, turning to run before the lighter hit the ground.

A whoomp! and a blast that lifted him by the seat of the pants, helped him along.

More yelling.

As Hedges turned the corner behind the big building another explosion echoed across the compound, the whole tank going off like a bomb.

Then he was clear.

Billy sat upright as Red Rock drew into view.

Same old shithole. Scattering of trailers and containers and shitholes of houses, a couple decent ones, the playground way back, tucked up against the mountains.

"Think asshole's here?" he asked.

Wilder had both hands on the wheel. He shrugged.

"Roger thinks he's on the way. Or here. Try calling Hedges again. There's good cell coverage here. He's got to be in and set up by now."

Billy pulled out his phone and looked at it.

"As always, four bars. the Old Man does like his internet."

He tapped out a text to Hedges: *WTF?*

Instantly, the bubbling ellipse of a reply coming.

where u? Pinned down, behind arena. Team in compound. C, T, A down.

Billy pounded Wilder on the shoulder.

"Step on it! Hedges is in there, alone. Under attack. Some kind of a team..."

Wilder stomped down on the accelerator and the truck shot ahead, bouncing over the rough road.

Billy texted Hedges back: *right outside. On the way.*

He clicked through his messages and pulled up Winter and texted: *Hedges pinned down. Under attack.*

"What team? From where? Who the fuck could get in there?" Jack asked.

"How the fuck would I know?" Billy said. "Let's get in there and find out."

The truck screeched around the final corner and the compound came into view behind the long steel fence with its glowing red lights on top, black bars glistening in the headlights.

An orange red glow from the back of the compound.

"What the fuck is that?" Bobby asked. "That ain't the burn barn."

Wilder narrowed his eyes.

"Can't tell for sure. It's right by the loading docks, though. Truck fire, maybe?"

"Hold up!" Billy called, raising a hand. "Stop!"

He pointed at a white van, idling by the gate.

"Who's that?"

Winter pounded Danny on the shoulder.

"Go, man! Go!"

Danny floored it and managed to keep Billy's truck in sight until it disappeared around the final corner before the playground.

He flew around the corner, tires smoking and screeching in the night, then slammed on the brakes, truck skewing sideways, barely avoiding rear-ending Billy's truck stopped in the road.

"What the fuck is wrong with that asshole?" Danny grunted.

And then he caught sight of the white van in front of the gates.

A grin split his face in half and he reached back into the weapons compartment.

"Hot damn, Winter. Gonna have us a party after all!"

Winter looked over at him, raised an eyebrow.

"That's the asshole's van! That's him!"

Rosita heard the first truck round the corner and come to a stop. She turned and watched the second come to a screeching halt beside it.

Cucuy.

She stepped out of sight and slid open the side door of the van, pulled the two other machine guns into reach.

Max had shown her how to use them all, and she'd already fired one.

She was confident she could fire all three.

Would, in fact, fire all three.

She reached into her pocket and slipped the little rosary over her wrist.

"Dios te salve, María. Llena eres de gracia: El Señor es contigo. Bendita tú eres entre todas las mujeres. Y bendito es el fruto de

tu vientre: Jesús. Santa María, Madre de Dios, ruega por nosotros pecadores, ahora y en la hora de nuestra muerte. Amén."

She pulled back the bolt on the machine gun in her hands to check that a round was in the chamber, just like Max had shown her.

There was.

She set the gun down and quickly loaded rounds into the chambers of the other two guns, checked the safeties were off, then picked up the first gun, the one she'd already fired, and slid carefully down the line of the van to peer around the corner at the two trucks.

The tall thin man remained in a tight arc, back of his head and heels jittering on the cold concrete floor, pants stained with urine and shit, the smell flooding the little hospital room. Froth bubbled out of the corners of his mouth, the little erk! erk! erk! nonstop. Mary Jane took her eyes off the stuttering freak show as movement by the door drew her attention.

The door was slowly edging open, revealing a growing slab of darkened hallway beyond.

Mary Jane rolled her head, eyes rounding with effort to see from her position, get a handle on what was coming. She reached down and squeezed her left hand again, tried one more time to ease it out of the cuff. Bright white lights of pain popped in her vision and she stifled a gasp.

No way that wrist was coming free.

The door eased open with about a foot's space between jamb and its edge.

Mary Jane watched a face appear out of the darkness, the light from the room illuminating its planes. A hard face, scar tissue around its eyes, sharp cheekbones, tight mouth, eyes alive and alert, radiating a sense of calm readiness.

Max?

"Oh my God! Max! Here! Help!"

Max raised a finger to his lips, slipped into the room, pistol low and back, left hand out. He glanced right and left, taking in the whole room.

He looked down at the jittering man, stepped around him and moved to the bed.

"Mary Jane. You're a sight. Are you OK?"

He slipped the MP5 up and around his back on its strap. His hands moved quickly over the railings of the bed, gently down the outlines of her body under the sheet, feeling for restraints and finding them.

He lifted the sheet at her feet, examined the restraints, moved his way up around the other side of the bed, examined her left wrist and handcuff.

"About messed yourself up trying to pull out of this, didn't you?"

Mary Jane nodded. Her vision of Max blurred as tears began pouring from her eyes. She fought back a sob, wiped the tears away.

"Get me out of here, Max," she whispered. "Please, please, please. For the love of God, get me out of here."

"That's what I aim to do, darling. Hold tight and we'll see what we can do."

Max laid a hand on her shoulder and looked her in the eyes.

"We'll get you out of this, Mary Jane. I promise you that."

His face blurred again and this time a sob broke loose.

He patted her shoulder.

"Shhh," he said. "It's all right now, Mary Jane. I've got you."

Danny popped out of the truck and approached Billy's truck on the driver's side. Winter did the same on the passenger side. Billy and Wilder stood behind the open doors of Billy's truck, weapons poking through the open windows, resting on the metal of the door.

The men leaned in to a huddle.

"What you figure asshole's doing there?" Danny said.

Billy looked over his shoulder, "I figure we interrupted his reconnaissance," he said. "Right about now, he's realizing there's no way in. We get lucky, we might get to see him grab the fence and fry hisself."

"How you want to take him?" Winter asked.

"Smartest thing to do would be to wedge him in with the trucks, blitz him, then clean up the body parts."

The men watched the idling van, exhaust pluming up into the night air.

"The Old Man wants him alive," Winter said.

"Which is why we're parleying now, rather than picking up pieces," Billy said.

"Well, I ain't dying trying to take this asshole alive," Wilder said. "Fuck him. I say we mow him down and deal with the Old Man. He'd rather have him dead than us dead and him getting away."

Billy reached over and pinched a handful of nipple and fat on Wilder.

Wilder grimaced in pain and knocked his hand away.

"I'm about ready to shoot you in the head myself," Billy said. "Shut. Your Fucking. Mouth. This is an adult conversation."

Wilder glared at Billy, then looked to Winter in appeal. Winter met his gaze calmly, interested in what might happen next.

Wilder looked down and kept his head down.

"That's better," Billy said. "Dipshit here does have a point, though. Asshole has burned his way through some good men. Might just be best to take 'im here and now. Deal with the fallout."

"Shit!" Bobby called from the backseat. "Look out!" He pointed out the windshield, then dropped to the floor.

A head had poked around the corner of the white van.

A small head, only about five feet off the pavement.

Light flashed in a long burst and bullets spattered across the breadth of the two trucks, punching out headlights, bursting tires, frosting the windshield.

Danny cried out, "I'm hit!" as he fell backwards, throwing his arms up for balance, his gun flying up out of his hand, arcing out in front of the truck and clattering to the street beyond.

Wilder slumped at the wheel, an oozing hole in the center of his forehead, meaty chunk of bone and brain splattering the headrest behind him.

Billy dove down to the floor, secure behind the engine block.

Jack made a burbling noise and raised a hand to his throat which was shooting blood out in a powerful jet. He felt a fleeting sense of surprise at the warmth and power of the flow of the blood before he fell to his side, gagging and choking as his vision dimmed.

Winter crouched behind the passenger's side wheel, waiting it out.

Raymond jerked his head up and around at the sound of gunfire at the gate.

Through a gap in the buildings, he could see two trucks stopped in the road, down from the gate. Their grills sparked from incoming fire, headlights shattered and the street went dark.

A hand on his shoulder startled him; he spun around and found himself face to face with Marcus.

"I'm going to grab Socrates and hustle out there to see what's what," Marcus said. "You follow Big John and help sweep the area for the asshole that got away."

Orange light from the truck fire illuminated the scene as they both looked over to Timmy—flat on his back, heels jittering as Tyler worked on him from a medkit spread out on the ground next to them. Chad stood over them, shoulder to the wall of the concrete loading dock, sweeping the area with his sight and weapon, standing guard.

Big John and Forrest were spread out, moving along the wall of the big building, alert, heading for the corner they figured the shooter had sprinted around.

Raymond nodded.

"How's Timmy?"

"He was standing right next to the truck when it blew. Shrapnel and burns. He'll make it, but he's messed up pretty good."

"Let me text Max what's up."

"Good idea. We need intel on what's going on inside there. Last thing we need is more shooters squirting out of the building and taking us by surprise."

Raymond pulled his phone out, texted: *Max? SITREP?*

Marcus leaned in to look at the screen.

The bubbling ellipse, then: *Got MJ. Building clear.*

Marcus clapped Raymond on the shoulder.

"Hot damn! Good news. Tell him to stay put for now. We got to find that shooter, check out what's going on at the gate. With the building secure, he and Mary Jane are safe for now."

Raymond texted the message, stuck the phone in his pocket and moved to join up with Big John's team, his heart pounding in excitement and relief.

Mary Jane!

Rosita held the trigger down, sweeping the barrel back and forth across the face of the two trucks thirty yards down the road from her.

Aiming was easy: the bullets sparked on the metal, frosted the windshield, popped lights and tires.

At first, the recoil had kicked the barrel up and over her target, but she quickly figured that out and brought it back down, hosing the trucks thoroughly until there was a click and the bolt of the gun jacked open.

Empty.

She slipped back behind the cover of the van and tossed the empty gun into the back, trading it out for a loaded one.

She eased her way back to her shooting spot in a crouch, peered around the corner.

Flashes of light and metal zinged off the edge of the van, inches from her head.

She dropped to the ground and rolled back out of the way.

The bullets stopped.

Heart pounding, Rosita gripped the weapon and prepared

herself. Got up, back against the van, worked her way toward the corner again. "*Santa María, Madre de Dios...*"

She tightened her grip on the stock of the weapon, gritted her teeth and held down the trigger as she turned the corner to fire down the line at the two trucks.

Movement in the dark, off to the passenger's side of the first truck.

She focused in on it, loosing thirty rounds at it.

A bark of pain from the truck made her grin.

She swept the fire up and through the trucks again until the trigger went limp as the breech clicked into place and held there, chamber empty.

Madré de Dios...

She raced for the last machine gun, raced back as she heard boot heels on the pavement.

Ruega por nosotros pecadores, ahora y en la hora de nuestra muerte...

Billy slipped out of the truck to take cover beside Winter.

"Motherfucker! I'm going to kill that asshole myself. Right here, right now."

Winter nodded at the van.

"If that's him, then who's got Hedges pinned down?"

Billy looked at him.

"Motherfucker got help. A team. How the fuck...?"

"Had to come from Krell's compound. Only thing that makes sense. What I want to know is how the fuck they got in. Gate's closed and live. Obviously."

Billy held Winter's gaze, their eyes playing back and forth a silent conversation—*cut and run? Go all in?*

"We need to take out that van," Winter said.

He stood and braced his gun on the pickup, taking careful aim.

A head slipped around the corner and Winter unloaded on it, massive .50 caliber bullets from the Desert Eagle sparking against the corner of the van.

The head disappeared.

Winter paused, held his aim.

"Get him?" Billy asked, slowly standing to survey the scene.

"Don't know," Winter said. "Maybe."

The strobing light of muzzle flashes answered him, bullets tinging off the hood, and Billy spun away, crying out in pain as he and Winter ducked down and took cover behind the wheel.

"Fucking asshole shot me!" Billy cried, a hand on his shoulder, blood oozing out between his fingers,

Winter popped out the magazine to his gun, slammed in another.

"Only one thing left to do," he said. "When he goes to reload, I'll rush him."

He pulled himself into a sprinter's crouch and readied himself.

The gunfire stopped.

Winter took off, boots scrunching on the grit of the road.

Marcus hustled into the guard shack as Socrates covered him.

A small woman crouched beside the van, her frame bouncing with the recoil of the machine gun to her shoulder. She was hosing down two trucks parked in the road behind her.

Marcus set up cover, waved Socrates forward.

Socrates sprinted the twenty feet of open ground to take cover next to Marcus.

"That's our van," Marcus said.

Socrates nodded. "And that's Rosita."

"Which means…" Marcus gestured at the trucks.

"Bannisters."

Rosita's frame stopped jittering as her machine gun fell silent. For a small woman, she covered ground quickly, back to the van, the clunk of the empty machine gun on the metal floor, another in her hands, and back to position.

As she moved, a tall man in a cowboy hat and boots sprinted

down the road for the van, gun pumping up and down in his hand as he ran hard.

Marcus brought his weapon up and sighted in on the man, finger tightening on the trigger, then let up, raising a hand for Socrates to hold fire.

"Marcus, what the hell?"

"It's a cop!" Marcus said.

Socrates looked hard and sure enough, the man had on a uniform and a badge.

Rosita hit the corner of the van firing.

The big man in the cop uniform had time to set himself and bring his gun up as a hail of bullets cut him down. He fired a single shot and collapsed in a heap on the street, his cowboy hat flying off his head, then rolling down the road on its rim, arcing around and coming to rest in front of him.

One of the trucks fired up with the rattle of a diesel engine and rumbled and bumped awkwardly backwards, its rims screeching and scraping on the road, then turned and limped for the corner.

A body on the road next to where the truck had been screeched in anger and anguish and raised a weapon and pointed it at the retreating truck, firing at it, bullets chewing up the road all around it.

The truck disappeared around the corner and the figure on the ground screeched again, "Bobby! You chickenshit motherfucker!"

The click of a hammer on an empty chamber sounded the end of his ammo.

Rosita rested with her cheek against the van, gun pointed down the road, taking in the sight.

The cop's body sat in a crumpled heap ten feet from the van.

Another body lay flat on its back down the road, next to where the fled truck had sat. A third squirmed on the ground spasming and waving its arms and legs, attempting to sit up.

A spatter of gunfire and the body lay still.

"Rosita!" Marcus yelled.

Rosita spun around, loosing two rounds before the bolt jammed open, gun empty.

She screamed and threw the weapon at the gate. A loud snap! and sparks as the gun made contact with the gate, then fell to the ground.

"Cover me," Marcus said.

He lowered his weapon and stepped out from behind the guard shack.

"Rosita," he said again. "It's me, Marcus. I'm from Krell's. We're here to help."

Rosita cocked her head and studied him.

She drew near the gate, stopped a few feet away, studied Marcus some more.

Marcus looked the street up and down.

After all the noise and fire, the street was quiet.

Marcus kept an eye on Rosita and the other on the truck slumped in the street near the two bodies.

He looked again at the cop, gestured at him.

"Cop?"

Rosita spit on the ground.

"Bannister *cochino*."

Marcus gestured at the van.

"You take cover in the van. I need to clear that truck."

Rosita frowned at him.

"Where is Max?"

"Max is fine. He's safe in one of the buildings in back. We've just about got this place clear, we think, but before I let you in, I have to know that truck is clear. So take cover in the van."

Rosita glared at him, then turned and walked to the van and climbed in.

Marcus kept his eye on the truck and called out to Socrates.

"That guard shack have controls for the gate?"

"Just a minute," Socrates called back.

A second later there was a snap and a click and the gate began to roll back on its tracks.

Socrates stepped out of the shack, braced himself against a

corner and took aim at the truck down the street.

"Go," he said.

Marcus sprinted all the way to the truck and crouched down below the front bumper. He waved at Socrates who loosed a quick burst into the already frosted windshield of the truck.

Marcus waited for the gunfire to stop, then popped up and around the hood of the truck, weapon in front of him, aiming at the window. He stepped in close, scanned the interior and raised a hand.

"Clear!"

He moved quickly to the two bodies in the street, crouched and reached out a hand to feel for a pulse.

Each man was dead.

He sprinted to the cop, leaned down and checked him, then ran back to the van, Socrates following his passage and watching his back, then climbed into the driver's seat and fired up the van.

He turned to Rosita.

"Stay down. We think the place is clear, but there are all these cottages and buildings we haven't checked. There could still be guys hiding."

Rosita nodded at him, her hands busy.

Marcus looked down to see what she was doing and grinned.

She was loading 9mm shells into the clips of the machine guns.

He grinned. *My kind of woman*, he thought.

Max unlocked Mary Jane's handcuff and held her as she sat up.

She buried her head in his shoulder, sobs wracking her body.

The tall thin man had finally stopped his convulsions and lay inert and gurgling, froth coming from his mouth, eyes bloody.

Max let her cry it out, her tears and snot wetting through his shirt and soaking into his shoulder.

The tears triggered the door in his head and he was

overcome with the violent legacy of Red Rock: the room filled with women in twisted, impossible positions, some with compound fractures, sharp edges of bones poking through the skin, some with horrible burns, all with bruising and cuts, all in agony; the Red Presence infused the visions with a sick version of lust bound up with pain and sadism and control and glee.

Max looked at the ghosts, at each one as an individual and acknowledged her—tried to convey to her his sorrow and determination to set things as right as they could be.

There could be no justice, no setting things right, not truly. But there could be a taste of it, a start by making the men who'd participated pay. By wiping this monstrosity of a place off the face of the earth, by tracking down the genesis of it and snuffing it out.

Max took a final look at the women in their frozen agony and promised them: *the Old Man will pay. He is going to die. Today.*

He held Mary Jane tight as her sobs subsided, then eased her legs over the side of the bed, and let her go.

"Let's find you some clothes and get you out of here, shall we?"

Mary Jane rubbed her eyes and wiped her nose with the back of her forearm and nodded.

Hedges thumbed the button releasing the clip to his Desert Eagle. He glanced at the side of the magazine, straining in the dark to see...sure enough, full clip, one in the chamber. That gave him nine rounds. Five left in the .38.

Pretty soon, men would be coming around the back, headed for him.

He studied the red rock wall, the V where the two sides of the mountains met.

He'd never been back here, always assumed it was an impossible climb, but now that he studied it, maybe not so much. He eyed the wall, searching for a place of concealment, or a ledge reaching out that might put him on the roof.

The roof was where he wanted to get. He could maybe wait it out there, or figure out a way to ambush the assholes.

He looked back at the smooth concrete walls of the building again.

Impossible.

His eye scanned the length of the building, caught sight of a protuberance way down on the far edge.

A drain pipe.

Hedges slammed the magazine back into the Desert Eagle and hustled for the far edge, gun out in front of him.

Every second counted. The blast from the truck had provided him with diversion and by the sounds of things had fucked up the guy by the stairs, and that also bought him some time. But they were coming, no doubt about that.

Hedges reached the corner, held himself flat against the wall, then peered around.

Clear.

He turned his attention to the drain pipe.

It was stapled into the wall with little metal brackets, the staples/nails/whatever the hell they were solidly planted in the concrete.

He gave the pipe a test tug, then pulled harder.

It held.

He slipped the big pistol into its shoulder holster, reached up and took hold of the drain pipe with two hands, and clabbered for a toe hold, his cowboy boots finding the tiniest notch between metal bracket and concrete.

Slowly, painfully, he pulled himself up the wall, heart in his throat.

Ten feet off the ground. Ten to go.

Two hand grip on the drain pipe, both toes in those tiny little notches.

He reached up a hand, got a solid grip, tried to raise himself up using the little notch on the top boot.

His boot slipped off and the momentum dragged both feet free and clear.

He gripped the drain pipe with all his strength as his face slammed into it, the wall knocking his hat off.

He heard it land on the hard dirt ten feet below.

Damn, damn, damn.

Go back down and get it?

Men rounded the corner in his imagination, guns out, feet away from his exposed position.

No.

Up. Get up!

His scrabbling toes found purchase and gave his aching hands some relief. He held his position for a moment, shaking with muscle fatigue and adrenaline, then found another toe hold, and carefully raised himself up.

Nine feet to go.

He forced away the imagery of men rounding the corner and lighting him up with gunfire and focused on the task at hand, shrinking the world down to his four points of contact with the wall, working his way up foot by foot.

He was going to make the roof, damn it.

And he was going to rain down vengeance on the sorry motherfuckers that put down his crew.

Nobody fucks with Hedges, he thought. *Nobody.*

Raymond followed Big John and Forrest as they swept around the corner, guns up.

Twenty feet of bare red dirt between the truck loading side of the building and some kind of an adobe hut—with a huge, smelter-looking type of chimney.

The three men paused, poised, ready.

Nothing moved.

Just the faintest sound of wind across the desert floor, the scritching of dry branches against one another.

Big John set himself and waved Forrest toward the little hut.

Forrest scurried to the door of the hut, got his back against the wall by the door, swept the area with the muzzle of his AR, scanning the bare ground and the flat wall of the big building, not able to see the back.

He motioned for Raymond to join.

Raymond raced to the wall and they took up positions on either side of the door.

Big John stayed flat against the wall of the big building.

Forrest held his AR up and ready, took a breath and slammed through the door and into the building. He scanned left and right, weapon poised, finger on the trigger.

Empty.

Just a huge metal furnace of some kind, still giving off warmth.

"Clear!" Forrest yelled.

Raymond stepped into the room.

"What the hell is this?" Raymond asked.

Forrest lowered his weapon and approached the furnace. He opened the door and the smell of burnt hair and flesh suffused the room.

"Holy shit," Forrest said.

Raymond stared at the furnace, slack jawed.

Forrest reached in and grabbed a handle and pulled. A long platform, about six feet long and four wide slid out on rails that extended as he pulled.

Raymond's mind flashed to the documentary footage of the Nazi furnaces he'd seen in high school.

"My God," Raymond said. "Is this what I think it is?"

Forrest reached in and pinched a handful of gray and black ash, ran it through his fingers.

"Yep," he said. "They've been burning bodies here."

He peered into the furnace, eyed the pile of ash under the platform. Whoever was running this place wasn't that keen on upkeep—the ash was piled nearly to the level of the platform, cutting the efficiency of the burn, which was why there were still pieces of bone on the platform. He fanned through some of the grit and came up with a piece of bone. He pulled it out and showed it to Raymond.

A human femur. Blackened, charred, mostly burned away,

but unquestionably human. A smaller human. Whoever once stood on this couldn't have been more than five feet tall.

"Holy shit," Raymond said. His gut clenched with a mix of nausea, horror, and a burning anger that threatened to envelop him.

Forrest stared at the femur, turned it over in his hands.

He looked up at Raymond.

"We've got to kill these motherfuckers," he said.

"Every last one of them," Raymond agreed.

CHAPTER FIFTY EIGHT

Max dug through the cabinetry in the room. There was a decent supply of medical equipment and goods: bandages, IV bags of saline and plasma, a refrigerator with blood of various types and a whole pharmacy of injection bottles and syringes. Plaster for casts.

He moved to a wardrobe and pulled it open. Stopped and stared.

Leather bondage gear, maid outfits, slinky lingerie, cocktail dresses.

No way he was putting Mary Jane into that.

She sat on the bed, blanket wrapped around her, watching his every move.

Max turned his attention back to the wardrobe, started opening drawers.

Sexy underwear. Panties, bras, garters, net stockings.

He pulled open another drawer and sighed in relief.

Blue jeans. Plaid shirts. Cowgirl stuff.

Max shoved jeans and shirts around, checking sizes. He looked back at Mary Jane, estimating, then pulled out a pair of jeans, and a shirt. Walked over to Mary Jane with them.

"Try these on," he said.

He turned his back to give her some privacy, heard her drop the sheet, the rustle of the hospital gown coming off, her legs sliding into the jeans, the *zzz* of the zipper closing, flapping of the shirt going on.

"Good enough," Mary Jane said.

Max turned to see Mary Jane standing barefooted on the concrete floor. The jeans and shirt were a little tight, but as she'd said, good enough.

She had two black eyes and her nose had obviously been broken, but she was clean and seemed steady enough.

"You going to be able to walk?"

Mary Jane nodded.

"Let's get out of here," Max said.

Hedges edged his way carefully towards the lip of the roof. From his vantage point he could make out all of Red Rock. The wall of the Arena shot up another twenty feet to his left, but it was all smooth concrete, no way to get on top. No cracks, no gutter, no handholds.

Out on the road, fifty feet down from the gate or so, a truck sat low on its rims, flashes of glass scattered on the road around it. Two men lay on the road beside it in the crumpled postures of death. Ten feet from gate another man was folded over, head on the pavement, arms splayed out. Something about the man connected in Hedges' brain... *Winter!*

"God damn it," Hedges muttered.

Hedges did some quick calculations. With Winter down, the other two men on the road—*Billy? Danny?*—there ought to be three more out there somewhere. Another truck. *Where were those bastards?*

Winter, he'd trusted. Winter would've blasted his way through, come in guns blazing. Danny, too. Billy, as well. The others? That fucking Bobby was a chickenshit, through and through. He'd cut and run first chance he had.

Would he have been able to convince Wilder and Jack to run?

Wilder was impulsive. Not a thinking man. *Yeah, he could cut and run. Easily.*

Fuck.

Looks like it's a one-man show.

He gripped the big .50 Desert Eagle and set himself.

Blaze of glory, God damn it. Blaze of glory.

He watched as a white van wound its way through the tangle of cottages, around the Rec Room, headed back his way.

The asshole. Had to be.

Hedges listened hard.

Down below a man yelled in pain.

The dipshit that got blasted when the truck blew up.

He inched closer, stopped, listened.

At least two teams had hit them, one from each side of the Rec Room, catching him and the boys in a crossfire.

They'd be circling the building he was on, looking for him.

Good.

He listened some more, ears straining for footsteps, conversation.

Two men stepped out of the burn barn.

Hedges lined up the sights of the Desert Eagle on the front man.

He could take him.

He could take them both.

He took a breath, held it, began the careful squeeze of the trigger, then let his breath out quietly.

No, damn it. He'd give his position away. He'd only get one shot at this.

If I'm going to die today, I'm taking the asshole with me, he thought. *Got go get that motherfucker. That low-life, motherfucking, cunt of an asshole that started this whole thing.*

He's the one.

I might die up here today...

But so will he.

He turned his attention back to the white van as it slid around to the back side of the Rec Room. His eyes narrowed as he squinted to see through the windshield into the cab of the van.

Big John watched Raymond and Forrest step out of the little hut with the huge chimney.

Forrest dangled something from the hand not clutching his

gun. Charred, grayish white. Bone.

They looked angry.

Which would be OK, except their postures were wrong. Rather than stealthy and ready, they were slump-shouldered and distracted.

"Hsssst," Big John hissed at them. "Get under cover, you idiots!"

Forrest startled and looked at Raymond. He tossed the white thing which landed with a thunk on the dirt at Big John's feet.

Big John looked down at it. Forrest and Raymond gripped their weapons, back in the ready position, and both scuttled across the yard.

The white thing on the ground resolved for Big John and he sucked in a breath as he understood. The whole truth crashed in on him at once: the little hut with the huge chimney, the white thing—charred bone, the bone—a human femur, the femur—small…

Horror, and a sense of evil washed over him.

"Cover and move, you idiots," he hissed. "You're bunched together and in the open. Damn it!"

He could feel the crosshairs on the two. Danger. He waited for the shots and for one or both of them to drop—dead or screaming.

And then they were on either side of him, up against the concrete wall of the building, under the lip of the roof.

"Any sense of how many?" he asked.

Raymond looked at Forrest.

"Couldn't tell for sure," Forrest said. "Hundreds. Had a furnace in there kind of like the type you'd see in a crematorium. Ash was piled up this high." He held out a hand at hip height, "mix of bones and shit in there…" He shook his head and looked at the ground.

"Holy shit," Big John said.

"This place is pure evil," Raymond said.

Big John wiped his face, pulled himself together.

"I wish we had some demo," he said. "We may have to make

a trip, come back. We need to remove this place from the face of the earth." He set himself, grabbed his gun and motioned the other two into place. "Let's stay sharp. Not sure how many there are here, but it feels like just the one on the loose. If there were others, they'd be on us by now."

Bakke strained against the handcuff holding him to the door handle of the chopper. The cuff bit into his wrist as he maneuvered himself around and got his head under the dash. The gunfire had stopped. He'd watched the white van roll by and disappear behind the Rec Room, headed back for the loading dock and the Arena.

Once they discovered all that was going on back there, they were going to be pissed. Want to take it out on someone. Someone like him, even though he was just the pilot. Had really nothing to do with it. Sure, he'd used the women a time or two or three, but that was just...a fringe benefit. Like a stock option or something. And he'd never hurt the girls. Not really. Shit, he was *nice* to them. Something they never got. He'd been the good guy there. He certainly didn't deserve what he had a feeling was coming.

He'd never tried to hotwire a chopper before, and had only seen cars hotwired in movies. Even movies didn't use that much anymore, ignition systems what they were these days.

But this was an old chopper. Been around for fifty years.

Old ignition system. Old everything. Well maintained—had to be, he built his business around it, couldn't have any problems—but old.

By stepping over his arm cuffed to the door, bending back and sliding down a bit, he was able to get his head under the dash.

A bewildering tangle of wires and knobs and conduits greeted him.

His shoulder felt like it was about to rip off. The blood was rushing to his face. Where were the wires to the ignition? He tried to follow some of the wires under the dash, but his position was so awkward and uncomfortable, he kept losing balance and having to use his arm to keep from sliding all the way down—and maybe not being able to get back up.

He followed a thick tangle of wires back, slipped, regained his hold, got back to the wires...*yes!* The ignition.

The problem was there were about seven wires there. He had a vague memory of guys in movies ripping all the wires apart, then touching a couple together to make the engine start.

He got a grip on the wires, gave them a little tug. Testing.

He stopped and considered. If he yanked these loose, there was no putting them back. At least not by him. And if this didn't work, and he crippled the aircraft...they'd be even more pissed at him.

The question was—how bad did they need him?

He gave the wires another test tug, considering.

Pain shot up the cuffed arm into the shoulder and he bit his lip.

Get back to sitting. Think it over a bit.

He tried to slip his leg back over his arm, swivel around, sit up, but he was jammed deep into the well under the dash.

Panic jolted him, and he flailed desperately, trying to right himself. When he finally sat back in the seat, he felt a warm trickle down his arm and looked to see blood running down where he'd gouged himself flailing around with his wrist cuffed securely to the door.

Panic and claustrophobia rose as he waited for the men to return.

What were they doing?

What would they do to him?

How was he going to get out of this?

Max and Mary Jane wandered the back corridors of the building, a rabbit warren of rooms and hallways and dead ends. Max could feel the women nearby, their low-level desperation and fatigue, but he couldn't center in on them.

Wait.

The hallway off to the right, off the final dead end.

That way.

He pulled Mary Jane by the hand and together they turned the corner.

A long, narrow corridor, tiny red bulbs illuminating the passage, casting a dim glow off the walls and floor, like a fire burned down low.

At the end of the corridor a set of steel doors.

Security doors.

Max placed a hand on one.

Desperation, resignation, pain, and terror oozed through the smooth metal and crawled through the door in his head.

The women were here.

He ran a hand down the line where the double doors met to the thick rectangular metal plate jutting off from the knob, covering the door latch.

It'd take a crowbar or better to get in there.

"They're here," he said.

"Raymond's outside?"

"Raymond and about nine other guys, by the sound of it," Max said.

"Let's go," Mary Jane said, "Get something to open this door."

Max gave the door a final pat, sensing the women scurry on the other side, frightened mice, and turned with Mary Jane to head out for help.

Dean peered around the corner of the big building.

Red rock running straight up for a couple hundred feet.

Flat, red earth.

Clear.

He motioned Chad to follow and stepped around the corner, ready.

Whoever had set off the truck and slipped away had to be around here, somewhere.

Dean leaned back and scanned the red rock wall, eyes following the contours, seeking out the cracks, looking for a route.

"Climbable," he said.

"Barely," Chad said. "About a 5.14, I'd say. Take some real skill."

"Yup."

Something brushed Dean's foot and he looked down.

A cowboy hat.

He'd missed it on first glance, his senses alert for a man-sized object, and the hat itself was a dull clay color that blended well with the dull red-orange dirt.

Dean looked back at the wall behind him, spotted the drain pipe stapled to the side of the concrete building with the little metal brackets.

Ten feet up, black scrapes.

Boot marks where someone had scrabbled and flailed on his way up.

A bolt of electricity shot through him and he grabbed the shoulder mic and keyed it.

"All teams. This is Dean. All teams. Target is on the roof. Repeat. Target is on the roof."

Dean and Chad stepped back from the wall carefully, guns trained on the lip of the roof, ready.

Sweat beaded on Raymond's forehead as Big John motioned him forward.

Five feet from the back corner of the big building, brushing up against the wall, gun ready, Raymond edged forward, Big John's massive shoulders blocking his view of what lay ahead.

Dean's voice on the radio; "...target is on the roof..."

Raymond flattened himself further into the wall and stopped as Big John held up a fist. The three men paused, waiting.

Big John reached for the shoulder mic, and Raymond heard the click as he keyed it.

Gunfire from the front of the building.

Something big, the shots booming and echoing off the red

rock and buildings.

Big John motioned for cover and move, then sprinted to the little building with the furnace, positioned himself so the building provided cover, set himself, then motioned Raymond forward.

Raymond ran, head down, fast. He could feel Big John and Forrest covering him, but the hair stood on the back of his neck, waiting for a bullet.

Marcus parked the van behind the long low building across from the loading dock.

A click and whoosh as Socrates slid open the van's big side door behind him, the scratch of his boots as he stepped down onto the red dirt.

Marcus opened the door and got a foot on the ground, turned to reach back in for his gun as Dean came on the radio.

The skin on the back of his neck, exposed to the big building behind him, bunched and crawled.

Marcus grabbed his gun and whipped around, raising the gun, seeking out the threat.

Hedges watched the white van crunch to a stop and the side door slid open. A compact, agile man stepped out onto the ground, alert and ready. The man pulled his gun into the ready position and Hedges sighted in on him.

The asshole?

Maybe.

The driver's door popped open and the driver got a foot out onto the ground, then turned and reached back in.

This one was taller. A little thicker. Had the same lithe athleticism as the first man, only more powerful. Hedges could see a guy like that dismantling Mack, beating down Roger.

The asshole!

Hedges shifted and brought the front sights to bear on the driver's neck.

The driver tensed, then moved in a blur, spinning around to

face Hedges.

Hedges grinned and squeezed the trigger, the big Desert Eagle slamming his hand back and up with the recoil.

The driver's hands came up, a sputter of gunfire into the sky, and a neat hole appeared in his forehead. A red and grayish jet of fluid—bone and brain matter —splattered up against the white van, a beautiful abstract splash of blood, and Hedges crowed, screeching in joy.

"Got you! Asshole! Die!"

Hedges kept firing, the big gun jumping in his hand, dragging the sight back down and over to the first man out of the van, his spirit jumping and capering with glee as he rained down death once again, glorying in the splatter and mess the big gun made.

Something moved off the passenger's side of the van, but the first man was still standing, bringing up his weapon....

Hedges focused on the front sight, bringing it onto the first man's forehead...

A bullet zinged off the concrete inches from his face, buzzing by his head like a bee zipping by, followed by a swarm of them, and then something hard and fast slammed into the side of his head and his vision exploded in a beautiful blaze of bright red light followed immediately by thick blackness.

The echo of deep and guttural laughter grew as his vision snapped off and the inky blackness swallowed him.

Rosita snapped her head up at the sound of gunfire, her eyes drawn to the muzzle fire on the roof of the loading dock.

She slapped the long banana clip, fully loaded, back into the machine gun, pulled back the charging handle and slammed a bullet into the chamber.

She swept out the door, gun up and moving towards the gunman on the roof, squeezing the trigger as she sighted in on the man.

Bullets sparked off the concrete and zinged back into the red rock beyond and she moved the barrel onto the man, tracking her fire by the concrete chips and dust kicking up. A splash of red and the gunman disappeared, and the firing stopped.

Rosita forced herself to release the trigger, the rage inside her demanding more blood, more vengeance. Payback.

A moment of profound silence.

Then she could hear the radios and the calls of men and the sound of boots across the hard red dirt.

She dropped the machine gun at her feet, put her back up against the side of the van and slid to the ground, folding up into a ball, head on her knees, arms around her legs, back pressed firmly into the passenger's door.

CHAPTER FIFTY NINE

Max was reaching for the door to the loading dock when the gunfire started. First the big boom of something large, coming from the roof above him. Then small arms chatter, a machine gun firing a long burst, the bullets spanging off the concrete above. The big gun stopped, then the machine gun stuttered into silence.

Quiet.

Max motioned for Mary Jane to stay put, slipped the MP5 around and held it ready, then eased the door open, peering out.

A burning truck was nosed up to the loading dock. Drag marks led to a man flat on his back twenty feet away, bloody dressings covering his face. Another man crouched over him, weapon ready. Thirty feet from the loading dock a white van—his van—paralleled the long low building which faced the loading dock. The driver's door was partly open. A huge splash of red dripped down the side of the van. The driver lay crumpled just by the door, the top of his head missing. Another man stood beside him, looking up at the roof.

He turned, bringing his weapon up as Max stepped out onto the loading dock.

Krell's man.

Max let his weapon fall slack on its sling and raised his hands.

"Hold your fire," he yelled. "It's me, Max!"

He had every man's in yard's attention.

The men held their weapons tight on Max and advanced.

"Keep your hands up!" the closer man yelled.

Max froze and waited.

Men came running from both sides to join the scene.

Max stood and watched the group assemble.

Raymond stepped out from the group and approached Max.

"Max!" he said. "You made it!"

The men lowered their weapons, but remained ready, alert.

Raymond climbed the concrete steps, his head craning to peer around Max into the building.

"Mary Jane?" he asked.

Mary Jane slipped around Max.

For a moment, she and Raymond stood staring at one another, and then Mary Jane ran to him and he met her halfway. They wrapped their arms around one another, Raymond picking her up and spinning her around.

Max looked out at the white van.

"Rosita!" he called.

The men looked at one another.

"Rosita!" Max yelled again.

Max edged his way through the men and approached the van.

The driver was clearly dead, the other man from the van now kneeling beside him, gently laying his body out.

Max rounded the front of the van and stopped.

Rosita.

Head on her knees, arms wrapped around her legs, her shoulders shaking.

Max slid over to her, sat down, and wrapped his arms around her.

"Max!" she sobbed, leaning in to him. "Max! You're alive!"

Her sobs intensified and Max held her tightly, stroking her hair.

"It's OK, now, Rosita. It's all OK," he said. "We got them."

Max led Big John, Forrest, and Raymond down the red-lit hallway to the big steel doors, heavy crowbar in his hands.

He fit the tip of the crowbar under the big steel plate over the latch and wrenched it, bending the plate up enough to reveal the latch and deadbolt. He rearranged the crowbar between the two doors, driving the tip as deep as it would go, then put his weight behind it and cracked the door open.

More red light spilled out as the door opened to reveal a concrete box of a room with blankets spread around, a stinking five-gallon bucket of a toilet and scattered water bottles.

The women had bunched into a protective knot in the corner, fear pouring off of them.

Max held up a hand and stood at the entrance.

"It's OK," he said. "You're safe now."

The knot of women, wearing bras and panties, squeezed together more tightly, trembling.

Big John stepped around Max and walked halfway to the women and stopped. He held up his hands.

"*Estás bien,*" he said. "*Estás seguro. Estamos aquí para traerte a casa.*"

The women turned as a group and faced him.

Big John opened his hands, a gesture of welcome.

One of the women detached herself from the group and approached him. She was a small woman, long raven-black hair to her waist. Bruising discolored her face, and ugly red welts ran across her breasts. Her bottom lip trembled.

"*Estás seguro?*" she said. "*De Verdad?*"

"*De Verdad,*" Big John said. He held his arms open.

The woman looked at him, then back at the other women still bunched in the corner, watching with round eyes.

Max felt something new slowly replacing the fear and terror, the desperation and despair:

Hope.

Socrates, Dean, and Chad headed up the other corridor to round up the men Max had put down. They moved in formation, guns ready. At each corner Socrates slid tight up against the wall and peered carefully down the hallway, moving them along until they came to the final corner before the rooms Max had cleared.

Two men lay stretched out at the corner, still out cold.

Socrates padded quietly to them, his boots silent on the concrete floor, leaned down and double checked.

Out cold.

While Dean and Chad covered him, he quickly searched them.

No weapons.

He reached into his pocket and pulled out some thick, heavy zip ties, rolled the first one over, and quickly secured his arms behind him, then zip-tied his feet together. He did the same with the second man.

The whole operation took less than a minute, and then he moved around the final corner.

A scuffing, and a tall man wearing only jeans was on him, hand on the muzzle of his weapon.

Socrates grabbed the man's hand, crushing it against the hard steel of the muzzle and pivoted, using the leverage to quickly bring the butt of the gun up, smashing it into the man's temple.

He went down hard, landing on his face.

Dean and Chad took up position on either side of Socrates as Socrates secured the third man.

A big bald man was in the center of the hallway, knees and forehead on the concrete floor, hands spread out in front of him. Behind him, another, this one with a ponytail splayed out behind him, flat on his back, arms folded across his chest.

Dean and Chad covered Socrates as he moved in and secured the men.

A door-to-door revealed only empty rooms along the corridor.

Socrates faced the steel security doors at the end of the hallway. Banged on them with his fist.

Solid.

The three men looked at the doors.

"Storage," Dean said.

"Likely," said Chad.

"We'll have to get in there," Socrates said.

"Leave a guard? Come back?" Dean asked.

Socrates pondered it.

"It's storage. No one's in there," he said.

"Could be," Dean said.

"Can't be sure," Chad said.

"All right," Socrates said. "Dean, you keep an eye on it. We'll sweep the rest of the building, find something, come back."

Max stepped up to the big loading door of the truck dock, released the catches on each side and raised it.

The pink light of a desert sunrise filled the room.

The women sat huddled in a group. Quiet. They wore jeans and plaid shirts taken from the supply in the medical room, clean blankets over their shoulders.

Raymond sat with his back against a wall, legs splayed, Mary Jane between them with her back up against his chest, head nuzzled in under his chin. He had his arms around her.

Max turned around and almost ran into Rosita.

She buried her head against his chest and Max reached out to enclose her in an embrace.

Socrates walked up to Max.

"Got all the prisoners back in that room you found the women in. Left 'em zip-tied."Max nodded.

"Looks like it's time to shut this rodeo down," he said.

The two men looked at one another.

"We should burn this place to the ground," Socrates said.

"All concrete. Not a lot to burn."

Socrates grimaced.

"We've got to do something."

Max walked to the edge of the loading dock.

The truck had burned down, the tires melted, thick black smoke curling into the pink sky. The blackened windows curled inward.

He looked over the truck to the buildings beyond.

"Well," he said. "We have to clear the place. Let's see what we can find."

Socrates looked at him.

"Assholes like this like to make things go boom," Max said. "I'm betting we'll find something that'll do."

CHAPTER SIXTY

The buzz of a low-flying small plane raised Chuy's head to the horizon. He elbowed Giorgio.

"That'll be them," he said.

Giorgio grimaced and straightened up, squaring his shoulders.

"You think Pelon will send the twins?"

Chuy shrugged, suppressed a shudder.

"The Barreras? Depends."

"On what?"

"How many bodies he wants."

The two men stood shoulder to shoulder on the apron of the small dirt landing strip and watched as the plane arced and settled into approach.

Puffs of dust rose as the wheels touched down, the plane engines winding down.

The pilot controlled the shimmy as the Piper Seneca braked on the dusty strip, slowed, and reached the end of the runway. The twin engines roared and he turned the plane around, taxied it back down the strip and brought it to a halt in front of Chuy and Giorgio.

The engines powered down.

The door behind the pilot swung open and a small man, dressed in all black, stepped down onto the dirt. He raised a black cowboy hat and settled it on his head.

Behind him, another man, dressed identically, stepped down onto the dirt, looked around, raised an identical black cowboy hat and fixed it in place.

The plane bounced on its wheels as a third man climbed down to join them.

This one was huge: 6' 7" and at least 300 pounds. Long, shiny hair, parted down the middle, hung over his face, doing a poor job of hiding the massive pox scars. A thick knot of scar tissue ran diagonally across his face, denting his nose at the bridge.

Chuy and Giorgio exchanged glances and approached the men.

"Señors Barrera. Ruiz," Chuy said. "*Bienvenido.*"

The three men regarded Chuy and Giorgio with flat, dead eyes.

Chuy waved them over to the waiting van as Giorgio popped open the luggage compartment and reached in to grab three long, black bags, then shouldered them and trudged after the men, his heart pounding with dread.

Max and Socrates rounded the corner to find Dean sitting on the floor, gun resting across his knees.

"That's it," Socrates said, pointing at the double steel security doors.

Max hefted the crowbar in his hands and approached the doors.

He paused, opened himself a little, listened.

The room pulsed with the Red Presence.

He tensed, opened the door in his head a little more, and closed his eyes.

The Red Presence...but...different. Mindless. Almost... secondary.

He opened his eyes, turned his head to look at the men behind him.

"No one's in there," he said, "but..."

"But?" Socrates prompted.

"Something..." Max said. "Be ready."

He fit the tip of the crowbar behind the security plate, put his weight into it and bent it up enough to see the deadbolts and door latch.

"This one's going to be a bitch," he said.

He fit the tip of the crowbar into the narrow gap between the doors and wrenched.

The door squealed and bulged outwards as he strained at it. He put more muscle into it, leaned hard against the crow bar.

With a loud screech the door popped open.

Max stepped quickly out of the way as Socrates and Dean swept by him, weapons ready. He dropped the crowbar, the metallic clang echoing down the concrete corridor, pulled out his small LED flashlight and popped it on.

It was a big room, twenty by thirty or so. Shelves rose to the ceiling on each side. A pegboard at the end of the room glistened with weaponry.

The Red Presence was there, but had a strange, secondary feel to it.

"These weapons have seen a lot of use," he said.

"We'll destroy them," Socrates said.

Dean found a light switch on the wall and flipped it.

Bright neon light filled the room.

The shelves were crowded with weapons of all kinds: pistols, long rifles, machine guns, boxes and boxes of ammo. At the end of the room, square cardboard boxes filled the shelves, stacked to the ceiling.

Socrates stepped down the room and whistled.

"I haven't seen a weapons locker like this since I left the teams."

He ran his hand over the cardboard boxes.

"And I've never seen anything like this," he said.

Max and Dean walked down to look.

"C4" in huge black letters on each box.

Dean stood back and craned his neck to take in the shelves.

"Got to to be hundreds of boxes here," he said.

Socrates gestured at a long stack of wooden boxes on the shelf next to the C4.

"Blasting caps," he said.

Max nodded.

"That looks about right," he said.

"All we need," Socrates agreed.

"Let's do this," Max said.

The men split into pairs and cleared the compound, leaving Tyler and Timmy with the women. Rosita protested at not being included in the sweep, but Max pointed out she was back up for Tyler—Timmy, face swaddled in medical dressings, wasn't helping anyone.

Neither was Marcus.

The long, low building across from the loading dock turned out to be the most innocuous on the compound. A dining hall and bar with a huge flatscreen TV. Nothing out of the ordinary.

Not a single ghost.

The cottages were another story.

Twelve of them dotted the compound, six on each side of the long, low building.

Max stood in front of the first he was to clear, gun ready. Raymond stood behind him, at an angle to give him a clear line of fire into the room.

Max raised a foot, kicked in the door, took a step into the room and positioned himself against the wall as Raymond swept by him into the room.

Max blinked. Blood spatter swept over the walls, and dotted the ceiling. The floor was thick with it.

The noisome stench of death hit him like a wave of concrete.

Raymond stood a few paces into the room, gun down, hand slack, body slumped.

The cottage was small, the center piece what looked to be a modified gynecological chair. The stirrups were shackles, and additional hardware provided shackles to hold the arms in place.

A long, steel table held a hideous arrangement of pliers and pinchers, clasps, alligator clips of all sizes, knives, spikes, whips in small, medium, and large—with and without spikes, pokers, what looked to be an old-fashioned branding iron with a circular "RR" five inches across at its tip.

Cattle prods, stun guns, other electrical-looking things.

A bewildering display of sex toys. Small, large beyond imagining, bulbous, curved. Latex, steel, and glass. Some glistened with what looked to be inlaid glass shards.

Max turned his head away.

A small, oven-looking thing on steel legs by the table.

He gestured at it.

"What the hell is that?" he said.

Raymond's mouth opened. Closed.

"Knife oven," he said. "Use 'em to make knives. Heat metal up to something like 2200 degrees."

He glanced at the array of steel implements on the table, his eyes straying to the brand, then away.

"Holy crap," Max said.

A battery charger up against the wall.

Off to one side, a thick ring in the ceiling. Chains against one wall.

Chairs lined another—for an audience.

Max looked back to the chair and startled.

A woman was looking at him with big, round eyes.

Overly big eyes.

He looked closer: her eyes had been stapled open.

On the table—a standard-issue staple gun.

The woman looked a lot like Rosita. Same small stature. Same long hair.

The woman faded into translucent waves, a mirage, then: another woman. Another gruesome pose. This one with thick, deep burn marks all over her, a big, pulsing "RR" stamped into her cleavage, another over her belly button. She faded into waves. Another woman, this one cut and bruised, another, and another, and then, kaleidoscopically, a long series of women flashed in front of him at a speed that blurred them into a stream of abused brown flesh.

He blinked again, and they were gone.

"Let's get the hell out of here," Max said.

The rest of the cottages were similar. Each had its own theme: there was one made up to look like a castle dungeon —with photographic wallpaper stone walls; another had Nazi flags and memorabilia; another a Japanese theme with swords and ninja-looking weapons; one with a slanted table, American flag, and a CIA wall plaque; another with Mexican cartel themes and cans of gasoline; and on and on. Twelve little torture theme park cottages. Each thick with death and suffering.

When the men met back at the loading dock, they were silent and pale, heads down. No one wanted to meet anyone's eyes.

Tyler watched them file in. He lifted his head towards Socrates.

"That bad?" he said.

Socrates glanced at him.

"You remember some of those torture rooms we found in Iraq?"

Tyler nodded.

"We found one exactly like that. And it wasn't close to the worst thing out there."

Tyler looked at Socrates a long moment, then at the others.

The men had grouped into an unconscious knot of protection.

Max stepped in. "Let's blast this place into oblivion, then burn the rubble. Wipe this shit off the face of the world."

The men straightened.

"I figure we bend the door on the holding cell back in place well enough to hold them for a while," Max said. "But once they get their act together and start really trying to get out, they'll get out. Let's bring the house down on them before they do."

Men nodded.

"Socrates, I think if we set the C4 right, it'll bring that whole mountain of rock down on this place, what do you think?"

Socrates rubbed his chin and looked up, imagining the tall

red rock walls behind the building.

"If we do it right," he said. "I'd say we also set a box or two on the building itself, to be sure. We got plenty."

"Great. We've got enough to set a box on each of those little cottages as well," He gestured back behind the men, "and a couple on the dining hall over there."

"I want three boxes on that cottage over there, with the furnace and the ashes," Forrest said.

Max looked at him.

"Works for me," he said.

CHAPTER SIXTY ONE

Old Man Bannister sat beside Roger at the big table.

Both of them had their feet up on the table, mugs of coffee on their bellies.

Both watched as the sky lightened and the stars faded.

Waiting.

Giorgio loaded the three long bags into the back of the van, slid the side door open, and gestured for the Barrera twins and Ruiz to get in. As Ruiz stepped up, the van tilted and rocked.

Giorgio slid the side door shut, walked around to the passenger's side and climbed in.

Chuy put the van in gear and headed out.

Mack sat in his cell, brain squirming with hatred and rage.

He rubbed the plastic knife he'd managed to palm after dinner against the floor, honing its edge as well as possible, filing the point down to a razor-sharp needle.

Stupid hippy motherfuckers. Going to kill them all.

But how? They were being careful, a guard standing well back out of reach every time they talked to him, never bringing all three men out together, only interrogating them one at a time.

On the other hand, they seemed to have lost interest.

Or maybe just catching some sleep.

He lay there, plotting, scheming, grinding his shank, elaborate fantasies of revenge populating his mind. Every time he moved wrong, his shoulder burned, and in his mind he made one of the men holding him scream, jabbed his shank into an eye, a neck, between the ribs....

When the men reached the helicopter, they found Bakke twisted sideways, under the dash, stuck. The hand sticking out of the handcuff was blue.

"Stupid asshole," Tyler said. "What are you trying to do? Hotwire this thing?"

Bakke whimpered in pain as Tyler reached in to uncuff him.

"Step out," Tyler ordered.

Bakke climbed out of the cab and stood on shaky legs.

Tyler leaned around him and peered under the dash.

"He got a few wires loose, looks like," he reported.

Socrates moved over to look.

"Maybe we ought to lock him in, back with the others?" Big John mused.

The men looked at Bakke.

Bakke quailed. "I'm sorry! I'm sorry! I won't do anything like that again! I promise."

Socrates looked down on him, his face an inscrutable mask.

Bakke quieted and settled into a barely audible whimper.

Socrates looked at him another long moment, then moved away.

"You going to be able to fix what he did?" he asked.

Tyler's voice came from under the dash, "Yeah, no problem. Wires are color coded and he didn't mess them up too bad."

"You figure you could fly this?" Socrates asked.

"Yeah, in a pinch," Tyler said. "But it'd be rough. Be OK for the flight up, but that's assuming I get this thing up without pitching into any walls or hills. And the landing'd be rough."

Socrates looked back to Bakke.

"Sounds like you're in luck," he said. "We need a pilot."

"Thank you!" Bakke said, "I promise..."

Socrates cut him off with a raised finger and Bakke settled back into his quiet whimper.

The men loaded Timmy's stretcher and Marcus' body into the helicopter. They'd covered his head with a blanket and arranged the corpse as well as they could.

The body of the copter was plenty big for the two stretchers to fit in the aisle, and the men clambered in and assumed their seats.

Max and Rosita squeezed up front behind the copilot's seat. Socrates eased his muscular bulk into the passenger's seat.

Bakke sat rubbing life back into his hand. The hand now glowed pinkish red with a nasty blue collar where the cuff had dug in.

"Get ready," Socrates called back to the men.

He motioned to Bakke.

"Crank 'er up," he said.

Bakke whimpered, massaged his hand some more, then reached out and started flipping switches, going through the routine.

"We got gas to get back to the compound?" Socrates asked.

Bakke glanced at the dials.

"Barely. We should stop at that little airport outside Freedom to fill up."

"There's an airport in Freedom?" Socrates asked.

"Tiny little strip. Private. But we can get gas there ..."

"We'll see when we get there," Socrates said.

He twirled his finger again and Bakke cranked up the helicopter.

The men strapped in, everyone put on their headsets, and Socrates nodded again at Bakke.

"Take us up, then hover about 250 feet over the compound," he said.

Bakke pushed twin levers yoked together forward and the chopper crouched, then rose straight into the sky.

Max looked down on the compound as they rose.

It was a picturesque little getaway: twelve cute little cottages flanking the rec room, pool and tennis courts out by the gate, the big building in back, little burn shack with the huge chimney to one side.

Hard to believe the hell it had housed. The misery and evil

that had lived there.

Max allowed himself a last feel for the place, opening the door in his head to scout it out.

Cries of the girls/women who had died there, the snorting lust of the men who feasted on their pain, their giggles of glee...

His mind snapped back to the cottages he'd seen, and the arena...

Good God.

The arena had been set up like a little rodeo, with a dirt floor. When they'd cleared it, it'd been empty, innocuous. Max had opened himself the tiniest sliver there and the imagery and horror that poured in nearly overwhelmed him.

He looked over at the arena, its square bulk rising above the section of the loading dock, the burned-out truck in front.

From 250 feet up, he could make out the bloody dark little dots where Marcus and Timmy had lain, along with those of the men they'd killed getting into the place. The body of the man on the roof lay splayed where Rosita had shot him.

They'd dragged the other bodies back into the building with the loading dock, and set a couple of bricks of C4 under them for good measure.

Max pictured the men in the holding room where they'd kept the girls. Each of them complicit. Each filled with the Red Presence, any trace of their humanity obliterated by the evil they'd not only welcomed, but nourished.

Yet a part of him balked at simply burying them alive.

Each of them a serial killer on a level that would make Ted Bundy blush.

Something about bringing a mountain down on them seemed, biblical, appropriate.

He shook his head, thinking about it, then looked over to see Socrates watching him.

Socrates raised the radio-control box in his hands and offered it to Max.

"You want to do the honors?" he said.

Max glanced out the window just in time to see the white

van turn the last corner out of town and disappear up the road that ran along the foot of the hills, heading south.

Chad had volunteered to drive the women back to Mexico, or wherever they wanted to go, leaping at the opportunity to get out and away, to clear his head.

Mack nodded to Socrates, who passed the box over.

He stood in a crouch and worked his way forward, between Bakke and Socrates, then turned back to address the men in the rear.

"Show's about to go down," he said, the voice-activated mic in the headsets carrying his words to all. "Anybody wants to watch, get ready."

Every head twisted to look out the windows.

Max locked eyes with Rosita.

Her eyes filled with sadness, and anger, and finally, resolve.

She nodded at him.

Max turned back and flipped the first series of switches.

Red dust and rock flew into the air from a dozen places along the wall behind the big building.

The red cliff shuddered, seemed to rise up a fraction, and then calved, like a glacier, a huge slice of red rock tilting and landing on the building below, followed by a waterfall of red rock tumbling after it, covering the building, pouring over it and around it, toppling the big chimney on the burn building, and spreading all the way to the dining hall, caving in the back side of that as well.

Max flipped a few more switches and the pile of red rock where the big building had been convulsed.

The Bannister crew died quickly, crushed under tons of rock.

Better deaths than they warranted.

Bakke swung the chopper around to face the forward section of the compound and Max ran through the switches in sequence, the rec room imploding and caving in, the little cottages exploding into white and black dust.

When it was over, a giant cloud of red dust filled the air, obscuring their vision.

Socrates signaled to Bakke, and the chopper rose above the dust.

They cleared the dust at a thousand feet.

Everyone peered down into the cloud below.

Max saw a throbbing black morass at the center of the dust, a black hole with the faintest red tinge. It pulsed with malevolence and pain and glee; something like lightning crackling within its depths.

Max handed the box back to Socrates and went back to his seat, looked out into the dust and darkness below.

Something clicked in his chest and a flood of warmth ran through him. In his mind's eye, the blond woman from the meadow smiled at him.

The ghostly remnants of the agony below dimmed, faded. Max closed his eyes and opened himself further.

The ghosts were slipping away…released.

Peace ran through Max and he leaned back into his seat, feeling more free than he had since he'd boarded the plane in Thailand. A final vision of the blond woman, ushering the spirits of those who'd been stuck here away to a better place, and then she was gone.

Rosita leaned into him, and he put an arm around her, holding her close.

CHAPTER SIXTY TWO

Mack sat with his back against the wall, waiting. They'd come to feed him soon. The room was a room, not a cell, and they'd have to open the door. He'd get a shot at them then.

Widrigs turned over in his narrow bed, unable to sleep.

The men had attacked them, yes. Mack Bannister had been captured after trying to kill Guy and Raymond, and snatch Mary Jane, yes. Mack Bannister had done many very bad things.

But they were men. Each of them had sustained grievous injury. Each would be better off in a hospital.

It went against everything he believed to hold them in cells. To allow them to suffer the pain of their wounds.

He'd been allowed him to give them antibiotics and some codeine. Had cleaned and bandaged their wounds the best he could.

But they really should be in a hospital.

This idea of holding them in cells was wrong.

Surely, if he explained the situation to the men, that he was letting them out, trusting them to simply leave, they'd bolt at the opportunity, never come back.

Mack Bannister was human—he'd understand.

Maybe this was the way to end it all!

Maybe one act of mercy and trust would allow the Bannisters to see the light. The truth of it. Eyes opened, they might even change.

Sure.

People were people.

Reasonable.

The Bannisters only behaved as they did because they'd

been conditioned to it, had hard lives, had never had the truth explained to them. Never understood their place in a community, the beauty of diversity and the wonderful sense of communion for which man was created.

He could explain it to them.

He could make them see the light.

Widrigs sat up, excited.

It was so clear to him, so vivid.

All he had to do was explain it to Mack and the others.

When they understood, they would see.

Widrigs stood, his heart thrumming in his chest.

He, Doc Widrigs, was going to put an end to the reign of the Bannisters.

Once they understood, they'd put their resources to work helping people, become a vital part of a flourishing community.

It was so simple, so easy, so *right.*

Why hadn't anyone tried this before?

He put on his shoes, grabbed his medical bag, and shuffled out of his cottage, headed for the barn.

Excited.

Happy.

Filled with love and hope.

He, Doc Widrigs, showing the Bannisters the light.

The idea put a spring in his step, and he moved up the hill, his heart dancing.

So simple.

So pure.

So sure.

Bakke looked over at Socrates, then leaned forward and tapped the gas gauge.

"We're getting tight," he said. "We've been fighting a headwind the whole way, I'm not sure we can make it to Krell's."

Socrates looked down at the gauge, then out the window,

considering.

The gauge was brushing up on "E." He had no desire to fall out of the sky in this thing and smash into the ground below.

"Where you thinking about? We don't want any interference, or cops, or someone leaning in and seeing..." He gestured at the stretchers in the aisle behind.

"There's a little strip outside of Freedom," Bakke said. "Private. Bannisters use it all the time, so do others."

"You want to put down on a Bannister strip and refuel? Are you out of your mind?"

"It's not a Bannister strip. It's private. I told you. You have to pay a fee to use it. The fee buys silence. No FAA, no cops, no nobody: just a couple of gas trucks, a strip, a hanger or two, some tie-down spots."

Socrates leaned into Bakke's face, stared into his eyes.

"If this is a trick, some kind of set up..."

"How?" Bakke asked. "There's nobody left. Between the attack on Krell's and taking out Red Rock, there's nobody left. Not really."

"Not really?"

Bakke glanced at the dials, out the window, then back to Socrates.

"Look," he said. "Most of the crews that work for Bannisters are a den of snakes. They're in it for themselves. They get to play with the girls, have a good time, and make a little money—not a lot of money, not most of 'em. You took out all the hardcore Bannisters. I mean, that one dude they call the asshole, Max, took out some of the family. With Mack up at Krell's and all those guys who hit the compound there dead, the guys at Red Rock...there are little knots left, here and there, but they're just good ol' boys who like a good time. None of them are going to risk their lives for the Bannisters. They certainly aren't getting organized. The Bannisters are done."

Socrates looked at Bakke for a long moment

"Not quite yet. Still have to cut the head off the snake," he said.

He looked out the window at the plains below.

"OK," he said. "But we'll be ready, and if you pull any shit, I personally am going to shoot you in the guts and watch you squirm. Tyler can take a shot at flying this thing, need be."

He adjusted the mic of his headset to rest up against his lips, then spoke into it.

"We are going to put down for gas in about ten minutes," he said. "I want you all armed and alert."

He turned around to make sure he'd been heard.

All the men were looking at him.

"This is a private strip we're landing on. Pilot says the Bannisters use it. And others like them. So stay sharp."

"Tyler and Dean will pop out, side arms only, and cover the pilot and anybody else who shows up. Low profile. The rest of us will arm up and be ready for support as needed."

The men picked up their weapons, popped clips out, checked them, thumbed more rounds in as needed, checked breeches and safeties.

Bakke pushed the stick forward and brought the chopper into a descending arc.

Max looked out the window, a hand on Rosita's back as she checked her weapon.

A narrow dirt strip down below: a couple of hangars, an office building of some sort, a gas truck, windsocks hanging limp.

As Bakke arced down and in, a private jet lined up on the runway.

All black.

Shiny.

Max sat bolt upright as if electrified.

The Red Presence filled the aircraft below.

Dust kicked up behind the jet as the pilot rammed the throttle forward and the little plane leapt into the sky.

The pilot made no allowances for the chopper, and the plane streaked by close enough for the jet wash created turbulence to bounce the chopper.

"Asshole!" Socrates said, broadcasting across the headsets, his lips still close to the voice-activated mic.

The chopper shook, and Max looked at the pilot.

All the blood had drained from his face and beads of sweat popped on his forehead, trickled down his cheeks. He raised an arm to wipe the sweat from his brow and Max saw his armpit was drenched.

Max adjusted the mic of his headset.

"Who was that?" he demanded.

Bakke shot a terrified glance back over his shoulder. He looked about ready to puke.

"Mexicans," he said. "the Old Man must've called in the Mexicans."

"Mexicans?" Socrates asked.

"Where do you think the Bannisters get their women from?" Bakke said. "They got a deal with a cartel out of Tenancingo."

"And?" Socrates said.

"And you think the Bannisters are bad? They're puppies compared to these guys."

The chopper hovered as Bakke brought it back under control.

"The Old Man must've called in a kill team."

Bakke began to whimper, his mic broadcasting it. The sheer terror in his voice unsettled the men, and they stirred in their seats, uneasy.

Hands clutched weapons, double-checked safeties and breeches.

Bakke brought the copter down on a marked-off square and powered it down.

Silence.

Just the whistle of wind across the plains, the quiet of men preparing themselves. Adjusting to the news.

It was not over. Not yet.

The Old Man stood at the big window, sun reflecting off the

sunglasses he'd put on against the glare.

A van turned off the main road and began the climb up the hill toward the house.

"They're here," he said.

Roger stood and walked to the window and stood next to him.

Both men watched the van climb the hill.

"Well, here we go," the Old Man said.

CHAPTER SIXTY THREE

Doc Widrigs shot a glance over his shoulder, back at the farmhouse below.

The compound sat quietly in the early light of dawn, a light on in the kitchen of the big farmhouse. He imagined Dallas making coffee and grinned.

Dallas was going to be so pleased with him. Turning the Bannisters into allies, solving this whole blood-soaked mess. Putting an end to conflict.

And the solution was so simple.

Put aside the animus. Talk to one another like adults.

Lay out the issues rationally, show the Bannisters the truth.

Community was what mattered.

Community was what made for happiness and fulfillment.

Not conflict.

Certainly not violence.

Doc shuddered, remembering the men laid out on the grass in the field behind him.

All buried out back now, he reflected.

That was what conflict bought you: an early grave.

With a last look down the hill, he slipped into the barn.

Tyler and Dean stood by the chopper, hands on hips, inches from their side arms.

The strip was quiet.

No rustle of men, no shouting, no commotion.

Peaceful.

They scanned the horizon, looked over the office building

and open hangars.

Nobody.

Tyler turned to Bakke.

"All right," he said. "How do you get gas here?"

"Someone will come. They know this chopper. The Old Man has an account here. They'll fill it, no questions asked. No one wants to chance pissing the Old Man off."

As he spoke, an old guy in coveralls exited the main building.

Bakke leaned out the window and waved at him.

The old man waved back, shuffled over to a gas truck, climbed up and in.

The gas truck fired up with the rattle of a diesel engine. Gears cranked and protested—an old truck, double-clutching still necessary.

The truck lumbered out toward the chopper.

Tyler leaned in toward the cockpit.

"Looks safe enough," he said. "But stay alert in there."

Max huddled with Socrates.

"What do you think?" Max asked.

"About these Mexicans?" Socrates asked.

Max nodded.

"Bannisters' about an hour's drive from here."

Socrates watched the approaching truck.

"If they just left, we should be able to beat them there. Set up."

"What I was thinking," Max said.

"We ought to drop Timmy off, though," Socrates said.

"Lose the element of surprise," Max said.

Socrates rubbed his chin, running the possibilities over in his mind.

"They got to be up here to get Mack back," Socrates said. "Which means they'll be coming to the compound. I don't care how good they are, if we set up for them like we did for the Bannisters, we'll take them out."

Max thought about it.

"Probably," he said. "But they won't be coming in like the Bannisters did. They'll try to infiltrate, quiet-like. Sneak through the wire and into the compound. Do some recon, get a handle on things. Quiet and quick."

"We can be ready for that, too," Socrates said.

"Maybe," Max said.

He had a bad feeling about the Mexicans. The jet had pulsed with the Red Presence. The men it had delivered were...*other*.

A new level.

"We need to get the drop on these guys," Max said.

Socrates sat up, decided.

"If we hustle, we can do it," he said. "Drop off Timmy...and Marcus. Just a touch and go. Won't take an extra ten minutes. Then we lock and load and head up to the Old Man's place."

Ten minutes seemed like a long time to Max. But he could see Socrates' mind was made up,

The truck circled up to access the gas tanks, and the old guy inside clambered down painfully, shuffled back to the hoses, selected one, then dragged it out by the nozzle to fill up the chopper.

"Howdy," the old man said, fiddling with the gas cap on the chopper. "Busy morning out here. Damn."

Tyler nodded at him, and Dean circled around the truck, clearing it, just to be sure.

"Yup, Tyler said. "We're in a hurry here. Get a move on, if you don't mind."

The old man glared at him, met Tyler's eyes, then looked down and fitted the nozzle into the gas tank and squeezed. Gas sloshed into the tank, the old-fashioned dials on the truck clicking off the gallons.

"I aim to please," the old man said.

An uneasy silence reigned. Just the slosh of the gas, the click of the dials and the faintest wind across the dry ground.

The Old Man and Roger stepped to the door and opened it, letting in the rose-hued morning light. The van had parked in the circle drive, passenger's side facing the house.

The driver sat motionless. A statue with sunglasses.

The passenger popped open his door and got out without acknowledging the Bannisters.

"Fuckin' spics," the Old Man muttered. "No fuckin' respect, no..."

"Easy, Pops," Roger said. "Keep it together."

"I got it fuckin' together, boy," the Old Man growled. He shut his mouth.

A metallic pop, and the side door slid back on its rails. The van bobbed as two men stepped out.

About 5' 7" each, maybe 140 pounds, with smooth, dark looks, the men stepped around and faced the Bannisters. They paused and looked the Bannisters up and down, surveyed the yard and land beyond.

"Señor Bannister," one of the men said. His voice was high and light, like a boy's. He and his twin tipped their hats, then let their arms hang loose at their sides.

"Señor Barrera," the Old Man said. "Come. Let's talk." He gestured into the house, and the Barreras strolled through the door and into the house.

Roger shot the Old Man a look. The Old Man raised his eyebrows, shrugged and followed the two men in.

"We're in it now, boy," he said. "Let's see where this gets us."

Roger shot a look at the van, the two men sitting in it, staring straight ahead. It made him uneasy, turning his back on them and walking in, but he had no choice.

He closed the door. Locked and bolted it, then turned and followed the Old Man into the den where the Barrera twins stood silhouetted in front of the window like two old-fashioned cowboys.

Or gunfighters.

Doc Widrigs nodded to Kane, then strolled towards the doors holding the prisoners.

"What are you doing, Doc?"

Widrigs came to a full stop and turned to look at Kane, who, light from the computer screens washing out his features, stared back at him.

"Checking on the prisoners," Widrigs said.

Kane stood.

"Now hold on, Doc," he said. "You come in here alone? You know better than that."

Kane glanced over his shoulder at the monitors.

Quiet. Peaceful. Trees and farmland and miles of wire fence. Lights on in the farmhouse, people beginning to stir after the long night.

Kane walked over and put a hand on Widrigs' shoulder.

"What are you doing, Doc?"

Widrigs looked at the floor.

"Just wanted to check on 'em," he said. He looked back up into Kane's eyes imploringly. "I couldn't sleep, thinking about it. These men should be in a hospital, somewhere more comfortable. They have serious wounds. They're suffering."

Kane looked at the ceiling. Gathered himself.

"You're a little simple, Doc, so let me remind you: These *men*," he said, "flew in here in the middle of the night with automatic weapons and tried to kill us all. They are lucky to be alive. They should be buried out back with the ones they came with."

Widrigs winced.

"Just let me check on 'em, Kane. Make sure they're OK. Talk to them a little. Then I can relax."

Kane fiddled with his keys, figuring.

Easier just to let the idiot do a quick check and send him on his way. Poor bastard never had been right since his wife had died in that car accident.

"Ah, hell, Doc. Just a peek, you understand? Then you go on back and leave it alone, got me?"

"I promise, Kane," Widrigs said.

Kane strolled to the door of Mack's room and selected a key.

"Now stand back, Doc, while I get the door open."

He slipped the key into the lock and turned it.

The men buckled in as Bakke cranked up the big chopper and took her into the sky.

Socrates looked over at Bakke, tapped him.

"How much longer to the compound?"

Bakke cast an eye over the flat terrain below, looked at his gauges.

"Twenty minutes, I'd say. Give or take."

Socrates passed word along to the men in back.

Rosita slid in beside Max again, one arm around him, the other her gun.

Max grinned and shook his head.

Quite a woman.

Roger leaned over the printouts and maps spread over the table, gesturing.

The Old Man stood to one side, cradling a steaming mug of coffee.

"This here's the compound where they've got him. We don't know where."

One Barrera twin studied the map thoughtfully, the other gazed out the window.

"And you sent in eight men in a helicopter, eight on the west gate and eight on the east gate."

"Yes," Roger said.

"And none of them returned to you," the Barrera twin said.

The twin at the window muttered something in Spanish and crossed his arms, leaned back on his heels.

The twin at the table smiled.

"My brother wonders if you are perhaps trying to get rid of us. Or, if perhaps you think we are stupid."

The twin at the window said something else. This time Roger caught it.

"Or if we're crazy," Roger said.

"Indeed," said the twin at the table.

He straightened up.

The smell of gasoline turned Roger's attention to the hallway leading to the front door.

His mouth dropped open.

A giant stood there, filling the hallway. The man had to be six and half feet tall and 300 pounds. Long, greasy black hair obscured his features, but a prominent scar dented his nose, the morning light glinting off the scar tissue.

But that wasn't the worst of it.

In one hand, the giant carried a red plastic jug of gasoline —the smell that had alerted Roger. In the other, a five-gallon plastic bucket.

Cold steel pressed hard into the back of Roger's head.

"No," said the high thin voice behind him, "I think that is not the way we will play this game."

Roger moved to turn, and the muzzle of the gun shoved into his head viciously, pushing him off balance, his arms windmilling.

"That's it," said the high thin voice. "Arms up. Keep them there, Señor Bannister."

Mack heard the murmur of conversation, and then footsteps approached. He gave his plastic knife a thumb check for sharpness and resilience, then crouched at the door, his wounded shoulder forward, shank in the other hand.

The key turned in the lock and the deadbolt snicked back into place. The key moved to doorknob. A click and the door knob rotated, and...

Mack put his whole body into it and slammed into the door —he'd been a defensive lineman in school who doubled as left tackle and he knew how to use his weight. He ignored the sharp flash of pain in his shoulder and pushed through.

The door flew open, catching the man who monitored the computers square in the forehead. He'd been looking down at the doorknob when it burst open.

Mack continued moving forward and the man went down

on his back.

Before he had a chance to recover, Mack was on top of him, his right hand a blur of motion, up and down, up and down. He snorted with glee as the shank found both eyes and burst them.

The man curled up and screamed in agony.

Mack let him turn, exposing the back of his head.

Never much of a student, Mack had retained one thing from high school Biology: how to pith a frog.

He'd honed the skill over the years on a variety of women and men, and when the man on the floor curled up, he sunk the shank deep into the soft dimple at the base of his skull.

The man jittered and spasmed, choking sounds coming from his mouth.

Mack stood and looked down at the man.

He threw back his head and laughed with joy.

"God damn!" he crowed. "You ever seen a more beautiful sight?"

He laughed again.

"Wait for it," he said. "He'll shit himself pretty quick."

He laughed again.

Doc Widrigs pushed into the wall behind the steel door and tried to make himself invisible.

Mack turned and looked at him, his grin ear to ear.

"Well, lookee here," he said. "Another one."

A shudder ran through Doc, making his shoulders tremble.

Mack threw back his head and laughed again.

"God damn!" he said again. "Got ourselves a real man here, ain't we!"

Still laughing, he reached out casually and gripped Doc Widrig's wrist as he attempted to cover up.

Mack leaned back with all his weight and swung Doc Widrigs around by the wrist, snapping him face first into the wall on the other side of the door.

Widrigs slumped to the floor and Mack grabbed him by the

hair and slammed his head against the concrete wall. He felt the skull crack and kept slamming, again and again, the man's skull shattering like the shell of a hardboiled egg.

He let Widrigs slump all the way to the floor, his head a mushy pulp.

Mack laughed again.

"Hot damn! Let the good times roll!" he said.

He leaned down and turned the first man over, pulled the key ring off his belt.

Widgrigs' black medical bag caught his eye.

"And what do we have here?" He snapped the bag open, pawed through its contents.

Dressings, medical tape, sterile cleaning solution, vials, and syringes.

"Ooo-eey!" he said. "Jackpot!"

He stopped for a minute, held a vial up to the light.

"Sweet Jesus," he said. "Dilaudid."

He fingered the vial for a minute, considered, then shook his head.

"No. Not now." He looked down at the men he killed, gave them a nod. "As much fun as it's been, it's time to go," he said.

He scooped up all the Dilaudid, shoved it into a pocket, and flipped through the keys. "Let's see…eeny, meenie, miny, moe…"

Bakke pulled the chopper down, coming in over the trees, aiming for the same spot he'd put it down just a short time ago.

Before everything went all to hell.

He pulled the chopper into a hover in the clearing in the orchard by the house and slowly lowered it to the ground.

Motion up the hill by the barn caught his attention.

A jolt of fear ran through him and he straightened in his seat.

Socrates noticed and followed his gaze up the hill.

"Incoming!" Socrates yelled.

The men in the back startled. They'd been relaxed, home-free. Ready to start putting this whole nasty business behind them.

'Incoming?'

It did not compute.

A knot of three men snaked down the hill, Mack Bannister in the lead holding a rifle ready. Behind him, two other men, one holding a pistol, another crouching for cover behind the other two.

All three visibly wounded with bloody dressings and medical gauze.

All three zeroed in on the chopper.

The chopper engine wound down into silence and Mack Bannister's voice crossed the clearing to meet them.

"Hot damn! Rescue mission! Ain't my old man the best!"

Socrates popped out of the chopper, gun rising to draw a bead on the three.

"Hold it right there!" he yelled. "Drop your weapons!"

The surprise on Mack Bannister's face was comical. He'd thought the cavalry had arrived, only to find a chopper full of hostile enemy.

Tyler and Dean scrambled out, weapons up, followed closely by the rest of the men.

Mack Bannister howled and brought the rifle up, a shot knocking Socrates off his feet and onto his back.

The men opened up on him.

Mack jittered and danced from the onslaught of bullets, rifle falling from his hand. Both arms raised up, hands flopping at the wrists, and he arced backwards and fell to the ground. The two men behind him dropped like sacks of grain and lay still.

The smell of gunpowder and aviation fuel drifted across the clearing, a haze of gray smoke wafting through the scene.

Socrates' grunts cut through the silence and Big John knelt at his side as Tyler, Dean, and Forrest eased up to the fallen men and checked them.

"Bullet penetrated the vest," Socrates said. "Not sure how bad. Hurts like hell, though."

Dallas Krell raced across the porch, down the stairs, and joined the men.

Men appeared on the edges of the clearing, armed and wary.

Big John had Socrates' vest off and was cleaning the wound with a field kit.

Dallas knelt beside them.

"Not too bad, I don't think," Big John said. "Doesn't look like the bullet went too deep, you can feel the lump here," he probed the wound with a thick finger.

Socrates bit back a yell.

"We'll have Doc cut it out, stitch him up, he'll be as good as new."

Dallas waved at the men on the periphery of the clearing—a signal to stay alert.

"Clear the compound," he yelled.

The men partnered up and began the patrol, disappearing back into the woods, back behind the barn, and into the fields behind the farmhouse.

One team entered the barn.

"Get the Doc!" Krell ordered.

A man peeled off from the pair headed for the farmhouse and ran up the trail towards the housing in back.

The team that entered the barn burst back out into the clearing, eyes wide, and trotted down the hill to the men clustered around the chopper and Socrates.

"Doc's in there," one of the men said, jerking a thumb over his shoulder. "And he's not helping anyone. Not anymore."

Dallas stood, heart thumping in his chest.

"Kane?"

The team from the barn looked down, then up at Dallas.

"Him too," said the first man. "It's ugly in there, Dallas. A mess."

"Aww, hell," Dallas said. "Damn it!"

He knelt down next to Socrates and put a hand on his shoulder.

Socrates looked up at him.

"Don't you worry about me," Socrates said. "I'll be fine. But we got to put an end to this. We're close now."

Max stepped in.

"Get me to the Bannisters," he said. "I'll end this. Guaranteed."

Old Man Bannister roared.

"You all are going to die! I'm going to get you down to Red Rock, have the boys soften you up a bit, then I'm going to take you slow. Real slow. You'll be begging me to die."

Chuy, Girogio, and Ruiz stood around the Old Man and Roger as the Barrera twins fiddled with the restraints holding the naked Bannisters to their chairs.

The twin who spoke English smiled.

"This is a lot of big talk for a man in your position, Señor Bannister," he said. "It is best to negotiate from a position of power. You do not seem to have a full grasp of your situation."

Roger licked his lips and looked over at the Old Man.

"Pops," he said. "Cool it a minute, will you?"

"You young pup! Don't tell me what to do. These fuckin' spics..."

"Pops!" Roger cut in.

He tried to look over his shoulder to address the twins. "This is not necessary. We can get you whatever it is you want. You don't have to do this. Just talk to us."

The Barrera twin behind him giggled. A thin, childlike peal of laughter that chilled Roger to the bone.

"But of course we have to do this, Señor," he said. "It is the only way to be sure."

"Sure?"

"Sure that we leave nothing behind. We are here to take it all. Every one of your little businesses. All of your bars, your hotels, your bank accounts...we will be taking possession of your...business. A change of management, if you will. What do you Americans call it? A hostile takeover, is that it?"

The Old Man coughed and spat a thick wad of phlegm at

him.

"Fuck you," he said.

Satisfied with the bindings, the twins circled around in front of the Bannisters and the other three men eased off and took up flanking positions. Ruiz stooped and picked up the Bannisters' clothes, then cast a glance at the twins.

"*Si*, Ruiz," one twin murmured.

"Ruiz is going to clean your clothes for you," the other said. "And then you will be allowed to put them back on."

Roger strained against the ropes, hands scrabbling for knots, desperately trying to free himself.

The English-speaking twin smiled at him.

Behind him, a rustling noise and the smell of gasoline.

CHAPTER SIXTY FOUR

"By the sound of it, these Mexicans might just take care of our problem for us," Dallas said.

Max, Tyler, Forrest, Dean, Big John, and Raymond sat around the table in the farmhouse with him.

"Maybe," Max said. "And maybe they'll do what the Old Man brought them up here to do. Maybe they're cutting through the wire as we speak."

Dallas glanced back over his shoulder at the computer monitors set up at the station behind him.

"Doubt it," he said. "And if they are, we've got them."

Max shrugged. "Only one way to be sure."

Big John leaned his bulk into the table, making it squeak.

"You should've seen this place, Dallas," he said. "It was like a torture theme park. They had a crematorium set up for the bodies." He gestured with a hand the size of a dinner plate. "Ash was piled yay high in there. We figure they done hundreds of people. Girls, mostly, by the looks of things. We can't take a chance with these people."

Dallas nodded.

"All right, so what's the plan?"

"Pilot says the Mexicans make the Bannisters look like Boy Scouts," Max said. "I figure they'll be taking some time with the Bannisters, feeling them out, seeing what kind of strength they still have. It'll be obvious to them the Bannisters are in trouble, and they'll want to know how bad it is...how weak the Bannisters are. Then they'll move. I think it's likely they'll go after the Bannisters and leave us alone here. We don't have anything to interest them, and even if they thought Mack was still here and alive, they wouldn't care. They'll be looking at taking over the Bannister operation, or at least scoop up every last penny of it they can."

"So we set up and wait? See if they come? Or if they take care of the Bannisters for us?"

Max shook his head.

"No," he said. "We mount up and move right now, before they get done with the Bannisters. Have the pilot chopper us in to the little valley behind the Old Man's spread, and walk in from there. Then we can have a look at the situation and see. Burst in on 'em and surprise them, or..."

"Or?"

"Well, if the Mexicans really are taking it to the Bannisters, we can wait a bit and let them get their job done..."

Dallas leaned back in his chair, and stretched his back. Looked at the ceiling, then straightened up, thinking.

"Do it," he said. "You guys are already geared up. Get some more ammo, load up the chopper, head over there and see what you can see. But Max..."

"Yeah?"

"We have to be sure this is the end of it. I'm not going to live my life on high alert, always wondering when and if someone's coming through the wire...."

Max rose from the table, walked over to Dallas and put a hand on his shoulder.

"Don't you worry about that, Dallas. We'll take care of it. 'In the end is my beginning.'"

Dallas looked up, raised his eyebrows in question.

"Misquoting T. S. Eliot. 'East Coker.' Rest easy, Dallas. I'm putting an end to this."

Roger bucked and writhed, but Ruiz' grip was unbreakable. The twins eased his feet into his underwear, then pulled them up his legs, had a bit of trouble at the hips, then snugged them up to his waist.

Gasoline dripped down Roger's legs.

The English-speaking twin grinned as his brother pulled the sopping wet pants out of the bucket.

"Ruiz, allow Señor Bannister to don his pants."

Roger bucked and writhed and kicked some more, but Ruiz held him and the twins dressed him as easily as a child dressing a doll.

"The socks, I think, no?" said the Barrera twin to the other.

He giggled again, that childlike squeal of joy colored with a tinge of cruelty, excitement building in him.

When they loosened his hand for the shirt, Roger attempted to stand and threw a punch at the twin holding the dripping garment.

The twin's head bobbed, and came up with a perfectly placed right hand that broke Roger's nose, blood splattering down his chest.

Both twins giggled.

"He has beautiful blood, does he not, brother?"

The Spanish-speaking twin giggled and nodded happily as together they finished dressing Roger.

Giorgio handed them towels he'd requisitioned from the bathroom and the twins carefully wiped all traces of gasoline from their hands and boots.

The English-speaking twin turned to the Old Man.

"I must confess, Señor Bannister, that this is my favorite part."

The Old Man clenched his jaw and kept silent, eyes pouring hatred, a spark of outraged helplessness deep down. If he was embarrassed by his nakedness, it didn't show.

"How many sons do you have, Señor?" the English-speaking twin asked. "We have done business with Roger, and Bill. And there is the wild one, yes? What is his name? The one you hired us to rescue?"

The Old Man spit at the twins, then shut his mouth.

The Spanish-speaking twin grinned and pulled a large Zippo

lighter out of his pocket, a US Customs logo emblazoned on its side.

He flipped open the top with one hand, snapped it shut, flipped it open again.

"Señor?" asked the English-speaking twin.

The Old Man moved as if to spit again, but satisfied himself with a deadly glare.

The grin on the English-speaking twin widened.

"Good," he said. "This is good. We will commence, now."

He nodded at his twin, who thumbed the wheel on his Zippo, spark igniting the butane soaked wick.

Flame rose from the Zippo and the Spanish-speaking twin approached Roger as the other men stepped back.

"Mack!" Roger screamed. "His name is Mack!"

The Spanish speaking twin paused and looked over his shoulder at his brother.

"We were not speaking with you, Señor, but with your father," said the English-speaking twin.

He nodded to his brother, who advanced again toward Roger, waving the Zippo ahead of him as if lighting his way.

Bakke piloted the chopper down low, close to the mountain ridge that ran along the main road toward Aston.

He brought the chopper in behind the town, rushing over houses with spreads pushed up against the rising hills, white picket fences and farmhouses and barns flashing by.

The Bannister compound looked down from its place on the hill above the town, like a medieval Lord's castle.

Bakke circled around the hill and slowed, scanning the valley for a safe place to put down.

Max, leaning forward, spotted a meadow and pointed.

Bakke nodded and the chopper drifted toward the meadow.

"All right, boys, check your gear," Max said. "We're about ready to roll."

Tyler, Forrest, Dean, Big John, and Raymond fiddled with their weapons, readying them.

Bakke set the chopper down gently on the field, testing its solidity, then powered down.

Max leaned over and pulled the key out of the ignition, stuffing it into a pocket. He pulled a pair of handcuffs out of his jacket and handed them to Bakke.

Bakke affixed a cuff to his wrist, wincing as the steel closed around his bruised flesh, and then the other to the handle of the door.

Max checked the cuffs, then squeezed the cuff on Bakke's wrist tight another two clicks.

Bakke grimaced, but managed not to whimper.

"Sit tight and don't try anything," Max said. "We'll be back."

Tyler opened the door in the rear, and the men filed out.

Max gave a last glance at Bakke, then popped open his own door and stepped onto the spongy grass of the meadow, stretched, and looked up the hill toward the Bannister spread above, just out of view.

Tyler looked at him, and Max nodded.

"Let's do this," he said.

The English-speaking twin nodded to his brother, who flicked the Zippo shut.

"And so Mack and Roger here are all that is left you," he said. "So sad. The death of the line. A great dynasty coming to an end." He sighed and looked at the floor as if lost in thought, then brightened and looked the Old Man square in the eye.

"But the Barrera dynasty will take its place. Instead of a mongrel American dynasty, a proud Mexican one with ancestry that goes back to the Aztecs. Yes."

The Old Man raised his chin.

"Fuck you. Fuck you and the horse you rode in on."

The English-speaking twin giggled again and clapped his hands.

"You bring me so much joy, Señor Bannister. We will begin anew."

He nodded to Ruiz, who thumped over to Roger on his huge

feet, then squatted down beside him.

Sweat poured down Roger's face, mixing with the tears from his inflamed eyes. Tiny puddles of gasoline collected at each of his feet where the gas had dripped down to the floor.

Ruiz patted Roger's hand, stroked the long fingers.

Roger jerked and cried out, then bit his lip.

Ruiz smiled.

Roger's other hand was a maw of meat, blood, and bone. Each finger had been snapped and curled up on itself like a ribbon. Raw shards of bone glistened, and blood dripped steadily to the floor beneath.

"And so we have ascertained that your son, the wild one, Mack—he is apparently a guest of these Krells. Of no real concern to us at present, though a loose end to snip, certainly. Roger, the business one, is here, sadly unable to pick up a pencil to do his calculations."

The twin walked behind Roger and patted his shoulder paternally, then gestured to Giorgio, who tossed him a towel.

"Is good, the shirt still well saturated. So, to the main course. Tell me, Senor Bannister—where do you keep your accounts?"

"Fuck you," the Old Man said. "You're just going to kill us anyway. Why the fuck should I tell you anything?"

Both twins laughed in unison. Identically.

The English-speaking twin clapped his hands again.

He turned to his twin.

"Es hora, sí? Deberíamos empezar?"

The Spanish-speaking twin smiled widely and pulled his Zippo back out of his pocket.

"Wait!" Roger said. "Dad doesn't know about that stuff. I'm the one who keeps the books. I'm the one who keeps it all running."

The English-speaking twin's shoulders slumped. He shrugged at the other twin, who put the Zippo away.

"We have one set of books on the computer," Roger said, voice high and wheezy with pain, "and a physical copy at the bank. In a safe deposit box."

"I see," said the English-speaking twin. He patted Roger's cheek, then circled the room to the desk and seated himself in front of the computer. "And how do I access this?"

"Roger, you shut your fuckin' mouth," the Old Man roared. "You silly fool! Just sit there and take it like a man. Ain't nothing you gonna say get you out of this."

The English-speaking twin wagged a finger at the Old Man.

"This is not productive talk, Señor Bannister. Ruiz?"

Ruiz straightened up, stalked over to the Old Man and planted himself in front of him, arms on his hips.

"If the elder Bannister opens his mouth again, I am thinking the proper course of action is to remove his tongue," the English-speaking twin said.

Ruiz glanced at Giorgio, who turned and walked down the hallway and out of sight.

"Now, Señor Roger, before we begin, perhaps you can enlighten me as to the location of the key for this safety deposit box at the bank, and the accompanying details?"

Roger licked his lips and looked at the Old Man.

The Old Man's lips curled into a grimace of disgust.

"Pussy," he said.

The English-speaking twin raised his eyebrows at Ruiz, who stepped forward and reached out an enormous hand to grab the Old Man, his fingers completely encircling his neck. Ruiz grunted, and lifted the Old Man, chair and all, off the floor so that their eyes were level.

The Old Man gurgled and made odd gagging noises, his face going red, eyes bulging.

Ruiz held him at eye level easily.

The Old Man began to buck and spasm in the chair, back arching, legs attempting to kick against his bonds.

"A second longer," the English-speaking twin murmured.

The Old Man spasmed more violently.

"That will do, Ruiz, thank you," the English-speaking twin said.

Ruiz lowered the Old Man to the ground.

The Old Man's face contorted as his mouth gaped for air, a thin wheeze that cut across the silence of the room as air made its way down the damaged passage of his throat.

"As we were discussing, Señor Roger, the key? And bank?"

Roger cast a sidewise glance at the Old Man, who still fought for breath.

"Key's in the tray of the locked central drawer of the desk. The one over the cubby hole. First National, downtown Aston."

The English-speaking twin pulled at the drawer.

"Yes, it is locked. As you say."

He pulled a thick stainless steel switchblade from his pocket, pressed the button on its side, and the blade snicked into place and locked. He stuck the blade into the crack of the drawer in question, fiddled around a bit, then pulled the door open. He folded the blade, put it back into his pocket and then held up the key. He looked over at Roger.

Roger nodded, "that's the one."

The English-speaking twin turned his attention to the computer.

"This requires a password. Señor?"

The Old Man wheezed out something incomprehensible. The English-speaking twin gestured lazily in Ruiz' direction, Ruiz stepped in and grabbed hold of the Old Man's left hand and rolled his pinky up backwards, splintering it into shards that drove through the flesh.

The Old Man bucked and moaned, but kept his mouth shut.

"Admirable, Señor Bannister," the English-speaking twin said.

He turned his eyes to Roger.

"'redrockweekend,'" Roger said. "All lowercase. Files are all clearly marked by place of business. Banks are under 'Banks,' like that."

The English-speaking twin turned his attention to the computer and the room grew silent, just the clattering of the keys on the computer keyboard, the steady platt, platt, platt of blood dripping from Roger's ruined hand, and the wheeze of the Old Man's breath.

Max crested the hill and the Bannister compound came into view. He held up a hand and Tyler, Forrest, Dean, Big John, and Raymond spread out to form a line hunkered down just out of sight of the back of the house.

A black van sat in the driveway, its sliding door open.

It appeared to be empty.

"Hold on a bit," Max said. "Let's suss this out."

Tyler pulled out a pair of binoculars and scanned the house and grounds carefully.

"Van's empty, unless someone's napping in back," he said. "Same for that garage."

"OK," Max said. "Better check 'em out."

Tyler gestured to the right and Dean hustled out to the garage, gun up and ready. He disappeared into the gloom.

"I'm on the van," Max said.

He slipped up to the van as quietly as possible and peered in.

Looked back at Tyler and signaled clear.

Dean popped out of the garage and also signaled clear.

Just then, the back door of the house opened.

A burly-looking Mexican guy strode out of the house, head down in contemplation, and made his way for the van.

Max crouched low and listened to the sound of the man's boots on the gravel.

As the boots came to the front of the van and turned towards the open door, Max rose up from his crouch, using the momentum to step forward and reach out with his rear leg in a front kick that caught the Mexican square on his chin.

The man folded up and dropped as if his spinal column had been removed.

Tyler slipped out to the van and together he and Max heaved the Mexican in. Tyler pulled some zip ties from his pocket and in seconds the man was secure.

"What do we have here?" Max asked, eyeing the three long black bags in back.

He reached in and slid one over, ran the zipper down its length.

Black steel and brown wood. Long rifle, machine gun, shotgun, pistols, an assortment of tools in black metal, a propane torch, some wicked looking clamps, knives and other things Max didn't have time to catalog.

"Someone's loaded for bear," he said.

"Loaded to torture a bear," Tyler said, reaching in and pulling out a vicious looking pair of pincers.

"Let's see what we can see," Max said.

Tyler signaled the men to move in.

Forrest moved to one side of the door of the house as Big John and Raymond gave cover, then Raymond moved to the other side. Big John joined them.

"Keep a man on each side of the door," Max said.

Tyler nodded.

"I'm going to slip around to the left and work my way around front," Max said. "You take the right. Post Dean and Forrest on either side of the house to cover us, keep Raymond and Big John on the back door. See what we can see, then meet back here."

Tyler motioned Dean and Forrest into position. Once each man had settled himself, prone and presenting as small a target as possible to the house, Tyler looked back to Max, then took off for the right side of the house.

Max moved to the left side of the house, pressed himself into the stucco wall and worked his way forward.

The drapes on his side of the house were drawn against the rising sun, but Max was able to peer through a crack in one set of drapes to see a jumble of furniture and thick brown carpet, the room apparently empty. The rest of the rooms held their secrets, and he moved to the corner.

In the brightening light of day, he was clearly visible against the white stucco of the house. Max looked out at the thick walls surrounding the compound, thankful they sheltered him from view of the town below. The last thing he wanted right now was some minion down below phoning the house to let them know they had unwelcome visitors.

He moved towards the front of the house, feeling exposed. Less cover from the wall, the rise in the hill giving the front portion of the house a commanding view of Ramsey and the plains below.

Tyler moved his way, and they flanked the front window, a floor-to-ceiling number at least twenty feet long, a huge piece of glass.

Max edged up and looked into the room.

A small man in black at a computer to one side, behind a magnificent teak desk. A giant: six and a half feet tall, at least, and as solid and blocky as a bull stood in the center of the room. A man in sunglasses leaned casually against the back wall, pistol dangling from his hand. Another small man in black circled a man strapped into a sturdy wooden chair… Roger Bannister? Same kind of outfit Max remembered from their meeting at that farm, which seemed years ago. Plaids and jeans. He looked smaller than Max remembered. At the moment, he seemed curled up inside himself. Miserable.

The Old Man was naked, and scrawny looking in the morning light, his chest rising and falling rapidly, curly gray chest hair dripping with sweat, face contorted.

Also strapped into a chair.

Max dropped down below the window, his back to the wall, gun cradled in his arms.

He looked over at Tyler, signaled retreat.

They met back at the van, crouched out of sight of the door to the house, still open.

"Looks like the Bannisters are getting a taste of their own medicine," Max said.

Tyler flashed a grim looking grin.

"Yup. What you want to do now?"

From inside the house, a whump! and then the screaming began.

"That sounded like..."

"Gas fire..."

The screaming rose in intensity, accompanied by hoarse yelling, the cacophony overlaid with a high-pitched giggling that sent chills down Max's spine.

Suddenly he was inundated with some of the most vicious imagery he'd yet been subject to...a flashing collage of writhing, twisting bodies in flames, women screaming, living people dismembered, limbs coming away spraying blood in massive arterial pulses...

Max shut the door in his head and closed it down.

Without a word, he stood and headed for the house.

Tyler stood and signaled to Dean and Forrest to stay put, then hustled to catch up to Max, who had already crossed the threshold and stepped into the house.

Big John and Raymond readied themselves as Tyler followed a rapidly moving Max into the house.

The English-speaking twin circled the burning Roger, rubbing his hands together and holding them out, warming them against the flames.

He giggled and looked over at the Old Man straining against his bonds, his mouth a clapping cavern, roaring into the room.

He brushed shoulders with his twin as they both squatted, hands on their knees, peering into Roger's thrashing face as the flames took hold of his body.

This was the best part.

The advantage to soaking a man's clothing in gas, rather than pouring it over him, was you could control the fire better, confine it. No need to burn the whole house down, not unless you wanted to, that was.

But perhaps for the Old Man...start with a pool of gasoline on his chair, let that burn out first, then...

Max stepped into the room, the smell of burning flesh and gas overpowering.

Aside from the Bannisters, lashed to their chairs, four men were in the room.

All had their attention centered on the screaming, writhing figure in the chair.

It was an eerie sight, as if the man were wearing clothing made of fire. It froze Max for a second, and he felt Tyler draw even with him.

Their presence alerted the man standing closest to them, and he pivoted to look.

As he did so, Max reversed his weapon and drove the butt into the dimple between the man's eyes, putting all his weight into it.

The man crumped and went down with an audible thump that turned attention in his direction.

The giant was on him in a flash—spooky fast for such a huge man.

But Max had slipped into combat mode, everything smooth, silent, and clear. He saw the big man's fist on its way, sidestepped, and kicked him in the solar plexus.

The man grunted and turned to face Max, but Max had already slipped back the other way, flanking him, and dropped a right to the giant's temple, tipping the man's head down and to the side to be met with a perfect left hook to the chin. The man dropped to his knees as the two small men in black stepped around the burning figure in the chair, grinning, guns up already, moving in Max's direction.

Gunfire over his shoulder and off to each side as Tyler and Raymond met the twins, neat holes appearing in each forehead, the twins nosediving into the floor as their momentum carried them forward.

The giant dove forward to tackle Max, and Max met his chin with a switch knee, driving the man's jaw up and off to one side, dislocating it.

The giant hit the floor and rolled, coming up yet again, implacable and unstoppable.

Max grinned, danced to one side, and laid his shin against

the side of the man's neck where it met his twisted jawline.

The giant dropped, hands opening and closing into fists he pushed into the floor, attempting to rise yet again as Max centered himself for a soccer kick, catching the man on the point of his chin, this time wrenching the jar far off center.

The giant's eyes rolled back in his head and he dropped to the floor, rolled to his back, arms waving spasmodically as Max lined up again and put the point of his boot to the huge man's temple.

Finally, the giant lay still.

Roger had grown silent and still, just the crackling sound of fire and burning flesh.

The Old Man hung in his chair, drool coming from a corner of his mouth and dripping down into his curly chest hair.

Nearly over now.

Max, Tyler, Raymond and Big John swept through the house, clearing it room by room. A bedroom, big poster bed with shackles at each of the four posts, drawers filled with sex toys and BDSM gear that edged toward a murder kit. A big den with a huge curved screen TV hooked up to all kinds of electronic goods, including some ancient VHS gear. A library of homemade tapes variously labeled; "Red Rock Ho Down '84," "Juarez Get Together and Tear 'Em Apart '86," "We Fire All the Maids—Literally ;-) '87.

A laundry room. Guest bath. Gun room. Near the end of the house, down a tiny corridor by the garage, a padded black leather door, with three gleaming brass twelve-inch surface bolts holding the door shut.

Max looked over his shoulder to Tyler, then approached the door.

Allowed himself to open the door in his head an inch.

Pain. Despair. Resignation. Defeat. A dark, hopeless, roil of emotion.

But no trace of the Red Presence.

Max stepped to the door and threw back the bolts, drew it

open.

A small woman in a French maid's outfit, her hands bound behind her, ball-gag in her mouth, knelt in front of the door. She was a striking young woman, a perfect specimen of feminine beauty. Movie star good looks.

Max took her gently by the elbow and raised her to her feet. He came around behind and loosened her bonds, then undid the ball gag, which came out of her mouth with a wet pop. The woman wiped drool from her lips and stood, head down, awaiting her fate.

Max realized she understood she had changed hands, but that her fate remained the same—a slave, a toy for men's amusement.

"It's OK," he said. "You're safe now. We have taken care of all the bad men. You are free."

The woman's lips moved, and Max realized she was trying out the word. Testing it.

He stepped back around her and spread his arms in a gesture of openness.

"Free," he said.

The woman looked at him, her eyes clear and sad. It was too much for her to believe. Too much, too soon.

Big John thumped down the corridor, his weapon loose in his hand.

"House and garage are clear. Two dead men in the front den, one fried and crispy Roger Bannister, two zip-tied men, and the Old Man himself naked and bound to a chair. Plus, there's that guy out in the van."

He stopped short in front of the woman, who looked up again, then crossed her arms to cover her breasts.

Big John murmured something to her in Spanish and a flicker of light sparked in the woman's eyes.

Max looked from Big John to the woman and back again.

"Why don't you see if you can get her to relax a little," Max said. "Find something else for her to wear, if there is anything. We have to clean up and get out of here."

Big John stepped closer to the young woman and stopped, giving her space. Her eyes followed his movements, and her shoulders relaxed, just the tiniest bit.

Back in the front den, Max clicked through the open windows on the computer.

"These are all the Bannister accounts, near as I can tell. We've seen a bunch of these in the ledgers I got from Bill's place. But the bank accounts are new. Windows are open and we could probably transfer all the money anywhere we felt like."

Tyler looked at the screen and grimaced.

"Damn," he said. "If we had Kane…"

Loss slumped his shoulders.

Raymond leaned in.

"I use the same bank," he said. "No problem. I can move this money. Where do you want it?"

"Search 'organizations to help victims of human trafficking' and pick one," Max said.

Raymond seated himself at the keyboard.

Max and Tyler leaned in as the results popped up.

Raymond clicked on the first link, scrolled through it.

"The top one," Max said, pointing. "'…provides services and support for trafficking victims, and works with survivors to develop long-term strategies to ending human trafficking.'"

Raymond nodded and got to work.

Max and Tyler turned around and surveyed the room.

The two zip-tied men were still, though the giant was beginning to twitch as if coming awake. Likely the pain in his jaw would revive him quickly enough.

The Old Man had straightened and was watching Max.

Max met his glare.

"You're the asshole," the Old Man said.

"You're the Old Man," Max said.

He walked to the Old Man, faced him.

"You killed my boy," the Old Man said. A tear worked its way loose and rolled down his cheek, hung on the edge of his jaw and dropped to the gray, curly chest hair below.

Max met his eyes. Nodded.

"I did," he said. "Didn't set out to…got a little crazy, seeing all that stuff out in the barn behind his place, finding Mary Jane… something came over me…I wasn't entirely myself."

A flicker of the Old Man's lips.

"You got a taste for it. Give it time, you'd be one of us. I can see it in you. That's the truth."

"No." Max said. "Everything you see is perverted by the shit you've filled your head with. You aren't capable of seeing things as they are."

"Is anyone?" the Old Man countered.

"What is truth?" Max muttered.

He turned away and looked out the big window towards Aston and followed the road out of town with his eyes, out into the plains.

CHAPTER SIXTY FIVE

Raymond turned the wheel of his truck and headed down the dirt lane for Krell's. It'd been a crazy couple of weeks. Feds in town. Police all over the place. News people.

The police had found the Old Man still tied naked to his chair, the dead men, the three trussed men, and the video library in the room with the big curved screen TV.

Turned out, there was an electronic library of even larger proportions than the old VHS tapes. Turned out, the Old Man had never made a tape he didn't like. There were thousands of hours of torture and murder on these tapes. Enough there to put him and everyone in them in prison until Jesus returned, angels at his side.

Raymond shook his head as he crossed over into the compound, nodding at the man guarding the gate.

He wheeled the big truck around in front of the farmhouse, shut it down and climbed out.

The door of the farmhouse opened, and Mary Jane stepped out, radiant in jeans, shirt and cowboy boots, her hair in a long ponytail.

Raymond climbed the steps to the porch where she enveloped him in a big hug, then grunted as she tried to lift him off his feet. The bruising on her face had yellowed and paled but was still visible.

It didn't detract from her beauty.

Raymond laughed, "You're getting stronger, I can feel it," he said. "But you're not quite there, yet."

"I will be, Raymond Ingersoll, you wait and see," Mary Jane said.

"No doubt in my mind. None at all," Raymond said.

Inside, Max sat at the table with Dallas and Tyler, coffee steaming in the mugs before them. Rosita had chosen a couch against the wall and curled up, legs tucked underneath her. Her dark eyes measured the room and its occupants as she turned something over in her mind.

Raymond and Mary Jane walked to the table and joined them.

"You two are looking good," Max said. "Comfortable."

The two exchanged looks, and Max grinned.

"Excellent," Max said. "Just excellent."

"Given any more thought to living out here with us?" Dallas said to Raymond.

"I like the life I've got," Raymond said. "Tending the bar, nice little cabin. And maybe someday…" A glance over to Mary Jane, "maybe someday…it won't be just me up there. I'm good."

Mary Jane reached over and took his hand.

"Maybe," she said.

Max stepped out of the bright sunshine into the gloom of the barn and gave himself a minute for his eyes to adjust.

"Max," Rosita said.

Max spun to face her as she stepped into a shaft of light. The light reflected off her raven hair, giving it a faintly purple sheen.

She was as beautiful a woman as he'd ever seen, Max thought.

Rosita put her hands on her hips and studied him.

"What kind of a man are you?" she asked.

Max met her eyes.

The two looked into one another's souls for a long moment, and then something clicked deep inside Max and a wave of imagery poured in:

A group of young women locked in a dark room with a dirt floor. Bolts and chains dangling from the walls. A sense of despair and fear, resignation…

The door to the room slammed open, and a handsome young man in pressed jeans and crisp white shirt dragged in another young woman by the hair, this one limp and loose limbed enough to be a corpse.

She was naked and bleeding from both her vagina and anus. Bruises discolored her face and body.

A jolt ran through Max as he realized it was Rosie.

The young man's face twisted into a caricature of pleasure and rage, a gloating slug lurking just under the skin coming visible. A faint glint of red in the depths of his pupils betrayed the Red Presence that ruled him.

Understanding flooded Max and he pushed the door in his head closed with an effort.

"Man enough," he said.

Rosita didn't smile, but nodded.

"That's what I thought," she said.

She leaned down to pick up a duffel lying in the shadows.

"Where we headed, exactly?" Max asked.

"Tenancingo," Rosie said.

"Well," Max said, "let's get on with it then."

The door of the back porch of the farmhouse swung open and Rosita stepped out and walked down the wooden steps, boots clunking, then up the path to the barn, a motorcycle helmet held in her hand, hair bound with a scarf. Leather jacket on.

Max put his arms on his hips and regarded her.

Rosita walked up to him, raised herself on her toes, planted a kiss on his cheek.

"You keep in touch," Raymond said. Mary Jane leaned on his arm, her head on his shoulder.

"You need anything…" Dallas said.

Max nodded, distracted, his mind already half the way to Mexico.

Got a few stops along the way. Places to see. People to kill.

Rosita flipped her long black hair out from under the collar of her leather jacket, and it cascaded down her back.

An image of the blond woman came to Max. She was smiling at him, nodding. Max blinked and looked at Rosita.

She looked at him.

"Well?" she said.

Max's shoulders relaxed and he grinned.

"Let's get on with it then," he said.

He climbed on to the big bike, fired it up and grinned at Raymond, Mary Jane, and Dallas and waved. Rosita slid behind and wrapped her arms around him. He aimed the bike down the driveway, past the gate, nodded at the sentry, then cranked open the throttle and blasted down the road.

The End

ABOUT THE AUTHOR

Peter J. White was born in Colorado and raised in SE Alaska. He has degrees in Education, French, and an MFA in Creative Writing. He taught ELL in Bangkok, Thailand for six years, and currently teaches high school English in Washington State. Hobbies, past and present, include writing, bicycling, mountain climbing, kickboxing, MMA, and yoga.

AFTERWORD

If you liked the book, please leave a review on Amazon. We indies rely on people like you to get the word out. Thank you!

A combination of real-life events inspired the story and the character. Visit PeterJWhite.weebly.com/the-hollow-men.html to read about them.

Sign up for the Ghost Hunter Newsletter at PeterWhite.Weebley.com/news to get the second book in the Ghost Hunter series: *Slouching Towards Tenancingo* for **FREE.** (And to be apprised of approaching publication dates, character info, interesting links and stories related to the series as well as free short stories and other bonuses. It's a win-win situation here. And how often do those come along? Go for it!)

To learn more about the five books in the Ghost Hunter series (number six is in progress) and other titles by the author, go to PeterJWhite.weebly.com

Ghost Hunter: The Hollow Men

Ghost Hunter: Slouching Toward Tenancingo

Ghost Hunter: Bangkok Redemption

Ghost Hunter: The Bad Beginning (prequel)

Ghost Hunter: What Lies Beneath

Ghosts of a Coven Past: A Tale of Witchcraft, Spirits, Satanism, and Possession

READ ON FOR MORE GHOST HUNTER:

Slouching Toward Tenancingo

Chapter One

Max geared the big Kawasaki down, and allowed the orange cones arcing across the pavement to direct him to the lane to the right.

The wing of the U.S. border crossing jutted out over the road, a tannish-orange canopy with dirty white framing, lanes demarcated by the cones.

Heading into Mexico, the traffic was light and moved steadily. He passed under the canopy and out onto the bridge which carried them across the border.

Rosita's arms tightened around his waist as they reached the peak of the arch of the bridge.

Max took his left hand off the handlebar and reached down to pat Rosita's arm reassuringly.

"We got this," Max said. "Been through worse."

Rosita squeezed harder and rested the side of her head against Max's back.

Max looked to the left as he tapped the brake to slow for the Mexican side of the border. Five lanes of bumper-to-bumper traffic throttled the road leading into El Paso, swarmed into the division where the lanes multiplied to become twelve and surrounded the U.S. Border station. People had their car doors open against the heat.

Max slowed further as they approached the Mexican side. He drifted left with the flow of traffic at the bifurcation of Avenida de las Americas and joined a line passing under a blue and yellow Nada que declarer/Nothing to Declare sign. Toeing the bike into neutral, he took his hands off the bars and leaned back.

Rosita straightened with him, but her grip around his waist was strong.

"Mexico," Max said.

Rosita opened her mouth, then closed it. She slowly released her hold on Max, straightened, and looked around.

Guards in uniform—navy blue trousers, light blue button-down shirts, blue jackets and baseball caps—wandered in a desultory fashion, waving cars over at random. Two guards had a Chevy Suburban pulled to the side and were busily pawing through the contents of the trunk.

Max felt eyes on him and glanced to the left to see a rotund guard with mirrored sunglasses staring straight at him.

His gut tightened as the familiar feel of The Red Presence descended.

Max understood The Red Presence as a quasi-spiritual thing of malice, lust, rage, and sadism. The devil that whispered into your ear, pushed you forward to the brink of hell, then—if you were willing to go—over the edge. His awareness of it had come on the heels of a series of events that began with some craziness a few years previous in Bangkok.

Max shook off the unease growing in his belly and pushed down the crowding visions. No surprise to find The Red Presence here. And the fact that it lived in the heart and soul of the guard staring at him fit nicely into Max's worldview. Good and Evil. Black and White. In conflict. A battle.

Max toed the bike into gear and inched forward with the line, the sun beating down suddenly hot. A bead of sweat worked its way from under his helmet and dripped down his cheek.

Rosita leaned into him again and patted his leg.

"Turn it off, Max," she said. "Think of the Blond Woman. The mountain top. Of peace and light."

She continued murmuring in his ear as the bike worked its way to the red and green lights just in front of the border guard's booth sitting on the lane divider.

Max ignored the rotund guard, and focused on the light ahead as it blinked to green: his turn.

The guard in the shack looked bored, but comfortable.

"Purpose of visit?"

"Family visit," Max said, nodding his head at Rosita.

The guard took a long look at Rosita, noting the braid of hair down to her slim waist, the curve of her breasts, the smooth beauty of her skin.

Max kept his mouth shut.

The guard took another look at Max, puzzling it over: at least fifteen years older than Rosita, taught and muscular, with a powerful don't-fuck-with-me aura.

Finally, the guard blinked and held out a hand.

"Passports and visas?"

Rosita handed them over.

The guard shuffled through the paperwork, raising his eyes to look at Max.

"You're a lucky *hombre*, no? She's a beauty. Much younger than you."

Max nodded.

"Tlaxcala?"

Max nodded again.

Rosita smiled at the guard.

"Tepatlaxo," she said. "To see my mother."

The guard looked back to her, sighed, and handed over the passports.

"Have a nice trip," he said.

Max toed the bike into gear and eased it onto the road ahead, working hard to keep his mind clear and calm, the Red Presence palpable as he moved away.

The rotund guard turned his head to follow them, twin reflections of Max and Rosita growing smaller on the lenses of his sunglasses until they disappeared from sight.

He pulled a shiny new top-of-the-line iPhone from his pocket and pressed a button, then raised the phone to his ear.

Chapter Two

Mexico 45 cut straight through Ciudad Juarez, four lanes in each direction.

Max checked his mirrors, signaled left, and drifted toward the center lane, the scene along the sidewalk disturbing.

The 45 was remarkably clean, moderately trafficked, the pedestrians on the sidewalk the hard-working type: men with big, round guts in T-shirts, jeans, and baseball caps, women in sedate dresses.

Max glanced to his right as he passed a Del Rio supermarket, spotted a big Coca Cola truck parked in front, cases of pop stacked to on the pavement.

Two men lay on the pavement, arms splayed, blood trails spreading across the lot.

Max tensed and looked away.

Keep it tight, Maxxy Boy. Rein that shit in.

Feeling his gut tighten under her hand, Rosita looked to the right, then straightened up and put her chin on his shoulder.

"More?" she asked.

"More," he said.

"You OK?"

"I'm fine. You just would not believe the number of bodies in this town."

Rosita settled back down and put the side of her head against Max's. She had a pretty good idea on that account.

Past the supermarket, they entered a section of town with luxurious houses behind thick concrete and stucco walls. The walls were solid up to about three feet above the sidewalk, then had open U-shapes with thick steel bars painted black topped with razor-sharp decorative points.

Not very secure, Max thought. *Easy to shoot through, and easy to hop over, using one of the pillars. Not afraid of drive-bys, kidnapping, assassinations?*

As the 45 climbed up over a through street below, Max felt the hair stand up on the back of his neck. He checked his mirrors again to see a big white Ford Excursion Stretch coming up on his right.

The Excursion limo pulsed with The Red Presence.

Rein it in, Max reminded himself again. *Now is not the time.*

He geared the Kawasaki down and let the limo slide past.

The windows of the Excursion were tinted an opaque black, the plating of the truck reinforced and bullet proof, yet still vibrating with the bass of the Hispanic gangster rap blasting inside.

Max tightened down on the door inside his head, leaned against it. If he weren't careful, the imagery pouring through the minds of the men inside the big Ford would overwhelm him. Next thing he'd know, he'd be off to the side of the road, head down, bike idling, fighting off the viscous evil that controlled the men in the truck.

Not the time or the place.

Max checked his mirrors, slowed some more, and eased the bike across the lanes into the lot of a strip mall.

"Let's get something to eat," he said.

Rosita patted him on the chest, and leaned with the bike as it climbed up off the 45 and into the strip mall.

A sushi place nestled in beside a dance studio flanked by a piano store and a small gym. A Kidz Burger sat in its own colorful building across the way.

A taco stand sat in the parking lot, and Max pulled in next to that and parked.

He let Rosita dismount, then clambered off himself.

He pulled off his helmet, ran his forearm across the crown of his head, wiping off sweat and took a look around.

Mexico.

The lot was clean, and a few customers sat at rickety metal tables in foldout chairs eating their tacos.

No one gave them a second glance.

Max set his helmet on the left-hand mirror to air out.

He stood for a minute and then carefully eased the door in his head open.

The tables in front of him shimmered, and he found himself looking at one off to the far right of the square where four men in jeans and plaid shirts lay sprawled in their seats. Nasty-looking bullet wounds blossomed like lurid flowers; their shirts and pants shredded. Each man had at least twenty bullets in him. The top of one man's skull had exploded, the lid of his cranium popping off and dangling to one side like a bad toupee.

Max eased the door in his head shut and blinked.

Just a quiet noon scene in an ordinary parking lot of strip mall in Ciudad, Juarez.

He dismounted and joined Rosita at a table.

"Just amazing," he said as he eased into the chair across from her.

Rosita raised her eyebrows at him.

"Bodies everywhere," Max said.

"I ordered you the pork tacos," Rosita said.

Max sighed and looked down at his hands, folded on the table.

"The world is an ugly place, Rosita," he said.

"You don't have to tell me that," Rosita said.

She rose from the table and went to the taco stand to grab their order.

Max watched her carefully, and a smile twisted his lips upwards.

Ain't that the truth, he thought.

Chapter Three

Max pushed the stained paper plates to one side up against the bottles of hot sauce and leaned back.

"I needed that," he said.

Rosita smiled at him, "I know," she said.

"They got more dead bodies per block here than anywhere I've seen," he said.

"You knew what to expect," she said.

Max looked down at the table, then up to meet Rosita's eyes.

"It's wearing on me."

Rosita reached across the table and took his hands in hers.

"Max," she said. "You've been given this...gift...for a reason. You've been chosen. Look at what you've done with it. The Bannisters are history. You've saved hundreds of women."

She squeezed his hands and pulled them closer to her.

"You saved me, Max. Without you, I'd be dead. Tortured and fucked to death in that little hotel outside of Mountain Cleft. Or still there, locked up in that room..." She shuddered.

"No Bannister is ever again going to set up one of those disgusting little hotels or bars. No Bannister or one of theirs is ever again going to torture a woman to death for his pleasure. You've made a difference."

Max shrugged.

"All we really did is open the door to the Mexicans. They're all over the Bannister operation. They'll have women flowing up across the border and into those little whorehouses and torture chambers in no time. Remember that little town just outside of El Paso?"

Rosita grimaced.

"I remember them all, Max," she said. "Every one."

She released his hands and leaned back.

"And I remember how we went in there and took care of it."

Max grinned.

"Burned that sucker to the ground," he said.

"And every one of those snake pits we came across," she said.

"You are quite the woman, Rosita," Max said.

"A match made in heaven," she said.

"It's going to be worse down here," he said.

"That's why we're here, isn't it?" she said.

Max sighed.

"It is," she said.

"You think we'll survive this?"

"Do you?"

"Seems unlikely. Seems like we'll end up just like those poor bastards over there," Max nodded his head at the unoccupied table on the right.

"Maybe. Maybe not. We've made it this far," she said.

"Yeah, well…."

Max sat up straight like he'd been poked in the spine with a cattle prod.

In one fluid move, he was on his feet and pulling Rosita away from the tables and back behind the taco stand.

He wrapped Rosita in his arms and hit the pavement behind the taco stand just as a big Ford truck with huge tires screeched into the parking lot and the chatter of machine-gun fire shattered the noon calm.

Printed in Great Britain
by Amazon

38865972R00274